NOBLE PRINCE

USA *TODAY* BESTSELLING AUTHOR

DEVNEY PERRY

NOBLE PRINCE

Copyright © 2020 by Devney Perry LLC

All rights reserved.

ISBN: 978-1-950692-81-1

Editing & Proofreading:

Elizabeth Nover, Razor Sharp Editing

www.razorsharpediting.com

Julie Deaton, Deaton Author Services

www.facebook.com/jdproofs

Karen Lawson, The Proof Is in the Reading

Cover:

Sarah Hansen © Okay Creations

www.okaycreations.com

OTHER TITLES

Jamison Valley Series

The Coppersmith Farmhouse

The Clover Chapel

The Lucky Heart

The Outpost

The Bitterroot Inn

The Candle Palace

Maysen Jar Series

The Birthday List

Letters to Molly

Lark Cove Series

Tattered

Timid

Tragic

Tinsel

Clifton Forge Series

Steel King

Riven Knight

Stone Princess

Noble Prince

Fallen Jester

Tin Queen

Runaway Series

Runaway Road

Wild Highway

Quarter Miles

Forsaken Trail

Dotted Lines

The Edens Series

Christmas in Quincy - Prequel

Indigo Ridge

Juniper Hill

Calamity Montana Series

Writing as Willa Nash

The Bribe

The Bluff

The Brazen

The Bully

CONTENTS

CHAPTER ONE

SCARLETT

I *loved you.*

I jolted awake, sitting up with a gasp as I clutched my racing heart. It boomed inside my chest as loudly as a gun's blast in my mind.

A nightmare. Just a nightmare. Were they nightmares when they attacked during the day? I rubbed my eyes, then looked around the room.

The vinyl blinds over the filmy windows weren't the right size for the frame and daylight escaped their edges, streaming onto the bedspread beneath me.

Pink, purple and white daisies dotted the canary-yellow fabric on the quilt, sheets and matching pillowcases. The print had likely been chosen for its attempt at cheer—and to hide the sad state of this room. Except every daisy in the world couldn't disguise the fact that I was trapped. Every pastel in the rainbow couldn't camouflage the reality of my situation.

My life was a series of hells and I kept trading one for another.

I stood from the bed, closing my eyes at the first dizzying step. My head pounded from the lack of sleep, food and water. But I wasn't hungry. I wasn't thirsty. And sleep was fraught with gruesome images I didn't have the energy to relive, so I'd forced myself to stay awake the past ten nights. I'd sat in the living room with the cop assigned to Scarlett duty and stared at the wall.

Napping during the day was dangerous too, but after dark, the nightmare felt more real. Probably because it wasn't actually a dream. It was a memory my mind kept pulling up over and over. Blood. Death. Fear. It was more terrifying than any horror movie.

Reality had a way of trumping our imaginations.

The stench from a pizza my current babysitter had brought over for lunch wafted through the large crack under the door. Bile rose from my stomach, but I swallowed it down and shuffled to the adjoining bathroom, cringing at the mirror's reflection.

I look like shit.

Worse than shit. My skin was tinged with gray. The circles under my eyes were so deep and purple they could have passed for bruises. My cheeks and lips had lost nearly all their natural pink flush.

I needed food. I needed rest. I needed the hideous dream that found me whenever I succumbed to my exhaustion to disappear. I needed . . . the list was so long it would take hours to recite, but it all came down to this—I needed out. After nearly a year of treading in a sea of my own mistakes, I was close to drowning.

It was time to start making my way to shore.

I splashed some water onto my cheeks, washing away the sheen of sweat from the nightmare. Then I buried my face in

2

the one and only hand towel. The terry cloth was embroidered at the hem with more goddamn daisies.

Tossing the towel aside, I leaned in closer to the mirror, inspecting my lower lip. The split had almost healed. My tongue darted out, feeling the slight rise where it had been. Eventually, the faint mark would fade, but not the memory. I could recall with absolute clarity how I'd gotten every bruise, every cut and every scar.

Jeremiah might be dead, but I'd always remember him hitting me hard enough to split my lip.

And for that, he could rot in his own hell.

I pushed thoughts of Jeremiah away and walked out of the bathroom to tug on a sweatshirt. It was part of three outfits I owned, and I preferred this matching set above the others only because my sister had given it to me. Somehow, knowing that these were her clothes made it easier to forget that I'd been wearing them the night Jeremiah had died.

These sweats were the only link I had to Presley at the moment. And my shoes.

I'd taken to sleeping with my sneakers on at this house. It would be easier to run if I was wearing tennis shoes, not that I had anywhere to go. I was stuck.

The bedroom itself was sparse, having only a bed and a wobbly end table. The rest of the place was more of the same, the few pieces of furniture staged for function, not comfort, in this dump of a house.

My home for the foreseeable future.

My prison.

And it was all Jeremiah's fault. *That son of a bitch.* I'd met his mother. The sentiment was true. If not for the anger and resentment, I'd be numb, so for now, I clung to my rage, letting it fuel me forward when sleep deprivation and starvation threatened to bring me to my knees. I'd survived enough, and a shoebox-sized house in Clifton Forge, Montana, was not the thing that would push me over the edge. Neither was Jeremiah.

He didn't get to fuck up my life, hit me, then kill himself, leaving me with the nightmares. He didn't get to be the one who broke me.

I loved you.

That's what he'd said before the bullet tore through his skull. *I loved you.* Bullshit.

My father had told me he loved me. He'd told my sister. He'd told my mother. Then he'd beat us under the guise of that love. Was there a man on earth who actually knew what it was to love a woman?

Jeremiah had claimed those three little words but they'd been as empty as his promises for the future. If he'd actually loved me, he wouldn't have kept me in that clubhouse. He wouldn't have hit me, hurt my sister and left me to suffer the consequences of his lies.

If he'd actually loved me, he would have let me go.

I flung open the door to the bedroom and the smell of garlic and cheese slapped me in the face, making me gag. Sucking in breaths through my mouth, I walked down the hallway toward the front of the house.

The officer on duty was in the living room, sitting in one of two overstuffed recliners. He'd taken the nicest of the pair, his attention fixed on his phone.

I passed him for the kitchen, my shoes squeaking on the linoleum floor.

"Have a nice nap?" he asked as I opened a cupboard.

"Yeah," I lied, taking out a glass and filling it from the tap. When I'd been brought to this safe house, the water had run orange from the faucets and even after ten days of use, it still had a rusty tinge and taste.

But I drank it regardless, then went to the other chair, plopping down and letting the spring in the back dig into my spine. I hated the brown upholstery nearly as much as I hated the daisies. Though neither could beat my absolute abhorrence of this house.

There wasn't even a television. The cop who'd been here with me last night had brought a deck of cards and a cribbage board, so the two of us had played for hours. But the cops assigned during the day never seemed to think of something to do to pass the time. They had their phones, their connection to the outside world.

While I was trapped. Never alone. Always alone.

Today's officer was young, his dark hair combed neatly at a harsh part above his right eyebrow. He had a pimple on his chin and his navy uniform—a starched, long-sleeve shirt and matching slacks—looked like they'd been washed less than five times. His badge was too shiny and his gun too new. But for today, he was my protector. One of three cops per day who'd come to stay here with me and keep me *safe*.

"What's your name again?" I asked. They'd all started to blur together.

He tore his eyes from his phone and gave me a tight smile. "Nathan."

"Nathan," I repeated and tapped my temple. Nathan, the pepperoni, sausage and garlic fiend. I'd remember him now.

The air currents from the heating vents sent a waft of pizza smell from the box still on the kitchen counter. Nathan must have left it out for me, thinking I'd be hungry. *Thanks, but no thanks.* One slice and garlic would be seeping through my pores for a week. Every few minutes, I stifled another gag, until the need for fresh air drove me from my seat.

I passed the collapsible card table and folding chairs in the dining area adjacent to the kitchen and walked to the back door. Nathan didn't even notice where I was headed until the slider scraped on its track.

"Hey." He shot out of his chair. "What are you doing?"

"Just getting some air." Before the stench made me dry heave. Pizza had never been my favorite food and after today, I'd be avoiding it for good.

Nathan hesitated, his gaze flicking up and down my body twice as he sized me up.

What he saw was a skinny, frail woman who looked like she was about to topple over from the emotional weight bearing down on her bony shoulders. A woman who'd fought her entire life and was running out of punches.

"It's only the backyard," I said, giving him my best version of a tired smile. "No one can see me if I stay inside the fence."

Just let me go outside. Please. I was suffocating in here, not just from the smell, but from the drab walls, reminding me with their ugly beige that the past year had been nothing but poor choice after poor choice. That I was here because of my own selfish decisions.

"Please," I whispered. "Five minutes."

Finally, he nodded. "Stay close."

I slipped through the door before he could change his mind.

The sky was covered in clouds, muting the light, but I lifted a hand to my face to shield my eyes. Then I pulled in a deep breath of the winter air and held it in my lungs. It had been ten days since I'd stood outside. Ten days that had felt like a lifetime.

Snowflakes drifted to the ground, dusting the empty yard with a fresh layer of white. The top of the tall fence had tufts on each picket, and like the inside of the house, the yard was nearly barren. Only one shrub grew in a corner, its branches barely wide enough to catch the snow. Otherwise, the yard was empty, square and flat.

To my left, the top of a swing set peeked over the fence in the yard next door. To the right sat a playhouse, the opening of its yellow tube slide gaping at me. These were family homes. Did the neighbors wonder what happened at this house? Did they wonder why it was so quiet and lifeless? Or why, three times daily, one police officer left as another arrived?

The cop on shift never parked here. He was always dropped off in another car, the same one that picked up the officer leaving. While yesterday's babysitter had been in the bathroom, I'd peeked through the front window. The driveway hadn't been shoveled and a red truck sat parked in front of the garage, covered in snow. Besides the path of footprints leading from the street to the front door, this house appeared abandoned.

The neighbors likely thought this was a sad, pathetic house and so was the person who lived inside its walls. They weren't wrong. I was as miserable and lonely and pitiful as this dismal house. My walls were crumbling down and when all that remained was a heap of bones and flesh, there'd be no one to mourn the desolation.

Not even Presley.

And I have myself to blame.

I took one step into the yard and glanced over my shoul-

7

der. Was Nathan watching me? No, he had returned to his chair and his phone. I took another step and the fluffy snow under my shoe gave way to the icy crunch beneath.

Two steps became fifteen and when I reached the gate that led to the alley, I brushed my fingers along the frozen latch and flicked it open. I cast one more glance at the door.

Screw this place.

If what waited for me outside this fence was just another prison, at least it would be one of my choosing.

I pushed through the gate, relishing the rush of adrenaline that spread through my veins as my foot stepped into the alley behind the house. It was trash day and large green bins dotted the narrow lane. They were all empty and askew from when the garbage truck had come through earlier. I picked the largest tire rut in the snow and started walking, my legs warming instantly despite the cold.

Presley's clothes were baggy on my thin frame, and I burrowed into the olive-green sweatshirt, pulling the hood over my hair, which hung limp past my shoulders. The ends dangling to my waist were a year overdue for a trim. My sweatpants were cinched tight and rolled at the band in an effort to keep them from falling off my protruding hip bones.

The frigid air bit at my cheeks as I walked but there wasn't a breath of wind. The snow floated as it fell, blanketing the world and cloaking me in its peace.

Clifton Forge, Montana.

This town had been my sister's choice. Presley had wanted a life in a small, sleepy town, and though I'd spent little time here, I'd say she'd definitely found one. With the mountains looming in the distance, there was a pretty view every direction you turned. But what I suspected Pres loved most was the community.

I'd come here once, last summer—well before my twin sister had even known I was in Montana. The few places I'd stopped, I'd been hounded by strange looks as people tried to place the familiarity of a face so much like one of their own. If not for my long, blond hair versus Presley's short, stylish cut, the two of us were nearly as identical now as we had been as toddlers.

Maybe if Presley had told people she had a twin, they would have put it together sooner. But from what I could tell, I was a surprise to everyone, even those closest to her. Not that I faulted her for turning me into a secret. I would have forgotten about me too.

She'd come here to start over, to build her own life, and though a part of me envied that she'd done it with such incredible success, mostly, I was happy that she'd found a home. A family.

They sure as hell treated her better than her real family ever had, me especially.

At the end of the alley, I turned, wanting to get out of view in case Nathan came looking. The sidewalks had been plowed but fresh snow covered the concrete and my footprints marked my path.

I turned again, winding through the neighborhood and past quiet homes. Not a car or truck passed me as I walked, probably because people were at work. It was a workday, right? Friday? I'd begun to lose track in the blur of sleepless nights and hazy days.

Block after block, I trudged, relishing the burn in my legs, until finally, I spotted a busier road ahead. I aimed my feet toward the bustle, picking up my pace as my stomach growled.

I was hungry. For the first time in days, I was hungry. A

smile tugged at my mouth. I should have ditched that safe house last week.

There were 179 dollars in my pocket. Like my shoes, I kept the cash with me always. It was all I had left of the money my mother had given me the day I'd escaped Chicago, and I'd kept it close ever since, in a pocket or tucked into a shoe.

After I'd caught Jeremiah trying to steal it from my purse, I'd started hiding it. That should have been my first clue he was no longer the boy from my youth. But even with the missing twenty-dollar bills, the strange disappearances at night, the paranoid behavior and the lack of affection, I hadn't realized just how far he'd fallen.

How far *we'd* fallen.

When I reached a busy intersection, I looked up and down, past the traffic, in search of a restaurant or coffee shop. A grocery store caught my eye.

I crossed the street, keeping my head down as I hurried. The smell of fried chicken greeted me in the store's parking lot and my mouth watered. I dusted off my sweats, damp from the snow, and pulled off my hood. I combed my fingers through my hair and parted it in the middle, creating a frame to hide most of my face. My reflection in the store's sliding doors showed a flush in my cheeks from the cold air.

Well, looking like a drowned rat is better than a corpse.

A blast of heat hit me as I entered and took a black basket from the stack inside the double doors. Then I followed my nose to the deli.

The woman behind the counter pasted on a smile, though her gaze was wary as she scanned me from the waist up. If I were in her hair net, I'd stare wide-eyed too. Nine months of living in a motorcycle club's compound hadn't done much for my looks.

"What can I get for you?" she asked.

"I'll have the lunch special, please." I pointed to the menu, where they had chicken and steak fries for five dollars. "Two piece."

She nodded and went about preparing the meal, putting it into a white to-go container. Then she slapped the price sticker over the latch and handed it over.

"Thanks." I didn't linger and made my way through the produce section, palming an apple for my basket. Then I found the dairy aisle, getting a small bottle of chocolate milk.

My stomach growled with every step as I wandered up and down the aisles, shopping by my hunger pangs. I added a jar of pickles and a package of Hawaiian rolls, the sweet ones Presley and I had begged our mother to get whenever she'd let us go to the store as kids.

Mom would buy them in cash so they wouldn't show up on the receipt Dad would pore over after work. Dad didn't like sweet rolls. He didn't like Mom spending his money on anything he deemed unnecessary.

So she would buy them with the small allowance he granted her each week. Dad thought she used that twenty-dollar bill for lattes on the way to drop us off at school when really, Mom spent it on us. Lollipops or slushies. An ice cream cone or a Hawaiian roll. Presley and I would scarf our treats down in the car and agree without hesitation when she'd make us promise to eat a good dinner so Dad wouldn't suspect that we'd snacked.

I missed my mother.

I missed my sister.

Presley was here, somewhere in Clifton Forge. And

though I had a phone in my pocket—the third item I kept on me at all times—I wasn't ready to call her yet. First, I had to eat something and regain my strength.

Because I'd need it.

I had one hell of an apology to make.

For ruining her wedding. For bringing death to her doorstep. For not returning one of the many texts she'd sent me in the past ten years.

For hating her strength. For being jealous that she'd been courageous enough to leave. For blaming her when I'd been the coward, too scared to make the leap.

Another long list. I only hoped she'd be able to forgive me.

My trip through the store came to a halt in the cookie section. I was debating between the chocolate cream and fudge swirl cookies when footsteps thudded down the aisle. I ignored them, assuming it was another customer in search of sugar, and put both packages of cookies in my basket.

I turned from the shelves, ready to check out, and ran into a solid wall.

"What do you think you're doing?"

Cringing at the familiar, gravelly voice, I lifted my gaze. It traveled up the broad chest I'd crashed into, past a square, clean-shaven jaw, to a pair of the deepest blue eyes I'd ever seen.

Luke's eyebrows were pulled together above the bridge of a straight nose that cleaved his face in two. I'd noticed the symmetry of his features ten days ago, when he'd sat me down in his office and questioned me about Jeremiah.

It had been easier to study the handsome Clifton Forge chief of police than relive the horrors I'd seen just hours before.

His dark brown hair was short and clean cut. He stood with a proud, authoritative posture, his strong shoulders pulled back and his hands fisted on narrow hips.

"I asked you a question," he clipped.

I hefted the basket hanging from my elbow. "Shopping."

"You're in protective custody."

"Am I?" I dared, then made the move to sidestep him and head to the register. The basket was heavy and I wasn't exactly at my best today.

But Luke moved in tandem, blocking my path. "I got a call from Nathan that you ran."

"Walked. I walked." *Right out the back door.*

His jaw clenched as he glared down at me from his towering height. He stood inches over six feet and I was getting a cramp in my neck trying to hold his scowl. Even irritated, he was handsome.

I hadn't seen Luke since he'd deposited me at the safe house. The night Jeremiah had committed suicide in my sister's house.

After the gunshot, a strange man had hauled me out of my sister's house. I'd fought hard, kicking and screaming as I attempted to rush to Jeremiah's body, but he'd dragged me from the scene. Call it shock or insanity, but I'd thought if I could just touch Jeremiah, I could put the pieces back together. I could erase the bullet's path and rewind time.

Except the man who'd had me had been too strong and had hauled me outside into the freezing March night. Then Luke had appeared. He'd stood before me, much like he was now, and had given me something other than blood to focus on.

His gorgeous face.

He'd taken me to his truck, put me in the passenger seat

and cranked up the heat. Then he'd told me to sit tight and wait. Maybe I should have run for it that night, but much like today, I had nowhere to go.

After Luke had done whatever cops do after an armed man holds two women hostage before taking his own life, he'd driven me to the police station, where he'd taken me to his office and asked me a sequence of questions.

I hadn't answered a single one. Instead, I'd noticed how his eyes had a ring so dark around the edge it was like the graphite tip of a freshly sharpened pencil. I'd studied the shape of his mouth, stern and serious, and wondered what it would look like with a smile. I'd concentrated on the bob of his Adam's apple whenever he swallowed.

I'd studied Luke and ignored his questions until he'd given up and gone in search of answers from someone else.

Presley must have enlightened him as to all that had happened with Jeremiah, because after two hours alone in his office, he'd returned and told me it was unsafe for me to be in public. That my life was in danger and he was putting me into protective custody.

That was the moment his words had registered and I'd stopped studying his face.

I'd gone along with it, too fatigued and shaken to argue. But that was ten days ago. Things were different now. Yes, I was still wearied, but the shock of all that had happened in the past nine months was fading. And I'd rather take my chances than waste my days staring at a beige wall.

"Do you mind?" I pointed down the aisle. "I'm hungry and would like to check out."

He glowered and stood to his tallest. "Give me the basket."

Maybe another woman would have caved, but there was

nothing truly fearsome about Luke Rosen. I knew exactly what frightening men looked like, and it certainly wasn't him.

"I'm good." I took another step, but he blocked me again. "Seriously, do you mind? I want to eat and then I'm going to go find my sister."

"You're going back to the safe house and I'm locking you inside."

Rage surged in my chest. "No."

"Let's go before someone sees you." Luke reached for the basket and I yanked it away with a feral snarl. "Scarlett, I will haul you out of here if I have to."

I tried to sidestep him again, but damn it, those long legs of his were a lot faster than mine. "Move."

"Give me the basket."

"Move!" The sleepless nights and the hysteria were catching up to me and the outburst came out as a wailing shriek. It came from the woman who'd been trapped for far too long.

Luke's eyes darted above my head. A couple stood at the end of the aisle, their cart immobile as they stared.

"Goddamn it, Scarlett," Luke said, lowering his voice. "Just put the basket down so we can get out of here. You're drawing attention to yourself."

And I did not care. Not at all.

"If you're not going to get out of the way, I'll just go around." I spun on my shoes, whirling the opposite direction, but when I went to take a step and carry my basket away, I suddenly found its weight missing from my arm. He'd stolen it from me before I'd had the chance to clutch it tight.

Then the world was spinning. The floors, the ceiling, everything flipped topsy-turvy.

I'd fainted.

No, that wasn't right.

I was being carried. *Hauled.* That had been Luke's threat and damn it, I'd underestimated him. The chief had made good on his word.

His shoulder dug into my belly as he walked. I lifted my face, pushing the hair out of my eyes. My basket of food sat exactly where I'd been standing. My chicken and rolls and cookies and chocolate milk. The items grew smaller with every one of Luke's strides.

"Put me down."

He kept walking.

"Put me down!" I shouted.

Still, he kept walking.

I lifted a hand and raised it above my head. My hair kept falling in front of my face, obscuring my vision, but that didn't stop me from using every ounce of strength I had left. I brought my fist down on Luke's lower back. Except my aim was shit so I didn't hit his back. No, my fist bounced off his firm, perfect ass.

Luke didn't so much as break his stride. "I promised Presley I'd keep you safe."

And without another word, without stopping, he carried me in a fireman's hold out of the grocery store and into the snow.

I was going back to the daisies, whether I wanted to or not.

Hello, Scarlett. I'm rock bottom.

CHAPTER TWO

LUKE

"Goddamn it, Scarlett." I slammed the door to my truck and wiped the flakes of snow off my face. "What were you thinking?"

She crossed her arms in the passenger seat, staring straight ahead. "I'm not going back to that house."

"Did something happen? Did Nathan—"

"This isn't about Nathan," she snapped. "It's about me. I'm sick of living in a prison."

"It's not a—"

"If you say it's not a prison, I'm going to scream."

I clamped my mouth shut and sucked in a deep breath. This woman was making me fucking crazy. So was her sister.

Was Scarlett really so cavalier with her own life? She'd been walking around the store like it was any other day. Did she not realize how much danger she was in?

The Arrowhead Warriors, a notorious and violent motorcycle gang in the state, might want her dead. It wouldn't take long for them to track Scarlett's whereabouts to Clifton Forge. There hadn't been any sign of them yet, but it was inevitable. A Friday afternoon jaunt to the grocery store was the epitome of reckless behavior. Did she have a death wish?

I opened my mouth to ask, but when I glanced over, Scarlett's face was as solid as stone. Any lecture would be pointless. She was locked behind her own mental fortress and if I actually wanted my warnings to penetrate those brick walls, now was not the time. So I started the truck, reversed out of my parking space and drove to the safe house.

The tension in the cab was thicker than the gray clouds above. Scarlett sat statue still, her eyes trained on the road ahead, and the crease between her eyebrows deepened with every turn.

She knew exactly where I was taking her.

I knew she wasn't going to stay.

For fuck's sake. I was sick of this goddamn mess. For the past ten days, all I'd done was try to stop the bleeding, but with every wound I staunched, five more cuts opened up.

First, it had been the investigation into the hostage situation and suicide. Clifton Forge was a small town with an equally small police force. This case had required my complete attention, and the hours I'd put in at the station had been long. The mayor called five times daily to check in.

Meanwhile, the media had swarmed. The only reporter in the state who hadn't called the station was the one in Clifton Forge—but that was only because her husband had been on the scene, and whatever information Bryce wanted she could get from the other people who'd been at Presley's house that night. Bryce had access to every facet of the truth, but ironically, her story had been written at the most facile level. There'd been no speculation. No mention of Jeremiah's affiliation with the Warriors. It had read like just a domestic dispute, though that wasn't entirely inaccurate.

Finally, ten days later, the endless phone calls were beginning to dwindle. I'd planned to spend this afternoon plowing through the mountain of backlogged work. Instead, Nathan had called to inform me Scarlett had made a break for it.

I didn't have time to deal with a snarky woman who lacked enough regard for her own life to stay hidden.

The closer we got to the house, the more Scarlett stiffened in her seat. Her fists were balled on top of her knees and with every block, I expected her to open the door and leap out. Stubborn woman.

Where was her head? Where was mine? I'd hauled her out of the grocery store. Literally hauled. I'd manhandled her down the aisle and through the front door.

What the hell was wrong with me? Damn it, that was not the man I was. This entire situation had frayed my nerves and shred my patience.

I pulled up to the safe house, parking beside the truck in front of the garage. This wasn't even a safe house. It was mine, a personal rental property that I'd bought cheap last year and was planning on fixing up. The red truck beside me was mine too. I used it to tow my raft and fishing boat in the summers.

The Clifton Forge Police Department didn't have a demand—or budget—for a safe house and when I'd needed a place to stash Scarlett, this had been the logical choice.

Sure, it wasn't much to look at. Yet. But this summer I planned to start remodeling and freshen it up before renting it out. For Scarlett, there weren't many other options. This ugly but functional house was the best place for her.

Until we knew exactly what threat she faced from the Warriors, hiding was Scarlett's best option. Maybe things would die down soon and she'd be free to leave. But it had only been ten days. Ten days that had felt like a minute.

My phone vibrated in my pocket as I shut off the truck. I pulled it out. Presley's name hovered above a text. She'd been hounding me relentlessly for information on her sister's whereabouts and I had no doubt she'd already heard about the grocery store incident.

You better know what you're doing, Rosen.

I looked over at Scarlett, then typed out a quick reply. *She's safe.*

I'd promised to keep Scarlett safe.

I was a man of my word.

"Come on." I climbed out of the truck and rounded the hood, opening Scarlett's door.

She didn't budge.

Why was she so difficult? Why? Didn't she realize I was on her side?

The snow had nearly stopped falling, so I stood in the cold, waiting.

Scarlett had to go into that house on her own. I'd done enough hauling her around today, and if she wanted to sit here all night, then fine. I'd wait.

The street was quiet. The neighbors on this block had been a godsend, watching over the house in my stead. This place had sat empty for two years before I'd bought it, and though I hadn't started renovations, everyone nearby was glad that it would soon be getting some much-needed care.

The man who lived next door shoveled the sidewalk in the winter, though his own was covered, so I suspected he was out of town. I'd come over later and clear them both. In the summer, I paid the teenager who lived across the street twenty bucks a week to mow the lawn.

Someday, this would make the perfect starter home for a young couple. Or if I could convince my dad to move here after he retired, I'd happily give this place to him.

But first, it needed paint and new flooring. Electrical updates. Plumbing updates. The bathrooms and kitchen would be overhauled. Normally, the prospect of a project gave me energy. Today, I was just too damn tired to think about the work I had in store.

Scarlett's teeth began to chatter. She'd walked to the grocery store in the snow and her clothes were damp. Her hair too.

But I didn't move or speak. I simply waited.

Minutes passed. Nathan stood at the front window. His shift replacement would arrive at five with dinner for Scarlett. I didn't have the rotation on me but I was pretty sure Chuck was up next.

Scarlett had had fried chicken in her basket at the store. I'd recognized the container, having grabbed the deli special a hundred times myself over the years. I dug out my phone and texted Chuck, telling him to stop by the store, get a fried chicken meal, some of those Hawaiian rolls and a chocolate milk.

When he replied with a thumbs up, I shoved my phone away and looked to Scarlett.

Her bravado was fading. The fight had drained from her eyes and her shoulders were slumped forward. And her teeth just kept on chattering, no matter how tight she clenched her jaw.

"Scarlett." I held out a hand.

She looked at my palm and the sadness in her blue eyes made my heart twist. *Fuck.* She looked miserable. She looked weary to the core.

21

"Come inside," I urged. "Let's talk."

Scarlett nodded but refused my hand. She hopped out of the truck herself, her feet landing hard on the snow. She wrapped her arms around her waist and trudged to the front door, her body shrinking before my eyes.

Her spirit hadn't just faded. She'd drained it dry.

I followed her to the door, giving her plenty of space while matching her glacial pace.

Nathan whipped the door open the moment her foot hit the single porch step. "Chief—"

I held up a hand, then waved for him to get out of Scarlett's way. When we were all inside, I closed the door behind me. "Scarlett, why don't you go change into dry clothes."

She nodded and shuffled down the hallway toward the only bedroom with an actual bed.

"I'm sorry," Nathan blurted. "She said she wanted some fresh air and I didn't think that was a big deal."

I sighed. "We'll talk about this tomorrow at the station."

"But—"

"Tomorrow." I jerked my chin at the door. "There should be a shovel in the garage. Would you mind hitting the sidewalk?"

"No, sir," he said, then disappeared outside.

Nathan would be reprimanded verbally for not watching Scarlett more closely, but I wasn't going to blow the kid up. He was new and hadn't realized she was a flight risk. Hell, I hadn't either. When I'd gotten a text from Bryce saying she'd recognized Scarlett at the grocery store's deli counter, I'd about fallen out of my chair.

I'd thought Scarlett understood the severity of the situation, but clearly, I'd been wrong.

Maybe I should have pushed her harder that night.

Instead of letting her ignore my questions as she'd sat in my office, huddled beneath a blanket, staring at my face, maybe I should have demanded some answers. But demanding anything from a woman in shock had seemed unnecessarily cruel.

Maybe I shouldn't have gone ten days without checking in here myself.

I paced the living room, dragging a hand through my short hair. Everyone expected me to have the answers. To know how to handle situations like this. I'd been a cop for a long time, but even this was new. I wouldn't admit it out loud, but I'd been fumbling for days, relying on instinct, not experience. Because if I overanalyzed my decisions, I'd second-guess them all.

So I'd focused on the facts.

Ten days ago, Scarlett's ex and a member of the Arrowhead Warriors Motorcycle Club had pushed his way into Presley's house, where she'd been staying with her sister. Jeremiah had held them hostage at gunpoint, demanding money.

Jeremiah had confessed to the women that he'd been stealing drugs from his club and reselling them. He'd also admitted that he'd pinned the theft on Scarlett to avoid punishment and certain death from his brothers. But he'd hoped that by getting money to repay the club, the betrayal would be overlooked.

So he'd driven the three hours to Clifton Forge in search of Presley. She didn't have the one hundred thousand dollars he'd been looking for but Jeremiah had hoped to get the money from Presley's boyfriend, Shaw Valance. After all, Shaw was one of Hollywood's most highly paid actors.

Jeremiah had been a foolish bastard. Even if he'd

managed to get the cash, no matter how much money he took to the Warriors, they wouldn't have let it go. When Jeremiah had finally clued in to the reality of the situation, the coward had taken his own life. He'd trapped Scarlett and left her behind to pay for his mistakes.

Behind me, Scarlett cleared her throat. She'd changed into another pair of sweats. The navy hoodie and matching pants were articles I'd snagged from the station. The police department crest was embroidered in stark white above her breast. The set was a women's small but it sagged from her body in bunches.

I hadn't thought to check if the things I'd sent actually fit. When I'd first set Scarlett up here, I'd had a female officer make a hasty trip to the store, picking up the necessities. Soap. Toothbrush. Deodorant. Bedding for the bedroom and towels for the bath. I'd told her to take two sets of sweats from the station's supply closet and make sure to pick up Scarlett some socks and underwear.

Each shift change was scheduled around meal time and my team was supposed to have been bringing Scarlett food, but had anyone actually made sure she ate? Scarlett looked to have lost five pounds she hadn't needed to lose.

A knock came at the door before it opened and Chuck stepped in with two plastic grocery bags on his arm. "Hey, Chief."

"Thanks." I went to the door and put my fingers to my teeth and whistled, stopping Nathan before he could get into the patrol car and disappear. "Hold up," I hollered at him, then took the bags from Chuck. "I've got tonight's shift. You can report to the station and grab a patrol car for the night. Watch out for the drunks."

"You got it." Chuck nodded, then lifted a hand to Scarlett. "Ma'am."

He left the house, hurrying across the now shoveled driveway to catch up to Nathan, and I closed the door, bringing the food to the living room.

"Have a seat." I gestured to the recliners, a pair that I'd had in my old house before I'd moved and upgraded furniture.

After I'd bought this place, it had become a storage unit of sorts. I kept my raft here so it wasn't crowding my garage at home, and any spare furniture in case my future renter wanted something partially furnished. These chairs weren't much but they were better than nothing, even if one of them had a protruding spring that poked into my spine. I took the uncomfortable chair, gesturing to its mate.

Scarlett perched on its edge as I hauled out the to-go container, popping the top.

The smell of fried chicken filled the room, chasing away the lingering scent of pizza Nathan must have brought over earlier. I handed it to her along with the package of Hawaiian rolls and her drink.

"Thanks." She set the meal on her knees but didn't eat.

"Don't mind me." I nodded at the food. "Go ahead."

She didn't hesitate. She tore into the chicken and rolls, eating with hurried bites and chasing them with gulps of chocolate milk. When was the last time she'd eaten? She'd been famished.

And when was the last time she'd slept? The circles under her eyes were bottomless and black. Her skin looked pale and her cheekbones hollow. Scarlett's eyes should have been a vibrant, blinding blue, like her sister's. But they had no shine. No spark.

25

Either she'd lost it in this house. Or she'd lost it a long time ago.

I waited, observing as she ate, and when she was done, I took the empty container from her and stuffed it back in the plastic sack.

Scarlett curled into a tight ball in the chair's seat, pulling her knees to her chest. Her hands disappeared into the hems of her sleeves. Her shoes were knotted to her feet, even though they had to be wet from her trek to the store.

Most people would look at Scarlett Marks and think she was broken. Maybe there were a few cracked and scraped pieces, but this woman was not broken. She was lost. Tired. Alone. But not broken.

"Time to talk," I said.

Her eyes flicked to mine. "No, thanks."

"I wasn't asking. I need to know what's going on. The truth."

"You locked me in this place and all but tossed away the key. Which tells me you already know exactly what is happening." Her eyes flashed and that bright blue I'd been searching for blazed for a split second. Maybe I'd missed the blue in the store earlier when I'd had her over my shoulder.

"Yes, I know what's happening," I said. "But I want to hear it from you anyway. Your words."

"Jeremiah was stealing drugs from the Warriors. He got caught and told them it was me."

Her statement was in line with what I already knew but I'd hoped for more details. Not that I'd get them. Scarlett had retreated behind her fortress, her chin raised and her gaze impassive.

Asking questions straight on wasn't going to work so it was time to try a new tactic.

"Do you know Dash Slater?" I asked Scarlett.

She paused. "Sounds familiar."

"He's the man who carried you out of Presley's house that night. He's Presley's boss at the garage."

"So?"

"Dash used to be president of a motorcycle club in town. The Tin Gypsies. Heard of them?"

She blinked.

That's a yes. The Tin Gypsies and the Warriors were known enemies. Even though the Tin Gypsy Motorcycle Club had disbanded years ago, the animosity between members hadn't disappeared. Anyone who'd spent any time with the Warriors had likely heard the Tin Gypsy name. And according to Presley, Scarlett had spent months with the Warriors, living with Jeremiah at their clubhouse in Ashton since last June.

"He thinks the Warriors will retaliate," I said. "I tend to agree."

Scarlett said nothing, though the worry line between her eyebrows lengthened.

"I want to help you."

"Why?"

"Because your sister asked me to."

She blinked and the look of surprise on her face, well . . . it took me by surprise. Why would Presley's concern be a shock to Scarlett?

"She comes into the station every day. She stomps in, demands to know where you are, even though she knows I won't tell her. Mostly, she wants to know you're safe, and she's counting on me to keep you that way."

Scarlett's gaze dropped to her knees.

"Let me. Let me keep you safe."

"I don't want to be trapped here."

"Then tell me everything. All of it. I can't help you if you're hiding things from me."

Her lips pursed together and when she lifted her gaze, it was ice.

"Talk to me," I pleaded.

Nothing.

"You'll do this? You'll really fight me on this? I can't keep you safe out there if I don't understand the threat." I threw my hand toward the door. "Where are you going to go? Huh? If you walk out that door, where are you going to go? To Presley? You'll be bringing trouble straight to her door."

"I would never endanger my sister on purpose."

"Then you don't have a choice. You must stay here. You must talk to me so I can help you."

Scarlett shook her head as she pulled her legs closer to her chest. "No."

Goddamn stubborn woman. "Scarlett—"

"Please don't leave me here." Her whisper was pained. Desperate.

"You have to stay somewhere. Until we learn more. Until I know what we're dealing with." *Until you confide in me.* "They call it witness protection for a reason."

Though this was the small-town, temporary version.

Scarlett turned her gaze to the wall, giving me her profile. Shutting me out.

I didn't have time for this. Was cooperating really so fucking difficult? I stood from the chair and went to the kitchen, taking a long inhale as I reeled in my temper.

Christ, it smelled in here. I walked to the garbage can and popped the lid, my nose scrunching at the stench inside. Nathan must have brought over the pizza place's infamous garlic deep dish. I refused to let the guys bring it to the station because it stunk up the break room so badly. Meal choice was another thing I'd address with Nathan tomorrow.

Slamming the lid back on the garbage, I yanked open the back door and set the entire thing outside. Then I closed the slider and scanned the kitchen.

The linoleum was cracked in a few places and worn thin in front of the sink. My plan was to put hardwood flooring throughout the entire house and get rid of the vinyl flooring and worn, ragged carpet. The refrigerator was yellow, the tinge of a sweat stain. If it had once been white, I couldn't tell. The cabinets were faded and dull. One of the drawers was missing a pull.

There was a reason I'd gotten this house for a steal. It was a shithole. The ugliest house on the block.

No wonder Scarlett had run. I wouldn't want to stay here either.

"Go pack your bag," I said, returning to the living room.

"Huh?" Scarlett unfolded.

"Your bag. Go pack it."

This was a stupid fucking idea I was sure to regret, but at the moment, I was fresh out of other options.

She hopped out of the chair, brushing past me on her way to the bedroom, her scent trailing behind her. The smell of wind and snow clung to her hair but there was a citrus sweetness underneath.

I liked that smell.

Which was a good thing.

Because it was coming to my house for a little while.

CHAPTER THREE

SCARLETT

I wasn't sure where Luke was taking me, but as he wound through the empty, snow-covered streets of Clifton Forge, I didn't ask. As long as I wasn't in that safe house, I'd be fine.

Luke wouldn't take me to Presley, not after his speech about putting her in danger.

Still, my spirits soared that she'd asked about me. Not just once, but every day. It was the only ray of hope I'd seen in ten days and I was clinging to it with a death grip.

Maybe, when this was over, I'd get my sister back after all.

I did my best to memorize street names as we rolled past intersections marked with signs. I wanted to know where I was, not in case I decided to run—I had nowhere to go, as Luke had so graciously reminded me—but because then I might not feel quite so lost.

Walnut Lane.

Maple Street.

Ash Court.

I recited them in my head as the headlights shone on their names. The sky above was pitch black, but the golden glow from porch lights and streetlamps reflected off the fresh snow, chasing some of the darkness away.

Luke had cranked the heat up for me and the inside of his truck was toasty compared to the frozen world beyond the windshield. Despite the warm air blowing through the vents, I shivered, mostly from nerves and adrenaline. From fear.

I'd spent my whole life trying not to shiver. Trying not to show when I was afraid. Most of the time it was easy. After twenty-eight years, faking happy was my specialty. But tonight, I didn't have the strength to keep the trembling at bay.

So I shivered.

Deep, bone-shaking quakes. They felt endless. They came from my soul.

I'd sat inside Luke's truck three times now but I hadn't really noticed the differences between it and a normal vehicle before. Between us, a computer was attached to the console. On the dash, there were rows and rows of buttons and switches. A flash of green lights moved up and down in a row beside a radio headset, like someone was speaking but Luke had turned off the volume.

The cab smelled like Luke. Like sandalwood and earth. He didn't give off a spicy scent or douse himself in cologne, something Jeremiah had done no matter how many times I'd suggested one squirt was plenty.

Luke's scent wasn't overpowering or noticeable unless you stood close. It was simply soothing. Rich and deep. Solid.

The truck smelled like rubber too. Because everything in the truck seemed to be covered in a layer of the black material, from the floor to the lining on the doors. The rubber made sense. If a suspect was bleeding or vomited in the back, rubber would be easy to hose clean.

Too bad our home in Chicago hadn't had more rubber.

Blood wasn't easy to extract from carpet fibers or cotton shirts. Unless Presley was the one doing the cleaning. She'd mastered blood-stain removal by the time we were preteens. Meanwhile, I was the one who'd learned how to apply a butterfly bandage to minimize a scar. I could wrap broken ribs in under five minutes.

The bodily wounds were easy to heal. The wounds to the heart and soul, well . . . those were a different story. Ignoring them was usually how I tended them. For better or for worse, shoving the hard truths away was my coping mechanism of choice.

Luke had pleaded with me to confide in him. To trust him.

I swallowed a laugh. Every man who'd ever asked for my trust had betrayed it. My father. Jeremiah. Maybe Luke was different, but I certainly wasn't going to test that theory.

Trust? *No, thanks.* I'd keep my secrets. Too much was riding on them, especially my life.

If word got out of the video on my phone, I'd die a slow, agonizing death at the hands of the Warriors. Or it would mean a one-way ticket to a new identity.

Maybe I didn't love Scarlett Marks. Maybe she'd been a coward her entire life. Maybe she should have fought harder, done better. But she was me. And one of these days, I'd find a way to redeem her.

Witness protection wasn't an option. Not yet. Not until I'd exhausted every other option to convince the Warriors I'd been Jeremiah's scapegoat.

How? *Not a clue.* But I'd figure it out. I'd fix this fuckup and rebuild my life. And until then, the best way to protect myself was by keeping my mouth shut.

I supposed I had my father to thank for my uncanny ability to bury my pain. He'd taught us young that a smile could be the greatest deceit.

No one had ever suspected what life had been like for Presley and me. Teachers. Neighbors. Pastors. When they looked at us, all they saw were two little girls who wore pink and curled their long blond hair in pretty ringlets. They saw my mother as the shy, soft-spoken woman who preferred to spend her days at home. And my father was the greatest deceiver of them all. He was a monster who'd shake your hand at church on Sunday and crack the best jokes during a neighborhood barbecue.

Sorry, Luke. My hard truths were none of your damn business. Telling them would be like slashing cuts through scars.

Luke slowed and took a right. The angle of the turn caused me to miss the street's sign, but the lights down this block seemed to glow brighter. Cleaner. Happier, even.

This neighborhood was newer than the one I'd walked through earlier. We passed an open lot where the ground around a large *For Sale* sign was blanketed with snow. Beside it was a house in the middle of construction. The walls had been erected and the windows installed, sporting their stickers, but there was no siding on the exterior and the front door was a sheet of plywood.

Curiosity won out and I couldn't stay quiet any longer. "Where are we going?"

Luke didn't answer, serving me with a dose of my own medicine. *Touché, Chief.*

He slowed in front of a two-story house with dormer windows protruding from the roof. The lights were off inside but the exterior fixtures shone bright.

The siding was an eggshell color, board and batten in some sections, straight horizontal in others. The windows were trimmed in black instead of the standard white and the wooden front door had been stained a grayish white to match the garage doors.

This was a family's home. It wasn't extravagant, though it did seem slightly bigger than other homes on the block.

Luke reached for his visor and hit a button to open one of the garage doors, easing inside. Then he shut off the truck and closed the door behind us, not moving until it had lowered to the ground. That was when he got out and came around to the passenger side, opening my door for me.

Luke held out his hand, like he'd done at the safe house.

It would be so easy to slide my palm against his. To take some comfort in a human touch. But if I gave in to his hand, then I might give in to his help. Bit by bit, he'd wear me down until my resolve crumbled.

So I hugged my bag, a navy backpack that held my worldly possessions, and hopped out of the truck to land on my own two feet.

Luke sighed but didn't speak as he led the way to the interior door. He opened it and flipped on a light.

I followed behind him, entering the house through a mud and laundry room.

Luke hung his keys on a hook beside the door, then

planted a hand against the wall, using it for balance as he toed off his boots.

This is his house. He'd brought me to his house. Why?

I stared at him, waiting for an explanation.

Luke didn't offer one. He simply walked away, turning on the lights as he strode through his home.

He had a confident walk, every step sure and unhurried. Without his boots on, the cuff of his jeans dragged on the floor, and the denim fell differently down his long legs, accentuating the strength in his thighs. Molding to that sculped ass. I could still feel the heat in my fist from where I'd hit him earlier.

My cheeks flamed. Was it from embarrassment? Or lust? There was no denying that Luke Rosen had one hell of a body and one hell of a striking face.

Not the time, Scarlett. This was, most definitely, not the time to study Luke's firm behind.

I dropped my chin, studying the brick pattern of the tiled floor as it disappeared beneath the washing machine. My toes were frozen in my shoes and my socks squished a little at the toes, but I didn't take either of them off. Instead, I carefully emerged into the kitchen, following Luke's path across the hardwood floor.

His smell wasn't as strong inside as it had been in the truck, but it was still there, an ever-present reminder that this was his personal space. And for some reason, he'd invited me inside.

The kitchen's bright lights illuminated the space. Black pendants hung above the island's shiny gray quartz countertop. The stainless-steel appliances broke up the rows of white cabinets.

He had a farmhouse sink.

My mother and I had taken to watching home improvement shows over the past five years. We'd curl up together on the living room couch, share a bowl of popcorn and watch HGTV. My father would read, keeping us under his watchful eye, but it was the one channel he didn't mind having on in the background.

If she could see this place—that sink—she'd swoon. Luke's kitchen had all the color schemes and features she loved most.

My heart clenched as I pictured my mother's face. Had she survived my escape? Did she regret shoving me out the door?

Luke picked up a remote from the wooden coffee table in the living room and pushed a button, sending the shades over every window scrolling down. Then he turned to me, his face gentling as he blew out a deep breath.

"This is my house," he said. "You can stay here. Until we have a long-term solution, this will be better than the other place."

I blinked. Was he serious?

Luke dragged a hand over his dark brown hair, mussing the neatly combed strands. I wasn't the only one who was tired of this day. "Come in. Make yourself at home."

I didn't move away from the kitchen island.

The couch looked cozy and there was a large flat screen mounted on the wall above the fireplace. It was homey and warm. The décor was manly, favoring the bold leather couches and dark tones of the wood furniture. The living room walls were painted a rich brown that reminded me of chocolate frosting.

It was so inviting. Too inviting. Too good.

Too good to be true was an adage for a reason. Or maybe

this was his way of earning my trust, showing me his so I'd show him mine.

"Did my sister ever spend the night here?" The question came spewing from my mouth before I'd even processed it mentally.

Maybe I asked because the quickest way for me to compartmentalize Luke Rosen and his handsome face was by picturing him with Presley. To picture him as hers.

"No." Luke shook his head.

"But you dated."

"Yes. For a short time."

Presley had told me she'd dated Luke but I didn't know how serious they'd been. I didn't know much at all about my sister's life over the past decade. Certainly not much about her lovers.

Though I guess *lovers* was the wrong term. For most of that decade, she'd been with Jeremiah. He'd found her after he'd left me. They'd been engaged until he'd jilted her on their wedding day.

Because of me.

"Did you fuck her?" I asked with too much bite.

Luke didn't so much as blink. "No."

Maybe he was telling the truth. Luke didn't seem like a man who'd lie, but I was a pitiful judge of character. For all I knew, he'd lured me into his den. I'd become his prey. Tonight, I was too tired to care.

I shuffled past the island, lifting a hand to skim the smooth surface of a white cabinet. Luke's cabinets were pristine. Clean and unmarred.

I hoped they stayed that way.

We'd had white cabinets at home. Mom would scrub their faces to keep them free of grease and grime. At least, that was the lie she'd tell herself. Really, she'd scrub them after one of Dad's outbursts. Just last year, not long before I'd left, he'd taken a plate of baked ziti and thrown it at a cupboard. Mom had used store-bought marinara sauce instead of making her own from scratch. I'd helped her clean that mess because he'd pushed her so hard that she'd fallen and strained her wrist.

Funny how being in a nice home brought back memories of my own. I'd been so consumed with Jeremiah and the Warriors that my parents had fallen to the wayside. Not forgotten, but not front and center. But it seemed today, I couldn't keep them from the forefront of my mind.

"What happened with you and Presley?" I asked Luke, joining him in the living room.

"You didn't ask her?"

"I didn't have a chance."

When I'd come to Clifton Forge, I hadn't seen Presley in ten years. Not since the night she'd escaped Chicago and I'd chosen to stay behind. But I'd known where she lived. Presley had picked Clifton Forge long before she'd fled our father's rule.

It had taken me a long time to join her. Too long. Instead of leaving Chicago and finding her, like I should have done, I'd gone to Jeremiah.

He was marrying her and I had to know if he'd ever loved me at all. Or if he'd always wanted Presley.

Me. He chose me. And in the process, he ditched Presley and their wedding.

The guilt of my actions, of humiliating her, would stay with me always.

That guilt was part of the reason I didn't go to Clifton Forge and seek her out. I stayed with Jeremiah at the Warrior clubhouse, pretending like things between us would be okay. If we could just get a little more money. If we could just get our own place. If we could just get away from his brothers.

If, if, if.

Months passed as I repeated those ifs. Until finally, I opened my eyes. Or had them opened for me.

The day I packed my bag and raced from the Warrior clubhouse was the day it should have ended. I hitchhiked to Clifton Forge but the truck driver only took me as far as the highway.

From there, I walked to a pay phone and called a cab, using up some of the precious money my mom had given me, money that I'd kept safe since Chicago.

When I arrived at Presley's doorstep, I was so tired, so relieved to be safe with her, that I fell asleep for days. Finally, when I woke up, we sat down to talk.

Then Jeremiah showed up at her door and pressed a gun to her head.

When I'd left the Warrior clubhouse, that should have been the end of it.

Now, the end was nowhere in sight.

"Like I said, we dated," Luke said, answering the question I'd nearly forgotten I'd asked. My brain was sluggish and heavy. "Movies. Dinner. She's an incredible woman. But it wasn't meant to be. She's in love with Shaw."

Shaw Valance. A movie star. I liked that for my sister. I liked that a lot. "Is he a good man?"

"Yeah." Luke nodded. "He is."

I raised my eyes to meet his. "Are you a good man?"

Luke stared down at me, his dark blue eyes unwavering. "If you don't know the answer to that already, I guess I've got some work to do."

Damn. That was a great answer.

"Come on." He jerked his chin for me to follow him through the living room.

We passed a staircase railed with wooden pickets. The steps turned at a square landing in the middle, then led to the floor above us and a small balcony that overlooked the living room. The main floor was finished with a dark hickory, but the carpet on the stairs was plush. My hands itched to run across the fibers. Was it as soft as it looked? It had been a long time since my bare feet had plunged into a soft carpet.

Luke pointed to the ceiling above us as we went down a hallway. "My bedroom is upstairs."

"Okay."

"This is yours." He leaned into a room on my right, flicking on the light. "Towels are under the sink. Shower is stocked but if you need something, let me know."

"Why is the shower stocked?" My question came out more accusing than curious.

Did he have a lot of overnight female companions? Why did it bother me that he might? Luke was a stranger with a perfect face. Nothing more. And after everything that had happened with Jeremiah, the last thing I needed was complications from another man.

"Never mind," I blurted before he could answer. "Not my business."

"For when my dad visits. Hope you like the smell of Old Spice."

"Oh." An odd surge of relief flooded my body, and I gripped my backpack tighter to keep it from falling. "I should have plenty of things. From before."

My first day at the safe house, a female officer had brought me some toiletries and clothes. I suspected that was from Luke's instruction. The woman had also hauled in some necessities for the house. I might have remembered her name if she hadn't brought all of the daisies.

"If you need anything, just make me a list," he said.

Tampons. That was going to be fun to put on the list.

"Okay."

Across from the bathroom was another doorway. Luke reached inside to flip on the light, then stepped aside, waving for me to go ahead.

The room was large with a king-sized bed positioned across from a dresser. The flat screen on top was enough to make me weep. Maybe if I had the TV on at night, it would keep the nightmares away.

The bedding was a simple dove-gray quilt embroidered with squares of the same color thread. The walls in here were even darker than the living room, a charcoal-like ash. Not unlike that ring around Luke's irises. The blackout blinds were down and I suspected that when I turned off the light, it would be like sleeping in a cave—if I could sleep.

It was all monotone, including the black and cream rug that extended beneath the bed, but with the wooden dresser and end tables that matched the chocolate hardwoods, it was cozy. Most importantly, there wasn't a daisy in sight.

"Thank you," I whispered.

He nodded and leaned against the door's frame. "Remote is in the top drawer."

"Okay."

"Come on." Luke jerked his chin for me to follow him back to the living room.

He took a seat on the couch, the one directly across from the fireplace and TV mounted above the mantel. I took the chair beside it, the furniture forming an off-kilter U around the coffee table.

"We need to talk about some rules."

Rules. The word made my spine stiffen, but I stayed silent to listen.

"Please don't leave."

I narrowed my gaze. Never in my life had someone included *please* when reciting rules. What was the catch? "Okay," I drawled.

"You've got the run of the house. TV. There are books in my office upstairs if you like to read. If you want something to eat, just give me a list and I'll hit the store."

I stayed quiet and unmoving, still waiting for that catch.

Luke leaned forward, bracing his elbows on his knees.

Here it comes.

"Stay inside," he said. "Keep the blinds closed. Don't unlock the doors. Don't open the doors."

He paused, waiting for me to acknowledge him so I gave him a single nod.

"The alarm will be set on the doors but I'll leave the motion sensors off," he continued. "When I leave for work, I'll turn the lights on. Leave them on. I'll shut them off at night. That way it doesn't look like someone is here during the day while I'm at work. It'll just seem like I'm an energy hog who can't be bothered to shut off the lights."

I studied his face and the small smile tugging at the corner of his lips. Was he was trying to be funny? On a different day, I might have laughed. But not today. Not when more was coming. Because that couldn't be all the rules. "What else?"

"That's it."

"Just stay inside?"

He nodded. "Just stay inside."

Another prison.

"I get it," he said. "I'd be angry if I were trapped too. But give it a little time. Give it a week or two to let the dust settle. Then, we can reassess the risks."

Maybe it was another prison. Maybe this one wouldn't be so bad. If I had the TV and a book to read, I could distract myself from the shit swirling in my head.

"Okay," I agreed. I'd try. Not for Luke, but for Presley. I wanted to live to give her the apology she was owed. Though when this place began to feel like a prison, I'd be gone. "What about babysitters?"

He chuckled, the sound so soothing and deep, it caught me off guard. "No babysitters. If you can promise to stay inside, you're on your own during the day. You're stuck with me at night."

Yes, I was definitely stuck.

Luke stood. "I'll leave you alone to get settled. I'm upstairs if you need anything."

I stayed seated as he gave me another polite nod, then went to the staircase, disappearing from the main floor. When he was gone, I went to the bathroom, shutting myself in and locking the door.

Then I turned on the shower, stripping out of my sweats. The steam enveloped the room and when I stepped under the spray it scalded my skin. But I stayed under the hot water, letting it chase away the chill in my bones and warm my frozen toes.

Finally, when my skin was red and tingling, I emerged from the shower and swiped a hand over the steam on the mirror. My reflection wasn't as awful as it had been earlier. The dark circles under my eyes were still there. I'd lost too much weight and the skin over my collarbones pulled too tight. But the food from earlier, the fresh air and hot shower, had given my skin some color.

And for the first time in ten days, my blue eyes weren't so flat. Maybe they even held a glint of hope.

I studied myself, from the widow's peak in my forehead to the tip of my chin. Had I ever looked in the mirror and liked what I saw?

No.

At least, not recently. I didn't like the woman staring back at me.

I didn't like myself.

Somehow, that had to change. Somehow, I had to become a better me. I wasn't sure how that was going to happen sequestered in a stranger's home, but I could start small by keeping my word and obeying Luke's rules.

I combed through my hair, the scent of Old Spice filling the room. I'd used what Luke had left in the shower, not bothering to unload my backpack. Maybe I smelled like a man, but it wasn't all bad. At least I was clean.

With a towel wrapped around my body and my clothes and shoes in my arms, I tiptoed across the hallway to the bedroom, glancing past the staircase to the living room. The lights were off except one above the sink in the kitchen. Luke must have come down and shut them off while I'd been in the shower.

I closed and locked the bedroom door behind me, then took out the last clean pair of sweats and panties from my bag. Maybe if I asked, Luke could get me some pajamas. I had a little money left over and something other than sweats would be nice.

Dressed and ready for bed, I picked up a shoe and

groaned. Did I really need to wear them? I wasn't going to run, certainly not tonight. So I tossed it aside and flipped back the quilt, sliding between the cool sheets and snuggling with a down pillow. The light was on but the cotton was so smooth and soft against my cheek, I couldn't muster the energy to open my eyes and lift my head.

Above me, the ceiling creaked under Luke's feet. He was moving around, doing whatever he did. The sound of a hushed television floated through the ceiling.

I took a deep breath, smelling my own soap and the fabric softener on the sheets. It was the same brand my mother used. Pressing my nose into the pillow, I dragged in a long breath.

I missed Mom. Maybe I should have stayed in Chicago. Maybe I should have stayed, sentencing myself to a slow death alongside her.

But now that I'd gotten out, I'd never go back. I doubted I'd ever see her again. No matter how many times Dad hit or raped her, she'd never leave that man. She didn't believe she deserved anything better.

Well, I did.

I deserved more than my father. I deserved more than Jeremiah.

My heart had broken countless times in the past ten days because I was so goddamn angry at him. But this . . . he hadn't deserved this end.

Without warning, a sob escaped my throat. I muffled it with the pillow, feeling the sting of tears as they flooded my eyes. Then, for the first time in ten days, I cried. For Jeremiah. For my mother. For my sister and all I'd put her through.

And I cried for me.

Whether it was the emotional release or my body physically shutting down, I didn't cry for long. I surrendered to the bed and the gentle sounds of Luke above me.

And for the first time in ten days, Jeremiah's nightmare didn't visit me in my sleep.

CHAPTER FOUR

LUKE

"Cause of death?" I asked.

Mike, the county's primary medical examiner, stared down at the body on the stainless-steel table. "I haven't done the full autopsy yet but given where he was found and the obvious signs, gonna say he drowned. Could have been hypothermia too. He was definitely in the water for a while."

I followed Mike's gaze, taking in the victim's hands. The skin was wrinkled and discolored, the same grayish blue as the man's bloated chest. There were welts and scrapes on the distorted skin, and his face was nearly unrecognizable.

Two purple lines slashed with cuts were once the man's lips, though the bottom one had nearly come off his face. One eyeball dangled from its socket. And he'd lost an ear completely.

There was a purple circle on the underside of his jaw, a birthmark about the size of a dime. It had taken on the same violet shade as the man's lips, and beside it, a cut so deep, jawbone peeked out.

"He looks like he was beaten to hell," I said.

Mike shrugged. "Remember that guy who got drunk and fell into the river about eight years ago? Washed up the next day?"

"Vaguely."

"He looked like this too." Mike seemed to remember every single body that had crossed his exam table. How he'd desensitized himself was a mystery. A day inside his mind would be creepy as fuck.

"That guy had cuts everywhere. Couple of holes." Mike spoke like he was reading a restaurant menu, not discussing a dead man. "He'd had an entire slab of skin torn off his back. His face was mush."

"Thanks for the visual," I muttered.

"That's the river for you. Those currents drag you down and pummel you to death. Then it drowns you. You don't fuck with nature, man." Mike accentuated his point with the scalpel in his hand.

"Uh-huh." The chemical stench in the morgue burned my nostrils even though I breathed from my mouth.

Mike was used to the corpses, but seeing a dead person never got easier for me. This one . . . well, my stomach had been churning since I'd walked into the room. To use Mike's word—the river had pummeled this man to death.

"Keep me apprised," I said, already heading for the door.

"Will do, Chief. Shouldn't take me long to have specifics."

The clang of metal instruments dimmed as I left the exam room behind me and took the stairs to the exit two at a time. When I pushed through the door, I filled my lungs with cold winter air, holding it there for a few heartbeats. I hadn't taken a full breath since I'd walked into the building.

How Mike worked with the smells, let alone the dead bodies, wasn't something I'd ever understand. Maybe it was the reason Mike spent most evenings and weekends at The Betsy, drinking beer and playing pool with whoever walked inside.

The afternoon sun rebounded off the melting snow. Beside me, the gutter dripped water onto the parking lot's pavement. It was a beautiful day, the sky cloudless and bright. A trip to see Mike hadn't been on my Saturday agenda, but as the chief of police, there really wasn't such a thing as a day off. The only time I really checked out was when I left town for a fishing trip.

I took the sunglasses from the brim of my hat, putting them on as I walked to my truck. Then I drove to the station, my agenda for the day good as gone.

Every morning, I worked out in the small gym that we had available to the officers and staff. A workout was part of my regular routine, something I never missed, even on the weekends. Lifting weights and doing some cardio kept more than my body in shape; it was an hour for me to organize my thoughts. I'd been on an elliptical, sweat dripping from my temples, when dispatch had called.

A woman had taken her dog for a walk this morning along the riverbanks and the pup had sniffed out a corpse. *So long, elliptical.*

I rolled the windows down as I drove, letting the air blow in my face. The stink from the exam room wouldn't go away until I was home and had showered. My T-shirt was grimy from the dried sweat and I didn't smell all that fresh either. But before I could go home, I had to kick off the investigation into the man's death.

After dispatch had called, I'd pulled on some track pants

and a ball cap, then made my way to the scene. Two other officers had beat me there but both had looked a shade too green after inspecting the body. So I'd been the one to question the woman whose dog had found it. The last thing I needed was a patrolman puking on the poor woman's feet.

This case was going to Chuck. He'd have no trouble working through the process and unlike some of my younger officers, he'd seen enough dead people to keep his breakfast down. Before I went home, I wanted to enter the woman's statement into our system and give Chuck an update on my conversation with Mike.

The bullpen was quiet when I arrived and most desks were empty. The clock on the wall showed it was after three. I'd missed lunch, not that I was hungry.

Today's activities had stolen my appetite. After questioning the woman, I'd hung around the scene as my team had photographed the body. Then while it had been transported to Mike's office, I'd canvased the scene with the other officers, making sure we hadn't missed anything. The only thing we'd found were rabbit tracks in the remaining snowbanks and mud.

Lots of mud. My new tennis shoes weren't so new anymore.

I sat behind my desk and pulled the small notepad from my pocket. Then I logged on to my computer and got to work, transcribing my hurried notes.

The victim's wallet had been stuffed in the back pocket of his jeans. Somehow it hadn't fallen out in the river, which made identifying the body a whole lot simpler. The cash and receipts in the billfold had been soggy, but the driver's license and credit cards were intact.

Ken Raymond. I stared at his name as I typed it in, along

with his address. Ken wasn't from Clifton Forge. According to his ID, he'd lived in Ashton.

On a normal day, I wouldn't have thought twice about his residence. But since Scarlett had come into my life, nothing had been normal. She'd invaded my life, my home and mostly my thoughts. Ashton wasn't just a town three hours away anymore. Ashton was synonymous with the Warriors and the risk they posed to Scarlett's life.

If there was a risk.

Since Jeremiah's suicide, there hadn't been a single sighting of a Warrior in town. And everyone had kept a close watch.

Dash and the guys at the Clifton Forge Garage, most of whom were former Tin Gypsies, hadn't noticed their rivals around town. I'd called Dash yesterday to check in, wondering if maybe the Warriors had been to town but had just been keeping a low profile. Dash had laughed and assured me that nothing about the Warriors would ever be low profile.

I wasn't sure if that should make me feel better or worse.

But at the moment, Scarlett didn't seem miserable. She'd been at my place for a week. That was what I'd asked of her, to try for seven days to stay put, and that was what she'd done. If the Warriors avoided Clifton Forge for another week, I'd have a hard time convincing her—and myself—that they were a real threat.

But I wasn't ready to open the front door and set her free quite yet. So I was going to ask her to stay for another week. Just one more. Then we'd reassess. I could survive Presley's continued trips to the station to harass me about her sister's whereabouts.

So far, no one suspected Scarlett was living under my

own damn roof. Or if they did, they hadn't tipped off Presley. If she knew Scarlett was at my house, Presley would be beating down the door.

The only person who might suspect Scarlett was with me was my buddy Emmett. He worked at the garage as a mechanic and, like Dash, was a former Gypsy. The two of us had met years ago at The Betsy. We'd gotten into an intense game of pool and I'd schooled three hundred bucks from him that night. Two weeks later, he'd won it all back. We'd been friends ever since.

But Emmett wasn't just a mechanic. He had an affinity for hacking, something I pretended not to know. Emmett knew I had that rental house and he'd probably put it together that I'd stashed Scarlett there. Though I doubted he knew I'd moved her. And I doubted he'd ask.

The guys at the garage hadn't pushed for information on Scarlett. I was taking it as a sign of trust, that they knew I'd do the right thing by her. They knew that to the best of my abilities, I'd keep her safe.

I wanted to believe that Ken Raymond's death was entirely unrelated to Scarlett and the Warriors. Chances were, it was. But there'd been a knot in my gut from the moment I'd rifled through the man's wallet while standing beside the river.

Maybe after Chuck ran his investigation, that knot would go away.

How Ken had fallen into the icy Missouri River was a mystery. It could be foul play. It could be suicide. Ken might have been out fishing and slipped on a patch of wet ice.

In the past week, the weather had undergone a swift change. Since the day I'd hauled Scarlett out of the grocery store, we'd had nothing but sunshine. One week of above-freezing temperatures and Clifton Forge was a slush pile. And the river was roaring.

I spun from my monitor, taking in the river through my office's window. We'd had a big winter with lots of snow. It meant lots of runoff. Ice chunks and dirty snowdrifts still spotted the shores, but the water was high and moving fast. The undercurrents were as lethal as the gun holstered at my hip. If Ken had waded in too deep at the shoreline, he'd have been instantly swept away.

Most Montanans knew to stay back from the water. Tourists were usually the sort who'd get themselves into a mess.

We didn't get a ton of visitors in the summer, nothing like other areas of Montana, but we'd see an influx of activity. Strange faces. Out-of-state cars.

It would be harder to identify a Warrior if one came to town. Maybe instead of one more week, I could convince Scarlett to last two.

A knock sounded behind me. "Chief."

I turned from the glass, Chuck at my door. "Hey. What'd you find?"

"Not much. Ken Raymond was clean as a whistle. No record. Not so much as a parking ticket."

That was a good thing. It meant the chance that he was connected to the Warriors was low. "Did you notify next of kin?"

He nodded, his eyes somber. "Called the Ashton station. Had them send a squad car over and notify his wife. Then I called to follow up and give my condolences while you were out."

Chuck was a long-time cop in Clifton Forge. We'd been colleagues much longer than I'd been his boss. Hell, he'd taught me a lot. And when I'd been appointed chief of police, he'd been the first to congratulate me and offer his support. He loved his job and keeping the town's people safe. He was also looking forward to retirement in two years, three months and twelve days—he had a countdown calendar on his desk.

He reminded me of my dad in that way. Dad had a countdown too. And even though retirement approached, Chuck was as diligent about his duties as he'd been for years.

"What did the wife say?"

"Not much." Chuck sighed. "She was pretty shaken up. The officer in Ashton told her that her husband's body had been found, asked if she'd be willing to identify the body. When I called and told her who I was, she started crying and that was about it. I'll give her some time and drive over to talk in person."

"Damn." It was hard to be the man who delivered heart-breaking news. "Sorry."

He nodded. "ETA on the autopsy?"

"Mike didn't think long. But I want to know what he was doing in Clifton Forge. Why he came here from Ashton. Let's be sensitive to Ms. Raymond's grief, but we need answers, sooner rather than later."

"I'll drive over first thing tomorrow morning. Check in. Gauge the situation. Go from there."

"Appreciate it. You're the lead on this. Holler if you need anything."

"Will do." Chuck backed away, returning to his desk in the bullpen.

I pinched the bridge of my nose, wishing my brewing headache a short life. *Stress.* I'd had more headaches in the past two weeks than in the past two years. What I really wanted was to finish up here, go home and shower, then collapse on the couch for a long nap. I hadn't slept well for the past week, ever since I'd moved Scarlett into my guest bedroom. One ear had been trained for any noise from her—an escape attempt.

But she'd been true to her word and stayed.

She was probably wondering where I'd gone. When I'd left this morning, I'd told her I'd be back in an hour. Now the day was spent and when I finally arrived home, it would be time for dinner.

It was for the best. Last weekend, after she'd moved in, I'd given her space. I'd spent more time in my home office than I had in months, working my way through bills and a stack of mail. Then I'd killed hours working in the yard. During the week, after work, I'd done more of the same.

Eventually, I'd get used to having her around. Maybe if she ventured outside of her bedroom for more than five minutes at a time we'd get to know each other. But she was holed up tight, and as long as she didn't leave, I'd let her be.

We were walking on eggshells, sharing awkward glances and muttered hellos. Maybe tonight, if I picked up a couple cheeseburgers from Stockyard's, she'd eat with me and we could muddle our way through a conversation.

Maybe eventually, she'd grow to trust me.

I hadn't pushed Scarlett for more information about her time with Jeremiah and the Warriors. That didn't mean I wasn't antsy to know, especially if the Warriors were in any way connected to Ken Raymond's death, but I was balancing my curiosity against her flight risk.

Should I ask her about Ken Raymond? *No. Not yet.* I'd leave it alone until Chuck determined if this was an accidental death or a homicide investigation. The last thing I wanted was to spook Scarlett and have to chase her down again.

If she grew comfortable at my place, she'd be less likely to run, right? She'd be more likely to see that I had her best interests at heart.

I finished up my report, then closed down my computer and dialed Stockyard's, one of the bars in town, and ordered a couple of burgers to go. Stockyard's wasn't the ruckus The Betsy was and catered to an older crowd. Their burgers were legendary and now that the stench of the morgue was fading, my appetite had returned.

The waitress didn't question my two-burger order, assuming they were both for me along with a heaping order of fries. I'd just ended the call when another knock sounded at my door.

A woman stood at the threshold, wearing a pair of black slacks and a matching blazer. Her white shirt was starched, the collar crisp and stiff beside her neck. The badge on her hip shone, as did the Glock holstered beside it.

What the hell was a fed doing here?

Chuck peeked over her shoulder, giving me a shrug. He must have escorted her in.

"Chief Rosen." She walked into my office, hand extended. "Maria Brown."

"Nice to meet you." I stood, returning her firm handshake before motioning her to take a seat in a chair across from my own.

"Maria, please." Before she sat, she took a card from her pocket, handing it over. "I'm with the FBI."

No shit. I glanced at the card, the words *Violent Gang Task Force* jumping out beneath her name. Son of a bitch. This was about Scarlett. I'd bet my pension on it.

I stared at Agent Brown, waiting for her to speak.

Maria's dark hair was pulled into a severe knot. Her brown eyes were warm in color but calculating as she held my stare. She was sizing me up.

"What can I do for you?" I asked.

"Do you always work on Saturdays?"

"Do you always answer a question with a question?"

The corner of her mouth turned up. "A couple of weeks ago, a man committed suicide here after taking two women hostage."

"I'm aware."

"One of the women is a person of interest. Scarlett Marks."

"And why is she so interesting?" I kept my face impassive, though my heart raced. Maria Brown had the upper hand, and if I didn't keep my wits about me, my bad day would turn into a clusterfuck really fast.

"We believe she has information that might help us on a case."

I steepled my fingers by my chin. "What case?"

"I'm sorry. I'm not at liberty to discuss the details. I hope you understand."

"Of course." Cooperation was a two-way street around here. She didn't get to show up at my door on a Saturday, whip out a business card and get my secrets. Not until she spilled some of her own first. Not until I knew the FBI had Scarlett's best interests in mind.

Maria continued to stare, waiting for me to speak. Most people did if you waited long enough.

Not me.

"After the hostage incident, you took Ms. Marks into custody, correct?"

"Correct. I placed her in a safe location and had officers assigned to her round the clock." All of which was documented in our reports. If Agent Brown started asking questions around the station, she'd have this sliver of truth and my team wouldn't have to lie.

"Where is this safe location?"

"Actually, it was a rental property of mine. It was empty and the quickest solution. She was staying there."

"Was?"

I nodded. "Was. Ms. Marks decided to leave that location." Another sliver. If Agent Brown talked to Nathan or Chuck, they'd know about the events leading up to the grocery store debacle and that I'd brought Scarlett back to the rental house. But the only person who knew what happened after that was me. "I didn't have the manpower to force her to stay. I offered. She refused."

"Do you happen to know of Ms. Marks's whereabouts now?" Maria asked.

"I don't." Scarlett could be in her bedroom. She could be on the couch watching TV. She could be naked in the shower. I didn't know of her exact whereabouts and wouldn't until I got home.

Maria's eyes narrowed. "Have you spoken to her about the incident at her sister's home?"

"I have."

"And?"

"And that's part of a closed case. I'm not at liberty to discuss the details. I hope you understand."

A flash of irritation crossed her eyes, having her own words tossed back at her, then her mouth split into a wide grin. "Of course."

"Sorry I'm not much help." I stood, holding out my hand.

Maria stayed in her seat, her eyes glued to mine, until finally, she stood and shook my hand once more. "Thank you, Chief. I'll be in town for a while. Maybe I'll swing by again soon."

"Happy to help any way I can, Agent Brown." It was a lie. We both knew it. But unless she showed up here again with a warrant, I wasn't talking.

Maybe the FBI could help Scarlett. Or maybe they'd use her as a pawn. I'd been involved in two federal cases in my tenure as a cop, both of which had left a bad taste in my mouth.

I escorted Maria out of my office and through the bullpen, neither of us bothering with small talk or pleasantries. When we left the station, I nodded a curt goodbye on the sidewalk, then strode to my truck and climbed inside.

Calm. Collected. Cool. It was only after she pulled away in a shiny black SUV that I blew out the breath I'd been holding.

What the fuck did the FBI want with Scarlett? Did they think she'd stolen drugs from the Warriors? Did they know she was innocent? Or was there more?

Maria Brown was from the gang task force, not the DEA. Though it wouldn't surprise me if both divisions were involved here. This had the Warriors' name written all over it.

My mind spun through the questions as I drove to Stockyard's and picked up dinner. Another death. The FBI. There'd be no relaxing when I got home. Only work, trying to get Scarlett to confide in me with the truth.

As I turned onto my street, my eyes darted everywhere, searching for anything out of place. The vehicles parked in driveways were all recognizable, neighbors' and a few construction workers'. A couple of kids rode their bikes along the sidewalks.

Yet the hairs prickled at the back of my neck, like someone was watching me as I eased into my garage. I waited until the door was completely shut before climbing out and going inside.

Scarlett stood in the kitchen. "Hey."

"Hi." I hefted up the bag in my hand. "I picked up burgers."

"Oh."

I toed off my shoes and padded into the kitchen. "Is that okay?"

"Sure." She nodded, darting to the cupboards to take out plates.

Scarlett had found her way around the house quickly. When I came home each evening, she'd already retired to her room, but judging by the dwindling food in the fridge and the dirty dishes in the dishwasher, she was eating.

The circles under her eyes had faded considerably. Her cheeks weren't as hollow as they'd been a week ago. Even her hair had a newfound sheen. It hung in long, silky strands to her waist.

She looked better. Much better.

Scarlett took a burger for her plate and I shook out some fries. Then she gave me a small smile before picking up her plate and making a hasty exit from the kitchen.

"Wait," I said to her back before she could disappear into her bedroom. "Let's eat together."

"Oh, that's okay."

"Please." The word was more of a command than a plea.

Her shoulders fell as I walked to the dining room and quickly drew the shades.

The room was located at the front of the house, off the entryway. I rarely sat at the table myself, preferring to eat at the kitchen island or in the living room. But that was only because sitting at a six-seat table alone was a bit depressing.

There was a large picture window that overlooked the neighborhood. I hadn't bothered to pull these shades earlier in the week because even if someone pressed their hands against the glass from outside, they couldn't see into the house. Scarlett was smart enough not to come in here and expose herself.

She hovered beyond the room as I took a seat.

I frowned. Did everything have to be a fight? "Sit down, Scarlett."

A flash of irritation crossed her face but she did as ordered, sliding into a chair. Then she popped a fry into her mouth, her eyes never leaving mine as she chewed.

I tore into my burger, eating like a starved man, but Scarlett picked at hers. "Don't you like burgers?"

She lifted a shoulder. "They're fine."

Lies. Was that why she'd been quick to disappear? So I wouldn't notice that she wasn't eating? It wasn't my job to learn everything there was to know about her. I just needed to learn what had happened with the Warriors. "I had a visit from the FBI today."

Scarlett froze, the fry pinched between her fingers stopping midair.

"They are looking for you."

She gulped.

"Want to tell me why?"

"No." She dropped the fry to her plate and made a move to stand, but I lifted a hand.

"Stop. Scarlett, please. You've got to tell me what's going

on. Today won't be the last time the FBI comes sniffing around. For all I know, they're watching the house. And until I know what we're dealing with, you're not going anywhere." One week. Two weeks. It was all off the table at this point.

Her shoulders tensed, rising toward her ears. Scarlett knew that with the FBI involved, she'd be hiding here for the foreseeable future.

"It would help me if I knew what happened while you were with the Warriors."

"Nothing happened."

"I believe that just about as much as I believe you like cheeseburgers."

Her nostrils flared and she picked up her burger, using both hands, before opening her mouth wide and chomping a huge bite. She chewed with fury, trying to prove me wrong. She might have done it if not for the grimace when she swallowed.

I hung my head and sighed. *Christ.* Couldn't this be easier? Did she have to be so damn stubborn? I was trying to help. "Fine. Let's try something else. How about some yes and no questions?"

She dropped the burger to her plate.

"Did you know Jeremiah was stealing drugs from the Warriors?"

"No."

"Has the FBI ever contacted you before?"

"No."

They probably hadn't been able to approach her if she'd been living with the Warriors. Now that she was out, Scarlett was fair game.

I popped the last bite of my burger into my mouth, still

hungry, and reached across the table to collect the rest of hers.

She didn't protest. Scarlett simply watched me eat, bringing her legs up in the chair so her knees were tucked into her chest. The posture seemed so natural for her. A habit. A protective shell.

There was no way I'd get past it with another round of questions, which meant it was time to switch it up.

"Did you do laundry today?" The house smelled like soap and fabric softener, one of my favorite things.

She gave me the side eye. "Yes."

"Whenever I walk into a house that smells like laundry, it reminds me of my mother. I'd come home from school and it would either smell like laundry or chocolate chip cookies." Mostly laundry. Mom had always teased me that it was the never-ending story of her life. But on the days when there was nothing to wash, she'd bake cookies. "Is the bed in your room comfortable?"

Scarlett let one of her legs drop to the floor, her eyes narrowing as she drawled, "Yes."

"Good." I nodded. "My dad always said it was but he's happy sleeping anywhere so I wasn't sure."

Scarlett studied me, lifting another french fry to her mouth as she put her other leg down.

My random questions were working. Thank God. Not that I was learning anything important. "Watch anything good on TV today?"

"No."

I leaned back in my chair, taking my last bite. The juicy flavor of the burger, the soft texture of the bun and the tang of the pickle and mustard were what I'd needed after a long day. How could Scarlett not like a good burger?

She was different than Presley that way. Pres and I used to go to Stockyard's often while we dated.

"You grew up in Chicago, right?" I asked.

"Yes."

"What did you do?"

It wasn't a yes or no question, but I hoped that she'd open up. *Come on, Scarlett. Give a little.*

She ate another french fry, her eyes fixed firmly on her plate. "I worked as a receptionist after I graduated from a local community college."

"Did you like it?"

"No."

It wasn't much, but it was better than nothing. Slowly, I was figuring this woman out.

Scarlett wasn't like Presley. Whatever came to Presley's mind usually came out of her mouth, snark and all. Scarlett had the snark, she had the edge, but she kept everything hidden.

There wouldn't be a hurried confession. Learning about her was going to take time. Trust. And after all she'd been through, I guess I couldn't blame her. That son of a bitch Jeremiah had done a number on her. Why would she think I was any different? She didn't know me either.

I had the power to change that.

"I went to college," I said. "Stayed all four years and graduated with a degree in sociology. Except for my criminal justice classes, I hated every minute. I always knew I wanted to be a cop like my dad, but I stuck out school anyway."

"Why?" Scarlett ate another fry, unable to hide the curiosity in her voice. She could ask me all the questions she wanted. Unlike her, I had nothing to hide.

"My mom. She wanted me to go to college for the experience and education. Secretly, I think she'd hoped I'd decide to be a lawyer instead of a cop." I always wondered if she was looking down on me, happy that I'd followed the path I'd been so set upon, or disappointed that I hadn't branched out. "I actually wouldn't have gone to college at all, but she died my junior year in high school."

Scarlett sucked in a sharp breath. "How?"

"Breast cancer."

"I'm sorry."

I gave her a sad smile. "She was a remarkable woman. Love of my dad's life. Best mother in the world, and I'll fight you on that one if you say yours is better."

Scarlett dropped her chin and shook her head.

"I grew up in Montana. Lived in the state my entire life. When Mom was alive, we lived in Great Falls. That's where I was born. Then after she passed, neither Dad nor I wanted to stay. Too many memories. We moved to Missoula and I did my senior year there, then stayed for college. He's been there ever since. Though I think he'll move here when he retires in a few years."

To this day, we both missed Mom. We both always would. But especially Dad. He'd stayed strong after her death, not letting his grief consume him. For me. And I hoped in some way I'd helped him too. We'd leaned on each other.

"Are you close?" Scarlett asked.

I nodded. "He's my best friend. I talk to him a couple times each week."

She kept her chin down. "Why are you telling me all this?"

"Because maybe if you get to know me, you'll realize I'm a good guy."

Scarlett scoffed, the noise barely audible. Then she lifted her face, her gaze defiant, and shook her head. "I don't believe in good guys."

I'd have to change her mind on that one. Luckily, I had time.

Scarlett Marks wasn't going anywhere.

CHAPTER FIVE

SCARLETT

Thirty days. It had been exactly thirty days since Luke had come home to tell me the FBI was in Clifton Forge. Thirty days since he'd asked me his yes or no questions about Jeremiah and the Warriors.

Thirty days—I'd been counting—and nothing since. No hint at what was happening beyond these walls. No interrogation about my past. Luke acted like I was his long-term guest. A roommate, even.

He went to work every morning, rising earlier than me. He'd leave the coffee pot on with enough left over for me to have three cups. Then he'd come home every evening and eat whatever I'd made that day. With nothing else to do, cooking had become a regular pastime.

A couple times per week, I'd leave a sticky note on the island with some things I needed from the grocery store and Luke would dutifully pick them up.

We didn't eat together. I made sure to finish my dinner before he came home, ensuring I wouldn't be forced into the dining room again. I hadn't set foot in there over the past thirty days either.

After he ate, sometimes we'd watch a movie together. Other times, I'd disappear to my room while he went upstairs. But the awkwardness between us was fading. Being around him was . . . comfortable. Easy. Or, it should have been.

As the days passed and he continued to show absolutely no interest in what had happened before I'd come to live under his roof, the anxiety was taking its toll.

I was sick to death of the pleasant smiles. His standard *How was your day?* followed by a standing report on the weather. The goddamn weather.

What was happening? Was the FBI still sniffing around? Had anyone seen or heard from the Warriors? The only reason I could come up with for his silence was that he already knew. But that was impossible. There was no way he knew what had happened in Ashton.

There was no way he knew what I had on my phone.

So why was he being so quiet? His silence was driving me up his chocolate-frosting-colored walls. It had pushed me to the edge and when he got home and saw what I'd done to his house, well, he only had himself to blame.

"Damn," I muttered to the ceiling as I flopped onto the carpeted floor. Sweat beaded at my temples as my heart pounded inside my chest.

God, I'm out of shape. My muscles were weak after a month of lazing around and doing nothing but watching Netflix, snacking and reading a couple of Luke's books—or trying. The man only had books about dead presidents and world wars in his library.

No, thanks.

The past month with little to no physical activity had turned my body sluggish. My time at the Warrior clubhouse hadn't exactly included regular exercise either. I'd spent months in Jeremiah's room, avoiding his *brothers*. More like avoiding assholes.

When you added up my time here and my time there, I'd been in Montana for ten months. Nearly a year of spending more time in bed than out. Nearly a year of terror and uncertainty.

Nearly a year, wasted.

No more. The minute I was out of here, I was going to change that. I'd find a job. I'd find a home. I'd find a flipping life.

Only, I had no idea when I was getting out of here.

Luke might not have clued me in to what was happening with the Warriors or FBI, but I had to believe that if there was no risk, he would have been the first to kick me out of his house.

In the meantime, I was stuck in Luke's house, desperate for a distraction and searching for ways to get into shape.

Hence my afternoon rearranging furniture.

In Luke's bedroom.

After a month of wandering around the house and shaking my head at the layout in each room, I'd finally had enough. Seriously, had he just left the furniture where the delivery crew had dropped it? There was no structure. No pattern. No flow.

Well, I'd fix that.

And work up a good sweat in the process. If Luke didn't like it, too bad. It was his fault for not having a home gym.

Certainly he worked out, but where? His body was insane and fit and tight in all the right places. His biceps bulged against the sleeves of the navy uniform shirt he donned each weekday. His jeans molded around those beefy, tantalizing legs. And his ass . . .

I swallowed hard, squeezing my eyes shut as a wave of heat rushed to my core.

Maybe it was boredom's doing, but damn it, I'd all but memorized Luke's features in the past month and not a single one was lacking.

His physique was unparalleled and so, *so* freaking sexy. His blue eyes had this way of drawing me in and putting me under his spell. And every now and then, he'd flash a smile, mostly when we were watching a comedy on TV.

That smile sent tingles down my spine each and every time it spread across his face. It wasn't devilish or flirty. No, Luke's smile was just pure, unfiltered confidence.

When something was funny, he smiled. When he was happy, he smiled. Luke wasn't the type who needed to fake a thing, certainly not his joy. He knew exactly who he was, and damn it, that was the biggest turn-on of them all.

You have no business being turned on, Scarlett.

No, I did not. Because whenever Luke did decide to ask me some questions, a crush wasn't going to make it easier to dodge them.

Besides his inability to stage a room, there had to be something wrong with him. If I could just figure it out.

I wiped my brow and sat up, inspecting the room.

The pieces had been a lot heavier than I'd imagined. Luke had invested in quality furniture. But I'd managed to wrestle them around regardless. Sure, I could have just watched a Pilates video, but I loathed them—there was something about a woman ordering you to *lift, sweep, circle* over and over that made me want to pull my hair out.

Tomorrow my plan was to tackle the living room. Then his office.

For the first week I'd lived at Luke's, I'd stayed on the main floor, keeping close to my room. But then curiosity had won out and I'd wandered upstairs. Much like the first floor, the furniture hadn't so much been arranged as it had been plopped.

Luke's bedroom had been the worst offender, so I'd decided to fix it first.

His bed had been pushed underneath the windows, leaving a huge expanse of empty wall space. Who didn't center their bed? Not only that, but it had been on the wrong side of the room. Why not put it opposite the doors to the bathroom and walk-in closet?

His sleigh bed was extremely heavy and had taken me nearly an hour to shove, inch by inch, and pivot in the room. The chest of drawers had taken nearly as long to drag into position across the thick, plush carpet.

I stood and surveyed my work, smiling to myself as my chest puffed with pride. There was so much potential with Luke's house. It just needed a bit of help.

In another life, maybe I would have become an interior designer. But no one was going to pay a woman with a generic associate's degree from a no-name community college to shuffle furniture around and pick out new pieces.

Besides, before I could think of another life, I needed to fix the one I was living.

I glanced at the clock. I had another hour before I needed to start dinner, so I hurried to the bathroom and showered. As I blow-dried my hair, I studied the small room, like I did most days.

The mirror was boring and frameless. The walls needed a color other than white.

Fixing those would be another woman's duty. I doubted Luke would grant me access to a paint brush.

I dressed in a pair of boyfriend jeans, cuffed at the ankles, and a simple T-shirt. It was a Clifton Forge Police Department shirt, one Luke had snagged from the station. He'd ordered the jeans for me online, along with a few simple tees after he'd offered and I'd given him my sizes. I hadn't gone crazy, just two pairs of Levi's, but it was amazing how much better I'd felt, acquiring a wardrobe not entirely made of sweats.

I hadn't worn a lot of jeans growing up. Dad had preferred his *precious angels* in dresses and skirts. If there were bruises on our legs to cover, then we'd slip leggings on beneath our skirts. Everything had been pastel or floral print.

If I never wore a flower again, I'd die a happy woman.

I worked my hair into a quick braid. It had grown thicker this past month. So had I. My pants and shirts didn't feel like the tents they had when I'd moved into Luke's home, though when I looked in the mirror each day, I still didn't love the woman staring back.

But she was growing on me. Each day I noticed my skin's healthy flush. The blue of my eyes was beginning to sparkle.

Maybe these thirty days were exactly what I'd needed.

I hurried to the kitchen, taking out one of two cookbooks from Luke's cupboard. The cooking was in part so I'd have something to do and something to eat. But it also served as a way to avoid another cheeseburger.

Tonight, I was making spicy mac 'n' cheese. I got to work, bustling around the kitchen that felt more and more like mine every day, boiling water and shredding cheese. I roasted a couple poblano peppers and added them to the casserole dish before placing the entire thing in the oven to bake while I pulled out plates and silverware.

I was just taking the dish from the oven when the garage door opened and the low rumble of Luke's truck grew louder.

"Damn." It was only five. He'd come home early and I'd gotten a late start on dinner.

We'd probably have to eat together.

The door to the garage opened and Luke jerked up his chin as he tugged off his boots and socks, tossing the latter in the hamper I'd learned he left in the laundry room specifically for that purpose. "Hey."

"Hi." I gave him a small smile, trying to ignore the skip of my heart.

It was a rush to see him. The biggest thrill of my day. The energy was always charged when Luke was in the room. Whether it was because I was waiting for him to finally ask me about the Warriors, or something else entirely . . . well, it was probably both.

He came into the kitchen and opened the fridge, bending to take out a beer. "Want one?"

"No, thanks."

He closed the door and twisted off the bottle's cap, tipping the rim to his lips.

My breath hitched and I forced my eyes away from his handsome face. I didn't let myself study the way his shirt accentuated the breadth of his shoulders. Or how sexy it was to see him walk around in bare feet.

Too much ogling and I might forget that I didn't trust Luke Rosen.

"Smells great in here. Have you eaten yet?"

I shook my head.

"Then I guess we can eat together for a change."

Ugh. He was going to force me into the dining room again. "Sure."

Luke took another long pull from his beer, his Adam's apple bobbing as he swallowed. It was a mesmerizing thing, this man's throat. Seriously, didn't he have a flaw?

I turned away to hide the flush in my cheeks. A flaw, a flaw. I needed to think of a flaw to focus on if I was going to survive this dinner. *Come on, Scarlett. Think of something.*

Lightbulb!

He'd dated Presley. There, that was a flaw. Okay, not exactly. Really, it just showed his good taste. But my sister and I had traded enough men. Well, one, but Jeremiah had been a doozy so I wasn't in a hurry to repeat that mistake.

Luke had dated Presley. Therefore, he was off-limits. Plus, he was the enemy. Two very substantial facts to focus on instead of his handsome face.

I grabbed a serving spoon from a drawer.

"What would you like to drink?" Luke asked.

"Water is fine. I'll get it," I said, walking to the sink to fill a glass. When I came back, he'd dished my plate.

It was very domestic. Easy. Then he took another drink of his beer and I found that bob of his throat again.

My mouth watered.

He looked up, beyond the amber bottle, and for the briefest of seconds, I could have sworn his eyes darkened with desire. But he was gone before I could analyze the look, taking both of our plates out of the kitchen.

And straight into the dining room.

It was just a room. The only room I hated in this house.

I had no choice but to follow, my steps heavy and slow. The table was nice enough, a lighter color wood than the floors. The tall-backed chairs were classic with clean lines. But everything about the room made me edgy.

"How was your day?" he asked as I sat down.

"Okay." My stomach twisted and I picked up my fork. "How was yours?"

He sighed. "Fine."

The days when Luke came home and immediately went for a beer, combined with a *fine*, meant he'd had a long day. But the details were something he didn't share, maybe couldn't share, so I didn't ask.

Luke lifted his fork, diving into the pasta. He put the first bite in his mouth, flinching and reaching for his beer as he sucked in some air. "Ah. Hot."

I froze, holding my breath, as I stared, unblinking, across the table.

He chewed openmouthed, swallowing his bite with a gulp of his drink. When he looked my way, his eyebrows came together.

Probably because the color had drained from my face.

"Sorry," I whispered.

"For what?"

"I should have warned you it was hot."

"I saw it steaming. I was the idiot who ate it."

"Right." I gulped, then focused on my plate.

Trauma and fear were horrible dinner companions. They'd stolen my appetite.

"Scarlett, it's not your fault."

"I know." And I did. It wasn't my fault he'd burned his tongue. But too many times I'd watched my mother get punished for the same thing. It hadn't been her fault either.

"Hey." Luke's gentle voice made me look up. His eyes, so

kind and concerned, were waiting, begging for an explanation.

And for the first time, I didn't want to shut him out.

"Did Presley ever tell you about our childhood?"

"No."

That wasn't a surprise. I doubted she'd told many people about our upbringing. Habits and all. "The table makes me nervous."

"The table."

I nodded. "My father's favorite place to explode was at the dinner table. If he burned his tongue on something my mother cooked and she hadn't warned him, hell, even if she had warned him, he'd use it as an excuse to blow."

Luke set down his fork, leaning his elbows on the table. "Define explode."

"Do you really need a definition?"

His jaw clenched. "I had no idea."

"It's not exactly something that makes great conversation."

"Because we have so many great conversations," he deadpanned.

I laughed. "True."

"How about we have one now?" Before I could object, he held up a hand. "You tell me whatever you want. Leave out whatever you don't."

Oh, he was good. Those eyes. That honest face. They shattered my resolve.

"My father is a monster disguised as the nice neighbor next door. From the outside, we were the perfect family. Picnics on Saturdays. Church on Sundays. Girls with straight As and parents who loved them so much, they kept them close. But on the inside, our home was a cesspool of fear and rage."

"Your father hit you."

"He *beat* us."

There was a difference between those who hit and those who beat. Physical blows weren't as powerful unless you paired them with mental torture too.

"My mother took the brunt of it. He'd punch her when she didn't cook something he liked. He'd rape her when she waved at the man who lived next door on her way to the mailbox. And for us . . . he demanded perfection."

Tension radiated off of Luke, rolling over the table in waves. But it was a different kind of tension, the protective kind. Something I'd only ever felt from my sister. And from Jeremiah.

"When he exploded, it was always physical. He wouldn't scream or yell. It was just this terrifying, silent rage. He'd hit me or Presley in the arm or kick us in the shin because we missed a word on a spelling test. Mom didn't work so he'd crack her in the face."

Luke flinched and the faint sound of molar grinding against molar caught my ear.

"For us, with school, he'd keep the bruises where we could cover them with pants or sleeves. He'd drag us around by our hair. Which is probably why Presley cut hers short. So no one would be able to do that to her again. If we complained about eating broccoli, he'd send us to bed hungry. If we cried, he'd 'give us something to cry about.'" I rolled my eyes with the air quotes. It felt good to roll my eyes, something I wouldn't have dared in my father's presence.

"And your mother didn't stop him?"

"She loves him."

"She just let it happen?" From the little he'd spoken to me about his mother, it was clear he'd adored her. And she him. Luke's sense of right and wrong was so noble. So definite. My mother wasn't someone I expected him to understand.

"It's a sickness," I said. "Presley hated her for it. But I don't. She'll always cower before him because she doesn't know any better. Because in between the bad days, he worships her. He makes her feel like she's his entire world and without her, he'd die. He's warped her mind. She doesn't work. She doesn't have friends. He is her entire world and it's his game. One that he never lost until Presley left."

"When was that?"

"Ten years ago. After we turned eighteen."

Luke nodded but otherwise sat motionless, hanging on my every sentence. Now that the words were shaking loose, I couldn't seem to get them to stop.

"I haven't told many people about this. It's humiliating," I confessed as my eyes blurred. "Much like my mother, I don't have friends."

"Scarlett, you don't have to—"

"No." I shook my head and blinked the tears away. "It actually feels good. I have very little control over my life. But keeping my secrets . . . no one can reach into my mind and take them. What I tell people, what I give to them, is my decision."

Understanding washed over Luke's face. Staying quiet about what I'd seen at the Warrior clubhouse wasn't just to protect my life. It was also me grasping for a shred of control when otherwise, I was at the world's mercy.

I was trapped here. Before that, I'd been trapped in

Ashton. And before that, I'd been trapped in suburban Chicago.

"Presley got out," I said. "I didn't."

"Why?"

"Because I'm a fool," I whispered. "After graduation, Dad was as bad as ever, maybe because we were eighteen and we were old enough to leave. He wouldn't allow Presley or me to get summer jobs. He didn't want us to have any money. One day, he came home from work with applications to the community college and told us to fill them out. That he'd pay for our classes and afterward, he'd find jobs for us at his company. Everything was planned. Presley joked that he'd find our husbands before too long."

Luke leaned his elbows on the table, the meal forgotten.

"Presley wanted out. So did I. And Jeremiah was going to help us because he loved me."

Luke nodded, like he'd heard this part before. After Jeremiah died, Presley had probably told Luke how Jeremiah and I had known each other from Chicago.

"Jeremiah was my high school boyfriend," I said. "My secret. My parents never knew about him, or maybe my mother did, but she never let on. He knew what life was like at our home and he wanted to help us get out. Presley and I scraped together money from babysitting and he covered the rest to buy us all an old junker to drive off into the sunset."

"But you didn't go."

"No." I dropped my gaze to the table. "Almost."

Luke didn't utter a word as I thought about that night. About the mistake I'd regret forever. Maybe if I had been brave, maybe if I'd just gone with Presley, Jeremiah would still be alive. Maybe none of this would ever have happened.

I couldn't blame him entirely for his death. Part of it had been on me too.

"Presley had her sights set on Montana. And I wanted California. I wanted to live beside the ocean, to fall asleep to the sound of the waves and be a world away from my father. Jeremiah was going to come with me. We'd drop Presley off in Montana, then continue on our way. But . . ."

"Your father found out."

I shook my head. "No."

"Your mother?"

"I got scared." I gave him a sad smile. "We'd been sneaking clothes and stuff from our room for weeks. Jeremiah kept them at his place since we lived in the same neighborhood. The only place Dad would let us go was the library but Presley used one of their computers to line up a job here at the garage. She'd found a place to stay. All she could talk about was her new life. Over and over and over. She never stopped. And I . . . wasn't prepared. I wasn't ready. Then it came time to leave and . . ."

I closed my eyes, the darkness from that night wrapping around me like cold tendrils of smoke, dragging me into a night I'd replayed more times than I could remember. "The air was so still that night. It was too thin, like I couldn't breathe in enough air to fill my lungs and I was dizzy. Every step I took away from our house I felt like I was stretching a string. Pulling it tighter and tighter. And it kept towing me backward. Like my father had a hand on the other end and he was letting me go just far enough to yank me back before delivering a punishment so severe it would become the ruler against which I measured all future discretions."

My throat went dry so I lifted my water glass, except my hand was shaky and it sloshed over the rim.

"Come on." Luke stood, collecting his plate and mine. Then he walked into the living room, taking a seat on the couch.

I followed, glad to get away from the dining room. In my mind, I knew it was different. Luke wasn't my dad and there was nothing to fear from a table and six chairs. Someday I'd conquer that irrational fear. Today was not that day.

Luke gave me time to settle into the chair across from him and catch my breath. He dove into the pasta and didn't say a word. No questions. No pressure. If I wanted to talk, it was my choice.

For a woman who'd just told him how little was in her control, it meant the world that he'd listened.

I tucked my legs into the chair's seat, the plate balanced between my knees. "Presley always tested the boundaries. She'd do things to see if she'd get caught. She was fearless."

The corner of his mouth turned up as he chewed. "Sounds like her."

"I wasn't like that. I didn't need to test the limits because I didn't like what happened when I was caught. Or when she got caught. I was the one to take care of her. I was the one to wrap her ribs when he cracked one. I was the one who raced for the ice pack when Mom got a bloody nose or black eye. Presley got mad at Mom, resented her. I just . . . I just wanted everyone to live and see tomorrow."

Luke set his nearly empty plate aside on the coffee table. "You didn't rock the boat."

"Why would I? We were sitting in a life raft in the middle of the ocean while a hurricane raged around us."

"So you stayed."

"I stayed." What I wouldn't give to go back and redo that

night. "We snuck out. Mom and Dad weren't asleep but there were noises and they were . . . occupied."

No matter how many years that passed, I'd never forget the sound of my father raping my mother. The slaps. The grunts. I'd been terrified to have sex with Jeremiah in high school because I'd been so sure it would hurt.

It had, but in the way that awkward teenagers lost their virginity. Then later, at the clubhouse, it had been cold. Distant. Sex was overrated. I couldn't even blame it on Jeremiah. The one who'd changed most in the years we were apart was me.

"We ran in the dark to meet Jeremiah," I told Luke. "Presley was so excited. She was so sure. She laughed and smiled. I took one look at that car and the string just *yanked*. If he caught us, we were dead. So I lost it."

Neither of them could calm me down. I'd been hysterical, crying and trying to tell Presley that it was wrong. That we'd be caught. My entire body had been shaking. I'd tried to tear her bags out of the car, to drag her home, but she wasn't going back to that house.

"I screamed," I said. "I told Presley I wasn't leaving. I didn't think she'd go without me, but she got behind the wheel of that old, shitty car, and drove away. She left me on the street."

"And Jeremiah went with her."

"No." I shook my head. "He stayed. For me."

"What did your father do to you?"

"Exactly what would hurt me the most. He almost killed my mother."

Luke closed his eyes, shaking his head. His shoulders were stiff. His hands fisted. I had the sneaking suspicion he was imagining strangling my dad. "I'm sorry."

"Part of me is glad I was there to care for her. So she didn't lose both her daughters."

Luke rubbed his jaw. If he disagreed, he kept it to himself. "So Presley came to Montana. Jeremiah stayed with you. But then he came here to find her and they got engaged."

"Yeah." I nodded. "We broke up in Chicago. He was angry at me for not leaving. He said he didn't want to watch as I became my mother or wait for my father to marry me off to some other man. We argued a lot. I promised I'd tell my parents about him soon, but there was never a good time. And I think . . . I think he resented being a secret. A secret I needed to keep, to control. Because Dad would have hated him. Or maybe not, I don't know. It doesn't matter. We broke up, and Jeremiah came to Montana and found Presley. They got engaged."

"Were you angry with her?"

"Yes," I admitted. "He'd always been mine. My one thing, and she took him from me. Looking back, I think I was mostly just angry because she'd had the courage I hadn't to break the tie."

"What made you finally decide to leave?"

"My mom. Presley texted me that she was marrying Jeremiah on June first. I showed Mom and she got this look on her face. In all my life, I'd never seen her so sad. Not even after Presley left." Granted, she'd been bedridden for almost a month thanks to Dad's punishment.

A lot had changed after Presley had left. Mom had grown more reflective. And the rebellious streak Presley had always carried had slowly crept into me.

So when my mother had told me to go, I'd been ready.

"Mom didn't realize Pres was marrying my ex-boyfriend.

She didn't know how much it hurt me to read that text. I was crushed. Angry. But I needed that anger. And I needed Mom to tell me it was okay to leave her behind. She gave me a roll of cash she'd been hiding from Dad and told me to use the bathroom during church the following Sunday and never come back."

"Have you spoken to her since?" Luke asked.

"No." I was afraid to tell her what a mess I'd made. And I was afraid to call the house and find out Dad had finally killed her.

Mom had given me the freedom and encouragement to run. To start a new life. There was no doubt she'd paid dearly for her actions. And that payment had been made in vain.

Because I'd run to the wrong damn place.

"I hopped on a bus to Montana. I found Jeremiah in Ashton. And he stood Presley up for their wedding, because I'm the worst sister in the world."

Luke didn't argue. It was a point in his favor because if he'd tried to tell me otherwise, I would have known he was lying.

"And you know the rest," I said.

"Do I?"

No, he didn't. But the rest was mine and mine alone.

I picked up my fork, ending the conversation by diving into my cold meal. When my plate was empty, I took it to the kitchen and put it in the dishwasher.

Luke came into the kitchen behind me with his own plate and put it away as I dealt with the leftovers.

Then, like I did most nights, I retreated from the kitchen toward my bedroom.

"Scarlett." Luke stopped me before I made it past the living room. "Thank you."

"You're welcome." I shrugged. "I like to cook."

"No, not for the food. For confiding in me. For trusting me."

"Oh." I guess I had trusted him, hadn't I? He could have learned as much from Presley, but in a way, I was proud of myself for telling my story. Telling it my way. "Good night, Luke."

"Good night, Scarlett."

I turned and walked toward the hallway, but then stopped at the base of the stairs. Shit. His room. "Um, Luke?"

"Yeah?"

"Don't be mad."

"For what?"

I fought a smile. "You'll see."

Luke cast me a strange glance before I disappeared into my room and closed the door. Then I sat on the edge of my bed and waited.

It didn't take long for his footsteps to echo upstairs. And it didn't take long for a muted "What the fuck?" to come through the ceiling.

I slapped a hand over my mouth so he wouldn't hear me laugh.

Not thirty seconds later he knocked on my door.

"Yes?"

He pushed the door open but didn't cross the threshold. He also didn't speak. He just arched an eyebrow and crossed his arms over his broad chest.

"What?" I feigned innocence. "Now the room has a better flow."

CHAPTER SIX

LUKE

"Scarlett!" I bellowed. Was nothing sacred?

I slammed the drawer where my toothbrush should have been and stalked out of the bathroom, through my bedroom and the changes I still hadn't adjusted to, then down the stairs.

Enough. This was enough. Wasn't this my house?

Apparently not. Over the past week, I'd begun to feel like a stranger in my own damn home.

All I wanted was to walk through my door each evening and have my things be in the same place where I'd left them that morning. When I'd left for work, I'd thought today might be that day. Today, I wouldn't come home to a minefield. She had to be done making changes, right? I mean, there wasn't much else to touch.

How wrong I'd been. I'd come upstairs ten minutes ago to put my gun in the safe and take a piss only to find another host of changes.

Scarlett had given me one month of peace, but the clock had run out. She was trapped here and clearly, she'd decided to retaliate.

Against me.

I should have seen it coming. This was the Scarlett I'd hauled out of the grocery store. The infuriating, stubborn woman who had no respect for the way I'd organized my life.

When she spotted me coming down the staircase, she scrambled from the living room to the kitchen, pretending like nothing was wrong.

"Enough," I snapped when I reached the island, planting my hands on the granite.

"What?" She lifted a shoulder, shooting me the same sly grin I'd seen every single day for a week.

I pointed a finger at her nose, opened my mouth, but damn it, her grin spread to an actual smile and my lecture about privacy and boundaries died on my tongue.

Scarlett's smile was marvelous. It transformed her eyes into brilliant, azure jewels. Damn, but she was lovely. Exasperating, but stunning. My frustration and anger didn't stand a chance against that kind of beauty.

I sighed and spun for the fridge, taking out a beer. I'd been working around the clock for weeks on end and the long, consecutive days were draining me dry. When I left the station each evening, I wanted to come home and relax. Instead, I came home on full alert, wondering what was different. At first, the changes had been easy to spot. My bedroom. Her bedroom. The second guest bedroom. The living room. Then Scarlett had gotten creative.

My books in the office were no longer organized by time period, but alphabetically by author last name. She'd spouted something about libraries and bookstores and convention. I'd walked away midsentence.

Then she'd turned the kitchen upside down. That had

been three days ago and I still wasn't sure which drawer had the silverware.

And today, my bathroom.

The woman had rearranged every single room in the house. How she'd moved the heavy furniture I had no idea, but I'd learned something in the past week.

Scarlett Marks was a powerhouse.

It didn't matter that she was petite, that she didn't stand much above five feet tall. This woman was a force.

"You're moving everything."

She waved it off. "It flows. And it's more efficient."

"I don't give a fuck about efficiency."

"Clearly," she muttered. "Who puts their toothbrush in a drawer?"

"Me."

Scarlett planted a hand on her hip. "Just try it."

"I never should have given you the login to Amazon." I dragged a hand through my hair.

The day after she'd confided in me about her parents—the same day I'd walked into my bedroom and caught her sweet citrus scent, savoring it before I'd even noticed the changes—I'd brought her my laptop along with a sticky note scribbled with the username and password.

I'd bought Scarlett a few items online, some jeans and shirts, but it was strange to pick out her clothes. Too domineering. Then after she'd told me about her father, I knew I'd never do it again.

She deserved to buy her own things. So I'd given her the login to my Amazon account. I had no idea how closely the FBI was monitoring my life. Much to my disappointment, Agent Maria Brown hadn't disappeared from Clifton Forge. Why they were expending so much effort and resources, I wasn't sure. It was enough to make me uneasy and careful. But to give Scarlett just a sliver of freedom, I'd taken the risk and let her shop.

It had backfired on me. Epically.

Every evening I got home to a stack of boxes waiting outside the door. Scarlett knew not to haul them in herself.

I cringed, thinking about how much she'd spent in less than a week. And every time I hauled in a load, ready to scold her or tell her to slow it down, I'd see that smile on her face as she tore into her purchases.

She'd bought candles. A tray for the TV remotes. Knick-knacks for the built-in shelves beside the fireplace. Books she had no intention of reading but that looked pretty.

I'd thought the toothbrush holder and drawer organizers she'd unboxed yesterday had been for her bathroom.

Wrong.

Maybe this was her way of testing my limits. Testing to see if I'd explode.

I wouldn't. Not only because I wasn't that kind of man, but because earning her trust was too important.

So I guzzled my beer—an amber bottle of patience— while she filled two bowls with rice and a stir fry mix.

"Do you want hot sauce?" she asked.

"No." I tossed my empty bottle in the trash, then went to the cabinet for a glass. Instead I found the plates. I moved down the line. Plastic storage containers. Spices. Coffee mugs. "Where are my glasses?"

Scarlett pointed to the cabinet directly beside the sink.

Efficient. *Son of a bitch.*

"Here." She took out a glass for me, handing it over. "It's a better flow."

If she said *flow* one more time . . .

I took the glass from her hand, breathing fire from my nose. Then I turned on the water to cold, letting it run for a second before filling my glass. I tipped it to my lips and chugged it all gone. Then I slammed the glass onto the counter. "You better not move my beer."

"Never."

What a damn liar.

Scarlett pulled her lips together to hide a smile.

"Are we done now? Can we be done?" I tossed an arm toward the rest of the house. "You've touched it all."

Her eyes darted toward the garage.

"No."

"But—"

"No."

Her eyes narrowed in a silent challenge. She'd do whatever rearranging she wanted, and there wasn't a thing I could do about it. While I was at the station, there was no way I could stop her if she went wild in the garage.

She knew it. I knew it.

For fuck's sake.

"Just keep the doors closed," I muttered, refilling my glass, then stalking to the living room and plopping down on the couch. She'd shifted it so it sat perpendicular to the television instead of parallel like I'd had it.

Scarlett came into the living room and handed me my bowl before plucking a remote from the carved wooden tray on the coffee table. Then she sat cross-legged in the chair that she'd angled against the wall, her own dinner resting in her lap.

Her chair.

Even after she left here, that would be her chair.

The way she'd configured the living room made it feel

bigger. It made watching TV from the couch easier. And it turned the french doors that led to the backyard into a focal point.

It looked nice, something I was never going to admit.

"What do you want to watch?" she asked.

"Whatever." I sat up to focus on my meal. The toss pillows on the couch were new and though four seemed excessive, they were easy to sink into.

From the corner of my eye, I caught Scarlett's smile as I relaxed into the downy comfort.

Damn it. The pillows could stay. And I'd use my new toothbrush holder.

Scarlett flipped on the TV, scrolling through channels until she landed on an action movie.

We settled in, eating and watching, like we'd done every evening this past week. Although we could have eaten at the island, the living room seemed to be Scarlett's preference. And I wouldn't ask her to sit in the dining room again.

There was another stack of boxes on the porch that I'd bring in after the dishes were done. She'd open them. I'd grumble. Then we'd retreat to our own areas for the remainder of the night.

The routine was becoming more and more familiar. Scarlett had lived here for over a month, and one thing was certain, she kept it interesting. Even her food choices had added some variety to my life. Gone were the predictable and simple days.

The lonely days.

Scarlett didn't initiate conversation. She didn't feel the need to fill the silent moments with idle chatter. But it was nice to have another person around, to come home to. It reminded me of life with Dad. When he came to town for a visit, our evenings weren't all that different.

Josh Rosen was a man of few words. Because he made sure the ones he spoke were the ones you needed to hear.

Maybe he'd meet Scarlett one day. Dad would get a kick out of her quiet wit and determination. Maybe if the FBI left town and we could ensure the Warriors weren't a threat, Scarlett would stick close to Clifton Forge to be around Presley. And Scarlett and I . . . maybe we could be friends.

"Presley didn't come to the station today," I said, setting my empty bowl aside.

Scarlett blinked. "I didn't realize she had been."

No, she wouldn't have. I'd been tight-lipped about the things happening beyond these walls. Not because I'd wanted Scarlett to feel isolated, but *because* she was isolated.

She didn't need to know all about the shit swirling in town, not when she was powerless to change it. So I hadn't told her that the FBI came to the station each day. I hadn't told her that last weekend when I'd gone outside to clean the windows, I'd actually been searching for any sign of electronic surveillance on my house. And I hadn't told her that two weeks ago, Dash had seen a Warrior in town.

I'd acted as her shield. I'd carry these burdens for her, for as long as it made sense, and let this woman live in peace. Scarlett had been through enough. And she'd need her strength. Because sooner or later, we'd have to face what was coming.

And before then, I wanted to remind her that Presley was on her side.

"She's come to see me every day since . . . you know," I said. "Today was the first that she missed."

Scarlett sat up straighter. "Is she okay?"

"She's fine. I texted to make sure. She said she was giving up."

"I see." Scarlett dropped her gaze to her lap, her shoulders sagging.

"Not on you. On me." Presley hadn't been as forceful in her recent visits. She wasn't giving up on Scarlett, but she'd finally realized I wasn't going to bend.

"Maybe on me too," Scarlett said quietly. "I betrayed her. I never should have gone to Jeremiah. I should have talked to her first."

"I don't think she's mad about Jeremiah."

Scarlett turned toward the windows, staring at the closed blinds like she could see through them to the yard. If she could, she'd see grass that was overdue for a mowing and weeds taking over the flower beds.

This weekend, I really needed to spend some time at home. But I was so far behind at work, I couldn't seem to catch up. Presley hadn't been the only regular visitor to my office. At least Pres had kept her trips short.

Agent Maria Brown came into my office each day and stayed. She didn't have anything to tell me. She refused to explain why she was so interested in Scarlett. She'd just sit in the same chair, ask if I'd heard from Scarlett, and when I gave her my standard no, one would think she'd leave.

Nope. She'd sit there, staring. Finally, I'd stopped staring back. Now when Agent Brown camped out in that chair each day, sitting statue still, I kept working. Fielding phone calls. Reviewing paperwork. Hell, I'd started inviting my staff in for meetings.

If the FBI wanted to know what was happening in Clifton Forge, then she had a front row seat to the drunk drivers, speeding tickets and petty crimes. This continued presence in Clifton Forge had to be costing them money. Eventually, they'd realize it was a waste. The only case Agent Brown hadn't been privy to was Ken Raymond's.

Chuck had closed the case on Ken's death two weeks ago. After speaking to Ken's wife again, it had been determined that Ken had gone out hiking. His wife hadn't been sure exactly where he'd gone. According to her, he had a tendency to choose random places. And his last random journey had brought him toward Clifton Forge. No one would ever know for sure, but Ken must have been hiking near the river. Somehow, he'd fallen in and been swept away.

The autopsy had confirmed water in his lungs and ruled the cause of death to be drowning.

On the day Ken's case had been closed, Dash had come into my office—thankfully *after* Agent Brown had vacated the premises for the day. Because he'd come to tell me that at lunch, he'd seen a Warrior at the gas station.

To anyone else, it might have looked like a man on a motorcycle stopping to fill up as he passed through town. But the Warriors didn't come to Clifton Forge. If they needed gas, they hit the next town over.

It was a message. A warning.

They wanted Scarlett too.

Dash had become a regular visitor to my office. He didn't ask where I was keeping Scarlett, and I got the impression he didn't know. That he didn't *want* to know.

His visits were purely educational.

I'd learned the names of Warriors and details about their leaders. He'd told me about old rivalries they'd had with the Gypsies. About what he suspected the Warriors did for money, mostly drug running.

It was all information in my arsenal, to use when the time came.

And that time was when Scarlett decided to talk.

Until then, we'd wait.

Maybe she really had told us everything. Maybe there wasn't much to her story and time at the Warrior clubhouse. But my gut said she was hiding something. Could be nothing. With the FBI involved, it could be something big.

Scarlett's confession about her childhood was a good sign. She was beginning to open up. If I was patient, eventually, she'd tell me the rest. But in the meantime, she was busy mixing up my house.

She was still staring at the covered window, lost in thought. Weeks ago, I might have prodded her to talk, but it would get me nowhere. Scarlett needed to do things on her own timeline, no matter how fast or slow. And I had the patience to hang back, to be there when she was ready.

So I focused on the television, letting her have the moment. And when her fork scraped the bowl, I knew whatever mental tunnel she'd traversed, she was on the other side now.

She sighed as she chewed a bite, a habit I'd noticed earlier this week. I thought all her meals were delicious, especially since I hadn't had to cook for myself, but when Scarlett didn't like something she'd made, she'd sigh as she chewed.

I doubted we'd be having stir fry again. That or she'd lay off the hot sauce.

"What?" she asked, her mouth full.

"Nothing." I shook my head, tearing my eyes away from her mouth. From those soft lips and that luscious pout.

Oh, hell. Each day it was becoming more difficult to stop

myself from staring at Scarlett. Somewhere between carting her out of the grocery store and coming home to a feng shui'd house, Scarlett had become more than the woman I was trying to protect.

What exactly, I wasn't going to contemplate. Not yet.

Maybe not ever.

Still, there was no denying we'd come a long way from the cookie aisle.

"Scarlett?"

"Yeah?"

I shifted to face her. "I should have told you last week, but I'm sorry for hauling you out of the grocery store like I did."

"Oh, um . . . it's okay."

"No, it's not." The last thing I wanted was for her to think of me like her father. "I apologize."

"It's fine."

"I'm still sorry."

She gave me a small smile. "Do you want to know something strange? I think I needed it. I don't want to ever be hit again, but I went for so long with someone else telling me exactly where to go and what to do, when those shackles came off, I went too far. When I was at the Warrior clubhouse, I did everything I wasn't supposed to do."

I held my breath, waiting for more. I didn't want to think about what she'd done there. Who she'd done it with. Mental images of a motorcycle club's wild parties were not something I wanted tied to Scarlett. But I stayed quiet. If she wanted—if she needed—to talk it through, I'd listen.

"I'm not proud of it," she said, shaking her head. "I partied. Hard. I drank too much. There were nights when I'd black out and wake up having no clue what I'd done the night before. It's humiliating."

"It's normal. The first few months of my freshman year in college were a blur." I'd spent my own drunken nights trying to drown the grief from my mother's death, until Dad had gotten my first round of grades and smacked me upside the head.

"I stopped. I made myself stop. It took me too long to get out of there but when I left, I was done. With Jeremiah and all the rest. When I pulled up to Presley's house, my God, I was so relieved. I thought to myself, *This is it. Day one of a new life.* And then it fell apart too."

My heart clenched at the pain in her voice. The lost hope.

"The day you found me at the store, I was lost. I walked all those blocks in the snow, knowing I had nowhere to go, but I was too mad to stop. I knew what I was doing was reckless, but I just . . . I didn't care. Every emotion was scratching at the surface, and then you showed up and I needed to fight with you. I needed to let some of it out. And I needed you to put me in my place. I was spiraling and you made it stop. You were steady."

The air was sucked from my lungs. Scarlett stared at me with so much gratitude and so much regret, it broke my heart.

She was the girl who'd followed the rules and still hadn't won. Then she'd rebelled, fighting to make her own way, just to be slammed down again. She stared at me like I was the hero. But I'd bet every possession in this house that even if I hadn't shown up at the store that day, Scarlett would have been fine.

She was a survivor.

Before I could think of what to say, to tell her that I admired her strength, she stood from the chair, taking her bowl to the sink and signaling the conversation was over.

I stood and followed.

"Dinner was great," I said.

She scoffed. "Not my best."

"I liked it. Thank you." I set my bowl on the counter. "You don't have to cook for me."

"Actually, I like it." She shrugged. "My mom always cooked. Every meal. She'd pack a lunch for Dad and Presley and me. After Pres left, Mom was . . . she wasn't able to cook for a while."

Because her father had probably beat the shit out of her.

"I took over for her and really enjoyed it. Cooking is kind of a connection to her."

"You said you haven't spoken to her."

Scarlett nodded. "She doesn't even have my phone number. She thought it would be better that way."

It probably was for the best. Scarlett didn't need me to tell her that what had happened in her childhood was fucked up. But she did need some time to come to terms with it. To decide where to go next without the influence of guilt where her mother was concerned.

"Here." I stepped close, nudging her out of the way. Dragging in the faint scent of orange—or what is grapefruit? —that clung to her hair. "I'll do the dishes."

"Okay." She backed away, then retreated to the living room. Except she didn't take her seat. She picked up the remote, shut off the television and disappeared to her room.

Damn. My time with Scarlett was over for the day. She hadn't even opened her boxes.

And I hadn't given her my gift.

I finished in the kitchen and went to the garage, flipping on the lights.

There were three stalls. The far one had my aluminum boat. The raft that I took on river floats used to take up the middle, but since it was at the rental house, I parked my truck there instead, giving me more space.

Plastic tubs were stacked against the wall. A tool chest on wheels sat in the corner. A stack of cardboard boxes was overdue for the recycling bin. By tomorrow evening, Scarlett would have moved anything she could lift.

The woman was turning my world inside out. And I really didn't mind.

I collected the small box from the passenger seat in my truck and brought it inside, taking it straight to her room and knocking.

The bed rustled before she opened the door. "Hey."

"Here." I handed her the box.

"What is it?"

"A sound machine. I had to stop by the hardware store today. They had these on a display. You said you wanted to fall asleep to the sound of ocean waves and it's supposed to have a setting."

Scarlett's lips parted as she stared at the box.

"You don't have to hide in here," I said.

"I, um . . . didn't want to impose."

"Let's watch something. Together. Unless you're sick of TV."

She shook her head. "I haven't been watching it much this week."

"Too busy moving my shit around."

"It—"

I pressed a finger to her lips. "—flows, right?"

She gave me the slightest of nods before her blue gaze dropped, slow and heavy, down my face to my lips.

The air around us crackled. The temperature spiked. The heat from her lips seared my finger but I couldn't pull my finger away. A jolt raced up my arm and I was about to replace my finger with my mouth when Scarlett gulped and stepped away.

Fuck. Me. I took a step away, letting my hand fall to my side and shaking the electricity out of my fingertip.

Scarlett's cheeks flushed as she raised the box between us. "Thank you for this."

"You're welcome." I jerked my chin toward the living room. "I'm going to watch something. You're welcome to join me."

"I think I'm going to turn in." The corner of her mouth turned up. "Good night, Luke."

"Good night, Scarlett."

The click of her door followed me down the hallway. I reached the center of the living room and stopped, replaying the last minute. *Luke, you fucking idiot.*

Either I'd made Scarlett uncomfortable. Or she'd felt that jolt too.

Maybe we'd been dancing around it all week, but there was chemistry here. A whole lot of complicated chemistry.

She was under my protection. Her ex had just killed himself. And I'd dated her sister.

Complicated was too tame a word.

Maybe it was strange that I'd dated her twin, but it didn't feel that way. They might have similar—identical—features, but they were different women.

When I looked at Scarlett, I didn't see Presley. Scarlett's beauty, her personality, was unique to her alone.

Her nose was straight and regal. Her top lip had this slight dip in the center, and the bottom lip had the perfect pout. Her hair hung in long, golden, shiny panels I ached to slide between my fingers. And those eyes. Scarlett could undo me with those blue eyes.

She had delicate and soft features. But knowing she was the furthest thing from fragile made her all the more appealing.

I cast my glance to her closed door. It didn't matter how beautiful she was, inside and out.

Scarlett was forbidden.

I shut off the lights and went upstairs, putting my floor and her ceiling between us. Trying something with Scarlett while she was here would be a mistake.

And damn it, if I couldn't do the right thing, who would?

CHAPTER SEVEN

SCARLETT

Another month had passed under Luke's roof. I didn't have much to show for myself other than a newly acquired skill at cribbage.

And a flourishing crush on the Clifton Forge chief of police.

"Fifteen two and I win." I put my peg in the last hole on the cribbage board and shot Luke a smirk. "That's, what, twelve in a row?"

His deliciously soft lips formed a thin line as he tossed his cards on the table. "Eleven."

"Ah. Eleven." Tonight, I'd make it twelve. I scooped up the cards and glanced over my shoulder toward the clock on the wall. "You'd better get going."

"Yeah." He stood from his stool at the kitchen island, taking his cup of coffee to the sink.

I stayed seated, concentrating on straightening the cards so I wouldn't stare at his ass.

This island had become a favorite hangout spot for us. We'd started eating here together, breakfast and dinner. And playing cribbage. We'd play a game every morning before he went to work and at least five more every night after he arrived home.

Hour after hour, day after day, I'd learned a lot about Luke Rosen as we moved the pegs on this board.

He was fiercely competitive. Even in the beginning when I'd still been learning the rules and strategy, he wouldn't cut me a break. When he won, he taunted me. When he lost, he pouted, demanding a rematch if there was time. But he was patient. My God, he was patient. More so than any person, especially any man, I'd ever met.

I never felt rushed to count my hand. He didn't hurry me along when it took me minutes to decide which cards to put in the kitty. And he indulged me whenever I wanted to play another game.

We talked as we played, sharing stories and random facts about ourselves. The inconsequential details of his life were the ones that endeared him to me the most.

He loved war movie remakes as much as books about those same wars. He kept his hair short at the sides because he hated when it touched his ears. And he'd told me stories about college, about his buddies and the trouble they'd get into on a Friday night. Like the time they'd driven into the mountains with a case of beer and gotten stuck in the mud, having to hike back to civilization the next morning.

Luke was happy with a cheeseburger every night of the week and when he'd asked me again why I didn't like them, I'd finally confessed.

When living at the Warrior clubhouse, I'd had one hundred too many cheeseburgers. Jeremiah would leave me there most nights while he ran off to play poker—I now knew that's where he'd been blowing the money he'd made from stealing and selling the club's drugs. When he'd come home, at three in the morning, he'd always bring along a greasy burger. We'd eat and he'd tell me about his night. Then he'd pass out, leaving me with a stomachache that had little to do with the burger.

Luke had listened intently, then promised the next time he brought home takeout, the Stockyard's made a good chicken Caesar salad too.

After a month of cards and conversation, I knew Luke better than any other person in the world. He was my best friend. My only friend at the moment. And this, watching him leave for work, was the worst part of my day. I'd spend the next nine or ten hours checking the clock as I waited for him to come home.

Mondays were the worst. Luke still worked on the weekends, but he was here a little more than during the week.

"Have a good day." I infused my voice with false cheer as I stood from the island and followed him into the laundry room. *Freaking Mondays.*

"You too." He tugged on his boots. "Any plans?"

"Hmm. Well, I did have some shopping to do," I teased. "Or maybe I'll go out for a mani-pedi. Probably meet up with girlfriends for a late-afternoon cocktail."

Luke chuckled. "So . . . TV."

"I might go wild and read."

He grinned. "See ya."

"Bye." I waved as he walked out the door to the garage.

I waited for the door to go up, for him to reverse out and for the door to go down.

And now I'm alone. Again.

My steps were unhurried as I shuffled to the living room, glancing around for something to do.

Nothing. There's nothing to do.

The television had no appeal. My mind wandered whenever I tried to read. The furniture had been staged. There wasn't a drawer, cabinet or shelf I hadn't organized. Twice. And once per week, I cleaned the house from top to bottom. My only new pastime was cataloging the neighborhood from behind the safety of the windows and their shades.

The only windows in the house that weren't covered were those in the dining room. Luke didn't want the neighbors to think he was a complete recluse, so he left them up most days. He knew I wouldn't go in there, not even to clean. If the table was collecting dust, too bad.

The front door had a window without a shade, but it was marbled and impossible to spy through—I'd tried. And given it was on the first floor, it didn't afford me much a view anyway.

The office, on the other hand, was perfect.

I scurried upstairs, drawing a deep breath of Luke's scent when I reached the balcony. The earthy smell, mixed with his soap, was intoxicating as I passed his bedroom and continued to the office.

It was brighter in here, where the morning sun glowed on the glass. The window overlooked the street and I knelt on the carpet, peeling back the shade to peek outside.

I was careful to maintain only the tiniest of openings, but just a sliver of sunlight on my face seemed to warm my entire body.

Two plus months inside and my skin was beyond pale. I was translucent and in desperate need of some vitamin D. But I'd obeyed Luke's rules and stayed inside.

Waiting. Waiting for him to tell me it was safe.

Dreading the day it was safe.

This home had become my sanctuary and though I was lonely, there was peace here. There was peace with Luke.

For a woman who'd waited twenty-eight years to wake without fear of the upcoming day, peace wasn't something I took for granted.

A car door slammed across the street and I shifted to get a better look. A pretty young woman with auburn hair stood beside a blue car. I hadn't seen her or the car before. Didn't that house belong to an older couple?

On cue, a man I did recognize rolled out a suitcase, loading it into the trunk.

Must be his daughter.

He kissed her on the cheek.

Yep. Daughter.

She said something to his back as he returned to the house that made him laugh. Then she slid behind the wheel and drove off.

The rumble of a large engine came from down the street. I leaned back to check the wall clock. *Seven thirty-two.* The bus schedule was nothing if not reliable.

It was nearing the end of May and soon there'd be no more school buses. I was actually looking forward to the days when the neighborhood was full of kids. They'd be more entertaining to watch than an empty street.

Minutes after her children had climbed onto the bus and disappeared, the neighbor in the blue house—across the street and three down—backed her Honda out of the driveway. The man in the green house one over drove a hatchback. From what I could tell, he lived alone, but on Wednesday last week, he'd had an overnight guest. I'd tried to wait and get a look at him or her, but after three hours, my knees had fallen asleep and I'd given up. The car hadn't been back since.

With that side of the street empty, I moved to the other side of the window.

The woman who lived in the tan house next door was in her late forties or early fifties, with a short brown bob. She left home around eight each morning and returned around two. I wasn't sure if she worked part-time or if she volunteered someplace during the day. The bumper sticker on her car read *I'm a Quilter. What's Your Superpower?*

The clock ticked by and away she went, off to quilt or meet friends or work. And that was it. *The morning rush.* There'd be mothers out pushing babies in strollers later. A jogger on occasion. The mailman swung by around noon. I'd spent an entire day here once, watching and pretending I was part of the outside world.

But sitting on the floor for eight hours wasn't exactly comfortable so I slowly eased the shade into place over the glass and made my way downstairs.

For my daily backyard inspection, I allowed myself a slightly bigger opening when I pulled the curtains away from the french doors.

He needs a deck.

The same thought hit me each and every day. Two long cement steps dropped straight from these pretty doors to the grass.

Oh, what I'd do to Luke's yard if I were allowed to go outside.

Saturday afternoon, after he'd returned from his regular trip to the station for a workout and some time at his desk, Luke had mowed the lawn in his boring, boring yard. The grass was thick and lush and green, but besides two trees in opposite corners along the fence, the space had no accents.

There were a few flower beds up front but since bushes didn't count as flowers, the front was more of the same. Yesterday, after his Sunday morning trip to the station, he'd spent an hour outside, sweeping the garage and pulling the few stray weeds from those beds.

I'd been in the living room when I'd heard voices in the driveway. I'd rushed to my perch upstairs. Luke had been talking to a beautiful woman with dark hair and a man— presumably her husband—with tattoos up both forearms. He'd had a baby wearing a pink bonnet strapped to his chest in an equally pink carrier.

Luke had laughed and smiled, flashing the dimple on his left cheek and straight, white teeth, as he talked to them for over twenty minutes. And I'd watched, longing to join them in the sun.

My hand skimmed the knob, aching to twist it and step outside for just a moment. To smell the summer and look at the sky and feel the breeze on my skin.

I yanked my hand away, dropping it to my side, before the temptation became too much. Besides, the alarm was on. I could read the status on the panel by the front door from here.

Luke would go ballistic if I opened a door.

So I went to the couch, obeyed the rules and cuddled into the buttery leather, cocooned in Luke's scent, which lingered on the throw pillows.

Hour passed.

Oh, look. Another soap.

Hours passed.

Lunchtime.

Hours passed.

Time for a walk.

I lapped the main floor three times, jogged up and down the stairs ten times, then wandered aimlessly through the rooms on the second floor, avoiding Luke's because my crazy might win out and the last thing I needed was for him to come home early and find me napping in his bed.

After months, I had this house memorized. There was a nick in one of the office's built-in bookshelves. I ran my hand over it as I swept through the room. The other bathroom on this floor was mostly empty, but the corner of the shower curtain had turned up, probably from when I'd cleaned, so I straightened it as I passed. Then I returned to the main floor, avoiding the creak on the fourth step beyond the landing.

What if the couch was switched with the chairs and the coffee table turned?

I tapped my chin, studying the layout. It had been over a month since I'd shuffled things around. And though I liked the layout . . .

I can do better.

So I got to work.

An hour later, sweat beaded at my temples as I surveyed the new arrangement.

Almost. It's almost perfect. But what if—

"Aha!" I kept experimenting, moving the couch back to where I'd had it originally, but changing the position of the chair and love seat.

By the time I looked at the clock, most of the afternoon had disappeared. If I didn't rush my shower, by the time I was ready to start dinner, Luke would be home. And that was exactly what I did.

I shaved my legs. I washed, conditioned and blow-dried

my hair. Using the wand I'd ordered online, I curled my hair into loose waves. Moisturizer. Makeup. Mascara. The only person who'd see my new eyeshadow was Luke. That seemed reason enough.

When I stepped back from the mirror, my reflection startled me.

Whoa. I looked . . . pretty.

Gone were any traces of my months at the Warrior clubhouse. The fear. The anxiety. I'd let myself fall in Ashton because it had been easier than admitting the wreck that was my life. It had been easier than facing my mistakes.

So many mistakes.

At least I'd refused to act like one of the Warrior club whores. They were passed around between members more often than the drugs.

Part of the reason I hadn't wanted to move out without Jeremiah was because I hadn't trusted him to stay faithful. I'd believed that if I was there, watching, he wouldn't stray. Maybe he had. Maybe he hadn't. It didn't really matter.

In the end, neither of us had a desire for the other. I'd been disgusted by him, by myself. And he'd been absorbed in the gambling.

Shoving those memories aside, I hurried to my room to get dressed, then to the kitchen to start dinner. My black bean enchiladas were in the oven when the rumble of an engine resonated from outside. I scurried to my spot upstairs beside the window, lifting the shade's edge just in time to see the man who lived in the white house, two down on the opposite side of the street, park in his driveway.

This was one of my favorite parts of my day.

The man's wife, pregnant, opened the front door to let a squealing toddler amble outside. The little boy raced on chubby legs toward his dad, who caught him under the arms and tossed him in the air.

"Dada!" The boy's laughter rang out loud enough to melt my heart.

Would I ever have children? Did I want them? *Yes.*

And I'd protect them. Unlike my mother, if I had to protect them, I'd die trying.

How had our neighbors missed what was happening in our home? How had everyone missed it? Teachers. Pastors. Relatives. We'd been isolated from others but not cut off. Anyone with two eyes should have seen the animus behind my father's gaze. It hadn't been love but obsession.

Not a single person had noticed the abuse. Or if they had, they hadn't stopped it.

Someday I'd be the nosy neighbor watching all the kids.

Until then, I'd do my best from this window.

The family across the street vanished inside their home and I returned to the kitchen, finishing dinner.

My days here had been boring, but the solitude had helped quiet my mind. It had helped me put Jeremiah's death in the past.

I'd always mourn the boy who'd loved me. I'd regret what had happened to the man who had tried. But the anger had faded.

One day, I hoped the bad memories would too.

With the island set, I turned the oven off to keep the food warm while I waited.

It was five thirty.

Any minute now.

The minutes dragged to six o'clock. I drank a glass of ice water, then two.

Where is he?

At six thirty I had to pee.

By seven, I was pacing the length of the couch.

Has something happened?

Maybe there'd been an accident in town. An emergency.

The Warriors.

No. Luke hadn't mentioned them. Not once in months. If they were in Clifton Forge, he would have told me. He wouldn't have stopped asking me for information.

It's not the Warriors.

Still, I walked to the front door, making sure the lock on the handle and the deadbolt were both secure. The alarm was engaged.

Needing to keep myself busy, I went to the kitchen and put away the unused plates. The enchiladas were covered and put into the fridge to reheat later. The countertops were cleaned.

Then I went to my chair in the living room, curling under the throw I'd ordered, and waited.

Please let him be okay.

Hours passed, slower than they ever had before. Darkness descended beyond the shades. And I stayed in my chair, anxious for a flash of headlights and the hum of the garage door opening.

By ten, my stomach was in a knot and sitting wasn't an option. So I put on my pajamas and tied up my hair. Then I washed the makeup from my face.

I returned to my chair, turning on the television for some added noise. The glare from the lights made it difficult to watch, but it wasn't like I could shut them off. And it wasn't like I could concentrate on the movie anyway.

Finally, at exactly midnight, the garage door opened.

I surged from the chair, my heart racing, as I rushed to meet Luke in the laundry room.

"Hey," I breathed. "Is everything okay? I was worried."

"Yeah." He shucked off his boots. "Just met up with some friends for a beer. Played a couple games of pool. Sorry I'm late."

"Oh."

It shouldn't have hurt as much as it did.

After all, he didn't owe me anything. He was probably tired of entertaining me every night.

Luke gave me a tight smile, not meeting my gaze as he brushed past me and strode through the kitchen. There was no comment, no raised eyebrow, at the new living room arrangement.

He just walked away, muttering, "Night," at the base of the stairs.

Night? I'd waited up for him. I'd been worried. And all I got was *night?*

Aliens had come to Clifton Forge today and abducted the chief of police. That was the only explanation. Because the Luke I knew, the man who was polite and kind and respectful, wouldn't blow me off like this. No, that was something Jeremiah would have done.

I slapped a palm to my forehead. *This is Jeremiah all over again.*

Why was I so pathetic? I'd been here, waiting for Luke to return. Waiting for a glimpse of his approval and a smile. Meanwhile, he'd been out living his life. Meeting up with friends. Drinking beer. Playing pool.

Replace friends with brothers, pool with poker, and things really hadn't changed, had they?

Well, they were about to.

I marched through the house, turning off the lights as I stormed to my bedroom. What was I even doing here?

The water turned on upstairs, trickling through the pipes. Luke was showering.

Oh my God. My stomach dropped. What if he'd been with a woman?

I didn't expect the man to be a monk but my foolish, stupid crush had blinded me to reality. Luke was a sexy, single man and he'd been here with me for months. I was a witness, nothing more. I was part of a case.

And after months without, he'd probably found a woman who wasn't carrying enough baggage to sink a battleship. A woman not intimidated by sex and intimacy.

Jealousy raged through my veins. Humiliation came next.

I had no claim on Luke. He wasn't mine.

Except I wanted him to be.

Screw this place.

I flew into action, rushing for the dresser. I swapped out my pajamas for jeans and a hoodie. I packed panties and bras into my backpack with one more change of clothes—Presley's olive-green sweats.

I went to the bathroom, shoving my toiletries into the bag until it was so full, I could barely close the zipper. Then I tiptoed into the living room, my shoes in hand, checking that the lights above were off too.

Luke had deactivated the alarm system when he'd come in and the panel beside the front door glowed green. He'd forgotten to engage it before jumping into the shower to wash off the scent of sex.

Was that why he hadn't lingered downstairs? Because he'd been afraid I'd notice the smell of another woman?

I tugged on my shoes beside the door, then gave the house one last glance.

I'd miss it here. I'd miss him.

Goodbye, Luke.

I reached for the deadbolt, twisting it slowly to muffle its click. I did the same with the lock on the handle. Then I held my breath, my heart jumping into my throat, as I turned the knob and—

"Scarlett."

I gasped, spinning around. There wasn't much light in the room, only the glow from the alarm panel, but it was enough to catch the glistening drops of water cascading down Luke's chiseled chest. A white towel was wrapped around his narrow waist. He had it fisted in his grip, but the cotton dipped low enough to reveal the V of his hips.

Luke's eyes narrowed at my hand still on the doorknob.

"Where the fuck do you think you're going?"

CHAPTER EIGHT

LUKE

My fingers dug into the towel, strangling the terry cloth, because at the moment, it was the only thing I could hold on to. The grip on my restraint was about to break.

"I asked you a question," I clipped.

Scarlett jutted out her chin but didn't answer.

Fucking hell. I was either going to kill her. Or kiss her.

I'd leapt from the shower, my gut screaming that something wasn't right. I'd swiped up the towel, haphazardly wrapping it around my waist as I'd hustled to the balcony, arriving just in time to see Scarlett by the door.

The zipper on her backpack was stretched so tight it was ready to come apart. Had she stuffed her entire dresser in there? Where exactly was she going to go?

"Scarlett," I growled.

She didn't budge.

So I crowded close, planted my hand on the door's face and shoved it tight before twisting the deadbolt. *Locked.*

Her face was tipped up to meet my gaze, and even in the

dim light she was stunning. Even though I wanted to lecture her up one side and down the other for attempting to leave, the woman stole my breath.

Her scent—citrus and soap—filled my nose and I backed away. One step. Two. Then three. She was too close. I was too keyed up and needed a minute to pull my shit together. I'd gone to the shower for a fucking reason. And despite the brutally cold water, I was still hard beneath the towel.

Scarlett had tormented me with that silky hair, those blue eyes and her magnetic smiles for months. I was a strong man, but there was only so much I could take.

I balled the towel tighter, keeping my fist in front of my groin to conceal the bulge. Thankfully it was dark, otherwise I doubted I'd be able to hide my arousal from her.

"Where are you going?" I asked. "Why?"

"I just . . . it's time."

" 'It's time,' " I mocked, my molars grinding together. "Are you serious? You can't leave here. It's too dangerous." Did she have a death wish?

She rolled her eyes. "It's been months. Nothing has happened."

"Because no one knows where you are." Because I was doing everything in my power to keep it that way. Keeping the vultures from circling so Scarlett could find peace.

"No one cares."

I scoffed. "Do you have any idea how many people are watching this house?"

"Please," she deadpanned. "No one is watching the house."

"Get away from the door," I barked, turning my back to her and dragging in a long breath. My nostrils flared as I summoned every last shred of patience. When I glanced over my shoulder, she still hadn't moved. The distance between us evaporated in a split second and I towered over her.

But I didn't touch her.

I wouldn't touch Scarlett again.

Unless she begged me to.

"Get. Away. From. The. Door." I swallowed hard. "Please."

"Fine," she muttered, sidestepping me for the living room. The backpack landed on the floor with a *thwop*.

God, I didn't want to have this conversation. Especially wearing nothing but a wet towel. But there was no more putting it off. It was my fault Scarlett didn't understand the risks. Maybe I should have told her from the beginning. A mistake I'd correct tonight.

I walked to the kitchen and flung open the fridge. Behind its cover, I adjusted the towel, making sure it was secure. Then I let the cool air rush over my damp skin, willing my cock to stand down. There was a sports drink on the second shelf, an extra I'd brought home from the vending machine at the station. I yanked out the bottle, twisted off the cap and, with my back to Scarlett, chugged the entire thing, using those few precious seconds to think of anything other than the woman whose gaze bored into my bare shoulders.

With my erection partly under control, I set the bottle aside and closed the fridge. Then I stalked to the living room, the newly arranged living room—hadn't missed that on my way in tonight—and faced Scarlett from a safe distance of three feet away.

"What happened?"

"Nothing."

Lies. "Scarlett, what happened? What made you want to

leave? Was it because I was out? Because I'm sorry. Plans came up last minute and there was no way for me to get here and tell you. And it's not like I can call."

Scarlett's eyes dropped to the floor.

That was answer enough. She was pissed that I hadn't come home like normal. In her shoes, I probably would have been too.

"I'm sorry."

She waved it off, still avoiding eye contact.

"You can't leave."

"Why?"

I sighed. "Agent Maria Brown with the FBI stops by my office daily. And every day, she asks about your whereabouts. She wants to find you, Scarlett. She's persistent. This is costing them time and resources, which tells me they're desperate."

Scarlett looked up and there was a crease between her eyebrows. Something I'd learned meant she was nervous. "Why didn't you tell me?"

"Because I didn't want to worry you."

"Oh."

Was that a good *Oh?* Or bad?

I pointed toward her bedroom and the side of the house that was closest to the tan home next door. "Guess who lives in that house?"

"I don't know. Some lady who likes quilting."

"How do you know she likes quilting?"

Scarlett shrugged. "Sometimes I peek past the curtains and watch the neighbors."

I swallowed a curse. She'd been spying? Christ. Hopefully no one had noticed. Though if the FBI had realized she was here, she'd have already been dragged out. And if the

Warriors knew, she'd have already been dead. Not a mental image I cared for, so I shoved it aside.

"The neighbor next door is not just some lady who likes quilting." If she even liked quilting at all. "That house was empty until two months ago. Also exactly the time that Agent Brown started coming to my office. Do you remember hearing a moving truck? Notice anyone unpacking boxes?"

"No."

"Because no one lives there. I'm ninety-nine percent sure that the lady you see is an undercover FBI agent." More time and resources, all to find Scarlett. I doubted they'd bugged the house, probably because they hadn't been able to get a warrant, but the FBI seemed to be here to stay. Not that I could prove it. But my instincts were rarely wrong.

The color drained from Scarlett's face.

That wasn't even the worst of it.

"For over a month, there have been regular sightings of Warriors in town. They haven't done anything or made a move, but they make sure someone from the garage sees them. Presley and Shaw were eating at the diner when a Warrior came in two days ago."

Scarlett gasped. "Is she—"

"She's fine. He came in, made eye contact, then he strode out with an omelet to-go."

"Shit," she hissed.

"Isaiah and Genevieve live down the street."

"Who?"

"Isaiah. He works at the garage. Genevieve is Dash's sister and a lawyer in town. They don't know you're here, but they've been on alert. Everyone has. Genevieve came home early last week and saw a Warrior parked three doors

down. He was just sitting on his bike"—I pointed to the floor
—"watching her house."

Scarlett dropped her gaze to the floor. "Then I should go.
I can't put these people at risk like this."

I scoffed. "You'll be picked up within an hour."

"You don't know that."

"I do. I do know that. We're lucky someone hasn't
decided to come inside and check for themselves. Somehow,
the Warriors must think you're hiding out with one of your
sister's friends. The FBI suspects me but without a warrant
or cause for one, there's nothing they can do. But the bottom
line is that it's not safe for you to leave this house."

She shook her head. "But I don't want to keep you from
living your life."

"What are you talking about?"

"You don't need to be here, entertaining me. If I was
gone, you'd be free. You can live your life. Be with friends.
Go on your dates."

Dates? "What dates?"

"Tonight. You went on a date, right?"

"No, I went to meet Emmett at the bar."

"Who's Emmett?"

"A buddy of mine. He works at the garage with Dash.
He used to be a Tin Gypsy and I wanted to talk to him about
the Warriors."

We'd been on our second beer, playing a game of pool,
when Emmett had stepped close, his voice covered by the
noise from the jukebox. Even on a Monday night, The Betsy
was packed with people ready to party.

*Better hurry up and let me beat you so you can get back
home. She's waiting.*

I'd blinked, jaw slack, then laughed. Emmett hadn't

outright asked if Scarlett was here. His statement might have been to trick me into admitting it, but there'd been something in his gaze that told me he already knew. Maybe all the guys at the garage knew she was here.

Maybe it was just a matter of time before the Warriors figured it out too.

The clock was ticking and the most important thing to do was keep Scarlett hidden.

"What did Emmett say about the Warriors?" Scarlett asked, but before I could answer, she held up a hand. "And don't say nothing. Don't keep me in the dark. Please."

I sighed. "The Warriors haven't said anything. They haven't asked around about you. But it stands to reason that's why they've been in Clifton Forge. They want you found."

She nodded, swallowing hard. "And the FBI?"

"I don't know," I admitted. "Agent Brown won't tell me anything. But they've been here for weeks. That's not a good sign."

"Damn it." She wrapped her arms around her waist, her shoulders curling forward. "I thought it was over. I thought . . ."

"Thought what?"

"I thought they'd forgotten about me," she whispered and the hopelessness on her face broke my heart.

I stepped closer, unable to keep my distance. "You're unforgettable."

Her blue eyes were so unsure. The confident, vibrant woman who'd invaded my home, turned it inside out, had withered right before my eyes.

"I should go. I should disappear. Or maybe I should just . . ." She shook her head.

"Should what?"

"Go home to Chicago." Her voice was so quiet I'd barely heard her. But when the words registered, rage began to boil in my chest.

"Over my dead body." She'd never return to her father's house. Never. "You're here. I know it sucks. I know it's boring and lonely, but this is it. You're here."

"It's not fair."

"I know. And I'm sorry."

"No." She shook her head. "Not for me. I landed myself in this mess. I mean, it's not fair to you."

"Why? I want you here."

"Luke, you had a life before I came here. You deserve to get back to it."

To long hours at work? To coming home to an empty house? She had no idea how much I liked having someone here with me. Not just someone, *her*. I liked wondering what surprise was waiting when I walked through the door. A new room layout. A new culinary experiment. My sock drawer reorganized and the clothes in my closet hung by color. I liked listening to her laugh at the television or brag when she beat me at cribbage.

I loved having Scarlett in my home. A confession precariously close to spilling off my tongue.

"Listen, the only reason I went out tonight was to keep up appearances," I said. "I need to look like I'm living my life. That's hard to do with you here."

"Then I should go."

"No, that's not what I mean." I blew out a deep breath and raked a hand through my hair. "I don't want to go out. I don't want to spend my evenings at The Betsy."

Scarlett had turned this house into a home. Maybe part of the reason I hadn't told her about the FBI or the Warriors was because I wanted to keep her here as long as possible. To have her as mine.

Fuck it.

Tonight, she'd get all the truths.

"If you give me the choice of anything outside these walls or being here with you, I choose you. Every time. Trust me when I say that I would much rather share dinner with you than lose fifty bucks to Emmett at the pool table."

Scarlett's mouth parted. "Really?"

"Yes, really. I didn't like leaving you here tonight. I didn't like that I had no way to call. All I wanted was to come home, have dinner and let you win at cribbage."

"Wait. You let me win?"

"No." I chuckled. Of course that was the thing she'd focus on. Scarlett was as competitive as I was. "Don't worry. You win fair and square."

The corner of her mouth turned up. "Why didn't you tell me any of this?"

"Because I was trying to protect you."

"By keeping me in the dark?" She shook her head. "That's not protection. I've been standing at the windows for days, bored, seeing what was out there. Someone could have seen me. I thought it was safe."

"I'm sure it's fine."

"But it might not have been." Her voice rose. "You should have told me."

"You're right." I held up a hand. "I'm sorry. I've never done this before."

She scoffed. "I should hope not."

"I'm doing what I think is best." Muddling through, day by day.

"I know." She sighed. "I know. Maybe your life would be better if I disappeared. Or went with the FBI."

"No." A tendril of hair had escaped the messy knot on the top of her head. My fingers ached to touch it. To tuck it behind the shell of her ear. But I kept my hands at my sides, my arms rigid. "No, it would not."

Scarlett's gaze dropped to my bare chest and I realized, during our discussion, I'd inched even closer. There was no need to be in her space, but damn it, I couldn't move away.

Her eyes turned up, finding mine, and her tongue darted out, licking her bottom lip.

Fuuuuck. My cock jerked beneath the towel, surging to life. I wanted to claim that mouth. To suck her tongue between my teeth. To hear her whimper as I kissed her senseless.

But she was forbidden. As much as I'd pretended, Scarlett was not mine. So I cleared my throat, grateful the room was still dark so she couldn't read the hunger on my face. "Let's get some rest."

"Okay." She bent to pick up her backpack, then turned, but before she could disappear into her bedroom, I stopped her.

"Scarlett."

"Yeah?"

"I like the living room."

She smiled. "Can I tell you something?"

"Of course."

"I thought maybe tonight you met a woman and wanted to bring her home but couldn't because I was here."

"There was no woman, Scarlett." Not when I only saw her.

"But if there is. If you need . . ." She fidgeted with the

125

strap on her backpack. "I can hide in my room. Pretend I'm not here."

Was she serious? She thought I wanted another woman?

"I don't want another woman."

"You don't?"

Crash.

My control shattered.

I closed the distance between us, holding her gaze, willing my next words to sink in deep. "The only woman I want is you."

Scarlett gasped, her eyes heavy as they dragged down my body. I ached for her and the towel did nothing to conceal the bulge. When her eyes reached my groin, they widened.

That night I'd given her the sound machine, I'd thought maybe there could have been something on her part. Maybe this electricity wasn't one-sided. Had I read it wrong? Shit. Maybe I had. Maybe I'd scared her away for good and now she'd run.

Why the fuck had I had two beers tonight? It had been over the course of hours, definitely not enough for me to be drunk, and I'd stopped well in time to drive home. But damn it, two beers had clearly rattled my goddamn mind. Because on a normal night, never would I have admitted I wanted her.

And damn, did I want her.

"I'll, uh . . . good night, Scarlett." I turned, ready to call this day done and hope tomorrow morning she'd still be here. But before I could leave, a pair of dainty fingers brushed over the skin at my shoulder.

"Luke."

I gritted my teeth, unable to turn. "I'm sorry. I didn't . . . I don't want to make this uncomfortable for you. Pretend I didn't say anything."

"No." The backpack landed at her feet with a muffled thud. Her fingers drifted across my skin, moving over my shoulder blade and toward my spine. "Turn around."

I obeyed. "I don't want to take advantage."

"What if I want you to take advantage?"

She was shredding me to the core. Unable to resist just one touch, my fingers found that tendril of hair, tucking it away and tracing the curve of her ear. Then I traced the smooth line of her cheek, her skin like satin. "Scarlett, tell me to stop."

"No."

"I'm doing my best to stay in control here." I jerked my hand to my side, closed my eyes and gritted my teeth. "Scarlett—"

She leaned in close. The whisper of her breath skated across my chest. "Lose control, Luke."

CHAPTER NINE

SCARLETT

*K*iss me.

My heart raced as he stood, frozen. Would he walk away? Would he do the responsible thing and put twelve stairs and a landing between us?

Kiss me, Luke.

Just one kiss. Just to see what it would feel like to taste and feel him.

Oh my God. What am I doing? This wasn't me. This brazen, daring woman who'd all but ordered a man to kiss her wasn't me.

But it was too late to take it back now. And if he didn't kiss me, I'd have to disappear to my room and no amount of begging would ever coax me out.

I'd gone too far. He probably thought I was a hussy.

Luke stood, unmoving, in nothing but that towel as the doubts crept into my mind like an ugly fog on a stormy night. I opened my mouth to mutter a good night, but before I could make a sound, Luke pounced.

Sure and bold, his lips crushed mine and his hands dove into my hair, pulling the strands free from its tie.

He swallowed my gasp. He conjured a moan with a sweep of his tongue.

Luke kissed me.

Luke *kissed* me.

And I melted.

My God, this man. He was sexy. Strong. Gorgeous. Kind. And wow, he was talented with his tongue.

He fluttered it against my own, the movement startling another gasp out of me. I'd only kissed one man. Jeremiah. He'd been my first and last. If Luke's tongue flutter was any indication, I was most definitely not prepared for what was to come.

He licked. I shuddered.

He devoured. I trembled.

I stood at his mercy as he explored, claiming me with a nip on my bottom lip.

Luke's hands were so big that with his palms cupping my cheeks, his fingertips could stretch into the locks of my hair. He held me captive, his willing prisoner, as his tongue plundered.

I reached for him but I wasn't sure where to touch so my hands just dangled in the air, frozen and stiff. His arms, maybe? His hips? Why had I encouraged him to kiss me? I didn't know what the hell I was doing.

All I knew was that I wanted him. More than anything, I wanted Luke.

He pulled his lips away from my mouth and peppered a trail of kisses along my jaw toward my ear. A shiver rolled down my spine. My legs wobbled.

"Scarlett," he moaned.

God, I loved the sound of my name in his voice. And I loved how he said it so often, like he wanted to make sure he had my attention. I concentrated on that, replaying it in my mind. *Scarlett. Scarlett.* But the insecurities wouldn't go away.

Luke brought his hands to my wrists, tugging them to his hips. When my fingertips brushed his skin, I jumped. His heat singed me straight to my core.

Then, with my arms no longer between us, he wrapped his own around me. Two strong ropes, pulling me into his chest as his lips returned to mine.

The space between us vanished. Another wave of searing heat spread through my clothes and the urge to strip them away stole my breath. Luke was only in a towel but that sheet did nothing to conceal the massive bulge between his legs.

Oh, God. He was nearly naked. He felt huge pressed against my belly.

The image of a penis, red and swollen and angry, filled my mind. It was a penis I'd seen at the Warrior clubhouse.

Before then, I'd only ever seen Jeremiah's penis. Then I'd come to Ashton and they'd been everywhere. The men in the club hadn't been shy about whipping themselves out at a party to publicly fuck the willing skanks.

There'd been one guy in particular, Ghost. Jeremiah told me he got off on sex in public and as I squeezed my eyes shut, all I could see was his penis. Penis. Penis. Penis.

Go away, Penis!

But no matter how much I willed the images away, all I could picture were those naked men. And whatever they'd been packing, or unpacking, in their dirty jeans seemed like dill pickles compared to Luke's . . . cucumber. Prize zucchini. Eggplant?

Great, I was thinking of his penis like a vegetable. I couldn't do this. Why had I instigated this? He was kissing me and my lips were moving against his but my mind . . . *Shut off. Shut off. Please, shut off.*

Luke tore his mouth away and leaned back, standing straight. "Scar—"

"How tall *are* you?" I blurted.

His eyebrows came together.

Shit. Thanks, brain.

If I'd hoped to give Luke the impression that I was a confident, sexy woman, that bubble had just burst. There was no hiding that I was just a pretender.

What was wrong with me? I slid a hand free from his warm skin and used it to cover my eyes. "I'm nervous."

Luke took my wrist, gently pulling it aside. "It's just me."

"Which is the reason I'm nervous. Sorry."

"Look at me." He hooked a finger under my chin. "I'm six two."

Twelve inches. He stood twelve inches taller. And judging by the tent in the towel, he had twelve inches in another place too.

Gah! Why couldn't I stop picturing penises?

My face flamed and this time, I buried my face in both hands. So much for our first kiss. Might as well call it the last. I swallowed a groan, repeating my apology. "Sorry."

"Don't say sorry."

"But . . . I am." I'd let my doubts steal something I'd wanted. Because I'd *wanted* Luke to kiss me. And then my mind had gotten involved and ruined the moment.

This was the reason sex had never been fun. Why I

hadn't had an orgasm in bed, unless you counted the ones I gave myself as a test to make sure my body wasn't broken.

I dropped my hands and bent to pick up my backpack but then the world turned upside down.

"Ah!" I cried as Luke tossed me over a very bare, very broad shoulder. A smile split across my face as he carried me to the stairs. "You're hauling me around again."

"Yep."

It was exhilarating. Sexy as hell. My heart swelled and a giggle escaped my lips as he walked, step by step, until we crossed the threshold to his room.

It smelled like Luke, rich and smooth, with a hint of sandalwood mixed with the soap from his shower.

"How did you know?"

Luke tossed me on his bed, then planted his hands beside my hips, leaning in close. "Know what?"

"That I was leaving."

"Had a feeling."

"A feeling?"

He nodded, inching closer, crowding me until I was flat beneath him. "I always trust my feelings."

I gulped.

Luke was ravenous. For me. Screwed-up head and all, he wanted *me*.

Why? He could have any available woman. He was the ultimate catch. So why me?

"Scarlett."

"Yeah?" I breathed. My hair fanned around me, bright against the dark quilt on his mattress.

He bent to whisper in my ear. "Stop thinking."

"How?"

"Like this." He moved, lithe and sure, lifting me deeper

into the bed. Then his mouth was on me again, tasting the skin of my neck.

His body pressed into mine and I spread my legs, making room to cradle his hips and that ever-present bulge. He rolled his hips, his thickness rubbing against the throb blooming in my center. Even through my jeans, the pleasure was mind-numbing. The thoughts in my head began to fade.

Yes.

He wrapped around me, holding me close, and it felt so good to have Luke's weight on me, the heavy strength of muscle and bone.

Jeremiah had stopped holding me. It had become very mechanical. Two minutes, our bodies touching in that one place, then it was over. Had he been like that with Presley too?

Was it strange that my sister and I had lost our virginity to the same man? Incestuous? Maybe he'd been a better lover to her than he had been to me. And here I was, repeating the cycle with Luke.

"Scarlett."

My eyes popped open.

Luke had stopped kissing me and he'd lifted up, staring down at me.

Ugh. Not again. "Sorry."

He blew out a long breath, then shifted away, rolling to lay on his side. His finger grazed my temple. "What's going on in here?"

I really, really didn't want to have this conversation but, as Luke propped his head on an elbow, I knew he wouldn't let it go. "I don't know. This happens to me."

"What happens to you?"

"I get . . . stuck." I tapped the bridge of my nose. "In here. During sex."

"Tell me what's on your mind."

"No way. Just . . . kiss me." I barked out a laugh. He'd think I was crazy. *Maybe I am.*

I reached for the fold on the towel that had somehow not fallen loose, but before I could give it a good tug, he caught my wrist.

"Tell me. Then I'll kiss you."

I frowned. "Bribery?"

"I'm not above it." He grinned. "Maybe I need to sweeten the deal. Tell me what's going on in your head and I'll kiss you here."

His hand released mine to trail over the sliver of skin above the waistband of my jeans. My sweatshirt had ridden up, exposing my flesh. The featherlight touch of his finger stole my breath and I stared at him in wonder as his hand moved lower. Lower. Until he'd followed the length of my zipper and his hand disappeared between my legs.

He stroked, gently at first, then gave me more. I closed my eyes, enjoying the delicious friction, as Luke leaned in close. His breath was a whisper across my cheek. "Tell me."

I shook my head.

A low rumble came from deep inside his chest as he quickly flipped open the button on my jeans, then slid his talented fingers inside the denim, stroking me through my panties.

"Yes," I hissed, arching into his fingers.

"Tell me."

I shook my head again.

"Tell me." His finger swirled around my clit, then it was

gone. He moved away, looking down at me while he waited for an answer.

"No fair. Tell me that's not an interrogation tactic."

He chuckled. "Only for you."

I sighed. "You're not going to let this go."

"Nope."

"Fine. I was thinking about Jeremiah and Presley. That it's strange we were both with him. And now here I am with you."

"It's strange if we make it strange," he said.

"I don't want it to be strange."

"Then it's not."

Simple as that.

And somehow, it was.

The past didn't need to influence the future.

"Did that earn me a kiss?" I whispered.

Luke was on me in an instant, his lips capturing mine.

I wrapped my arms around his shoulders, blanking my mind to anything but his taste. His heat. His strength. My hands roamed down the firm planes of his back, tracing and memorizing the long, firm lines. I reached between us and dragged my knuckles across Luke's washboard stomach, searching until . . .

Flick.

One tug on the towel's fold and it broke free.

Luke groaned into my mouth, swinging a leg over mine to straddle my body as his mouth tore free. He was naked. Perfect. "How about that kiss?"

I nodded, breathless, as he maneuvered me, lifting and pulling until my sweatshirt was sailing across the room. My tee came next. Then he freed my breasts from their simple white bra.

"What are you thinking about?" he asked as he moved, graceful and powerful, down the bed. There was nothing to hide his body now, nothing to cover his thick, long shaft.

My mouth watered. "You."

"Good." He stripped my jeans from my legs with a swift pull, my panties gone with them.

I brought my legs together. My arm slid down to cover my bare mound.

Luke took my wrist in his hand, kissing my pulse, then placed it to my side as he lowered his head to my body. He pushed my knees apart to bracket his ears.

"I've never—"

The words disappeared from my tongue as he dragged one long stroke through my folds.

I whimpered as he cast me a wicked, sinful look with his blue eyes.

Then his tongue was on me again. "First I'm going to fuck you with my tongue."

"God, yes." I arched into his erotic kiss.

"Then I'm going to fuck you with my cock."

Yes, yes, yes. I wanted it all. I melted into the bed, my legs falling apart as he urged them wider.

"You taste so good. Fuck, Scarlett." My name in his voice had never sounded better. "So good."

Luke sucked and lapped, alternating his rhythm until I writhed beneath him, panting and racing toward a release.

The orgasm built so fast, I wasn't ready when it came upon me, shattering me into a senseless mess of cries and moans.

As the white spots cleared from my vision, I brought a hand to my chest, feeling the pounding of my heart against my palm. Now this was sex. Toe-curling, phenomenal sex. And we were just getting started.

Luke's skin slicked against mine as he returned to the bed. He stretched an arm to the nightstand, opened the drawer and pulled out a condom. The crinkle of foil. The rustle of the mattress. It was all background noise to the blood still rushing in my veins.

"Scarlett."

"Yeah?"

"Open your eyes."

I pried them open and found his gaze waiting. "Thank you."

"Don't thank me yet."

I lifted my hand to his cheek, my thumbnail dragging across his lower lip.

He sucked it into his mouth, rolling it on his tongue. Then he positioned himself at my entrance, waiting for a nod, and slid inside.

My body stretched, my back arching off the bed as he filled me.

"Hold on to me, beautiful."

I gripped his triceps. "Like this?"

"No." He shook his head and brushed a lock of hair off my forehead. Then he touched the corner of his eye. "Hold on *to me*."

Luke didn't need to worry. He had me transfixed.

He eased out, then rocked his hips forward, slowly and gently, until he was buried deep.

"Luke," I moaned as my legs trembled. My heart raced. With every one of his languid, sensual strokes, pleasure spread through my veins.

And I held on to him, mesmerized by the lust on his face.

The want and sheer desire for me and only me. Thrust after thrust, he coaxed me higher and higher.

Luke dropped his mouth to my breast, taking a nipple between his lips for a long, hot suck. Then he did the same to the other, blowing on it as it popped from his mouth to cool the hardened bud.

"Yes, baby." I threaded my fingers into his hair, the shorter strands like velvet against my palms.

Luke's hips pistoned harder, faster, until I came apart.

I screamed, clenching around him as stars exploded in my eyes and I surrendered to the most intense pleasure of my life.

"Yes," he crooned, his hips rolling and moving as my inner walls pulsed.

And finally, as I returned to earth, he buried his face into the crook of my neck, shaking through his own release with my name on his lips.

It required no effort to keep my mind blank through the aftershocks. I was in a haze as Luke slid out and went to dispose of the condom in the bathroom. And I was in a state of bliss when he returned to bed, tucking us both beneath the sheets.

"Sleep here," he whispered into my hair.

I snuggled deeper. "I didn't know."

"Know what?"

I must have been delirious because the words spilled from my mouth. "I didn't know it could feel like this. Before, it was always fumbling. Awkward. I thought that was just how it was for me. That it wouldn't be good."

"That wasn't good."

"What?" My eyes popped open.

Luke pulled me into his chest. "That was explosive. Fuck, beautiful. You ruined me."

I smiled, snuggling closer. "I guess I won't have to rearrange furniture for a workout anymore."

"No. No more furniture. I'll give you a workout every night."

"Good. I'm going stir crazy."

Luke was quiet for a long moment. "I have an idea."

"What?"

"Well, the whole point of this charade is for it to seem like I'm living my life, right? For people to think everything is normal. So I guess I should do what's normal."

"Okay," I drawled, shifting to face him. The room was nearly black but I could make out his face from the yard light's soft glow seeping past the shade. "What does normal mean?"

He smiled, flashing me his dimple, and wagged his eyebrows.

"Luke." I poked him in the side. "Tell me."

"Do you trust me?"

"Yes." The word came without hesitation. Without doubt. I hadn't realized it until tonight, but after two months of getting to know this man, I trusted Luke more than I trusted myself.

Normally, that would be a good thing.

But for me, it meant everything was going to change.

Sooner rather than later, I'd have to trust him with my secrets.

CHAPTER TEN

LUKE

"Now will you tell me where we're going?" Scarlett handed over the dry bag I'd told her to pack with clothes, shampoo and a toothbrush.

"Nope." I tucked her bag into the raft, beside my own, then dropped a kiss to her lips. It was one of many we'd shared this week, but the spark was as alive as it had been from the start. And it came easy. Natural. Like it was the gesture, the part of us, that had been missing.

"Tease," she muttered, poking me in the ribs before she stepped closer to the raft, standing on her tiptoes to peer inside. "Are we camping at a lake or a river?"

"It's a body of water."

"Come on." Her pout was goddamn adorable. "Just tell me."

For five days, since the first night we'd slept together, I'd been torturing her with my plans. I'd asked her to pack certain things. She knew we'd be camping but I hadn't told her where or for how long. I'd bought her some wet gear to wear in case of rain but had hid it from her in my truck. And every evening this week, I'd worked to prepare for this trip, all while she watched along, begging to know what we were doing.

The coolers were loaded and jammed tight with ice. The tent was loaded along with two sleeping bags I'd zip together. Normally I slept on the ground, but with Scarlett along, I'd bought an air mattress. Excitement and anticipation buzzed through my nerves. God, we needed this week. Starry nights. Open air. No hiding.

"This is not the same boat that was here," Scarlett said.

"No. My boat is at my rental house. I normally keep this there." I'd swapped them out last night so I could pack the raft.

"You have a rental house?"

I nodded. "I didn't tell you that?"

"Uh, no."

"Oh. You've been there. It's your safe house."

Her mouth fell open. "That's yours?"

I shrugged. "I needed a place for you to stay. It seemed logical since it was empty. I'm planning on remodeling soon."

"Good." She grimaced. "It needs it."

I chuckled and took one last look around the garage to make sure I hadn't forgotten anything.

Scarlett had rearranged this space, like she had inside, and though I still wouldn't admit it and concede defeat, her setup had a nice *flow*. My tools were organized above my work bench. Coolers had been stacked, tackle boxes sorted. She'd even found some hooks to hang my fishing rods.

It had made packing for this trip a breeze.

"I've never been camping before," she said.

"You'll like it. Trust me."

"Okay." She breathed. "Can I help?"

"It's all done. Want to load us up some travel mugs? I'm going to open the garage doors and get the raft hitched to the truck."

"So I need to disappear." She raised her hand in a mock salute. "Got it."

I grinned, catching her by the elbow before she walked away, and pulled her into my arms for another kiss.

She moaned, sinking into my embrace, and when I licked across the seam of her lips, she opened for me, letting me sweep in and savor.

Our tongues dueled. Her fingers gripped at my biceps and she gave just as good as she got.

This woman could kiss. She poured everything into it, her spirit and her fire. Gone was the hesitancy from our first night together. If I sensed Scarlett getting stuck in her head, I'd do something unexpected, like swat her ass cheek or flip our positions, until she came back to me.

But after five days, it happened less and less. Her walls were coming down. Her inhibitions were disappearing the more we were together—which had been often. I'd had more sex in the past five days than I'd had in three years. Combined.

I found myself hurrying home each evening, ravishing her on every surface available. The couch. The kitchen island. Her bed and most definitely mine. We'd eat, barely clothed, then go at it again.

It was impossible to keep my hands off her body, and she felt the same about mine. Her fingers made constant trails on my skin. She lingered close whenever we were in the kitchen doing dishes, purposefully brushing against me as I put a plate in the cupboard and she reached to rinse a glass.

And the kissing. I hadn't had this much fun kissing a woman since I was a teenager and I'd snuck my high school girlfriend under the bleachers during basketball games to cop a feel. Back then, it had been exploratory and new. This thing with Scarlett was consuming. My lips were practically chafed raw but I couldn't get enough.

I growled against her mouth, angling my head for a deeper angle. She clung to me, whimpering when I cupped a breast and squeezed. My cock wept for more but if I started there, we'd never get on the river, so I tore my mouth away.

"You're irresistible," I panted, tucking a tendril of hair behind her ear.

Scarlett's hands snaked around my waist, her palms flattening over my ass. "Not so bad yourself, baby."

"Coffee." I dropped one more kiss to the corner of her mouth, then let her go with a playful swat on the behind.

She sashayed to the door, giving me a finger wave as she disappeared inside.

I adjusted my swollen cock and got back to work, opening both garage doors and backing the truck to hitch up the raft. I was bent by the ball hitch, hooking up the safety chains, when a voice carried across the driveway.

"Good morning."

I glanced over my shoulder to see my neighbor—and suspected FBI agent—walking down the sidewalk.

Her eyes darted into the garage, searching.

I stood and brushed off my hands, extending one her way. "Morning."

"I thought I'd come over and introduce myself," she said. "I'm Birdy Hames."

"I'm Luke Rosen. Welcome to the neighborhood."

"Thanks." Her gaze drifted over my shoulder to the door that led inside.

I shifted, blocking it from her view. "Are you new to Clifton Forge?"

"Yes, I am. It's a lovely town."

"I think so too."

She gave me a tight smile, then looked to my truck and the raft. "Where are you off to?"

"Fishing for the week. I go as often as I can get away in the summers."

Her eyes scanned my red truck, probably because she'd never seen it before. The wheels in her head were visibly turning as she took it in and memorized the license plate.

I stifled a laugh. This truck wasn't going to help them find Scarlett.

I'd brought this, too, home from the rental house last night. The rig I used for work was parked at the station.

"Well, I'd better get back to packing. Nice to meet you, Birdy." *If that's even your name.*

"You too." She waved. "Have a nice trip."

She retreated to her own home, walking slower than a sloth. Every third step, she cast a long glance at my house. She couldn't see anything but dark windows and drawn shades.

Ever since I'd warned Scarlett that my place was being watched, her neighborhood spying had ended. I hated to deprive her of anything, especially her freedom. Those little glimpses out the window had been important to her, but not as critical as her safety.

What the hell were we going to do? Scarlett couldn't hide forever. Eventually, we'd have to face both the Warriors and the FBI. I'd been stalling these past couple of months because I'd been waiting for Scarlett to tell me about her time with the Warriors.

Was there anything to tell?

Maybe all she'd seen was exactly what she'd already confessed.

And now the only reason I was stalling was because I was afraid I'd lose her when this was over.

I returned to my task, getting the raft hitched. A week on the river would help clear my head. Sooner rather than later, I'd have to make some decisions and there was nothing like the open air and fresh water to clear my mind.

Birdy lingered in her driveway, bending to pick at a weed growing in the crack of the cement. I walked to the raft, retucking bags as I waited. It took her five minutes to finally go inside, and when she was gone, I strode into the house.

If I'd suspected Birdy was with the FBI before, today confirmed my suspicions. One would think the FBI would be better at blending in.

Why were they still here? If they knew Scarlett was inside, they would have taken her by now. Why was finding her so critical? I was missing something. A big something.

"Scarlett?" I called when I didn't see her in the kitchen.

She came rushing down the stairs. "What did she want?"

"To be nosy," I said. "How'd you know?"

"I went to check that the lights were all off upstairs and I heard voices so I peeked through the office window while you were talking to her. Does this change the plan?"

"No." I'd promised Scarlett a chance to get outside and live normally for a week, and Neighbor Birdy wasn't going to stop us. We both needed this trip.

"How exactly am I supposed to get in the truck? It's not like I can waltz outside and climb in the passenger seat."

Damn. My original plan had been to have her get into the truck while it was in the garage, but then she'd kissed me and well . . . I'd forgotten. And now that Birdy was watching, I couldn't exactly unhitch the truck, park it and close the garage doors, only to redo it over again.

"Feel okay riding in the raft until we get out of town?" It wasn't ideal and I didn't like that she'd be without a seat belt, but it was about our only option.

Scarlett nodded. "Okay."

"Then let's get out of here."

We collected our coffee mugs from the kitchen, then I returned to the garage, closing one door to provide Scarlett some cover. Then I led her to the raft, taking her hand and helping her up.

"Sorry," I said.

"It's okay." She gave me a smile, then settled into the middle row, folding her small body between the bench seats on the rubber floor.

"Feel okay?"

"Yeah. It's not that uncomfortable. But should you cover me up with something?"

"Just stay low. There's no way anyone will see you."

"I look ridiculous," she muttered, shifting her feet.

"You look beautiful." I touched her leg and hustled to the truck, wanting to get the hell out of town.

The minute the raft was out of the garage, I punched the button to close the door. Then I rolled down the street, holding my breath as I navigated through town. Only when we were on the highway and there was no one behind us did I finally take the nearest pullout.

When I rushed to the back, Scarlett was laughing. Her smile eased all my worries.

"What?"

"That was actually kind of fun."

"Come on." I waved her out, keeping a watch on the road to make sure we were alone as she climbed out and jogged to the truck.

When she was buckled into the passenger seat and I was behind the wheel, I got right back on the road.

"Now will you tell me where we're going?" she asked.

I took her hand, lacing my fingers with hers on the console. "Every year, I take a week-long fishing trip. There's this float on the Smith River that's completely secluded. You can't get in by vehicle and it's bordered by public lands so there aren't any private homes or cabins. It's my week to unplug. No cell phones. No radio calls."

"No motorcycle clubs or federal agents."

I grinned. "Exactly."

"And you're okay to leave the station?"

"Yeah. My senior officers will deal with anything that comes up. I've got a good crew." And at the moment, there were no cases that needed my direct supervision.

Since Ken Raymond's death, the most exciting thing to happen in town had been a bar fight at The Betsy. Fights there weren't uncommon but this one had been unique because it had been two women. Both ladies had been hauled to jail, where they'd sobered up and left embarrassed and hungover the morning after.

If something big did happen, I had a good relationship with the county sheriff and her deputies. She knew I would be on the river this week, and like she did every year, she'd be around as an on-call resource. I did the same for her when she took her family on their annual February trip to Hawaii.

"Think you can rough it with me for a week?"

"I think I can do anything with you for a week."

I brought her knuckles to my mouth, brushing my lips across her smooth skin, then focused on the road. The trip to the drop-off point took about an hour. Normally, the drive was my time to relax and get excited for the trip, but with Scarlett beside me, I couldn't seem to settle my fears.

My eyes flew to the mirrors constantly, checking for cars that might be trailing us. Whenever a vehicle approached us going the opposite way, I tensed, hoping we were going too fast for a passerby to notice the gorgeous blonde riding shotgun.

Finally, the turn-off for the river approached and I'd never been happier to get off the highway. "Okay, beautiful. You'll have to crawl in the back and stay low. Once we get there, I'll sneak you into the raft."

"Will there be a lot of people?"

"No," I said, turning onto the gravel road. "There'll be a ranger from the park service who checks my permit. This is a special section of the river and to float, you have to draw an annual pass. Mine is normally in August, but a buddy of mine offered to trade for this week instead. It'll be colder than in August, and the water is running higher. Fishing won't be as good, but it will still be fun."

"I've never caught a fish."

"You will this week." I reached behind us, taking a blue ball cap I'd tossed in the truck for Scarlett. "Put this on."

She tucked it over her bright blond locks, tucking the long strands behind her ears and tying it all into a ponytail.

"There will be other rafters too, but the launch times are staggered so we won't cross paths. If we do, just smile and wave."

"And what if someone sees us?"

"Then we'll tell them the truth. I'm taking my girlfriend camping and floating for the week."

Scarlett looked over, her cheeks flushing. "I like being called your girlfriend."

"Good. Because I like saying it."

In a small town, there weren't many single women around and I didn't date much. I hadn't had a girlfriend in ages, unless you counted Presley. And even with her, the two of us had been more friends than anything. Two lonely people who'd go out to eat on a Friday night instead of coming home alone to a frozen lasagna.

Scarlett was different from Presley, different from any woman.

I craved her company. I longed for her smile. When we were apart, I counted the hours until I could be with her again. My desire for her was a living, breathing beast I had no plans to tame.

Maybe it was risky to bring Scarlett to the river, but I wanted to share this with her. To bring her into my world because I had no doubt she'd love it here too.

Camping was something my parents had always done together. Dad had taught Mom about rafting and boating. She'd grown up in town and her parents hadn't been outdoorsy. Then she'd married Dad and all that had changed. Dad wouldn't go on the Smith trip with me. He hadn't done it since Mom had died.

Because it had been her favorite week out of the year.

It was the last week of May and as expected, the parking lot ahead was nearly empty except for one other party at the drop-off point. The float was better later in the summer after the spring runoff had slowed. But as far as keeping Scarlett as hidden as possible, this week would be perfect.

She sucked in a shaky breath, then climbed into the back and tucked herself behind the passenger seat. Then she grabbed the blanket I left back there in case of emergency and draped it over her head. "Can you see me?"

"Yes."

She lifted the blanket and shot me a glare. "You know what I mean."

I chuckled. "You're fine. You don't need the blanket. No one will check the truck."

She covered herself again anyway.

I pulled into the loop of the unloading zone and parked, getting out to greet the ranger on duty as he walked over. He was a younger man who'd been working here for two years in a row and recognized my name from the permit.

We bullshitted about the weather and the fishing, then he shook my hand again, warned me that the water was running high and wished me a good trip.

"Almost set," I told Scarlett as I pulled farther down the stretch to reverse the raft onto the riverbank.

"How am I supposed to get out?"

I glanced around the gravel lot, making sure the ranger had returned to his camp trailer. There was only one other group here, three rafts and about eight people, but they didn't look anywhere near ready to launch. And none of them were paying me any attention.

I didn't want to get stuck behind a big, slow procession, so I hurried to beat them into the water. "Go ahead and hop out. I'll meet you at the raft. You can climb in where you were before."

"Okay," she whispered, then carefully untucked herself. We met at the side of the raft and I helped her into the seat, then secured the oars in the oarlocks so they'd be ready for me when we shoved off.

"Hang tight," I told her, pushing the raft into position.

With it ready, I parked the truck and trailer in the empty lot beside the loading zone and jogged back to the raft. One good shove and we were in the water. I leapt onto the bow and took up my position on the main bench seat.

Scarlett stared up at me with wide eyes as the raft bounced and bobbed with the water.

"Here we go, beautiful." I grabbed the oars and gave us a good shove forward.

"I already love this." She smiled, closing her eyes as she dragged in a long breath.

I rowed hard to get us around the initial bend, where we'd be out of sight.

The cool air blew in my face. The sunshine warmed my skin and the familiar burn from rowing built in my arms.

God, this felt good. If I'd had any doubts about taking her along, they were washed away with the river's current. I'd needed this trip, not just for Scarlett, but for me.

One week. I'd take one week and quiet the noise. I'd ignore my worries about the future.

By the time we rounded the first bend, I'd already adjusted to the rock and sway of the river. I glanced over my shoulder, double-checking we were out of sight, then grinned at Scarlett. "All clear. Come on up."

Scarlett sat and took in the surroundings, her eyes wide as she settled into the bench across from mine.

Her eyes were the cerulean blue of the sky. The breeze played with the loose tendrils of her golden hair. Her smooth, flawless skin soaked in the sun.

My heart skipped. Damn, but she was beautiful. So pure

and bright. The view around us was stunning, but it was nothing compared to Scarlett.

"This is . . .." She struggled for words. "It's gorgeous."

"Yes, it is."

She met my gaze and her cheeks flushed as she threw out a hand. "Not me. This."

Cliffs rose from the water like walls, towering into the sky. The nude rock was striated with streaks of red, orange and yellow. High above us, green grass swayed over the cliff's edge.

The natural landscape was the reason this float was so isolated. There were no beaches. No boat ramps or commercial campsites. The only way in was by water. And it was the only way out.

Scarlett tore her eyes from the view and flashed me that heart-stopping smile. "Thank you for bringing me here."

"My pleasure."

One week. This one week would be all about my pleasure. And hers.

Because my gut was screaming that the minute we got home, time would be up.

CHAPTER ELEVEN

SCARLETT

There was magic here. In all my life, I'd never seen anything as beautiful as the Smith River.

The rush of the river enveloped us as we floated past the sky-high and colorful cliffs. I understood what Luke meant now—we were in a world apart.

We'd been floating for about an hour. The cliffs had been like a gate early on, both sides dropping straight to the water and disappearing beneath its rolling surface. But as we'd traversed turns and small bunches of rapids, they'd retreated, giving way to a shoreline filled with lush, green grasses, leafy bushes and thick evergreens.

"I've never seen any place like this." I'd told Luke the same no less than five times as he rowed.

"This was my parents' favorite place to float. They did this trip on their honeymoon, ages ago."

This would be the perfect place to lose yourself in love with a new spouse. There was privacy. Adventure. Just two people alone somewhere in Montana.

I tipped my chin to the sky and let the sun warm my face. The air was cool and it, along with the slight spray from the water, kept me from getting too hot.

Would we sleep under the stars? Had Luke packed a tent? Had he brought sunscreen? I shoved the questions aside, wanting to live in the moment.

The questions, the worries, would take care of themselves. I'd been peeved at Luke for not telling me about the FBI and the Warriors, but I understood why he'd done it. And the truth was, he'd made the right decision.

With nothing to do most days, worrying about them would have driven me insane.

"When I lived in Chicago, I was always worried about tomorrow," I said. "What would happen to my mother tomorrow? What would I wear to appease Dad? Would he be in a good mood? A bad one? I don't think I even realized how much I worried about the mundane things until I left. Not that my worries disappeared after Chicago. They just paled in comparison to their replacements."

Would my mother survive my disappearance? How would I find Jeremiah? What if he and Presley didn't want to see me?

"What do you worry about now?" Luke asked.

"The Warriors. The FBI. But mostly, I worry about Presley. About our relationship. What I did to her was . . . unforgiveable." I showed up and took Jeremiah back. He'd ditched their wedding, for fuck's sake, because of me. Afterward, I'd been scared to face her. To admit that I'd been jealous.

She'd left home. She'd chased her dream.

While fear had ruled my life.

But I missed my sister, so much it ached.

"Think she'll ever forgive me?" I whispered.

"From my seat, I don't believe that Presley thinks there's anything to forgive."

Oh, there was. I'd seduced her fiancé because I'd convinced myself that he still belonged to me.

Jeremiah had been my first and only. After we'd broken up and he'd moved away from Chicago, I hadn't wanted to date. Too many questions. *Why do you still live at home? Why do you spend all your free time with your parents? Where did you get that bruise on your arm?*

I'd stayed single, dodging any guy who showed even the slightest interest. So when I'd left Chicago, only two people in the world had known what I was running from—Presley and Jeremiah.

I'd made the wrong choice.

Jeremiah hadn't been hard to find. There'd been a woman on the bus who'd sat across from me. I'd confided in her that I was going to Montana to look for my old boyfriend. She'd whipped out her phone and five minutes later, she'd found his Facebook profile.

When I'd shown up at the Warrior clubhouse in Ashton, Jeremiah had been shocked to see me. For a brief moment, it had just been us. Unchanged. Kids who thought there was enough love between them to beat all odds. To last a lifetime.

But that moment had faded fast as reality had come crashing in.

"I came to Clifton Forge once, about a month after I left Chicago. The guilt had been eating me alive," I confessed. Something about the surroundings made it easier to let the secrets free.

"What happened?" Luke asked.

"Once a coward, always a coward." I sighed. "There was this woman at the Warrior clubhouse who was nice to me. She was one of the girlfriends. I told her I wanted to go see my sister and she let me borrow her car. So I drove over to see Presley, but when I got to town and parked on the street by the garage, I couldn't do it. I went to a bar to try and work up the courage."

"The Betsy?"

"I think so. I didn't pay much attention to the name. I stayed for a while, sitting alone. There was this drunk guy who kept staring at me. Pointing at me. Probably because I have my sister's face. After a while, it started to freak me out, so I left."

By that point, Jeremiah had called me a hundred times, begging for me to come back to Ashton.

I'd made the wrong choice again.

"I'm going to tell you a secret," Luke said.

"What's that?"

"Presley got married."

I blinked, sure I hadn't heard him right. "What?"

"She got married to Shaw last month. It was a low-key thing. They flew to Vegas and spent a couple weeks in California."

"Why didn't you tell me?"

"Because I wanted you to hear it from her."

My forehead furrowed. "Then why are you telling me now?"

"Because you're beating yourself up and that's not what Pres would want. Yeah, maybe you should have done things differently. But Scarlett, I can tell you with certainty that the best thing that's ever happened to Presley was *not* marrying Jeremiah. Stop punishing yourself."

My shoulders slumped. Easier said than done.

"She loves you," Luke said. "She's happy."

"I just want to see her again. To tell her I'm sorry and make it right."

"You will. I swear, we'll figure out a way to give you back your sister."

At the moment, it felt like an impossible feat. Like climbing the cliffs around us without a rope. "Thank you for telling me about Presley and Shaw."

He nodded. "You have to act surprised."

"I can do that."

We were quiet for a while, Luke rowing while I took in the scenery.

"It's my turn to say something," Luke said, breaking the silence. "It bothers me when you call yourself a coward."

I flinched at the bite in his words. "Oh."

"Don't discount who you are, Scarlett. You're strong and courageous. Your life might be strange at the moment but remember how far you've come. I've seen people in your situation. People who've never broken free."

"Like my mother."

"Yes. And you're not your mother."

I studied his face, the stern sincerity.

Luke was like a mirror. When I looked into his blue eyes, I was reflected there. I saw the way he saw me.

It was a glorious image.

False, but glorious nonetheless.

"How will we get to the truck?" I asked, ready for a lighter subject.

"A shuttle service. I left my keys in the gas cap. They run vehicles from the drop zone to where we'll haul out."

"Ah." I nodded, once more looking around. "How far will we go today?"

"Not far. We'll float for another couple of hours, then stop to set up camp. There's no rush any day. We can sleep late. Float for a few hours and camp at our leisure."

"Sounds good to me." I wanted nothing more than to slow down. Not for my sake—I hadn't done much of anything lately—but for Luke. He deserved this trip and the chance to unplug from the stress of his job. And the stress of me invading his life.

"This place really is breathtaking," I said, soaking in the surroundings. "I've never seen anything like Montana. Not that I've traveled much. Or at all."

"My parents took me to Disneyland once when I was a kid," Luke said. "But this type of trip was much more our speed. Have you ever been?"

"To Disney? No." Before I'd come to Montana, my life had been confined to a small circle. My parents didn't travel, ever.

We never took a family vacation to Disneyland or a trip to the Great Lakes. We stayed in our neighborhood and for most of my childhood, I didn't think twice about it.

But when I started middle school and other kids would talk about a trip to Texas for Christmas or a vacation to California, I realized that my family didn't travel. Not even small weekend trips. It had been another oddity to my life, something that had kept Presley and me apart.

My freshman year in high school, the popular girl in my class sat three seats in front of me in algebra. She bragged to her friends about a new shirt that she'd bought in California when her family had traveled there for spring break.

She had beautiful skin, dark and smooth. She had a

perfect white smile and had always been nice to me. To everyone, really. The popular girls in our school weren't popular because they were mean. They earned it the right way.

I'd wanted to be her so badly.

Her love of California had been the reason I'd chosen it when Presley had chosen Montana.

What had happened to that girl? What was her name? I'd forgotten it over the years. It wasn't like we'd been friends.

Presley had been my friend. I'd been hers. Inviting others into our two-person circle hadn't been an option because friends asked questions.

And my parents had taught us from the beginning, what happened in our house was not to be shared.

We don't talk about Daddy's bad moods, okay? That was Mom, buttoning our cardigans on the first day of kindergarten.

If anyone asks where you got that bruise, tell them it was from Presley. That was Dad, tugging a sock over my shin in first grade.

Why hadn't they homeschooled us? That had always baffled me. Maybe because if we went to school, people would suspect less than if we stayed home. Or maybe it was because Dad didn't think Mom could string two coherent thoughts together. She was good enough to bear his children and use as a punching bag, but not good enough to teach.

Mom was quiet, but she wasn't stupid.

School had been our sanctuary. We hadn't had friends, but our teachers had loved us because we'd worked hard for our grades. They'd boast about how amazing a job our parents were doing.

Those Marks twins are so smart and sweet.

Fools. They'd all believed the façade. Straight As had been our only option.

"Hey." Luke nudged my foot with his. "You okay?"

"Yeah." I shook myself out of my musings. "Just thinking."

"I can see that." Luke could always tell when I was deep in my own head. "Want to talk about it?"

"No." I inhaled a deep breath, holding the clean air in my lungs.

"Change your mind, I'm here."

Yes, he was. But he didn't press me to confide the worries and fears plaguing my mind. He was simply there, as constant as the river flowing through the land. Strong and bold and steady.

Luke was a good man. The best part about him was that he didn't want anyone to put him on a pedestal. He was happy with his boots in the dirt.

I studied him as he rowed, taking in the strong lines of his face. Normally he shaved before work, even on the weekends, but not today. The dusting of dark whiskers the same color as his hair accentuated his handsome features. The stubble, combined with the small white scar above his left eyebrow, gave him a rugged edge.

"Where'd you get that scar?" I asked. "On your eyebrow."

"Guess." Luke smirked. He'd made me do the same with a scar on his shoulder.

That one he'd earned in the line of duty as a younger cop. Some asshole, high on meth, had pretended to go along with his arrest for breaking into an auto-parts store. Right before Luke had put him in cuffs, the guy had slashed out with a knife.

"Breaking up a bar fight?" I asked.

He shook his head.

"Did someone throw a punch at you?"

"No." He shook his head again and jerked his chin to a small box at my side. The top was clear and inside, it was separated into tiny compartments. Each held a hook adorned with a brightly tied fly.

"A fish hook?"

"Yeah. About three years ago, the mayor asked me if I'd take him fishing. He was in my office and saw a picture of me holding this big rainbow I caught the summer prior. It wasn't all that long after he'd appointed me chief, so of course I had to go. The guy's my boss."

"And he hooked you." I had a sudden dislike for the Clifton Forge mayor.

"Yep. We went out one afternoon, not far from town. I got him all set up, showed him how to make a cast. I bent to pick up my own pole when a wasp came after him. He freaked out, started flinging his pole everywhere. Hooked me right above the eye."

I hissed. "Ouch."

"I'm just glad it didn't get me *in* the eye."

"Me too." The world would be a darker place without his shining blue gaze. "Did you get your eyes from your mother or father?"

"My dad. My mom always used to joke that the only thing she passed down was her dimple."

I giggled, wishing I'd had the chance to meet his mother, that Luke still had her. "Genetics are weird. Take Presley and me. She had to get glasses when we were in fifth grade but I have always had perfect vision."

"And your eyes are bluer than hers."

"They are?"

He nodded. "Without a doubt. You're brighter."

"You're biased."

"Definitely."

He rowed us for another hour, steering the raft down the best channel as its current propelled us forward. We traded bits and pieces about ourselves, much like we did over the cribbage board, until Luke pointed ahead. "That's our campsite for tonight."

"Okay, great." *Where was the campsite?*

"You have no idea what I'm pointing at, do you?"

"Not a clue."

He chuckled. "You'll see."

I clutched tight to the raft as he maneuvered us toward the riverbank. The raft dug into the gravel on the shore, stopping us with a hard bump.

Luke sprinted into action, his movements quick but graceful, and hauled the front of the raft farther onto the shore with a strong heft. Then he secured a line from the raft to a nearby tree.

"What can I do?" I asked.

"Let's set up camp. Then we'll explore."

I took orders as he told me where to take things from the raft. The firepit was nothing more than a ring of stones, the insides charred. It sat in the middle of the campsite clearing. We unloaded a rubber tub of dry goods and one of the two coolers he'd packed. Luke told me that we'd leave one for the latter half of the week, and as long as we kept it sealed, it would stay cold for the next few days.

"Can I help with the tent?" I asked after hauling out my own dry bag.

"I got it. Why don't you get us out a couple of waters? We'll take them with us when we hike around."

My task took a whole thirty seconds, but it gave me plenty of time to appreciate my sexy camp director as he erected the tent.

The T-shirt Luke had worn today was stretched tight across his broad chest. The sleeves strained against the strength of his biceps and triceps. I'd learned a lot about those arms, how they could pin me in place as Luke drove inside me. How it felt to be wrapped in their warmth.

A shiver rolled down my spine and excitement for the night to come in our sleeping bag stirred in my belly.

The show was over too soon and Luke took my hand as we set off into the surrounding area.

Trees towered above us, shielding the afternoon sun. The grasses around the tent and firepit were short, probably from people treading on them, but as we made our way through the evergreens, the stems brushed my knees. Pine scented the air. The rush of the river beyond reverberated off the cliffs.

"Is this a hiking trail?" I asked, following Luke down a narrow dirt trail.

"Not exactly." Luke shot me a smirk over his shoulder as we walked single file.

A foul stench tainted the clean air and I ducked my nose into my armpit. Not me. And it wasn't Luke.

"Did something die out here or—"

Luke stepped aside and my question became pointless.

"No." My jaw dropped. "I can't use that."

There was a metal circle on the trail, about three feet in diameter. On the top, a stained toilet lid.

There were no walls. No protection.

There was no toilet paper.

"Need to pee?" Luke asked, taking a fold of white tissue from his pocket.

I scrunched up my nose, muttering, "Yes."

I hadn't gone since we'd left the house this morning.

"I'll wait over there." He turned his back and walked toward some trees, out of range.

I stared at the toilet, then gulped and opened it with the toe of my shoe. The stench was unbearable as I squatted, hovering as I peed faster than I ever had in my life.

The smell wasn't nice, but I could breathe out of my mouth. This wasn't clean by any stretch but I had strong thighs. What freaked me out most was the exposure.

Ahead of me, the river sparkled under the early-evening sun. Our tent and the cliffs were visible on the opposite shore. And here I was, peeing, for the world to see. If another raft came floating by, they'd find me squatting with my jeans bunched at my ankles.

I hurried to cover myself, then cringed as I walked away.

"That was an experience," I said when I reached Luke's side. But if that was the worst part of camping, I'd survive.

"Hungry?" he asked. "We can have an early dinner and chill by the fire or we can hike for a while."

"Dinner. But only if you let me help."

He shook his head. "This week, dinner is on me."

"But—"

"Let me spoil you."

"Okay." Had I ever been spoiled before? I had a feeling

Luke's version would be amazing, so I nodded and stood on my toes to brush a kiss against his lips.

We loaded our arms with fallen branches for firewood as we made our way to the tent. Luke found a few larger logs that he cut apart with a hatchet. And while he kindled a fire, I sat in a collapsible chair and decided camping was definitely my thing.

"I expected hot dogs," I said as Luke set a grate over the red coals in the pit. On the grate were colorful kabobs of chicken, peppers, onion and potato.

"We eat good on the river."

"What else can I expect?"

"Steak and potatoes. Shrimp scampi. Barbecue chicken. Greek burgers. Eggs and pancakes for breakfast. And hopefully trout if we catch any."

"Wow."

"There's not much I can't cook over a fire."

"Apparently." I laughed, sipping my beer.

After my days at the Warrior clubhouse, I'd stopped drinking entirely. Even when Luke had one at his place, I hadn't wanted one. But with him, I didn't need to worry about losing control or lowering my guard. There wasn't a person on earth who'd protect me the way he would.

It was entertaining to watch Luke cook. He was in his element here, so comfortable and relaxed. And when he handed me my plate, I devoured the meal and slipped into a blissful food coma.

I'd put on some weight over the past two months, but it felt necessary. I felt stronger. Capable. When the time came for a fight, the enemy wouldn't find a woman who'd wasted away under the weight of her fears and doubts.

Not that I'd stand a chance.

"This is peaceful, isn't it?" Luke asked from his chair beside mine.

I hummed in agreement.

"This is my favorite thing to do."

The evening light was fading, though there'd be hours before darkness settled, but the lowering sun made everything glow. Even the bugs flying between the trees glittered.

Birds chirped. The fire crackled. Luke didn't stay seated for long. He'd pop up and down, busying himself with tasks like tying up the garbage and making sure the cooler and food boxes were sealed tight. And he pampered me, not letting me do anything more strenuous than lifting a drink to my lips.

When he finally settled into his seat to stay, we watched the world move around us. The sun dropped and with it the temperature, raising goose bumps on my arms.

"You're cold." Luke shot out of his chair, going to the tent. He rifled around inside before coming back out with a blanket to drape across my lap. Then he stoked the fire, adding more wood.

When he sat down, he turned his face to the sky. There was enough of a clearing in the trees that we'd be able to see the stars.

"There." He pointed to a glimmering flicker, the first star of the night. "Out here, we'll see the Milky Way after dark."

It happened faster than I'd expected. The heavens morphed from cobalt to midnight. The velvety black was dusted with diamonds as billions upon billions of stars shown down onto our paradise.

"When I was a little girl, I read this book that said stars were actually fairies watching over us as we slept. I don't know why, but that story always stayed with me. As I got older, I wondered what the fairies watching me would have said."

Luke reached over from his chair and laid a hand over my wrist. "That your beauty is unmatched. Your bravery runs deep. And that you guard your pure heart."

He flattered me, this man.

I wished that what he'd said was true. Mostly, I suspected the fairies would be disappointed. Maybe disgusted. But I wanted to make them proud. And for the first time, I was beginning to understand how.

It would begin with a story.

The truth.

"What do you want in life?" I asked Luke.

He sighed, his grip on my wrist loosening as his fingers drew tiny circles on my skin. "I want a nice home. A good job."

"You have those."

He nodded. "I do. And I aim to keep them."

"What else? What's something you don't have?"

"A dog for a best friend. To talk about life every day with someone I love. To get my wife pregnant on a rainy day and raise my children the way my parents raised me. To end each day with a smile."

My heart melted. "Great answer."

"What do you want in life?" He turned my own question onto me.

I don't know. "A smile at the end of every day sounds nice."

I turned my cheek to study Luke's profile. The stars above were stunning. But still, he had them beat.

"Presley and I used to cuddle together in the middle of the night when our parents were asleep and talk about what we wanted in life. Her answer was always the same. She wanted to live in a small town where everyone knew her name. Some place old-fashioned."

"And you?"

"My answer always changed because I don't think I ever found the right answer. I picked things other people loved and hoped that if I got them, maybe I'd love them too." Like California.

"I think that's normal. To change."

"Maybe." Except it felt indecisive. Like if I really knew myself, I'd know what I wanted for the future. I'd have dreams.

"What is your answer now?"

"I don't have one," I admitted. "Which I think is better than guessing, don't you?" At the moment, I was content to just be . . . lost.

"Yeah, I do." Luke stood and held out a hand to help me from my chair. Then he led me to the tent.

"What about the fire?"

"I'll take care of it."

While I changed into some sweats, he collected a bucket of water from the river and doused the fire's red coals. Then he joined me, stripping off his boots, jeans and shirt, then slipped into our campsite bed.

Luke made love to me, long and sweet, before curling me into his embrace as he gently drifted off to sleep.

We'd spent every night together since the first, and he'd never fallen asleep first. But here, he must have felt safe to let down his own guard.

So I breathed him in, soaked in the strength of his arms.

What do I want from life?

I wanted to be the woman Luke got pregnant on a rainy day. I wanted to love the dog who'd be his best friend.

I was still choosing other people's dreams and trying to retrofit them as my own. If I was going to find my own answer, I had to make sense of my life. I had to unwind the mess.

Starting with the truth.

It was time to tell Luke everything.

CHAPTER TWELVE

SCARLETT

"Did you put on sunscreen?" Luke asked.

"Not yet."

He reached into the backpack beside our feet and plucked out a bottle, tossing it over. "Your knees and shoulders are a little pink."

I doused my arms and legs, then stood and sprayed the back of Luke's neck.

"Thanks, beautiful."

"You're welcome." I kissed his cheek and returned to my seat.

The sun was warm today but the spray from the river kept my skin cool, which was probably why I hadn't noticed I was starting to burn. My ghostly white legs and arms hadn't seen the sun in months, but wow, had I missed it.

My hair was tucked into the same cap I'd worn the whole trip, Luke's cap, and my ponytail draped down my spine. I hoped the ends would pick up some highlights because I didn't see a trip to the salon in my future.

"I need a haircut," I said.

Luke frowned. "What kind of cut are we talking here? Because I might have an opinion. Short like Presley's?"

"Do you like her hair?"

"It's fine. But I love yours."

"I just want a trim." My sister could pull off the short style. It suited her personality, spunky and free. She stood out and her hair made a statement.

I understood why she wanted it short. Long hair had been one of Dad's requirements. But still, I loved the long, bright-blond strands. They gave me something to hide behind. They gave Luke something to toy with. His fingers always seemed to find their way into my hair, even when we slept.

We'd woken up to the sun's warmth on the tent's walls and the birds singing their good-morning song. Luke had kept me in his arms all night, our legs twined together. As he'd promised, there'd been no hurry, no race to get on the water. He'd built a fire to cook breakfast and brew coffee. Then we'd slowly packed up camp and headed out.

Luke turned an oar, steering as we floated. His forearms flexed. His biceps and shoulders strained against his T-shirt. By the time we made it to camp, I'd be so hot and bothered from drooling over him all day that I might not be able to wait for him to set up the tent before I pounced. Raft sex? *Oh, yeah.*

That was, if he was still speaking to me.

I didn't want to ruin this trip, but the niggling sensation in my stomach couldn't be ignored. Now that I'd made the decision to tell Luke everything, the truth clawed at my throat, scratching to get out. I'd swallowed it down at breakfast, but this was as good a time as any to set the words free.

Just tell him. My hands trembled at my sides so I tucked them under my legs. My heart raced.

I trusted Luke to keep my story safe. I trusted him to help me figure this out.

I trusted Luke.

With my life.

Here goes.

"I need to tell you something."

The easy, relaxed expression on his face disappeared. "Want me to stop?"

"No." It would be easier to talk this through if he was rowing. If we were moving. "You asked me a while ago what happened at the Warrior clubhouse. I wasn't ready to tell you. The truth is, I didn't know if I could trust you."

"You can."

I gave him a small smile. "I know."

He nodded for me to continue and I had a hard time holding those navy irises. There was shame in my story. Regret.

"Jeremiah lived at the Warrior clubhouse," I said. "He kept telling me that he was getting an apartment. I believed him for a while, but he had no intention of moving out. Besides, stealing from the club would have been harder if he hadn't lived there. I justified living there too, waiting and believing his lies, because I was in love with him. I told myself it was temporary."

Luke swallowed hard. "You really loved him, didn't you?"

"No," I admitted. "I thought I loved him. I loved the boy he once was but not the man. I think I stayed with him because of fear. I was scared to go out on my own. And the irony of that isn't lost on me. I'm more like my mother than I want to admit."

"I don't know your mom, Scarlett. But I do know you. You're loyal. You're stubborn." The corner of his mouth turned up. "You stick things out, even when they're hard. Staying with him isn't a sign of weakness. You just weren't ready to give up."

My reflection was there again, shining in his soulful eyes. What would it be like to see myself that way? Emotion bubbled in my chest and I choked down the urge to cry. There was more to my story.

"Anyway, I didn't have a job or any money. Every time I talked about finding someplace to work, Jeremiah told me to wait. Just a couple more weeks and he'd have enough for a deposit on an apartment. Then I could find a job close to our place. I didn't have a car so it made sense. But a couple weeks turned into months. Then more months. I should have realized sooner he didn't actually want to leave the clubhouse."

"What was it like?"

I cringed. "Disgusting. Dark. Raw. The realness appealed to me. In a way, it was refreshing. They weren't trying to hide their demons behind floral prints and pastels. And I needed that kind of honesty. It was like taking my feelings and my fears from Chicago and smearing them all over the wall in black, bloody strokes."

The violence was never hidden. Women were shoved around and slapped. Men fought with other men.

"It's weird to think living there was healthy, but it was healing. That place was so much like my parents' house but there was no pretending. And because nothing was covered up, no one made excuses for why they hit and hurt. It was eye opening. I needed to stare at the ugly for a while and find the urgency to change my life."

That was not the life I wanted for myself. Neither was the life I'd had in Chicago. Neither was Jeremiah. I only wished it hadn't taken me so long to figure out. Because maybe if I had clued in sooner, I wouldn't have been in the clubhouse basement on that horrific day.

"The first few weeks were fun," I admitted. "The parties were exhilarating. Jeremiah gave me his undivided attention. He took me for rides on his motorcycle and we were in our own world. Then one day I woke up and was starving. I hadn't eaten the day before. Jeremiah was still asleep. He'd told me not to go wandering around the club-house, but I thought he just meant during the parties or at night since they had a lot of people come over who weren't Warriors."

Luke's hands squeezed tight on the oars. He knew where I was going with this.

"I went to the kitchen, hungover and out of it. I got some-thing out of the refrigerator and when I closed the door, this man was there. I didn't recognize him but he was wearing a Warrior cut." I could still see the arrowhead stitched into the black leather on the back. "He came at me. I wasn't sure what he was on, but I managed to scramble away and raced back to Jeremiah's room."

"I hope Jeremiah beat that guy's ass."

I scoffed. "Jeremiah was better at taking a beating than delivering one. He promised that he'd told the guys to leave me alone, but from that point on, I started to see things for what they really were."

Women being treated like whores. Some raped. Some beaten. Men who didn't care about anything other than drugs, money and violence. Men who would kill anyone who got in their way. All in the name of *brotherhood*.

"That was about the time I wanted to see Presley and came to Clifton Forge but chickened out. I shouldn't have gone back." *Stupid, stupid Scarlett.* "But Jeremiah promised to make some changes, to get us an apartment and a real place to stay. It was all bullshit, but I was so used to believing promises that I stayed the fool."

"Scarlett—"

"Don't." I held up a hand. "I love the way you see me. No one has ever looked past my mistakes and shortcomings the way you do. But I don't want to see past these. Does that make any sense? I need these mistakes. I need these regrets. Because this is the only way I can make sure they won't happen again."

Luke sighed. "I get it. But I still think you're too hard on yourself."

Maybe I was, but hard was the fuel driving me forward.

"Jeremiah promised to change and I guess, in a way, he did. Just not for the better. He started staying out later and more often. Most nights, I watched TV in his room and fell asleep hours before he got back. He was jumpy. He was edgy. A few times, he came back beaten to a pulp, but he wouldn't tell me what had happened. So I did what I'd always done. I cleaned him up like I had my mother a hundred times before."

I'd convinced myself that he needed me. That I was necessary to his survival.

Just like my mother.

"I was stuck. The money my mom gave me had almost run out. Every week that passed, I dreaded finding Presley. The longer I stayed, the harder it would be to tell her I'd been in Montana since June. Then one snowy morning, Jeremiah was asleep. He'd come home about dawn with a broken pinky finger—he wouldn't tell me what had happened. I assumed he'd been at the tables but maybe he'd been with another woman. It wasn't like we were sleeping together anymore so I didn't care. It was early and the clubhouse was quiet. I needed to get out of that room, so I tiptoed out. I finally decided it was time to get out. I was going to call Presley."

Luke nodded, his attention fixed on me as we floated. The sun had lost its heat. The sky had dulled. Because I was back in that dark place.

"I hadn't explored much of the clubhouse. There was a TV room where I watched movies sometimes. The kitchen was normally a safe place if I just waited until lunchtime. There were some women who stopped by regularly and cooked meals. I didn't know them well, but they were friendly enough once they realized I had no intention of sleeping with their men."

"Remember any names?"

"Some, but everyone went by their nickname. Even me. They called me Goldilocks." Repeating it made me grimace. "Their president at least went by his real name, I think. Tucker. He wasn't around much during the parties, but I saw him occasionally. He was always surrounded by the same group of guys. They were different than the partiers. They gave off this energy."

"What kind of energy?"

The terrifying kind. "Everyone watched them. When they walked into a room, everyone, even the scariest assholes in the room, held their breath." The first time I'd seen Tucker had been at a party. He'd come through the clubhouse doors and it was like the party was put on mute. The music still blared. The air was still sweaty and thick. But all eyes went to Tucker as he strode through the room and disappeared down a long hallway.

"Tucker Talbot." Luke rubbed his jaw. "He's one serious motherfucker."

"Do you know him?"

"I know of him. But that's another discussion. You were going to call Presley."

I nodded, my hands shifting to grip the edge of my seat. "I have the same phone I had in high school. Jeremiah bought it for me. He got one for Presley too. We hid them from my parents because Dad didn't want us to have phones. I kept it all these years. Presley would text me on occasion. I never texted back, but I had her number. I knew that if Jeremiah found out, he'd stop me from leaving, so I wanted to be far away from his room in case he woke up. I wandered down this hallway and into the basement."

I'd chosen the basement because I'd been trying to escape the stench. The hallway had reeked of alcohol and sweat. But the basement had been cold. Sterile.

"I was quiet. I didn't want to accidentally wake up one of the guys who'd forget I was Jeremiah's. I thought the basement was empty, but then I heard a noise. It was the same kind I'd heard at home for years."

The sound of flesh pummeling flesh. Of bones being broken.

"I snuck close, curious. Dumb. And through the crack of the door, I saw Tucker and three other Warriors standing around a man they'd tied to a chair. The guy was beaten and bleeding out of his eyes and ears and nose and mouth. I don't know why I did it, but I watched. I watched as the three men took turns hitting him until finally Tucker told them to stop."

Luke closed his eyes, shaking his head. "Did they see you?"

"No."

"You're sure?"

I nodded. "They didn't see me. I was barefoot and backed away. But . . ."

"But what?"

"I recorded it on my phone." I gulped. "I videoed the entire thing."

Luke flinched. "Fuck."

Pretty much. "Tucker started talking to his men. The guy in the chair wasn't dead, just unconscious. Tucker said they needed to make it look like a suicide. Like Draven Slater. I didn't know who Draven was, but I didn't stick around to find out."

Luke's face was stone, his grip on the oars impossibly tight. "Who knows about the recording?"

"You."

Luke nodded and looked past me to the river. He gave the raft a few strong rows, like he was forcing his anger into the water.

"Who's Draven Slater?" I asked. "Was he related to Dash?"

"His father. He used to own the garage and for all intents and purposes, he was like a father to Presley too. A good father."

My stomach plummeted. "And he died. Tucker killed him." This was just getting worse.

"Apparently," Luke muttered, shaking his head. "I don't

know if Dash knows. If he doesn't, this could mean a war between the Tin Gypsies and the Arrowhead Warriors."

"But I thought the Tin Gypsies weren't a club anymore. What about Presley? Would she be in danger?"

"I don't know." He sighed. "I don't fucking know. Who was the man in the chair? Did you recognize him?"

I shook my head. "I'd never seen him before. He was older, maybe in his forties or fifties. But with all the blood, it was hard to tell."

"Do you still have the video?"

I nodded and stretched for my dry bag. In the months I'd spent with Luke, I'd kept my phone close, hidden in the dresser in my bedroom. And I'd brought it along on the trip, not wanting it out of my reach. I dug it out of my bag and turned it on. Then I pulled up the video and handed it to Luke.

The noise from the device brought me back to that place. To the cold concrete. The shivers on my arms and the fear snaking its way through my veins. I shifted sideways, facing the river and focusing on the splash of the raft with its ripples. I studied the cliffs and their serenity.

It's just a nightmare. And here, on the river with Luke, I was safe.

I'm safe.

Luke cleared his throat when the video ended and I turned to face him. He handed me the phone and I stowed it away.

"What do you want to do with that?" he asked.

"I don't know," I whispered. "Throw that phone in the river and pretend it never happened. Run and never look back. But I'm worried they'll come after Presley. And right now, that video is the only thing I have to use against them if they do."

"If the FBI knew you had that, they'd make you testify."

"Should I?"

Luke stayed quiet for a long moment, staring off to the shoreline. "I don't know. I don't know what to do."

"How screwed am I?"

He turned and gave me a sad smile but didn't answer.

Not that he needed to.

His silence was answer enough.

CHAPTER THIRTEEN

LUKE

S carlett and I didn't speak of the video, the Warriors or Jeremiah again. We spent four days on the river, savoring each other and pretending like her confession hadn't happened.

But it was on my mind. Our minds.

I wasn't the kind of man who made wishes, but if I had one to make, it would be to stay here. Stay on the river with her forever and let the outside world disappear.

It wouldn't. But . . . I wished.

Because I couldn't ignore what I'd seen on that video. The violence. The murder.

And Ken Raymond. The man who'd been tied to the chair.

His face had been so bloodied and swollen, it had taken me nearly the entire length of the video to put it together. But toward the end, one of the Warriors had grabbed a fistful of Ken's hair, tipping his face to the ceiling. And there had been a birthmark, a purple circle about the size of a dime, on the underside of Ken's jaw.

My gut had been right. When Ken had been found on the riverbank and we'd learned his home was in Ashton, I'd worried there might be a connection to the Warriors. Now there was.

They'd murdered him. Those fuckers had murdered him and deserved to pay. But why kill him? What was his connection to the gang? What had he done to deserve that beating?

He hadn't died in the chair. Scarlett had left Ashton about two weeks before Ken's body had been discovered. The Warriors had made sure to keep Ken alive and breathing so that when they tossed him into the river, his lungs would fill with water. His cause of death had been drowning, but only because someone had thrown him into the river in the first place.

The river's beating had hidden the injuries from the Warriors. The autopsy hadn't been exact, but the coroner had estimated Ken had spent multiple days in the water before washing to shore. Hell, maybe they'd let him heal up a bit so he'd been awake when they shoved him into the icy water. *Sick bastards.*

Ken had managed an indoor shooting range and gun shop in Ashton. Maybe that had been his link to the Warriors. Maybe he'd been into drugs. According to the autopsy, there hadn't been any substances in his system, but all of my assumptions had flown out the window the minute I'd watched that video.

Did the Warriors know Scarlett had been there? Was that why they'd been in Clifton Forge? Or were they clueless and still hunting her because of Jeremiah's stolen drugs?

My guess was the latter. If they knew that Scarlett had evidence that could send them to prison, they wouldn't have been so docile in their visits. They would have torn my town apart to find her because Tucker Talbot wouldn't go down without a fight.

Prison was exactly where a motherfucker like Tucker Talbot deserved to rot for the rest of his life.

Scarlett had the video to make that happen.

Except giving it to the FBI would mean she'd lose everything. They'd make her testify and then strip her identity for witness protection. *Actual* witness protection, not the version where she lived in my house.

Scarlett Marks would cease to exist anywhere but in my heart.

Two months ago, I wouldn't have thought twice about it. If she'd shown me that video, I would have escorted Agent Maria Brown to my home and handed over Scarlett without question.

But that was months ago, before she'd captured my heart.

Later. I put it away until later and enjoyed the tail end of our trip.

This week had been refreshing. No hiding. No pretending. Other than the occasional moment when I found her staring off into space, the worry line between her eyebrows deep, she'd relaxed on the river. She'd found some peace.

Scarlett had needed this vacation more than I had.

As expected, she loved it out here. She was constantly turning her face to the sun. She giggled when we cruised through a set of rapids and the water splashed on her skin. She was never in a hurry to turn in each night when the stars were out in their magnificent force.

And as far as rafting trips went, this was the best time I'd ever had on the Smith.

God, I didn't want this to be the last time. I didn't want this to be one of the last memories I had with her.

Later. Put it away.

With Scarlett's eyes on the riverbanks, I lifted an oar out of the water, then I brought it up as high as it would pivot in the oarlock before slapping it down on the water, sending a splash of cold water onto her shoulders.

She gasped, her mouth forming a perfect O before flattening as she cast me a smirk. "What was that for?"

I shrugged. "You were looking a little flushed. Thought I'd help cool you down."

"You'll pay for that," she warned, taking the hem of her tank top in her hands. She tore it over her head, her blond ponytail flying. Then she laid it out on a cooler to dry, leaving her in just a bikini top.

Exactly as planned.

Scarlett was more beautiful now than she'd ever been. She grew more beautiful each and every day. Her face was flushed and over the week, she'd developed a tan. It brought out a small line of freckles on her nose. I'd taken to kissing them whenever I had the chance.

Her hair was in kinks—what did women call those? *beach waves*—and the texture thicker than when it was straight. The urge to touch it was as strong as ever. I'd brought along a camp shower, a plastic cube that hung from a tree. I'd fill it full of river water, then add water I'd boiled in a pot over the fire so it was warm. Scarlett would wash her hair and body, dress in sweats, then sit in her camp chair and brush it out.

If there was such a thing as spun sunshine, that was Scarlett's hair. And her eyes were jewels mined from the sky.

Seeing her there, wearing next to nothing and smiling,

stirred my blood. The stretch of river ahead had some tight curves and the last thing we needed was to capsize, but otherwise, I'd take her right here on the boat.

Later. In the safety of our tent, I'd ravish that delectable body and show her how I felt, even if I wasn't ready to say it aloud yet.

It was too soon for words. For promises. There was too much looming on the horizon.

There had to be a solution. There just had to be. I'd figure this out. Somehow. Because the alternative wasn't feasible. If I lost her . . .

"What are you thinking about?" Scarlett asked, her gaze roaming my face.

I'd been staring, lost in my head. "You."

"What about me?"

"Just how stunning you are."

She ducked her chin, hiding from the praise.

"Does it embarrass you?"

"A little." She looked up and shrugged.

"I don't give compliments when they aren't earned."

"You're biased."

"No." I shook my head. "I just see what you can't yet. But stick with me, beautiful. We'll get there."

Her eyes turned glassy and her head lilted to the side as she stared at me with an expression so grateful, it humbled me. Then the look was gone, replaced with such a bone-deep sadness, it hurt me as much as it seemed to hurt her. "We have to talk about it, Luke. We can't keep ignoring it."

"I know." I shoved the oars hard into the water, feeling the strain in my shoulders and arms as I pushed my frustration into the river. "I don't know what to do. That's not a feeling I enjoy."

Scarlett smirked. "Chief Rosen always has the answer."

"Or I fake it until I come up with the right one."

"How would you fake this?"

"I don't know." I sighed. "What do you want to do?"

"What are my options?"

"Hide away in my house forever," I teased, though part of me was serious. I'd keep her there until we were old and gray if that meant her safety.

"Tempting." She laughed. "But eventually you're going to get sick of me rearranging furniture."

"Never." I winked, giving us another strong row.

"I could disappear."

"What do you mean?"

She shrugged. "I could leave town, never look back. Cut off all ties to Presley."

A lump formed in my throat. Had she considered this before? Was that what she'd planned to do the night I'd caught her at the door? "Is that what you want?"

"No." She didn't hesitate. "If I have to, then I'll do it. But I'm not done fighting yet."

"That's my girl."

She squared her shoulders. "So how do we fight?"

"We need to make a copy or two of that video. I don't want to risk something happening to your phone." I suspected my email was being monitored by the FBI but we'd find a way to get that video into cloud storage or something. Maybe I'd create an account under Dad's name.

Scarlett nodded. "Then what?"

"The way I see it, we've got two options. The first—that video disappears and we find a way to get the Warriors to believe you didn't take their drugs."

"The second?"

"We take that video to the FBI. There's a chance they won't put you in witness protection."

"But there's a chance they will."

I nodded. "If they think the Warriors will retaliate and threaten your life, yes. If they want you to testify, yes."

"What happens if you give the video to the FBI anonymously?"

"They'll know it came from you," I said. "They'll make you testify."

"Can't I refuse?"

"They'll make it nearly impossible. They might threaten you with an accessory charge or something to force you into it. They can't build a case from that video alone. To make it rock solid, they'll want the person who took it to corroborate its legitimacy."

She dropped her gaze to her bare feet. Her toes wiggled on the bottom of the boat, tapping on the water droplets.

Fuck, what was I doing? We shouldn't even have options. My conscience raged in the back of my mind, scolding me for even presenting her with option one. I was a cop. The only option here was justice. Scarlett had the power to put those murdering thugs away. Each and every one of the Warriors likely deserved a prison cell.

But I'd lose her.

I wasn't just a cop, but a man falling in love who wasn't ready to give Scarlett up. Which was why as I watched her internal deliberation, my heart screamed *option one*.

"Option one," she said, lifting her chin. A part of me soared. Another part sank. "We try option one."

"Okay. That means we need to involve the guys at the garage." Even with Dash's frequent trips to the station recently, I wasn't an expert on motorcycle gangs. If we were going to approach the Warriors, I needed all the help I could get from the former Tin Gypsies.

"Tell me about them."

I took a long breath—it was a long story. "The Tin Gypsies brought a lot of trouble to Clifton Forge. In their prime, they were like the Warriors, though maybe not quite as reckless. But every bit as brutal."

Scarlett blinked. "And Presley worked for them?"

"She worked for the garage. It was owned and operated by Draven Slater. From what I understand, the garage was there first. The club came second. Some of the guys in the club, like Dash and Emmett, worked at the garage as mechanics, but it was technically separate from the club. I don't know how much Presley knew about the Gypsies or was involved in club business. My impression is not much. I think Draven wanted to protect her so he kept her out of it."

Scarlett sat up straighter. "Draven was the man Tucker mentioned in the video. Who was he? Why would they kill him?"

We'd been sidetracked the day she'd showed me the video and I hadn't wanted to go into all the history. But now was as good a time as any. "Draven was the president of the Tin Gypsies and one of their founders. When he retired, he passed the garage down to Dash. Same with leadership of the club before it disbanded."

"Why'd they disband?"

"From what Dash and Emmett have told me, the culture changed." Maybe it was the truth. Maybe it wasn't. But I'd never pushed for more than what they'd told me. The Gypsies were history and as long as they didn't break any laws, I'd left history alone.

"Emmett's dad was murdered," I said, watching as Scarlett flinched. "I don't know who killed him, but I suspect the Gypsies do and made that person pay."

"The Warriors," she murmured.

"Maybe. Afterward, Dash told me that the club changed. Emmett's dad had been one of the founding members alongside Draven, and his death really shook the club."

"So Dash shut it down."

"More or less. The garage is a fairly lucrative business. They do a lot of custom bike builds and classic remodels. Real high-end stuff that doesn't come cheap. I'm speculating here, but my guess is the garage started to make up for any income the club made through not-so-legal channels. The older members probably stepped away. I know for a fact that a handful of former Gypsies who wanted to stay in the club life joined the Warriors. And the younger guys all settled in at the garage, working for Dash."

Scarlett raised an eyebrow. "That's it? What about their 'brotherhood'? That's all I ever heard at the Warrior clubhouse. Brothers. Everything was for their brothers. It was like a cult. It seems strange to just walk away."

"Oh, I'm sure there's more to it, but good luck getting anyone to admit the truth."

Scarlett frowned and her eyes narrowed, like I'd just issued a challenge.

In a way, she reminded me of Bryce Slater, Dash's wife. Bryce had moved to town years ago to work with her father as a reporter at the local newspaper. She'd had a big career in Seattle as a news anchor, so when she'd come here and heard the story of the Gypsies, their sudden disbandment without much explanation, she hadn't bought it either.

She'd gone after Dash for answers.

He'd married her.

I had no doubt that she'd gotten the truth, but neither of them would ever share it with the authorities.

Not that it mattered. All I cared about was that the Gypsies were over and my town was relatively peaceful.

"They're good men," I told Scarlett. I didn't want her to have any misconceptions about their character, because we were going to have to trust them to get her out of this cluster-fuck. "They want an honest life. I'm not going to dredge up the past and risk taking it from them."

That was what had cost the last chief of police his career. And his life. Marcus Wagner's obsession with the Tin Gypsies had driven him mad.

Scarlett tapped her chin, talking more to herself than to me. "Okay, so the Gypsies fell apart. The guys went to work at the garage. If they weren't a threat to the Warriors, why would Tucker kill Draven Slater and make it look like a suicide? What am I missing?"

My smart, beautiful woman. She caught on to things quickly, so it was no surprise she was putting the puzzle together faster than I could supply pieces.

"About three, almost four, years ago, a woman was murdered at a motel in town," I told her. "Stabbed to death."

"Murdered?" Scarlett froze. "Who?"

"Her name was Amina Daylee. She was an old friend of Draven's. A lover. And their daughter is a friend of mine. Genevieve is married to Isaiah, one of the mechanics at the garage. She's Dash's half-sister. Remember I told you they live down the street."

"Ah." She nodded. "The pretty brunette and the guy with the tattoos. They have a baby."

"That's them."

"Everyone is tied to the garage, including Presley," she said. "That's how she fits in this thing."

"Pretty much. Long story short, Marcus couldn't handle the fact that Draven and the Gypsies got away with whatever it was they got away with. So he killed Amina and tried to frame Draven for her murder."

"But he didn't get away with it. Otherwise you wouldn't be chief."

"Correct. He'd disguised himself as a Warrior. Tried to get the former Gypsies to think it was them who'd set up Draven. Meanwhile, the county prosecutor put Draven on trial. Draven probably would have been convicted, but he killed himself first."

"No." Scarlett's eyes widened. "That's what Tucker meant. He didn't kill himself. They killed him. But why? If Draven was going to prison, why fake a suicide and murder him?"

"That, I don't know. Until you showed me that video, I thought Draven killed himself to avoid a prison sentence."

"Oh my God." Scarlett slumped and closed her eyes. "This is such a mess."

"And it might get messier. If Dash doesn't know that the Warriors killed his father, this could be a disaster." I didn't want to know what that might do to my friend's life. Or my town.

"What if he does know?"

"It means Dash and the guys at the garage chose to let it go. To protect themselves and their families. I wouldn't blame them. They're outnumbered. Dash and Bryce have little kids. Genevieve and Isaiah have their baby girl. A fight with the Warriors will only mean putting those kids in harm's way."

"I'm doing that, Luke." The color drained from Scarlett's face. "I am endangering those kids. You told me the Warriors have been watching them. What if they do something stupid? What if someone gets hurt? It would be my fault."

"No, not you." I shook my head. "Jeremiah."

"How could he have joined the Warriors? He was engaged to Presley. Isn't that some kind of betrayal?"

"Well, from what I understand, the Gypsies thought about as much of Jeremiah as they do dog shit on their boot. None of them wanted her to marry him. None of them knew their history. Now that they do, I don't think they blame her. Pres was loyal to him for helping her escape."

Scarlett turned and gave me her profile as she stared across the water. "He was a mistake. For us both."

"You didn't know."

"No, I didn't. And neither did Presley." Her fists clenched at her sides. "This is on him."

"Damn right." Scarlett might want that regret to fuel her forward, but I didn't want that burden on her shoulders. "That's the short of it."

"More questions than answers."

"Yeah. Which is why we have to involve Dash and Emmett. Leo too. He's another former Gypsy who works at the garage."

"Can we trust them?"

"Yes." And we didn't really have a choice.

"Okay," Scarlett whispered with no hesitation.

Because she trusted me. And I wasn't going to let her down. Not with this. Not ever.

"What's next?" she asked.

"We show them the video. They know more about the

Warriors than anyone else in Clifton Forge. We need to get their input."

And hope like hell that Dash didn't go ballistic when he learned the truth about his father, if he didn't know already.

Scarlett faced the river, thinking it over. I didn't rush her to agree, I just gave her time to process. Finally, she whispered, "Presley loves them. You trust them. So I will too."

"I'll reach out to Dash when we get home."

"Can you do this? Is it illegal?" Scarlett's hands flew to her cheeks. "Oh my God, Luke. I didn't even think. You're a cop. I showed you that video and put you in a position to lie and—"

"Don't." I lifted an oar from the water, setting it alongside the raft. Then I shifted in my seat, stretching an arm for her. I pulled one of her hands free and replaced it with my own, brushing a thumb across her cheek. "You let me worry about that. Right now, all I care about is keeping you safe."

Her eyes softened and she leaned into my touch. "I'm sorry."

"We'll figure it out." I circled my thumb once more, then returned to my bench, taking up the oar.

The two of us sat quietly, the sound of the river whirring around us and the magnitude of what was to come weighing heavily on our shoulders.

We had a fight ahead of us. One hell of a fight.

It was hard to enjoy the river today. This was one of the best areas to fish, and though I loved casting my line into the water, I couldn't bring myself to touch a pole.

"Should we have lunch?" I asked Scarlett as the sun reached its peak.

"I guess." She shrugged, probably not hungry. Our conversation had stolen my appetite too.

I pointed down the river. "There are some curves and rapids ahead. Nothing major, but enough that we won't want to be up and down opening coolers. Let's take a break. Pull off for a while. Then we'll continue on and make camp before an early dinner."

She nodded, twisting sideways to watch as I guided us toward the bank. When we were close, she moved to the front of the raft, grabbing the rope to tie us off like I'd taught her earlier in the week. She held the raft, her arms straining, as I secured the oars and climbed out, taking the rope to tie us to a tree.

Then I walked to Scarlett and took her in my arms.

She melted into my chest, her hands snaking their way around my waist. "I'm sorry."

"Don't apologize."

"I've brought so much trouble to your life."

"Hey." I leaned back, waiting for her to look up. When she did, I tucked a lock of hair behind her ear. "I'll take the trouble. I'll take it tenfold if that means I get you."

The doubts, the internal conflict, I'd put away. *Later.* They'd be there later.

She blushed again, then stood on her tiptoes, ready for a kiss.

I bent, sweeping my lips against hers, letting my tongue drag across the seam of her mouth. My arms banded around her back as I hauled her closer. I was about to flick the string on her bikini top loose when an eagle cawed above our heads, the noise breaking us apart.

Scarlett's gaze flew to the sky, her hand shielding her eyes, as the magnificent bird swooped down over the river. Its splayed talons plunged beneath the surface, grabbing a small trout and heaving it from the water.

"Whoa." Scarlett's jaw dropped. "That was—he was so close. And so big."

"There." I pointed toward the bird as it rose into the sky, toward a nest in a tree beside the cliff on the opposite bank.

"I've never seen a bald eagle in person."

"They're amazing creatures." I let her go and scanned the area. It was surprising the bird had come down when we were so close but the two of us were standing in the shade of a tree. The raft was fairly well hidden too. "My father taught me that eagles are good omens."

"I'll take all the good omens we can find." Scarlett's attention stayed fixed on the bird as it settled into its perch and began devouring its own lunch.

"Dad loves the old mountain-men customs. Trapping. Tanning hides. Hunting. Fishing. His best friend is a Chippewa Cree and the two of them will set out each year to do something 'the old-fashioned way.' I have a pair of gloves they made one year out of a beaver pelt and sewed with sinew. While they're doing these projects, his friend always tells him stories about Native American customs."

Dad would then impart them to me.

It was one of my favorite things about fishing trips with Dad. They came with history lessons and tales from a different era when survival was hard and the trivial worries of today . . . well, there hadn't been time for trivial.

I glanced around the shoreline and a flicker of white caught my eye. I stepped away from Scarlett and walked over to the feather resting on the gravel between two tufts of grass.

An eagle's feather. Perfect and pristine. Like the bird had dropped it here, knowing we'd come along to claim it.

"Here." I took it to her and placed it in her palm. "For

some tribes, whenever a battle was won or a warrior was particularly brave, they were awarded a feather. It's believed by some that the feathers hold the bird's spirit or energy, and when they fall, it's a gift."

Scarlett took the stem, twisting it to inspect every angle. Then she ran a fingertip along its dark brown vane. "It's so pretty."

"Earning an eagle's feather was for the bravest and strongest. You should take it home." That feather was meant for her.

"You don't think I should leave it here?" she asked.

"No."

Maybe it was superstitious, but my instincts screamed we'd need that eagle's bravery.

And more.

CHAPTER FOURTEEN

SCARLETT

"Ugh," I groaned as a bump in the road slammed my knees into the raft's bench.

Hiding was getting old. Fast.

I was curled into a ball on the floor of the boat, bumping and jostling between the seats and the bags stuffed around me. With the air open above me, I stared at the blue sky and the clouds as Luke drove away from the loading dock.

I missed the river already. I missed the tent we'd packed away this morning. I missed campfire meals and starry nights.

We'd been gone for all of fifteen minutes and all I wanted was to repeat this past week again on loop.

Today was June second—I'd asked Luke this morning before we'd reached the unloading zone.

I'd arrived in Montana exactly one year and two days ago. Presley would have been married for a year if I hadn't arrived. Jeremiah would be alive.

This past year had been filled with mistakes. Regrets.

But there were happy moments too, and each was thanks to Luke. Those moments, I wouldn't trade for anything.

I was not the same woman who'd ridden a bus to Montana. She'd been naïve. Scared. Lost.

My life was still a mess, but I was confident I'd found my path. I was confident that I could right my wrongs.

I was confident.

The feeling was heady and new. Maybe that confidence had been lurking under the surface my entire life, but I was embracing it, clutching it to my chest and not letting go without a fight. I wasn't sure how tomorrow would go. Or the next day. But I was certain that with Luke's help, we could figure it out.

Together.

It was time to take my life in my own hands and face the world. Well, not at this moment. Right now, I was hiding.

The truck slowed and dust from the gravel road flew overhead before disappearing into the ether. Luke's door opened and I sat up, shoving myself off the floor to meet him at the edge of the raft.

"You okay?" he asked, helping me down.

"All set."

He kissed me on the cheek, then I hurried around the boat to climb into the passenger seat.

"I want to come back someday," I said as he resumed our journey down the road.

Behind us, the river had disappeared behind green hills and leafy trees. There were no other vehicles around, but it was different to be out in the open again, unprotected and unshielded from the cliffs and hillsides that had bordered the river during our week-long float.

"I'll bring you back." Luke reached across the cab and took my hand. "Promise."

"Maybe we'll catch more fish next time."

He grinned. "Definitely."

Though we'd caught three, fishing hadn't been the primary objective of the trip. Luke had taught me how to cast my line from the front of the raft. He'd helped me reel in one trout and I'd ridden the high of my first catch and release for hours.

Luke had done hardly any fishing, instead being a steady rock at the oars. But two nights ago, he'd stood on the shore of our campsite and cast his line into a slower pool, bringing in two fish. We'd eaten them for dinner, baked over the fire with lemon slices and some campfire potatoes.

It had been delicious, as had breakfast this morning, but my stomach churned.

"I'm nervous," I confessed.

"Me too."

"When will you talk to Dash?"

"This week. Let's get home. Get settled in. Then I'll make an appointment to get the oil changed in my truck and head to the garage."

"Okay." I blew out a shaking breath, my fingers gripping Luke's as he drove one-handed.

The trip to Clifton Forge went by in a flash. As we approached town, I didn't wait for Luke to give me a signal. I gripped his hand, gave it one last squeeze, then wiggled free of his hold to crawl into the backseat, crouching down low.

We didn't speak as Luke navigated the town's streets. When we arrived at the house, he opened the garage door, got out without a word and went about unhooking the raft. When the garage door thunked closed behind the truck, I pushed my way out, my legs and back stiff from the uncomfortable position, then darted inside.

Luke would back the raft into the garage and then we could get to work unloading. Until then, I'd stay out of sight.

The scent in the kitchen welcomed me first, the air infused with Luke's rich and woodsy smell. It was slightly stale from our week away, but I drew in a deep breath anyway.

Home.

Luke's house had become home, and it had nothing to do with the place. Home was the man himself. Whether we were here or in his truck or on the river, wherever Luke went was where I belonged.

Luke was home.

I kicked off my flip-flops in the laundry room, then padded into the kitchen. The hickory floors were cool on the soles of my feet. The sleek countertop on the island was smooth beneath my palms.

Luke was home, but that didn't mean I was ready to give up this house yet.

Please, let this work.

I closed my eyes and sent my prayer to the heavens once more. Then three times. *Please. Please.*

If the Warriors wouldn't give up their hunt for me, my only other option was the FBI. Part of me wanted them to have that video. If it meant that evil men would get their just punishment, that was what I wanted.

Luke hadn't said as much, but I suspected he felt the same. He was noble. His honor and duty ran marrow deep. Was Luke really okay letting the Warriors off the hook for murder?

The churning in my stomach intensified because I knew

the answer. Luke couldn't feel right about this, but he'd go along with it.

Just because I'd asked him to.

The garage door closed and I made my way back through the laundry room, opening the door.

Luke had his arms loaded with our dry bags. "I can unload, beautiful. You can relax."

"No, I want to help." I smiled and took a bag from his arm, dropping it by the washing machine. Everything we'd taken was dirty and I'd spend the next day doing laundry.

I was grateful for the upcoming task. It was going to be hard returning to *normal* life—if sitting around doing nothing could be considered normal. The next two or three days would be restless as I waited for Luke to get in touch with the guys from the garage.

Luke brought the coolers to the kitchen next, leaving me to unload the little food that remained. But there was next to nothing because we'd feasted on the river. On food. On the scenery. On each other.

"I'll clean up the raft later," he said after hauling in one last load of our things. Then he kicked off his boots in the laundry room, tugged off his socks and joined me in the kitchen, surveying the fridge as I put away a bottle of ketchup. "How about pizza for dinner later?"

"Sounds good." I hadn't had pizza since we'd come here. My vow to never eat it again at the safe house had been a bit premature. I cooked every night and besides the one night of burgers, Luke hadn't brought home delivery. "Do you eat out much? When you're not harboring a murder witness?"

He chuckled and closed the fridge, pulling me into his arms. "Yeah. There are some good spots in town and I like to support the local businesses. But I try to limit it." He let me go and patted his stomach. "Gotta keep up my figure for the ladies."

"Watch yourself, Chief." I laughed and poked him in a rib. "There'd better be no ladies."

"Just one." He tugged on the end of the braid I'd done this morning in the tent.

"This one needs a shower." I wanted shampoo and conditioner and a razor.

I patted his washboard abs, marveling at this man's muscles and hard lines, then headed for the stairs. When I reached the bottom one, I paused and looked over my shoulder. Luke's gaze was waiting. "Are you coming or not?"

A wicked grin spread across his face. He stalked my way, those long, strong legs of his moving with purpose and stealth. The hunger in his gaze intensified with every step.

My pulse spiked as I stood frozen, waiting. He stopped before me and even with the step beneath my feet, Luke towered over me. It put his chest exactly in front of my gaze.

There was a chance—a big one if I was being honest with myself—that our time together would end soon, and if that was the case, I wanted every one of his minutes. I wanted his body. His attention.

His heart.

My lashes lifted to meet his heated stare.

Luke jerked his chin, a silent command for me to lead the way.

I moved in slow steps, savoring the feel of his heat at my back and his appreciative gaze. He didn't touch, but the whisper of his breath skittered across my neck as he crowded close.

At the top of our erotic stair climb, before I could saunter to his bedroom, Luke swept me into his arms, spinning me and slamming his mouth onto mine.

I gasped, my arms winding around his neck as I opened my mouth and let his tongue slip inside. He did the flutter that drove me wild and stole my breath, so I wrapped my legs around his waist, pressing my center to his growing arousal.

Luke repeated the tongue flutter, then nipped at my bottom lip as he walked us to the bathroom. His hand snaked under the hem of my denim shorts, sliding right to my center. He dipped inside quickly, then brought his wet finger to my rear entrance, circling it slowly.

His tongue fluttered against mine and I jerked, my eyes popping open. Once more, his were waiting with a hint of mischief behind the lust.

I tore my lips away, already panting for breath. "What was that?"

The corner of his mouth lifted. "Like it?"

"Yes," I admitted. It felt forbidden. Naughty. I wasn't ready for that but maybe someday.

"Good." Luke stopped so abruptly that I nearly fell, but his grip on me was firm. He set me on my feet, then stripped me of my shorts and tank top.

I went to open the walk-in shower's door and turn on the spray but his hand caught my wrist before I could even touch the handle. "We need showers."

Luke dropped his mouth to my neck and traced the line of my neck to my ear with his soft lips. "What if I wanted you right here on the counter?"

"I won't complain," I whispered. We both knew he was in control here.

When it came to bedroom play, I didn't need to be in charge. In other aspects of my life, that control was becoming more and more important, but here in Luke's arms, I relinquished it completely.

Because I trusted Luke to never abuse the power I'd handed over.

Luke grinned and opened the shower door, turning on the water. Steam quickly enveloped the space, clouding the walls lined with square, stone tiles. Their color was so much like the cliffs from the Smith River that I suspected Luke had picked them out for that reason.

"Naked," he ordered, reaching behind his neck, fisting a handful of the T-shirt he'd worn today and yanking it over his head.

The combination of Luke's broad shoulders, his taut abs and that delicious V at his hips was intoxicating.

"You're not moving," he warned.

"I'm appreciating the view." I smirked, then obeyed. The bikini I'd worn underneath my clothes fell away with quick tugs at its strings.

Luke's gaze zeroed in on my pebbled nipples.

I cupped my breasts in my hands, pinching the hard buds between my fingers. That earned me a growl.

The steam from the water escaped the open door as Luke stepped out of his jeans, his cock bobbing free. He'd barely kicked his pants free when I was swept into his arms again, his length hard and thick against my belly as he swept us into the shower.

"Hmm." I closed my eyes, leaning into the warm water as it cascaded down my face.

Luke's hands roamed my ribs and my breasts until he took my face in his hands. "Tip back."

With the top of my hair wet, he untied the elastic at the end of my braid. With gentle efficiency, he worked the strands free before letting me go to squeeze shampoo into his palm and massage it into my hair.

"Wow," I moaned as he worked up a lather. "I should make you do this every day."

"Feel good?"

After a week of marginal showers and sunshine, Luke's hands in my hair were a miracle. I hummed my agreement as he rinsed the shampoo free.

He stretched for the soap next, lathering a shower puff. Then he traced my body, dragging it in a torturous trail across my heated skin. He worked down and up, my arms and my legs. The suds collected on my small breasts, sliding with the water down over my nipples and into the drain.

When the puff came to the apex of my thighs, I let my neck loll to the side, enjoying the feel of Luke washing me clean.

It was erotic. Trusting and intimate. I stood bare, vulnerable and exposed, letting him clean my most sensitive place. It was maybe the most tender gesture we'd shared.

The puff made a splat as Luke dropped it on the floor. Then he cupped me, his palm pressing into my clit as his deft fingers slicked through my folds and inside my body.

My knees shook and I fell forward, leaning against his body for balance.

His other hand stretched down the line of my spine, his arm holding me against his side as he reached my ass and squeezed, all while his fingers toyed with me. Played me.

"Baby," I gasped as my orgasm came on fast and hard, shaking against him as I shattered into a thousand pieces. When the white spots in my vision cleared, I opened my eyes to find Luke staring at me.

"Damn, you are beautiful."

I smiled, falling into him as he slid his hands free and reached for the bottle of my conditioner. Its citrus scent filled the shower as he kneaded it into my hair.

"My turn." Bending, I picked up the puff and moved past Luke to let him under the spray.

He tipped his face to the stream, his eyes closed as I started with his shoulders, washing him from neck to arms to the dimples above his ass. The muscles in his back strained with every one of my strokes. His hands were in fists and his cock so rigid it made my mouth water.

I made it to his ass and let the puff drop over the perfect globes. Then I took one of his wrists, pulling him to turn. With his broad shoulders blocking the spray, I dropped to my knees.

The soap forgotten, I took his shaft in my hand, stroking the velvety flesh as I dragged my tongue across the tip.

"Scarlett," he groaned, his hand coming to my cheek.

Then I took him in, all the way to my throat, sucking and licking and stroking and savoring, until his legs trembled.

"I'm gonna come," he warned.

I kept at him, hungry for his pleasure, until he groaned my name and gave me his release, fucking my mouth as I swallowed every last salty drop.

When I popped my mouth free, I looked up at him through wet eyelashes. Maybe I was the one on my knees, but the power was mine. This sexy man was at my mercy.

Maybe I hadn't given up complete control after all.

Luke's fingers found their way to my wet hair and he opened his mouth, then closed it without a word. Instead, he helped me to my feet and turned me to the water to rinse out my hair.

"What were you going to say?"

"It's nothing."

"Tell me."

He sighed. "You've ruined me."

"Is that such a bad thing?"

"It's the best thing that's ever happened to me. *You* are the best thing."

"You're the best thing that's ever happened to me too."

There was so much adoration in his blue gaze, so much awe, it stole my breath.

The urge to blurt three little words rushed through my mind, but I shoved it aside. It wasn't time. Not yet.

So instead of telling Luke that I'd fallen in love with him, I memorized every line on his face. Every sparkle in his eyes. Because that look was the look I was going to fight for.

I was fighting for this man. For fishing trips. For sexy showers. For the chance to tell him that I loved his pure and gentle heart.

For us.

Luke framed my face with his hands and dropped a kiss to my lips, the water cascading over us as we clung to one another. We kissed and kissed, holding on to our naked and slippery bodies until the water turned cold.

Then we reluctantly released one another to dry off and make our way to the bedroom. Luke didn't need to ask if I wanted a nap. Though we'd slept plenty on the river, I was exhausted and fell into bed beside him, curling into his body.

"I need to ask you something," I whispered.

"Okay," he whispered back.

"If we do this, if we convince the Warriors that I didn't take their drugs, you'll be letting murderers go free. Don't you want justice?"

"Of course I do."

"Then why?"

"Because it means I get to keep you."

That answer should have made my heart leap out of my chest. If there was ever a moment to tell Luke I loved him, it was this. Except a deep, aching sadness spread through my soul.

He was going to go back on everything he knew. For me. He was going to put the oaths he'd sworn as a cop aside. For me.

Was I asking too much?

"What if they come after you?" I asked.

"Then we'll deal with it."

"They could kill you."

He scoffed. "They could try."

"Don't be cocky." I shot him a frown. "This is dangerous."

"Yeah." He nodded. "It is dangerous. So is being a cop. But I knew what I was signing up for when I earned my badge. I know what I'm getting into here too."

"I don't want to lose you."

Luke tucked a lock of my damp hair behind my ear. "You won't."

Please, let this work.

But if it didn't, if we failed and I lost the battle, I'd let Luke go. I'd turn myself and that video in to the FBI.

It would be heartbreaking to walk away. But Luke deserved to have that dog one day. He deserved to get his wife pregnant on a rainy day and have her at his side beyond these walls.

So I'd walk.

Because if I didn't have dreams of my own to fight for, then I'd fight for his instead.

CHAPTER FIFTEEN

LUKE

"Good afternoon, Agent Brown." I didn't bother looking up from the stack of papers on my desk as she walked into my office. The staccato click of her heels always preceded her entrance.

"Chief Rosen. How was your vacation?"

"Too short." I stuffed a report into its folder and leaned my elbows on the desk as she took her regular seat across from my desk.

"You went fishing."

"I did."

Maria's expression was as blank and unforgiving as usual, not a tell in sight. This routine was getting old. But she wasn't going to tell me what she wanted, just like I wasn't going to tell her where I was keeping Scarlett.

Stalemate.

I doubted they'd followed me out of town last week. I'd checked often, and once we got to the river, unless the FBI had secured a raft, they wouldn't have been able to follow. Maybe if they'd gone to the trouble of drone surveillance they would have seen me with Scarlett. But I was fairly certain they thought she was stashed in some backwoods cabin or someone's basement. And after Birdy had seen it was just me leaving with the raft, they'd let me go on my way without a tail.

"You go often," Maria said, taking a chair.

"Is that a question? Or a statement?"

Her mouth turned up in a small smirk. "A statement."

She didn't bullshit, I'd give her that. "While stating the obvious is definitely a way to pass the time, I've got a lot stacked up from a week away." I patted the file folders in front of me. "Have a nice day, Agent Brown."

Despite my dismissal, she wouldn't leave. She was going to sit in that chair for hours, scrutinizing my every move. Something I hadn't missed on vacation or over the past two days.

I'd been surprised when she hadn't paid me a visit on Monday or Tuesday. Not that I'd had time to talk with her. My days had been slammed trying to catch up on all that I'd missed. Shift questions. A phone call from the mayor about staffing and payroll. Reports to review, including a DUI and a couple of minor misdemeanors. Plus everyone in the station had wanted to stop by and say hello. My office had been a revolving door of people welcoming me back.

You'd think I'd gone off to war.

Agent Brown crossed her legs and leaned forward. "I think it's time you call me Maria."

I arched an eyebrow. In all the days that she'd stopped by my office, we'd stuck to formalities. "If I call you Maria, does that mean you'll start telling me more about what you want?"

"I want Scarlett Marks."

"Why?"

Maria steepled her hands in front of her chin. What she didn't do was answer my damn question. *Typical.* I didn't have time for this. The FBI's games were growing old.

I flipped open a new folder, picking up the report and starting at the top. Today I needed to leave early.

I had an appointment at the garage in an hour that I wasn't going to miss.

Maria didn't budge as I worked my way through the first page of the report. At the second, I shot her a glance, then cast my eyes to the door.

My message couldn't have been clearer unless I tattooed *Get Out* on my forehead.

She uncrossed and recrossed her legs.

Pain in the ass.

If she wanted to watch me work all day, so be it. I finished reviewing the report, jotted down a question for the officer on a sticky note, then stuffed both back in their folder, moving on to the next in line.

When my desk phone rang, I picked it up off the cradle. "Chief Rosen."

"Why are you coming in for an oil change at three?" Presley asked. When I'd called down to the garage this morning, Presley had been out for an errand, on a run to the bank or something. One of the mechanics had taken my appointment for me. I'd wondered how long it would take for her to realize that I did not need an oil change.

Four hours, apparently.

I chuckled. "Hello."

"Hello," she mimicked with what I suspected was an exaggerated eye roll. It was something I could see both her and Scarlett doing. "We did an oil change on your truck two months ago. It's not due."

"No, it's not due. But I saw a drip in the garage. Might be a leak," I lied. It wasn't like I could explain with Maria staring at me.

Presley went quiet, the silence stretching. "Okay. Dash and Emmett are both here. They can take a look at it for you."

Dash and Emmett hadn't done oil changes or routine tune-ups in years. "That would be great."

Thankfully, Presley was smart enough not to mention Scarlett's name. I wouldn't put it past the FBI to have tapped our phones, mine at least. I would have denied it if Pres had asked, but she'd been around the Gypsies long enough to read between the lines.

She started typing, her fingers clicking rapid-fire in the background. "Can you come in a little later? How about four?"

Presley was probably scrambling to rearrange their jobs so I'd be the only one in the garage's office and we'd have privacy for our conversation.

"Four it is," I said and hung up, then met Maria's gaze.

She looked smug and confident in that chair. Maybe as a younger cop, I would have let that intimidate me. But if the FBI knew where Scarlett was, Maria wouldn't be in my office. I still had the upper hand and wasn't going to waver.

So I turned my attention back to my work, opening another case file. I read the report and hid the nerves rattling my insides behind an impassive face.

Scarlett had made the decision to try this route first. It was her decision. It was her life.

It was something I could give to her, but it meant setting aside my oaths. My pride. My conscience.

Maybe that made me just as much of a criminal as the men I was going to meet later.

Dash, Emmett and Leo—the Tin Gypsies weren't innocent. They'd committed their fair share of offenses in their day. Hell, Emmett was about as good a hacker as he was a mechanic and metal fabricator. I was sure he'd broken countless privacy laws in just the time I'd known him.

Was I any better?

Was I just as bad as the man who'd sat in the chair before me?

Marcus Wagner had been a mentor. A good cop, at least I'd thought so for a long time. But then he'd crossed a line.

Was I guilty of the same?

Yes. The knot in my stomach tightened and I had to start at the beginning of the report, forcing myself to concentrate.

This wasn't right. What I was doing wasn't right. But it was *right.* Because it was Scarlett's best chance at a life. With me.

And maybe there was another way to get Tucker Talbot and the Warriors. Maybe I'd find a way to pin Ken Raymond's murder on them without Scarlett's video. How, I wasn't sure. The initial evidence hadn't shown any signs of foul play but we'd look again. And again. And again. There had to be something in Ken's past that tied him to the Warriors. We'd dig and dig deep.

The decision to reopen Ken's case eased some of the guilt and I finished one report, diving into the next one. With an added hour before I had to leave for the garage, I might actually finish these up so I could return them to the assigned officers for any corrections. I flipped open a third file, still ignoring Maria.

She sat as stoically as ever, her posture impeccable.

I worked through the entire stack as the clock turned closer and closer to four, all while Maria didn't budge. Was she even breathing?

Finally, with ten minutes to get to the garage, more than enough time in Clifton Forge, I loaded up the files, shut down my computer and collected my wallet and keys from my desk drawer.

"Pleasure spending time with you, Agent Brown," I lied and stood. "Any plans for your evening?"

She looked up at me, still seated, and the hardness in her expression turned to stone. There was ice there. Frustration. I wasn't cooperating and it was pissing her off. "No."

"If you haven't been to Stockyard's for a cheeseburger, I recommend it."

Maria stayed in her chair. "Is that where you're off to?"

"No, I've got an appointment."

"For what?"

"To get my oil changed."

Her eyes narrowed. Yeah, she knew exactly where I was going. I'd let her speculate why. If she followed me, all she'd see was me sitting in the office at the garage, bullshitting with some friends.

I waved a hand to the door. "I'll escort you out."

For a moment, I thought she'd have the gall to stick in her seat. But then she swept out of the chair and walked past me for the door. But before she disappeared, she stopped at the threshold. Her shoulders, normally ramrod straight, slumped, just slightly. It was the first sign of defeat I'd seen from her in months.

She glanced over her shoulder but didn't turn. "I have reason to believe Ms. Marks can provide me information on a crime."

"What kind of crime?"

"That's classified."

Was it about the stolen drugs? Or Ken Raymond's death? I suspected it was Ken. But why was Ken Raymond's murder a classified case? Was he an informant? A witness? My curiosity was piqued, and we would definitely be digging deeper. Maria could keep her classified information. I'd find answers another way.

"If you get the burger, add bacon," I said. "It's worth the extra dollar."

Maria crossed her arms over her chest. "You're impeding a federal investigation, Luke."

I guess she was ready to move on to first names. "Do me a favor. When you talk to your Agent Birdy, tell her to mow the lawn. The weeds are taking over and if they creep into my yard, I'm afraid I'll have to report her to the homeowner's association."

Her face broke into a scowl before she turned and marched out of the station.

I waited until she was through the exit before closing the door to my office and depositing the file folders on various desks in the bullpen. Then I headed out, waving goodbye to the officer stationed up front.

When I pulled onto the road, I wasn't surprised to see a black SUV follow me through town to the Clifton Forge Garage. But when I pulled into the garage's lot, they kept on driving, disappearing as I eased into one of the large, empty shop bays.

"Hey, Luke." Emmett raised a grease-smeared hand as I hopped out. "Dash and Leo are inside already. I'll be right there."

"Thanks." I nodded and made my way to the office door.

The garage was spotless, one of the cleanest I'd ever seen. Everything had its place. There weren't many stains on the concrete floor and the surfaces were free of clutter. Toolboxes and work benches and chests hugged the walls. The smell of oil and concrete and metal tinged the air.

The aisle to the office was free of clutter. This place had flow. Scarlett would approve.

As I opened the office door, Emmett hit a button to bring the bay door down before going to the sink and pumping a squirt of orange soap into his palm and lathering up.

Inside, Presley was behind her desk, waiting.

"Hey," I said. "Long time no see. I've missed you at the station."

She smiled. "Liar."

Her hair was the same short, bright blond. It swept artfully over her forehead. She was wearing a fitted black tank top today, the matching straps of her bra peeking out at her shoulders. Her baggy cargo pants sat low on her hips as she stood and walked to the office's door, flipping the lock and sign to closed.

Presley's style was her own, different from Scarlett's. Though she didn't have a big wardrobe, Scarlett seemed to prefer items that fit her trim body and hugged her slight curves. It was all casual, jeans and tees, but with a feminine edge. Presley seemed to favor dark colors, whereas Scarlett was happy with light. My favorite swimsuit she'd ordered had been the palest of blues, nearly white. It had brought out the color of her sparkling eyes.

With the door locked, Presley returned to her chair. The blinds on the window overlooking the parking lot were drawn.

Dash came out of his office, hand extended. "Luke."

"Hey, Dash." I shook his hand, then Leo's as he followed behind.

Both men were about my height, tall and fit. Dash looked more and more like Draven every time I saw him. There were a few gray hairs at his temple. Draven had always worn a beard and if Dash let the scruff on his jaw grow a bit, he'd look like a younger version of his father. Before Draven's death.

My heart hammered as we all took a seat. When was the last time I'd been nervous? Not even arresting Marcus had twisted me up. If Dash freaked out about the video, if he decided to take revenge on the Warriors for Draven's death, Scarlett would be the one to suffer. Which meant I had to tread carefully. It was a shame that Bryce wasn't here. If anyone could calm a raging Dash, it was his wife.

"Been fishing lately?" Leo asked, relaxing in a chair against the wall.

His dirty-blond hair was longer than I'd seen it in a while, almost enough to pull back like the way Emmett wore his. I wasn't sure how any of them could handle having their hair touch their ears. As soon as mine got long enough to touch the shell, I went to the barber in town and had it trimmed.

"Floated the Smith last week," I said.

"How was it?"

"Good. Best trip I've had in ages." Not because of the fishing, but the company.

"One of these days, I'm going to tag along with you and Emmett."

"You're welcome anytime."

Emmett and I often went fishing together in the summers, but it wasn't exactly Leo's thing. He was more of a

217

party guy. Most nights, he was at The Betsy searching for a good time.

Leo's face was covered in scruff and the backs of his hands were flecked with blue paint. He loved beer and women, but the man was an artist. Give him an air gun and a paint booth and he'd work magic on a classic car or custom bike.

Beside him, Dash leaned his forearms on his knees. I sat across from Presley at the desk, giving her a small smile. She was faking one of her own, but her hands fiddled with a pen on the desk. I was as anxious as she was to get this over with.

Emmett's bootsteps preceded him as he came into the office, closing the door behind him. His coveralls were streaked with grease at the knees, but he'd unzipped the top half to uncover the white T-shirt beneath.

He sat beside Dash and Leo, the three of them sporting an array of colorful tattoos.

"Where's Isaiah?" I asked. Isaiah hadn't been a Tin Gypsy, but since he was married to Genevieve and connected to Dash by family, I'd expected him here.

"Sent him home," Dash said. "I gave him the option to listen in, but he wants out of this one. With Genevieve and the baby, they don't need trouble."

"Understood." They might be my neighbors, but I wouldn't be bringing this to their doorstep. I circled my finger in the air. "We good?"

Emmett nodded. "Sweep it every morning. No one is listening."

"Good." With all the players here, I took a long breath, then jumped right in. "I'm here because of Scarlett."

"Is she okay?" Presley asked before anyone could get a word in otherwise.

"She's good," I promised. "She misses you, but she's good."

Presley blew out a deep breath. "Where is she?"

I hesitated, not wanting to answer. I'd kept her location to myself for months now and though I trusted Presley and the guys here, Scarlett's safety was everything to me. Except we were at the point where secrets were going to have to come out.

I sighed. "My place. She's been with me."

"Since the grocery store?" Presley's eyes widened.

"Yeah. It was the safest option and the only place where I could get her to promise to stay put."

Emmett smirked but stayed quiet. He'd known, no surprise, but he'd kept it to himself. Though Dash didn't look all that surprised either.

Presley opened her mouth to say something else, but Dash held up a hand. "What's going on with the FBI?"

"Nothing new." I'd told Dash that the FBI was looking for Scarlett, though I hadn't shared other details because there weren't many to share. I wasn't sure what Dash had told the others, and for today's discussion, I wanted us all on the same page. "They want Scarlett. The lead agent has been a regular visitor at the station. They've got an under-cover agent living next door to me and I'm sure others around town. They're tailing me too."

"Who's the lead?" Emmett asked.

"Agent Maria Brown."

He rubbed a hand over his bearded jaw. "Doesn't ring a bell."

"Me neither," Leo muttered.

Dash shook his head. "New to me too."

"You know FBI agents?" Presley asked her boss.

Dash only shrugged. "The club had some run-ins with the FBI years ago but they weren't in Clifton Forge for long."

"No evidence," Leo explained.

"And compared to the California clubs, we were tame," Emmett added before turning to me. "How long have they been watching your house?"

"My guess? Months. Probably since the day they rolled into town."

"They're watching the garage too," Dash said, raking a hand through his dark hair. "Bryce hasn't seen anyone around the newspaper office, but I'm sure they've put her on the patrol route."

"I've seen them drive by my place now and again," Leo said.

Emmett nodded. "Same here."

Both of them lived in town. "Dash? Anything at your house?"

He shook his head. "No, but we're out of town far enough that there's nowhere for them to hide."

"Why would you keep Scarlett at your house if it was being watched?" Presley asked.

"Where else would you have me put her? It's not like I have a safe house at my disposal. I don't have a big enough staff to assign one person to watch her and it was the one place where she promised to stay and not run. Better me than the feds."

"Yeah," she muttered.

"It's the right call," Dash said. "So why now? You've kept her locked away for months without bringing us into the mix. What's changed?"

"This can't last forever. Scarlett wants her life back. I want to help her."

Emmett studied my face, then the corner of his mouth twitched.

Of all the guys here, I'd known Emmett the longest. We had the most in common—a shared love of the outdoors and general appreciation for a simple life.

When the crew here had suspected Marcus of killing Genevieve's mother, he'd called me. He'd asked me for help. We trusted one another. We had mutual respect. I considered him a friend.

He knew there was more to my helping Scarlett than the police chief helping a citizen in trouble, but he kept it to himself. They'd all learn soon enough that Scarlett was the someone special in my life.

Tomorrow night, hopefully.

"Scarlett's only chance at being free is to convince the Warriors she didn't steal their money."

"They won't just take her word for it," Leo said.

"No, I don't expect they will. But she has leverage."

"What leverage?" Dash asked, sitting straighter.

I blew out a deep breath. "I need to tell you something. About your father."

His face turned to ice and the room went still.

"Remember the guy who was found on the river a couple months ago? Scarlett has a video of him being murdered by the Warriors. A murder staged as an accident. Or suicide." The tension in the room spiked, but I kept my eyes on Dash. "On the video, Tucker Talbot admits to doing the same to your father."

Dash's jaw clenched and his nostrils flared, but he didn't seem shocked. He didn't seem enraged. He was angry, no doubt. But this was an anger that had dulled over the years.

This was a permanent fury, one that settled under the surface of his skin, always there but in control.

"You knew," I said.

"I can assume you're here on personal business," he said, pointing to the badge on my hip. "That if you haven't turned Scarlett over to the cops, you're acting as Luke Rosen. Not the chief of police."

"I'm both."

He shook his head. "Can't work that way."

Dash was right. It couldn't work that way. Something I'd been denying since Scarlett had played me that video.

Something I was still denying.

"Just tell him, Dash," Presley said. "If it can help Scarlett, then we need to trust Luke."

My face whipped to hers. So they all knew about Draven?

"Dad made an arrangement with Tucker," Dash said. "His life for mine and Genevieve's."

"What? Why?" Before Dash could answer, I stopped him. "Wait. I don't think I want to know. I'm guessing it has something to do with Marcus."

Emmett nodded. "You want the full story one day, we'll tell you. But the deeper you get, the dirtier it is."

"Okay," I said. "If it becomes relevant, clue me in. Until then, let's figure out a way to get Scarlett out of trouble."

There was a limit to how much I could overlook. That limit was higher where Scarlett was concerned. And I'd learned enough about the former Tin Gypsies to know that some skeletons were better left as bones.

"I'd like to see the video," Dash said.

"Scarlett has it. She'll tell you all about what happened at the Warriors."

"When?" Leo asked.

"What are you doing tomorrow night?"

"Sounds like we're coming to your place," Emmett said. "We'll need an excuse. We can't just show up. It'll be too suspicious."

"Got any old cars out back you could sell me? Cheap?"

Dash nodded. "We'll think of something."

"I'm coming," Presley said, crossing her arms.

"Not this time, Pres," Dash said.

"That's my sister. I'm going." The expression on her face dared us to argue.

We were smart men. We shut up.

"Garage only," Dash warned. "Shaw has to sit this one out. It'll be too suspicious."

"He'll love that," she muttered. "You know how he feels about being left out."

Her husband wasn't one to be excluded. The night Jeremiah had held Presley and Scarlett hostage, Shaw had been there. He'd bought the place next door to stay at while his production company shot a movie in town. That's when he and Presley had hooked up.

So he'd known that when a bunch of cop cars had shown up on her lawn, there'd been trouble. Shaw had once been a cop himself.

I'd told him to stand down, to let me and my team handle it. But Shaw had disobeyed my orders and gone in to rescue Presley himself. Stubborn asshole. Dash had gone in too and for the stunt, I'd arrested them both.

They'd paid a fine and I held no hard feelings. I understood why he'd gone into that house. If Scarlett had been my woman that night, I would have killed Jeremiah myself for touching her.

But I agreed with Dash. If Shaw showed up at my place, it would look suspicious. We weren't exactly known for hanging out anywhere but at The Betsy for an occasional beer. Something we hadn't done since he and Presley had eloped.

Since Scarlett had come into my life.

"Fine, no Shaw," Presley said. "I'll deal with him."

"Good." I stood, glancing at my watch. I'd stayed long enough to have my hypothetical oil change. "See you tomorrow. Five?"

"Should we bring anything other than a reason to be there?" Emmett asked.

"Whiskey."

We were going to need it.

CHAPTER SIXTEEN

SCARLETT

"They're here." Luke stalked out of the dining room, where he'd been staring out the front windows ever since Emmett had texted that they were on their way.

They're here. My heart jumped into my throat.

She was here.

Luke came into the kitchen and walked right for the garage door. "I'll go outside and help them with the trailer. Then we'll come inside. Hang tight."

"Okay." I nodded as he disappeared.

The second the door closed behind him, I sprinted upstairs for the office, taking my place by the window. I carefully peeled the shade away from the window, giving myself no more than half an inch to peer through.

A large black truck eased along the sidewalk and came to a stop. Behind it, on a long trailer, was an old rusted car that had seen better decades. My breath caught in my throat as the driver's door opened.

Dash Slater stepped out, every bit as tall and built as I remembered from that awful night months ago.

Luke strode out of the garage, his gait slow and easy. From the outside, he looked so calm and collected. You wouldn't know that he'd been restless since his meeting at the garage yesterday. Last night, he'd barely slept.

As had I.

I struggled to fill my lungs as the other doors opened.

Two men stepped out. One had dark hair tied in a knot at the nape. He was wearing a white tank top, his arms covered in tattoos. And there was a lot of arm to cover. I'd thought Luke was strong and muscular, but this man was like a mountain, sturdy and tall.

The other man was leaner, though still as tall as both Dash and Luke. He shoved the sunglasses off his eyes and into his messy blond hair, then shot a devilish grin over his shoulder at the truck.

Her boots came out first, one pressing into the blond guy's ass before giving it a good shove to move him out of the way.

Then she hopped out, Presley's hair reflecting the sun. She gave Luke a beaming smile as he put an arm around her shoulders for a hug.

I gasped, my hand flying to my mouth.

I hadn't seen Presley since that night. Since Jeremiah had pulled the trigger. Luke had promised that she was okay. But not seeing her with my own eyes, it was hard to go on faith. It was hard not to picture her in that house, stuck in an endless nightmare.

Tears blurred my vision.

She looked happy. She looked healthy. Her smile was partly for show. Her eyes swept the house, searching. But even if her smile was fake, I didn't care. My sister was here.

There were times when I'd dreaded this apology. Probably because apologies had been associated with pain for the majority of my life. The words *I'm sorry* brought back memories of my mother leading me into my father's den, then leaving me to apologize for whatever thing I'd done that apparently deserved his wrath.

I'd swallowed my pride so many times it was a wonder I hadn't choked.

But today, there was no dread. I wanted to apologize so badly, to make things right with Presley, that I felt like screaming it through the window.

Luke exchanged handshakes with the guys before the group clustered around the trailer.

Yesterday, they'd decided to bring a car over to Luke's place as cover for this visit. The rusted junker would sit in the driveway and Luke would give the neighborhood a good show of tinkering on it occasionally.

If Emmett or Dash or Leo came over to talk about the Warriors, it would be under the guise of restoring an old car.

Maybe if Luke had hosted more barbecues with his friends, we could have just passed this off as a regular summer gathering, but the man worked too much to play host. If he did meet with his friends, it was at The Betsy, a place I wasn't allowed to go.

Yet.

Work. Please, let this work. Anticipation and hope raced through my veins. Being on the river had given me a taste of freedom and now I was starved for it.

We had two big hurdles to leap first. The Warriors. And the FBI. But Luke's meeting at the garage had started the race. And maybe, just maybe, I'd get my life back. No more hiding. No more fear.

Dash hopped up on the trailer and motioned for Luke to

join him. The two of them walked to the hood and Dash popped it open, bending to point out certain things with the engine.

Luke nodded along, playing the part of an interested hobby mechanic. Then he nodded, held out his hand and shook with Dash before motioning toward the house. I read the word *beer* from his lips.

The men and Presley all followed him into the garage, strolling. Every step felt like twelve as I waited and waited for them to disappear from my view.

I set the shade to rights, careful not to move it more than necessary, then pushed out of my crouch and hurried down the hallway for the stairs. The door between the laundry room and the garage opened as I reached the balcony, and I froze at the railing.

Presley stepped inside first. She hurried to the kitchen, looking around the empty living room. When her gaze lifted to the stairs, finding me, she sucked in a short breath.

Then we were both running.

I flew down the stairs, my hand gliding over the banister as my feet nearly tripped over themselves.

She bolted through the living room, passing the couch just as I leapt off the last two stairs and collided with my sister.

We'd always hugged tight, but this one was like a vise. Between us, we could have pressed a lump of coal into a diamond.

"I'm sorry," I blurted at the same time she asked, "Are you okay?"

I nodded, hugging her tighter. "I'm sorry."

"For what?" she whispered.

"Everything. For not leaving Chicago when you begged me to. For ruining your wedding. For Jeremiah. All of it. It's my fault and I'm sorry."

Presley let me go and leaned back, giving me a smile. "Have you been beating yourself up about this for months?"

I opened my mouth to answer, but Luke spoke from across the house. "Yes."

I shot a glance over Presley's shoulder at the audience of handsome men watching. My cheeks flushed but I ignored them, focusing on my sister. "I'm sorry."

"You're forgiven." She waved it off like it was nothing and with the gesture, I caught a shiny glimmer on her left hand.

She wasn't Presley Marks anymore. She was Presley Valance.

And I was supposed to act surprised.

"What's that?" I pointed to the stunning ring on her finger and the wedding band resting beneath it.

"Shaw and I got married."

I feigned a gasp. "Shaw Valance?"

"I didn't want to plan a wedding. Not again. Not without you there. So we flew to Vegas and got married. Just the two of us."

I'd missed it, being here. I'd missed a milestone in my sister's life. But she was so happy, I didn't care. "Congratulations."

I pulled her into my arms once more, our embrace fierce. Maybe if I didn't let go, maybe if I held on long enough, some of her strength and resiliency would soak into my bones too.

"I missed your hugs," she whispered.

"And I missed yours."

My mother used to tell us that we were born hugging, that we'd come out of the womb together. We both knew she'd been teasing, but part of me had always wanted to believe it was true.

My earliest memory was of hugging Presley. We'd been huddled in the kitchen, on the floor beside the fridge, clutching one another. Dad had just come home from work and he'd had a bad day.

That was the first day I could remember hearing the smack of his palm meeting my mother's cheek. I was sure I'd seen it before as a baby, but that day, something about the sound had made it stand out. It was like the crack before a boom of thunder.

Presley and I had held each other through the whole thing, and I remembered knowing that if I had her, we'd survive it together.

I'd believed it then.

I believed it now.

We'd survive it together.

"Pres, you want a beer?" Luke asked, opening the fridge.

"No, thanks." She let me go and stepped deeper into the living room, plopping down on one of his couches and looking around. "You rearranged things. It's so much better."

I covered a smile with my hand. Luke caught my eye, giving me a slight headshake as he took beer bottles from the fridge and handed them out to the guys.

"Have a seat," he said, gesturing to the living room. "I need to grab something."

He brushed past me, bending enough to drop a kiss to my hair, then jogged up the stairs.

I walked into the living room and took the seat beside Presley, inching close so Luke would have plenty of room.

"Uh . . . you're together?" she asked.

"Yeah."

A slow smile spread across her face. "He's one of the good ones."

"I know."

She took my hand, holding it as the guys came into the room.

Dash sat first, lifting a hand as he sank into a chair. "Hi. I'm Dash."

"I remember." I nodded, meeting his gaze with a silent thank-you.

He tipped his beer bottle my way before putting it to his lips.

"Emmett." The large man with the dark hair came over, hand extended. "Nice to meet you."

"You too." I returned his shake with my free hand, which was childlike in his grip.

Emmett sat in the chair beside Dash as the blond man came into the space, giving me a wave as he perched on the stone ledge in front of the fireplace.

"Hey, I'm Leo." He shot me the same grin he'd given Presley outside by the truck. It was sexy and a little bit mischievous. This guy was the playboy.

Wait a minute.

Recognition dawned. The night I'd come to Clifton Forge, the night I'd gone to The Betsy instead of finding Presley, he'd been the man who'd kept pointing at me in his drunken haze. He'd been the guy who'd kept saying her name to my face until I'd finally gotten the hell out of there.

Luke jogged down the staircase with a manila envelope in his grip. He sat beside me, putting the folder and his beer on the end table. Then he put his hand on my knee.

That was my cue.

I sat straighter, holding on to Presley's hand. "Where should I start?"

"The beginning," Dash said.

"Okay." And I did just that.

I told them all about how I'd left Chicago and come to Montana. How I'd reconciled with Jeremiah before Presley's wedding. How I'd come to Clifton Forge once, only to return after Jeremiah had begged me for another chance. Then I told them how his behavior had changed. How he'd become edgy and nervous. How'd he spent less and less time at the clubhouse.

Presley held my hand through every detail.

Luke's palm never strayed from my knee.

Then I reached the end of my story and I shifted, taking the phone from the back pocket of my jeans. I opened it, pulled up the video, and handed it to Emmett as he stretched a hand across the coffee table.

The guys watched it twice. When Draven's name was mentioned, Presley flinched and her eyes flooded, but she blinked them away.

"I'm sorry," I whispered.

"You didn't kill him."

One day, I hoped I'd hear the story of Draven Slater. I hoped to hear how Presley had found him and who he'd been to her. For now, I was content knowing that she'd found a family here. She'd found people who would protect her.

When the video was over, Dash handed me my phone. "How many copies of that are there?"

"Two." I glanced at Luke, earning a small nod. "It's on this phone and we put it on a cloud storage site."

Luke had written the username and password in a letter. That letter, along with Agent Maria Brown's card, were currently in his gun safe. He'd assured me that his dad would know the code, and if something happened to Luke, his dad would know what to do.

Leo, who'd gotten up from his seat to watch over Emmett's shoulder, began pacing in front of the mantel. "Who's the guy in the chair?"

"Ken Raymond. The guy who washed up on the river this spring." Luke picked up the file folder he'd brought home from work this afternoon. He placed it on the coffee table and flipped it open, greeting me with a gruesome photo of a blue, bloated body.

I cringed, both Presley and I looking away.

"Anyone recognize him?" Luke asked.

Emmett and Leo both shook their heads.

Dash narrowed his gaze, studying the picture before moving his scrutiny to my face. There was a glower to his features. A stern and threatening scowl that dared anyone to challenge him.

Yeah, I could see him leading a motorcycle gang. He had the same air of confidence that Tucker Talbot had always oozed. If not for Luke's and Presley's trust in him, I wouldn't have told Dash a damn thing.

"Do you recognize him from your time with the Warriors?" he asked.

"No. I'd never seen him before this."

"Did you ever hear the name before?" Emmett asked.

I shook my head. "No, at least, I don't think so. Most everyone went by a nickname."

"Who was he?" Leo asked Luke.

"According to his records, an upstanding citizen. Married. No kids. Worked as the manager for an indoor shooting range in Ashton. No arrests. No record."

"Upstanding citizens don't get mixed up with the Warriors," Dash muttered. "It's too clean."

"Agreed. I did some digging this morning. I'll do more tomorrow, but on the surface, everything looks normal. Exactly how I was supposed to see it. But according to my database, Ken Raymond has no next of kin. And his wife has left Ashton. After living there for ten years, she left ten days after he died. No forwarding address. She's just gone."

"Well, her husband just died," Presley said. "Can't blame her."

"Unless she's running. Or dead," Dash said. "Maybe they got tied up with the Warriors because of his job. He could have been selling them guns on the sly. They took him out. Took her out too."

"Definitely possible." Luke nodded.

Dash turned to Emmett. "Let's dig. See if we can find out who Ken Raymond really is."

Emmett nodded, then turned to Luke. "How far did you get?"

"Not far. I don't have a warrant."

Emmett grinned. "I don't need one."

Presley leaned closer. "Emmett does some hacking in his spare time."

"Ah." I nodded. "But how does this help me? The Warriors don't know that I videoed them. I don't like that this Ken guy had to die, but why is it important that we figure out how?"

"Information," Luke said. "Right now, we're coming to the table with more questions than answers. We need leverage and the more we know, the better we're positioned. Because even if we convince the Warriors you had nothing to do with Jeremiah's theft, the FBI is going to want you. I don't like walking into meetings with federal officials being the dumbest guy in the room."

"Exactly." Dash nodded. "If we can figure out the connection between Raymond and the Warriors, it might give us a clue about what the FBI is after."

"I've been thinking about this all night," Emmett said, his fingers tented by his chin. "Why would the FBI want Scarlett?"

"Because they think I stole the drugs?" I shrugged. "Maybe they want to arrest me?"

"No." Dash shook his head. "I'm on the same track as Emmett. They don't want to arrest you. Jeremiah said he stole how much?"

"A hundred thousand dollars," Presley answered.

"That's nothing to the DEA," Dash said. "They're working to bring down cartels and gangs, not one small-time drug deal by a woman from the suburbs. They're here because of this murder."

"Here's what I'm thinking." Luke squeezed my knee, then leaned forward. "The feds are going after the Warriors but they don't have enough evidence to take them down. They've probably been monitoring the Warriors for years. They see Scarlett go in and come out a year later. Days after she leaves Ashton, Jeremiah holds her hostage, then commits suicide. You're a woman I'd want to talk to."

"If she goes to the FBI, no matter what happens, the Warriors will think she's a nark." Leo tossed up his hands. "She's dead."

I flinched and Luke's entire body went rigid.

"Leo," Presley hissed. "The only person who's going to die is you because I'm going to strangle you if you can't keep a better hold on your tongue. This is my sister."

"They already think she stole their money. If they think she's turned informant, they'll put her in the ground, Pres. Just saying it like it is."

"Watch it, Leo." Luke's molars were grinding together. "Say it like it is but respect the fact that Scarlett is sitting right here."

Leo held up his hands, then muttered, "Sorry."

"How do we change their minds?" I asked, keeping the conversation on track. The important thing here was convincing the Warriors I was innocent. "I have no proof that I didn't take the drugs. It's my word against Jeremiah's."

"He hid it well, whatever he did with the money," Emmett said. "After . . ." *After he died.* "I looked into his records to see if I could find an influx of cash. Bank accounts. Credit cards. All normal. There's no sign of the money."

"There wouldn't be," I muttered. "He lost it all gambling."

Jeremiah had been so sure he'd strike it rich. He'd wanted to prove himself to the world. To his parents, who hadn't bothered to give him any attention as a kid and had granted him even less as an adult.

The money was gone. With it, the proof of my innocence.

"We'll figure something out," Leo said, giving me a small smile to make up for his bluntness earlier.

It was an odd feeling, to be helped by strangers.

No one had ever come to my rescue until I'd come to Clifton Forge. Not even Jeremiah. He'd taken orders from

236

Presley and gotten us a car, but when push came to shove, he hadn't rescued me.

And I was woman enough to know that I needed a rescue. I simply hoped like hell these men knew what they were doing.

"Thank you," I breathed.

Dash nodded and stood. "Let's head out. Get the car unloaded. We'll be in touch."

Everyone made their way through the living room and kitchen.

Presley hadn't let go of my hand, not since we'd started talking, and her grip was as strong as ever. She tugged my arm, holding back from the others.

"Say the word and we'll get you out of here," she said, her voice low. "Shaw and I have been talking and if you want a new life, we can make it happen. Europe. Australia. Wherever you want to go, we'll figure it out."

"No. Not unless I have to. I don't want to give you up." And I didn't want to give up Luke.

"Good," she breathed. "I was hoping you'd say that."

If I was going to give up my life, then damn it, I was going to take some of the Warriors down with me. I'd go to the FBI. It was doubtful they'd set me up with a new identity as cushy as one Shaw Valance could afford, but at least there'd be some justice for those bastards in Ashton.

"Be careful." I pulled her in for another tight hug.

"You too. I can't believe you've been here this whole time."

They had been the best months of my life. And if it all came crashing down today, I'd be grateful for every second. "Can I make a confession?"

"Uh . . . sure." She let me go, her forehead furrowed.

"I thought I was brave enough. Like you."

"I'm not brave, Scar."

"No, you are. And I'm not. It's true. I'm okay admitting it too. When I finally left home, it was my chance to stand on my own and I blew it. You took yours ten years ago and flourished. I wasted mine on Jeremiah because I wasn't brave enough to forge my own life. And I've felt guilt for that for a long time. I was jealous of you. I was disappointed in myself. I'm not fearless or independent. I'm scared of the future. I was as a kid. I am now."

"Why are you telling me this?" she whispered.

"Because I want you to know how sorry I am that my lack of courage hurt you. I didn't want that. Will you forgive me?"

Presley's eyes flooded. "There's nothing to forgive. You don't have to explain."

"Yes, I do."

Luke appeared at my side, his arm snaking around my shoulders.

I hadn't realized he'd been listening. When I glanced past him, they were all listening. I blushed, embarrassment creeping in, but then I looked at Dash's face. I looked up at Luke.

And there was respect there.

"Being unafraid isn't what makes you brave, beautiful," Luke said. "Being brave means you look that fear in the face and admit that it scares the shit out of you. But you don't give up anyway."

I gave him a sad smile. "I'm not giving up."

"Me neither." Presley nodded.

"We'll fix this," Emmett said, clapping Luke on the shoulder.

"Damn straight." Dash nodded. "One of these days, that son of a bitch Tucker Talbot is going to get what's coming to him. I want to be there when he does. We'll do some research, then I'll make the call. And we'll do our best to get the bastard out of our lives."

CHAPTER SEVENTEEN

LUKE

"Dash and Emmett are coming over."

Scarlett froze. The dinner plates she'd just lifted from the cabinet hovered inches above the island's countertop. "Already? They were just here yesterday."

I took the plates from her and set them down. "Maybe Emmett found something."

It had only been twenty-four hours, but I wouldn't put it past him.

Scarlett busied herself with plating the chicken and rice dish she'd made.

We sat down in the living room to eat, balancing plates on knees like we normally did, but neither of us did much more than push the food around as the clock she'd bought to hang on a bare wall ticked louder than ever. The knot in my stomach was beginning to feel permanent.

"It's all happening so fast," Scarlett whispered.

"Yeah."

"I'm glad, I guess. I want it over with but I just . . ." She sighed and put her fork down. "I want it over with. But I also just want to go back to the way things were."

Living here. The two of us in a bubble. The time on the river. "We'll get back to that. Just no more hiding."

There was a confidence in my statement that I didn't feel, but I was trying my best not to clue Scarlett in to my own anxieties.

She stood and took her plate to the sink, giving up on dinner. I forced myself to eat half, shoveling more than tasting, then helped her put the kitchen to rights.

I'd just shut the dishwasher when the thunder of two motorcycles filled the air. "Be back."

Scarlett nodded as I kissed her cheek, then wrapped her arms around her middle as I went out to the garage and opened the door.

Dash and Emmett eased into the driveway, their bikes both gleaming black and oozing menace and money. Those motorcycles likely cost more than two of my trucks combined. It had been years since I'd been on a bike and never one as nice as the custom models these guys built at the garage.

Maybe when this was over I'd find something fun to ride around the countryside. Scarlett and I could spend our evenings exploring together. Though I suspected she'd rather take the raft out on the river.

So would I.

Dash kicked down the stand on his bike, swinging a leg over the machine to stand.

Emmett did the same, shoving his sunglasses into his hair. "Hey."

I shook his hand, then Dash's.

"Got something for you." Dash walked over to his bike,

opening one of the saddlebags and taking out a greasy part wrapped in a red rag. "For the car."

"Thanks." I made a good show about unwrapping the part and inspecting it. Then we all walked over to the rusted wreck that we'd parked in my driveway last night.

I knew enough about cars to be dangerous but not enough to restore an old one. But my neighbors and Agent Birdy next door didn't know that. With the hood popped, we all bent over the hood and stared at the engine. My plan was to spend a few hours out here every so often to keep up the charade. But this old heap wasn't ever going to run, at least not if I was in charge of the repairs.

"Find anything?" I asked, keeping my voice low.

Emmett pushed at a loose bolt beside the battery. "Yes and no."

Dash set the part on top of the engine block. "How about a beer?"

"Come on in."

We left the hood open as we strode into the garage and to the house.

Scarlett was waiting in the kitchen, her lower lip worried between her teeth.

"Hey, Scarlett." Dash waved as I went to the fridge.

Emmett surprised me by going over and draping one of his large arms around her shoulders. "I'm going to need you to give me all the dirt on Pres so I have some new ammunition to tease her with at work."

Scarlett smiled and some of the anxiety left her face. "I hate to disappoint you, but I'm on Presley's side."

Emmett frowned down at her and took his arm away. "Shit."

Dash chuckled and took the beer I handed over. "You'll fit right in."

Goddamn, I hoped so. I wanted Scarlett to find a good place here. Because then maybe when this shitstorm was over, she'd choose to stay.

I'd been focused on making it so she would be free to live anywhere, but soon, I was going to focus on something else—convincing her to live in Clifton Forge.

If she wanted to see the world, I'd work my ass off to give her the best vacations we could afford. But I didn't want to lose her to wanderlust or lost dreams. There had to be a way to get a real shot at a relationship. No rules. No locked doors. No shaded windows.

I wanted time to see if this thing between us had staying power.

With Presley here, she had family. And with other good women, like Bryce and Genevieve, Scarlett could have a life with so much friendship and love and laughter.

But first, we had to get her free. Free to choose her life. And hopefully, free to choose one with me.

I handed Emmett a beer and opened the top of my own. "What did you find?"

"Not much." Emmett shook his head.

"Same here," I said.

I'd spent my day with the office door closed—*sorry, Agent Brown*—and my nose in the computer, searching for information on Ken Raymond. There was nothing to find. The guy had been a model citizen. He'd had a speeding ticket three years ago and that was all. His wife was spotless. His parents were deceased. So were hers. The wife had a sister who lived in Florida. Maybe she'd left Ashton to go there, but I doubted it.

"There is nothing suspicious," Emmett said. "And that's the problem. He owned a stock Harley. Boring. His house and car were paid for. Boring. He hasn't left the country in twenty years. Boring. His job was managing the range and gun shop, a straitlaced eight to five. Boring."

"So?" Scarlett asked.

"Boring men don't get mixed up with motorcycle clubs like the Warriors," Dash answered. "Neither do men of Ken's age and financial position. He wasn't rich but he wasn't poor either. If a guy like Ken wanted to get into a club, he'd join a local riding group with a bunch of lawyers and doctors and bankers who buy the same fifty-thousand-dollar bike and grow a beard for Sturgis every August. Those clubs do summer rides and their cookie-cutter Harleys are tarped in a garage each winter."

"That's not the Warriors," she said.

"No, it's not," I muttered. "My gut says he was mixed up with them because of his job at the range. But it's strange there's no pattern leading up to it. Financial troubles or something to show he would need extra cash."

"Maybe they were blackmailing him for something," Dash said. "Drug habit. A woman on the side."

"Maybe. We're definitely missing something. But what?"

Ken's life read like any normal middle-class man's. There was no reason for him to be affiliated with the Warriors. There was no reason for him to be taped to a chair, beaten to a pulp and tossed in the river to drown.

The Warriors were ruthless. They were a gang of men who were good at escaping the law. Every known member and affiliate had rap sheets. But they were good at dodging punishment for major crimes, the ones that meant a lifetime in prison. When the Gypsies had been around, they'd been good at avoiding prosecution too. The Gypsies might have disbanded to become law-abiding citizens, but the Warriors were every bit the cutthroat criminals they'd always been.

And they were growing. With the Gypsies gone, Tucker Talbot had expanded his criminal empire. Maybe he'd gotten greedy and was beginning to rumble with the motorcycle gangs in California.

Was that why the FBI was in Montana?

There was no reason for Ken Raymond to be affiliated with the Warriors unless . . .

"Damn it." I barked a laugh. I should have thought of this months ago. "Either Ken Raymond got busted doing something dirty and the FBI turned him into a rat as part of his plea deal, or . . . Ken Raymond is a shell. Son of a bitch."

"What's a shell?" Scarlett asked.

"Fake identity," I clarified. "Probably created by the FBI for one of their undercover agents."

Scarlett's mouth fell open. "You think he was an undercover agent?"

"Yeah. I do." It explained why the FBI had been lingering in town. Why they'd committed so many resources to this. They were hoping that Scarlett could help them prove one of their agents had been murdered.

"It's the most logical explanation," Emmett said. "Otherwise he'd have a record. A rat would have a record. Something the FBI forgot to wipe. Even a mention in a newspaper archive that he'd gotten into trouble. But there's nothing. He's too clean and it's been bothering me all day. My guess is the FBI planted Ken at the gun shop. He sold the Warriors guns on the sly. Maybe tried to get in with them or maybe not. But he fucked up somewhere along the way and they found out he was a fed."

"He's been in Ashton for years," I said. "At least, that's what his records show. Though my guess is it's all bullshit. I doubt the FBI would station him there for so long for just one club."

Though I'd underestimated the extent they'd stay to find Scarlett too.

"It might not be just one club," Dash said. "I bet the FBI has had a file open on the Warriors for decades. It all depends on how aggressive Tucker has gotten lately. But there are rumors that he's been growing over the past twelve months. Fast. And the same rumors say he's controlling a major drug transport ring. That he's got ties to a cartel and some major clubs in California. The FBI might be after the Warriors as a means to crack the door on other clubs down south."

Maybe Tucker wasn't as small a player as I'd assumed. Then by that logic, the FBI probably had a similar file on the Tin Gypsy Motorcycle Club.

"You really think they'd put an agent in Ashton, long-term?"

Dash shrugged. "Tucker is an ambitious son of a bitch. He's close with other clubs in Oregon and Washington. Could be he's trying to get them to come under his patch. If he expands, then links up with the California clubs, the FBI is dealing with an entire coastal gang. Maybe using a local resource was a shot at keeping that from happening."

"It's all speculation. About Tucker. About Ken. I found nothing to back it up," Emmett said. "Without the wife to question in person, it's impossible to know if he was an agent. Though her disappearance makes it more plausible. Maybe she's an agent too and has left to cover her tracks. If the Warriors knew Ken was a fed, they probably suspect her too."

I scoffed and pointed to the far wall. "The wife is probably my new neighbor." Agent Birdy had likely left Ashton and her role as Ken's pretend wife to come to Clifton Forge and find evidence of his killers.

"Do you think the Warriors knew he was with the FBI? Or do you think they killed him for another reason?"

Dash shook his head. "Your guess is as good as mine. Though I'd wager they figured out Ken was undercover and killed him."

I rounded the island and pulled Scarlett to my side. If the FBI was so desperate to talk to her, it meant they had nothing else. No proof to tie an agent's death to the Warriors.

And Scarlett had the video.

Fuck. My stomach churned. This was getting more complicated every second. It was one thing to turn a blind eye to a criminal killing another criminal. Not acceptable, but slightly easier to swallow than a criminal murdering a fellow officer of the law.

To make it worse, Ken's role in the FBI's scheme hadn't been enough. Whatever evidence Ken had found, if any, must have fallen short if Agent Brown was hounding me daily for Scarlett's whereabouts. And she must not have enough evidence to get a warrant to raid or bug my house.

If I were in her position, I'd be desperate to punish the people responsible for a colleague's death. I'd stick around Clifton Forge too if it was my only lead.

The Warriors needed to pay for his death. For all the lives they'd taken and ruined.

Other than Scarlett's video, there had to be evidence in that clubhouse.

"How good of a job do you think the Warriors did at cleaning up that room where Ken was killed?"

"There won't be any physical evidence," Dash said. "They'll have bleached that room clean. But there might be something electronic. Scarlett's probably not the only one who recorded what went on in that room."

I blinked. "What? They'd record a murder? Why?"

"My guess is Tucker has all of those rooms on video," Emmett said. "But you won't see his face. He'll have stood right underneath the camera so his face wouldn't show but everyone else's would. He'd keep his voice low, maybe not speak at all."

"That makes no sense. Why *create* evidence?"

"Because you're thinking like a cop." Emmett clapped me on the shoulder. "Not the president of a motorcycle club. Let's say one of his brothers gets an idea that Tucker isn't fit to lead and starts convincing the brotherhood of the same. What's to stop them from putting Tucker in the chair next time and tossing his body in the river?"

"You think they'd stage a coup?"

Dash nodded. "If the club wasn't making enough money. If someone was ambitious and wanted to call the shots. Tucker would guard against it."

"Was it like that for you and your dad?" I asked. Draven and Dash had both been presidents of their club. Had they always watched out for other members stabbing them in the back?

"Yes and no. We trusted with caution. And we were selective about who we allowed to join. We didn't bring just anyone into the Gypsies." Dash looked at Scarlett. "No offense, but if Jeremiah had shown up at our clubhouse door, he wouldn't have made it over the threshold."

"None taken." She leaned in closer. "So you think Tucker records what happens in that room, and that he has evidence on the other members in case they try to betray him."

"Guaranteed," Emmett said. "But you are the only one who can put him down. There is no way anyone but him knows that room is being recorded."

"Do you think he could have the whole clubhouse monitored?" I asked.

"Possibly." Dash took a sip of his beer. "Maybe he already knows that Jeremiah was the one to steal his money. But then why would they keep showing up in town? Tucker's looking for someone."

"Me," Scarlett mumbled. "He's looking for me. And if he knows I took that video then—how did Leo put it?—I'm dead."

"If Tucker knew you took that video, I don't think you would have made it to Clifton Forge," Emmett said. "Maybe he didn't have the hallway recorded. Maybe he did and never checked the video. My guess is he only scans it when he needs to. So I don't think he knows you have it. Yet."

"Then he just wants me because he thinks I stole money."

"Probably." Dash nodded. "Tucker doesn't allow theft. He's ruthless with his money."

"How do you know?" I asked.

"Because I was once the president of a motorcycle club. Someone steals, they pay. End of story." The cold, hard edge to Dash's voice made Scarlett wince.

"I think Tucker's covering his ass right now," Emmett said. "If Ken Raymond was an FBI agent, Tucker made a bold play by dumping him in that river. And if the FBI is as prevalent in Ashton as they are here, he knows they're looking for Scarlett. You are probably one of the only few who's lived in that clubhouse and not loyal to their club. You're a wild card. My guess is Tucker wants to find you to figure out what you know. And what you are going to say. Hell, he might think you were undercover too."

"This is so frustrating." Scarlett pushed out of my hold and dragged a hand through her hair, pulling at the roots. "We're guessing. We're all guessing."

"Want to drop that video anonymously?" Dash asked. "Might work."

I shook my head. "Scarlett and I discussed it. There's no way the FBI doesn't trace it back to her and make her testify."

Mostly, I suspected that the FBI needed Scarlett to give them an excuse to get through the clubhouse doors. If they could use her as a witness, they might be able to get a judge to issue a warrant for a raid on the Warriors.

Scarlett moved away from the island, pacing the width of the kitchen. Four steps. Turn. Four steps. Turn.

There was so much regret on her face and for once, I didn't know what to say. How could I promise her a future when I wasn't actually sure she could get out of this?

"Okay, let's back up," I said. "Let's assume the Warriors don't know about the video. Before we can deal with the FBI, we need to get the Warriors out of Clifton Forge and away from Scarlett. How do we do that?"

"Leverage," Dash said.

Leverage. Hadn't I used that word yesterday?

"We tell them she has the video," Emmett said. "It disappears when they do."

Bile rose in my mouth. Except if we worked with the Warriors, it meant letting killers go free. It went against everything I believed in as a cop. Everything I believed in as a man.

The prize for my morals was Scarlett.

"So we just lay it all out there," I said.

Dash nodded. "It's about the only option I see. We go to Tucker. Tell him Scarlett didn't take his drugs. Tell him the FBI wants her and that she's got video proof of a murder. Tucker's always been a man to make a deal. We set it up so that if anything happens to Scarlett—"

"Or anyone," she interrupted. "They have to agree to leave everyone alone."

"Agreed," Dash said. "They leave us all alone, leave Clifton Forge for good, or the video goes to the FBI."

Scarlett stopped pacing. "This seems crazy. Will it work?"

"I don't know," Dash admitted. "But if it was me in your shoes, that's what I'd do."

The kitchen went still.

Scarlett looked to me.

"It's your call, beautiful." This wasn't a decision I could make for her.

It was the river all over again. We were still left with only two options.

Negotiate with the Warriors.

Or go to the FBI.

Scarlett gained her life back if we blackmailed the Warriors into her safety. And the Warriors would get away with murder. Another murder.

Could I live with it? Knowing that a cop, a guy who'd started out like me just hoping to make the world a better place, had been killed while doing his job? And doing nothing about it?

Ken Raymond deserved justice. Scarlett deserved her life.

My insides were being torn in two, like a bullet ripping through my chest, shattering bone, splitting my heart right down the center.

For years, I'd acted as chief of police, upholding the law, keeping citizens safe. I'd vowed to do a better job than Marcus Wagner had before me.

But was I better than Marcus Wagner? He'd killed a woman, snuffed out her life with his own hands. Maybe I hadn't committed a murder, but if Scarlett chose to make a deal with the Warriors, I'd be an accessory to one all the same.

At the moment, my crime seemed just as grave as Marcus's.

Some things were easier to overlook, like Emmett's propensity for hacking. A mom in a minivan driving nine miles over the speed limit. A jaywalker on Central. But this was murder. Could I really let that go?

Yesterday, I'd promised myself I'd find another way to pin the Warriors with Ken Raymond's murder. But a deep, soul-crushing hopelessness settled into my bones.

If the FBI hadn't found evidence, I sure as hell wasn't going to either.

I turned for the sink, pouring my beer down the drain. Then I braced my hands on the counter, staring at the thin covering over the window like I could see out to the yard.

I couldn't look at Scarlett. She'd want me to decide and damn it, I couldn't do it.

Finally, she whispered, "Call Tucker."

"Okay," Dash said. "I'll let you know what we find. We'll get out of here."

Then without another word, he and Emmett set down their beers, the glass bottles clanking on the island, and walked out the door. The thud of their boots echoed through the garage until they were gone, replaced by the roar of their bikes coming to life.

Then it was silent.

The silence stretched. Minutes passed. Until Scarlett's bare feet padded across the wooden floor and her arms snaked around me from behind.

"I don't want to lose you."

Fuck. I hung my head and turned, pulling her to me in a fierce hold. "I don't want to lose you either."

"I know it's selfish. I know it's not the right thing. But I don't want to lose you."

With her chin in my hand, I tipped up her face. Her eyes were swimming with tears. I pushed the hair away from her temples, then released her chin to frame her face before dropping my lips to hers.

The kiss started slow. Smooth. Then a frenzy built in my veins, an urgency to savor her taste and memorize the slide of her tongue against mine.

Scarlett's arms banded tight, holding me closer as I devoured her mouth. As much as I was soaking her in, she was doing the same.

A moan escaped her throat when I picked her up off the floor. She took her arms from my ribs, one at a time, looping them over my shoulders. Her legs wrapped around my hips. Then the frenzy became a wildfire.

I strode across the house, practically jogging to the stairs. On the way to the bedroom, I tore at her clothes while she tore at mine. Hands roamed. Fingers fumbled. The urgency to get her naked, to feel her skin on mine, was like a siren blaring in my mind, blocking out any other noise.

Scarlett pulled and tugged at the buttons on my uniform shirt until it was free. I had her stripped to only a bra with her jeans and panties bunched at her ankles.

I picked her up, tossed her onto the bed and tore off her pants before shoving mine away. Then I ripped at her bra, breaking the center clasp, before settling into her arms.

Her lips found the skin of my shoulder, nipping and licking and sucking. My cock found her center, and with one hurried thrust, I drove home.

"Luke," Scarlett cried, ecstasy straining her voice.

"Fuck, you feel good."

She moaned her agreement as I slid out and slammed inside once more. Over and over, we moved together like practiced lovers, taking and giving pleasure from each other's flesh.

It wasn't slow and elegant. It wasn't lazy and gentle. We fucked, wanton and rough, surrendering to the need to just be together. To connect as one.

The fears disappeared, as did the worries about tomorrow. Sinking into Scarlett's tight body was the balm to soothe my troubled soul.

Scarlett's nails dug into my skin. Her moans filled the room as she chased her release. The scent of her shampoo and our sex clung to the air.

This was what we were fighting for. This, right here. Us.

My hips thrust harder and harder, our skin slapping together, until her legs trembled and the pressure built in my lower spine.

"Baby," she gasped.

"Come."

She detonated around me, clenching and drawing out my own release. I poured into her in long strokes, collapsing onto her, spent. Then I held her, my arms banded tight.

The decision I'd shoved away, the doubts, came rushing back like a tidal wave.

"Can you live with this?" Scarlett asked.

I slid out and rolled us both, tucking her into my chest so she couldn't see my face. So she couldn't read the lie. "I'll be fine."

We didn't speak of it again.

Scarlett fell asleep in my arms, and when darkness crept across the floor, I slipped from our bed and went downstairs. I shut the garage door. I turned off the lights. I stood at the sink and replayed the options in my mind, desperately hoping to think of another.

But there wasn't one to explore.

I sighed, ready to head upstairs, when my phone buzzed on the kitchen counter with a text from Dash.

Tomorrow. Meet at the garage. Noon.

Tomorrow, we'd talk to Tucker. Tomorrow, we'd make a deal with the devil.

Could I live with it?

Only time would tell.

CHAPTER EIGHTEEN

LUKE

"Be careful," Scarlett whispered.

"I will." I nodded and kissed her forehead, then turned and strode for the garage.

"Luke," she called as my hand skimmed the handle.

"Yeah?" I glanced over my shoulder.

She stood in the living room, her face ashen. Her arms were wrapped around her belly. The worry line between her eyebrows was etched deep. It reminded me of the day I'd hauled her from the grocery store and she'd been sitting in that old recliner at the rental house. She looked lost. Tired.

I knew the feeling.

Things between us had been quiet this morning. I hadn't gone to the station for my regular Saturday morning work-out. I'd stayed home and we'd lain in bed, both of us pretending to sleep.

This would get easier, right? That's what I kept telling myself. That one day, years from now, I wouldn't care that we'd let the Warriors get away with murder. Because if I had Scarlett, it would be worth it.

"I'm sorry," she whispered.

"I know." I gave her a sad smile, then opened the door and disappeared into the garage.

It was nearly noon. Time to meet Dash.

There was a bar about halfway between Clifton Forge and Ashton. It would take us over an hour to get there, and for the first time in months, I was looking forward to some space from Scarlett. Not because I was mad at her. None of this was her fault. I wasn't angry. I wasn't upset. I was just . . . what the fuck was I?

Conflicted. Frustrated.

And angry.

Okay, so I was angry. And if I had to aim it somewhere, I was sending it full force at the Warriors. Jeremiah had been one of them and that son of a bitch had put Scarlett in this situation. The rest of them could rot in hell just for existing.

Angry. Yeah, that was definitely the correct word.

I rammed some of that emotion into the gas pedal, my hands choking the steering wheel all the way to the garage.

Dash, Emmett and Leo were all waiting, their bikes in a short row in the parking lot. The minute Dash spotted me, he raised a hand, then pulled onto the street with Emmett and Leo following. The three of them roared onto the road in a single-file line and led the way out of town.

I glanced at the clock. Noon, exactly. It would take over an hour to get to the bar. An hour to return. With the meeting time in between, it would probably be dinner by the time I made it home. That was if everything went smoothly. That was if the guys didn't want to stop and talk on the return trip.

I'd told Scarlett to eat without me, to not wait if she was hungry, but I doubted she would. She hadn't eaten much in the past few days, not since I'd gone to the garage on Wednesday.

I didn't like that she wasn't eating. I didn't like the faint blue circles under her eyes. It was too easy to look at her and picture the woman from months ago—starved and pale and exhausted.

Maybe with some luck, I'd come home tonight with good news and all that would be left for us to tackle was the FBI.

Then, hopefully, we'd get normal. I craved normal. No more visitors on repeat to my office. There wasn't much happening, but I had hardly checked in with my staff since I'd returned from the river.

Or my dad.

As we pulled onto the highway, the bikes roared ahead, breaking away and speeding down the road. I caught up, the engine's rev shoving me deeper into my seat. We settled into a fast cruise, the rumble of the engines ahead louder than my truck's wheels on the pavement.

I hung back where it was quieter, then took out my phone and scrolled for my dad's number. The call went straight to voicemail.

"Hey, Dad," I said, leaving him a message. "Just calling to say hi. You're probably out fishing. Catch a big one. Call me when you can."

Damn. I tossed the phone aside. It would have been nice to talk to him. I wouldn't have told Dad what was happening, but he was the constant in my life. He was the one to ground me, to remind me of what really mattered. Family. Honesty. Integrity.

I was falling down on a couple at the moment.

What the fuck would he say if he knew where I was

going and why? He'd shake his head and curse under his breath. Dad had no use for murderers, thieves or thugs.

Was I any better? I was on my way to blackmail Tucker Talbot. I'd get Scarlett. All it would cost was my moral compass.

But I loved her.

God, I loved her. If there was ever a doubt, this trip proved how far I would go to keep her in my life. When this was all over and done, I sure as hell hoped she'd feel the same.

As the miles passed, all I could think about was Marcus Wagner. He'd been on my mind more in the last few days than he had in years.

Marcus had been a cop his entire life. He'd grown up in Clifton Forge, had served the town and its citizens for decades. He'd had a family. Friends. A good life.

And he'd thrown it away for love.

Marcus had been having an affair with Amina Daylee. According to his confession, he'd loved her. But she'd chosen Draven instead, and to Marcus, the price for that betrayal had been her life.

His *love* for her had compromised his integrity. He'd thrown his life away all in the name of love.

Was I doing the same thing?

I knew the answer. Deep in my heart, I knew the answer was yes.

But I kept on driving.

There was a black SUV tailing us. It had been since Clifton Forge. The FBI agents inside weren't trying to hide themselves anymore. They could follow but I doubted they'd come into the bar where we were going to meet with Tucker.

Maybe it was Agent Brown herself behind the wheel.

I'd see her Monday whenever she decided to grace the station with her presence. For once, I was looking forward to her waltzing into my office. Because if Tucker agreed to leave Scarlett alone, I'd be bringing her to work with me on Monday. And she could tell Maria that she'd been off on an unplanned vacation—or whatever we decided to say was the reason for her disappearance.

I expected they'd try to bully Scarlett into something, but my woman was no pushover. She'd keep on fighting because she was strong as steel. Her will was pure iron.

And she didn't even realize it.

Which made her even stronger. Scarlett believed she was weak, that she wasn't brave, so there was no ego to cloud her decisions. Every action was made with vulnerability and hope.

I put a lot of stock in hope. And I'd take it any day over blind confidence.

The rest of the trip passed quickly and by the time the bar came into view, my anxiety levels were record high. Thankfully, after years of being a cop, I knew how to shove it down and stay steady. The anger bubbling in my veins would stay safely trapped until I unleashed it on a punching bag at the station's gym tomorrow morning.

I pulled into the bar's gravel lot, the dust flying past us as we parked. The guys climbed off their bikes and I got out of my truck, my gun secured in its holster. I'd decided to wear a uniform shirt today with my jeans. My badge was clipped beside my gun.

There was no use pretending I was something I wasn't, and Dash had likely told Tucker who'd be at this meeting.

The four of us strode into the bar. My eyes needed a moment to adjust to the dim light.

It was a typical rural Montana bar. The focus here was on serving booze, not providing ambience. The scent of old cigarettes clung to the air. It was illegal to smoke in public places, but after thirty or forty years of smoking before that law had passed, the scent had ingrained itself into the walls, floor and ceiling.

"What can I get you guys?" the bartender asked, shoving away from the place where she'd been leaning, watching the television mounted above the bar.

"Four beers," Dash said. "Don't care what they are. Just make them cold."

She nodded and opened the cooler as we sat at a high-top table in the center of the room. We were the only patrons in the place.

None of us spoke as the bartender brought our drinks.

Dash handed her a couple of twenties and as she went back to her TV, we sat without speaking. Not one of us touched a beer. The bottles dripped with condensation, puddling on the scratched table.

"You good with what's about to happen here?" Emmett asked, his voice low.

"Yeah," I lied.

"You always were a shit liar."

I chuckled. No, I wasn't good with this. As a cop, I knew that Scarlett's testimony could save countless others. Innocents who crossed paths with the wrong men, like Tucker Talbot. "There's no justice in this."

"This isn't black and white, Luke," Dash said. "Never will be. There's justice for Scarlett. She holds no blame here. She was in the wrong place at the wrong time. You can't balance the scales. You'll go crazy if you try because there's no such thing. We live in a gray world and you've got to pick the shade closest to white. So do what your heart tells you."

And my heart told me to save her life.

Always. This was always for Scarlett.

Throwing Tucker in prison would feel fucking great, but Scarlett didn't deserve to pay that pound of flesh.

There's justice for Scarlett.

And it outweighed the injustice. A million times over, this was right.

I wasn't Marcus Wagner. And I'd needed to be here, in this dark bar, sitting beside three former criminals, to realize the difference.

This was right. We'd get justice for her. And I had no problem living with that, no matter the means. "Thanks."

Dash nodded.

I'd chosen the seat facing the door, and when it opened, the flash of sunlight brightened the room as three men wearing black leather vests strode inside.

Without an introduction, I knew which was Tucker. He walked with the arrogance of a man in charge. He thought himself untouchable. It oozed from his easy posture and the way he stayed one step ahead of his two subordinates. He was ready to give an order and they stood poised to take that command.

I imagined I looked somewhat similar at a crime scene.

Dash, Emmett and Leo stayed in their chairs beside me, but a slow grin stretched across Leo's face and he held out a hand to one of the men flanking Tucker.

"Hey, man."

"Long time, Leo." The guy grinned back. "What's new?"

Leo shrugged, sagging into his chair and finally picking up his beer. "Painting cars. Drinking beer. Chasing women."

"So nothing's new."

"Exactly." Leo chuckled and tipped the bottle to his lips. Then he shoved a booted foot into the stool beside him, moving it away from the table for the man to take a seat.

Leo's posture was relaxed, and his cavalier attitude defused some of the tension. He seemed at ease, like this was a normal Saturday afternoon drinking with friends. But how many guns did he have tucked away? I was guessing at least two. One in the waistband of his jeans, covered by the leather jacket he'd worn on the ride over. And there was probably another in his boot.

Dash and Emmett probably had the same, if not more.

Like me, the Warriors had theirs in plain view. All three had sidearms holstered beside their ribs, barely concealed beneath the fabric of their vests.

The other man beside Tucker went to grab himself a chair since there was only one empty at our table. As he turned, he flashed me the back of his vest and the Warrior patch. It was a simple white arrowhead framed by the club name and a year. Probably the year they were founded.

The guy returned with a stool, though I'd been wrong. It hadn't been for himself. He pushed it to the table, directly opposite me, and Tucker slid into the seat.

"Dash." Tucker held out a hand.

Dash hesitated for just a moment before returning the shake. It wasn't much, but we all noticed. The last thing he wanted to do was touch Tucker Talbot. But he'd do it and act civil to protect his family. To protect Scarlett.

"You remember Emmett and Leo." Dash jerked his chin in their direction.

Tucker nodded, not sparing them a glance as his gaze locked on mine.

I sat motionless, pretending to be indifferent, when really, I wanted to reach across the table, tackle him to the floor and fit his wrists nice and tight into my handcuffs. But the anger stayed hidden as I took in his features.

Tucker Talbot had dark hair, nearly black, that was heavily speckled with gray. The skin on his face and his forearms was tanned and weathered—according to his record he was fifty-seven. His gaze was cunning. His expression merciless.

I hated him with every fiber of my being, and later today, if all went as planned, I'd have to shake his hand too. My respect for Dash was growing by the second for the sacrifices he was making to endure this.

"There's an FBI agent outside," Tucker said, his eyes still trained on me.

I nodded. "Probably."

"Since when did you start working with cops, Slater?"

"Since one of your men came to my town, took my friend and her sister hostage, then decorated her walls with his brain matter." Dash picked up his beer, taking a long swallow.

The corner of Tucker's mouth turned up.

"Let's talk about that." I leaned my forearms on the table. There was no point stalling this thing so I jumped right in. "Your man—Jeremiah—was stealing your drugs. Selling them on the side. Burned his profits at the poker table."

"My men don't steal from me. And my club isn't affiliated with drugs. Those are illegal, Chief Rosen."

"Sure," I deadpanned. Not a surprise he knew exactly who I was.

"Like I said, my men don't steal from me or their club. Jeremiah said it was his woman. The sister."

"It wasn't," I said.

"How do we know? I heard she's gone underground. I'm not an expert, but in my experience, only guilty people run. Unless you know where she is. I'm sure if we had a nice talk with Goldilocks, we could clear this all up."

He tossed her nickname out there like he had some ownership of *my* woman. Fuck, I wanted to nail this guy. I wanted him in orange for the rest of his natural days. Instead, I was going to let him walk out the door. "The FBI is after Scarlett."

"Is that so?"

"They think she might be a witness to a murder that happened at your clubhouse while she was staying there." It wasn't something they'd confirmed, but Tucker didn't know that.

Tucker's jaw clenched. Not by much, but enough. Either he hadn't known that Scarlett had seen them kill Ken Raymond. Or he was pissed that we knew what was going on.

His secrets were escaping their dark corners and maybe one of them would come back to serve up revenge ice cold.

"What do you want?" he asked.

Dash leaned forward on the table. "Get your men out of Clifton Forge."

"We had a truce once. After you killed my father," Emmett said.

"After you killed my men," Tucker shot back. The Warrior standing at his back stiffened.

So Tucker had killed Emmett's father too. *Motherfucker.* I'd suspected something like that had happened. Every cop in Clifton Forge had their theories, all of which involved the

Tin Gypsies. It had been one of those crimes that had gone unsolved. No evidence. No witnesses.

Emmett never spoke of his father or his death. And here he was, sitting across from his father's killer.

For Scarlett.

For me.

"We go back to that," Emmett said, his gaze cold and cruel. "You stay away from us and our families. We'll do the same."

Tucker looked at Leo, whose laid-back posture was a sharp contrast to the serious expression on his face. "And what do I get? I made that agreement with the Tin Gypsies years ago. Club to club. From what I can tell, you three are all that are left of your club. Not exactly a threat."

"We'll get to that," I said as ice ran through my veins. This son of a bitch deserved to rot in hell, but damn him, he wasn't getting a rise out of me. "We're not done with our terms quite yet."

Tucker's lip curled. "Continue."

"Scarlett didn't steal your drugs. Believe me or not, I don't really give a fuck. But as of today, she's a distant memory. You'll forget about her. For good. In exchange, she'll assure the FBI that she knows nothing of the murder that happened in your clubhouse basement. The one where you tied an undercover federal agent to a chair and beat him within an inch of his life before tossing him in the river to drown. You remember that? The murder you staged as an accident?"

The Warrior seated next to Tucker immediately looked to his president. He'd been in that room. His fist had connected with Ken Raymond's face. I hadn't watched the video many times, but I had a good memory and his face was on it.

Tucker leaned forward, his eyes narrowing. Did he think I was bluffing?

My cards were on the table and I had a royal flush. Maybe I couldn't make these assholes pay the way I wanted. But I was taking this.

I was stealing their vengeance.

"What's keeping me from killing you all and the woman, right now?" Tucker said, his voice low. If he was going for menacing, it might have worked on someone else. "Dead people have a hard time testifying."

"If any of us die from suspicious circumstances, the video evidence finds its way to the FBI."

Tucker didn't flinch. He didn't so much as breathe. But he knew he was on the losing side. "I don't like dealing with cops."

"And I don't like dealing with murdering motherfuckers, but we don't always get what we want, do we?"

Without another word, Tucker slid off his stool and stood. Then he gave me a grin that sent my heart plummeting to my stomach. "We'll see."

CHAPTER NINETEEN

SCARLETT

My handwriting was sloppy.

It had been months since I'd had to write anything longer than a grocery list, and the pen felt awkward and heavy in my grip. The slash that crossed the double *t*s in my name was crooked.

A tear dripped down my cheek as I ran my hand across the paper on the counter. My gaze was locked on the last three words above my name.

I meant them. To the depths of my soul, I meant them. They looked insignificant on a cheap page lined with pale blue stripes, but I hoped that as Luke read them, he'd feel their power. That he'd know he was the best thing in my life.

Telling Luke that I loved him in a letter wasn't ideal. It certainly wasn't how I'd planned to share my heart. But if he were here, if I had to look him in the eye, I'd cave. I'd crack and lose my nerve.

And I had to do this today. I had to make this right.

When he'd left earlier, there'd been so much regret etched into his handsome face. Asking him to overlook another cop's murder was asking too much. No matter how he lied or pretended, Luke wouldn't be able to live with this decision.

He was too good of a man. So good that he'd do it for me just because I'd asked. Because maybe he loved me too.

Except I wasn't going to watch this decision eat away at his conscience for the next fifty years. So I was taking it back.

I was taking control.

I was fixing this on my own, something I should have done months ago.

Another tear fell before I forced myself away from the letter to dry my face. With a fortifying breath, I glanced around the house.

For as long as I lived, I'd remember every detail, like the way Luke looked when he was lying on the couch, one arm behind his head and a grin across his face as he laughed at a joke on TV. I'd remember the way he had to have a napkin at every meal. He rarely used it, but he always kept one handy. I'd remember those deep blue eyes staring into the center of my soul. The silk of his hair sliding through my fingers.

I'd remember how he taught me about love. That real love existed without judgment. Without conditions. Without perfection.

A love that would last my lifetime.

Whether we were together or not, I'd never stop loving that man. Which was exactly the reason I had to let him go. I loved him too much to let regret destroy him.

I closed my eyes and dragged in a long breath, finding his rich scent in the air and holding it in my lungs. The ache in my chest doubled and I slapped a hand to my sternum.

You can do this.

I had to do this.

My backpack was beside the front door, waiting. I couldn't take everything I'd collected over the months here. The dresser drawers in Luke's guest bedroom were nearly full of my clothes, and inside was a letter I'd tucked away for Presley. But I had clothes for a couple of days along with what I was wearing.

My skinny jeans were comfortable. I'd stolen one of Luke's T-shirts, the hem tied in a knot at my waist. The edge of it covered the phone I'd tucked into my rear pocket.

And I had my feather. I'd washed and dried my hair in case I wouldn't get a shower again for a while, and my hair hung to my waist in straight, thick panels. Behind my ear, I'd twisted a small braid, then tied on the feather.

I was stealing all its strength.

You can do this.

"Forgive me," I whispered, sending that plea into the air. Like my letter, I hoped Luke would feel the sincerity of those words.

Maybe he'd curse me for this. Maybe he'd hate me for that letter and stealing a sweatshirt from his closet. It was the one he'd worn on the river at night when we cuddled together beside the fire. Maybe he'd be angry at me for a while, but eventually, he'd see this was for the best.

With my belongings packed, all that was left to do was make one more phone call.

I took my phone from my pocket and turned it on. I'd charged it while I'd tidied up around the house, not wanting Luke to return to a mess. Other than the clothes, he wouldn't have much to take care of to put my time here in the past.

Maybe Presley could help rid the guest bedroom of my things.

I wasn't worried about my sister. She'd live a happy life.

She'd thrive—she already was. This phone call was not to her.

I rounded the end of the couch and sank onto its edge, then dialed a number I'd memorized years ago. It was the only number she had. Then I held my breath as it rang once. Twice.

"Marks residence."

Tears flooded my eyes. I covered my mouth with a hand to keep quiet.

"Hello?"

I love you, Mom.

Get out.

Get away from him.

All things I wanted to say, but I remained silent.

When I'd left, I'd offered to give her the number to this phone. She'd thought it was better if I kept it to myself. Maybe that had been another mistake.

"Who is it?" The voice in the background sent a surge of panic through my veins. No matter how many years passed, I doubted I'd ever stop fearing my father.

Fearing for my mother.

Dad had stopped hitting me a long time ago. Not just because I went to work with him every day, but because he knew the worst thing he could do to me was hurt Mom.

"I don't know," Mom told him. "No one's there."

I expected her to hang up, but then there was a shuffling and Dad's voice was on the line. "Hello?"

I stayed silent, my heart racing.

"Who is this?" There was a familiar edge to his voice. The beginning of fury. Had I just called to hear my mother's hello and sent Dad into a fit that she'd pay for?

I tore the phone from my ear and ended the call. *Stupid,*

Scarlett. I was screwing up everyone's life. But not anymore. I couldn't right Mom's world, but I could fix Luke's.

Dad deserved to rot in prison.

So did Tucker Talbot.

And at the moment, he was the only person I could punish.

I shoved off the couch, tucked away my phone and trudged to the door with heavy feet. I slung my bag over a shoulder. Then I punched in the code to the alarm. Luke had done it enough times I'd memorized the code.

Eight. Four. One. Two.

They were the last four numbers on his badge.

If he got a notification, he'd be hours away. And I wasn't traveling far.

The door's metal handle was cold against my clammy palm as I twisted it open. The sunlight hit my face and I squinted against its light as I stepped outside. The clean air filled my lungs along with the sweet scent of summer. Any other day and I would have savored the scent of cut grass. The blue sky and laughter of children playing in their yards.

Not today.

I closed the door behind me and hurried down the sidewalk. My courage faltered with every step but I kept on moving. *You can do this.* A car's trunk slammed shut, catching my attention, and I looked to the house directly across the street.

A young woman stood beside her blue car, watching as I walked. I'd seen her before. She was the daughter of the couple who lived there. Her auburn hair was in a thick braid, draped over one shoulder. Her eyes narrowed in suspicion as I marched.

I raised my hand in a tiny finger wave and forced a smile, then focused on my destination.

The grass was too long at the place next door. There were no summer planters filled with petunias or geraniums. Now that I was outside and taking in the street from a different perspective, the tan house stood out like a sore thumb. No wonder Luke had suspected the FBI of moving in.

I crossed the driveway and made my way to the stoop, hopping up the steps to the front door. Then I sucked in a long breath and jammed my thumb into the doorbell.

Part of me was surprised that I'd even made it to the door. I guess I'd expected to step outside and immediately be surrounded by federal agents. That I'd be swept into an SUV and hurried away to some undisclosed location.

There was no sound beyond the door. No footsteps rushing to answer. It was a Saturday. I hadn't spied much on Saturdays just because the neighborhood was busier and Luke was normally home from his workout at the station by this time of day. But shouldn't she be here?

I rang the bell again and before the chime had died down, the door flew open.

It was not the FBI woman who answered. She was lying on the floor in a pool of blood behind the tall, angry man looming above me. He wore a black leather vest. The same style I'd seen many, many times on Jeremiah's back.

And before I could turn and run, before I could scream, the world went black.

I GASPED AWAKE, then flinched at the pounding in my skull. The rhythm of the painful throbs matched the bass beat of whatever music was blaring outside the room. There was no point in looking around. The sterile, cold smell of the concrete floor beneath my cheek was enough for me to know exactly where I was.

The Warrior clubhouse.

My hands were bound behind my back and when I tested the bond, the hard plastic ties dug into my skin.

This wasn't happening. It wasn't supposed to be like this.

I'd planned to go to the FBI, hand over my video evidence and agree to testify against the Warriors. Right now, they should have me in some sort of interrogation room. I should be drinking lukewarm coffee as agents listen to my confession. Then they'd whisk me away to some suburban town in Oklahoma or Oregon or Ohio, and Scarlett Marks would cease to exist.

So much for doing the right thing.

I closed my eyes and pressed my temple into the cold concrete, willing the pain in my head to subside.

"Are you okay?" The voice startled me and my eyes flew open. A woman was sitting beside me.

The redhead from across the street. Luke's neighbor.

Shit.

"What happened?" I croaked out.

"They hit you."

Uh, yeah. I'd figured that one out.

Bringing my knees to my chest, I used what little strength I had to roll off my hip. Then I hoisted myself to a seated position on the floor. The room began spinning and the effort stabbed needles through my eyes. I collapsed against the cinderblock wall behind me, sucking in a few deep breaths until the pain was manageable.

"Who are you?" the woman beside me asked. "Why do they want you?"

"Scarlett Marks," I answered, turning my head to take her in.

Her face was pale and the braid she'd worn earlier had fallen out. A mass of auburn hair fell over her shoulders and down her green tee. Like me, she was in jeans but hers had a fresh tear at the knee. There was a red mark on her cheek and her caramel eyes were flooded with tears.

Even terrified, she was beautiful. Too beautiful for this place.

"What's your name?" I asked.

"Cassandra Cline." She kept her voice low, her gaze alternating between me and the closed door.

We were in one of the basement rooms—it could be the one where Ken Raymond had been killed. The floor pitched to a drain in the center. There were no windows, only a flickering lightbulb hanging from a black wire.

"I'm sorry," I said.

"Why?"

"Because trouble seems to follow me everywhere these days." And now I'd dragged this innocent young woman into the mix.

"What else happened?" I whispered. "At home."

"Chief Rosen lives alone and I wasn't sure what you were doing. My parents are part of the neighborhood watch. I thought maybe you'd broken into his house or something and were moving on to the neighbor's."

I huffed a laugh. With my backpack and as quickly as I'd been walking, I probably had looked like a criminal.

"I was still beside my car when that man opened the door. One second, you were standing there, then he took out a gun and hit you over the head. It happened so fast. I tried to get out my phone and call the police, but he saw me. I tried to run but . . . there were three of them."

Had the Warriors known I was at Luke's? Or had they gone after the FBI agent?

"Did you see another woman?"

"No." She shook her head. "It was just us. One of the men, the one who caught me, hit me across the cheek. Things are fuzzy after that. There was a van. They threw us in and tied us up. You were unconscious the whole time."

"Damn." Then I most likely had a concussion. I breathed and closed my eyes. "Did anyone else see us?"

"I don't think so."

It was a Saturday. People mowed the lawns on Saturdays. Kids played in their yards. Someone might have seen two women being thrown into a van, but even if they had, clearly the police hadn't been able to stop the Warriors from getting us to Ashton.

We were three hours away from Clifton Forge and when Luke got home, he'd see my note and think I'd gone to the FBI. Eventually they'd find the agent in the house next door, but how much time did we have before the Warriors killed us next?

"Where are we?" Cassandra asked. "Why is this happening?"

"Have you ever heard of the Arrowhead Warriors?"

She gulped and nodded, her eyes going back to the door. "One of my roommates is from Ashton. She's told me stories."

More like nightmares—except they were true.

"I shouldn't have gone to The Betsy," she whispered.

"Huh?" God, my head hurt. I was struggling to keep up with Cassandra, much less what was happening in my own mind. "What about The Betsy?"

"Two weeks ago, I came home with a friend. My parents go camping a lot in the summer and let me stay at their place. I go to grad school in Missoula and have a few summer classes. My roommates like to party so I come home to study whenever I have a break. But a couple weeks ago, my friend wanted to come with me and see where I grew up. We went out to The Betsy and there were these guys . . ." She shook her head. "I didn't get any work done, so I came back this weekend to catch up."

"Huh?" I was stuck on repeat.

"I have a paper due in two weeks. Except the weekend I brought my friend home, we went out and I only wrote two pages. So I came home this weekend to escape my roommates and finish it."

And now she was in the basement of a motorcycle gang's clubhouse.

While a party raged above.

It had to be getting closer to night. The music drifting through the ceiling was a tell-tale sign that one of the Warriors' Saturday-night ruckuses was underway.

The two of us sat quietly, the music a third person in the room. Cassandra sat rigid, her eyes on the door.

I closed mine and stretched for my jeans pocket. My phone was gone. *Fuck.* Maybe it had fallen out during the abduction but I suspected it belonged to the Warriors now.

This is bad. God, this was bad. I wasn't sure how I was going to get out of here myself, let alone sneak Cassandra out too.

My hands were strapped together tight and Cassandra was sitting in a similar position. Our ankles weren't bound, but even if we managed to open the door, there was no way we were getting out of this compound unnoticed. This place was probably crawling with people.

The ache in my head spiked and I focused on my breathing, taking in long breaths that smelled of concrete and bleach and death.

Had Luke made it home? Was he worried?

Damn it, I should have stayed put. I should have stayed hidden. Unless the FBI had been the Warriors' first stop and Luke's had been the next. Maybe I'd just saved them a trip next door.

"Scarlett." Cassandra's shoulder nudged mine.

I snapped up, not realizing I'd almost drifted to sleep. "Yeah?"

"You probably have a concussion."

"Probably." The crown of my head felt strange, sticky. It was probably dried blood.

"It would be best if you stayed awake."

"Okay." I forced my eyes open, the room spinning.

"Talk to me. Tell me about anything."

"Like what?"

"Um . . . what's your favorite place to visit?"

"Smith River." If I could just take a small nap, I'd be there again in my dreams. Instead of music, I'd hear the rushing river. Instead of feeling cold and scared, I'd be warm under the sun. And Luke would be there.

Maybe we'd talk about our dreams again. And this time, I'd have my own answer.

What do I want in life?

Luke.

A life with Luke.

"Open your eyes."

I obeyed, concentrating on a spot on the wall across from us. "Okay."

"How old are you?"

"Twenty-eight."

"I'm twenty-four." She had delicate, youthful features. Cassandra was thin but taller than me by quite a few inches, given where my shoulder reached hers. With the lack of makeup and her flawless skin, she could pass for a high schooler.

"You don't look twenty-four."

"I get that a lot," she muttered. "What month is your birthday?"

"August."

"Mine's in May." She shifted, sitting up straighter and wiggling her legs. Hers were probably numb like mine from the cold floor. "How do you know Chief Rosen?"

"I love him." I sagged to one side, my eyelids heavy, but I managed to keep them open.

Enough so when the door flew open and four men strode inside, I didn't miss the look on Tucker Talbot's face as he took me in.

One of the men was the one who'd hit me. I couldn't remember his name from when I'd stayed here. The other two were Tucker's lieutenants. Where he went, so did they. Both were younger than Tucker and hadn't spared me much of a glance when I'd been living here with Jeremiah.

Now, I was the center of attention.

White light streamed into the room from the hallway and made me wince. Maybe it wasn't night after all. I vaguely recalled a row of thin windows along the hallway from my one and only time in this basement before. The summer days were long, but it was still bright outside.

We hadn't been here as long as I'd thought.

Tucker studied me, the cold expression on his face unreadable, as he crossed the room and crouched in front of me. His eyes flicked to my hair, lingering on the place where I'd been clubbed. "Goldilocks."

I wanted to spit in his face.

So I did.

His jaw clenched as he reached into his rear pocket and pulled out a bandana. He wiped his face dry, then tossed it in my face. It smelled of gasoline and grease as it hit my nose, then dropped to my lap.

He didn't speak. He didn't move. He just stared at me with those haunting, dark eyes.

And I stared right back.

One of the other men came over, a lanky man with dirty-blond hair, and kicked at Cassandra's knee. "Who's this?"

"She saw us," the man who'd clubbed me said.

"So you took her?" the blond man asked. "Stupid motherfucker. Have you not noticed the federal agents surrounding this place? I knew I should have gone myself."

Tucker held up a hand, silencing the conversation. His eyes never wandered from mine as he reached into his back pocket and pulled out a phone. My phone.

"Your boyfriend tried to blackmail me." Tucker set the device on the floor. "I didn't like it much."

I stole one of Luke's moves and arched an eyebrow.

A slow grin spread across Tucker's face. Chilling. Deadly.

I wasn't leaving this room alive.

My heart dropped. "I have a backup of that video."

Tucker shrugged. "I've spent enough time dodging the law to know what sticks and what doesn't. A judge might rule it admissible. Or maybe he won't. Wherever you've saved the backup, we'll find it."

This evil man was going to kill me and take his chances.

"See you soon, Goldilocks." Tucker cast his gaze to the ceiling. "When things quiet down, then we'll have some fun."

The sick son of a bitch was going to enjoy killing me. He'd probably torture me relentlessly until I told him exactly where I had the video saved. Maybe he'd cut off my fingers, one by one. Or maybe he'd hurt Cass, knowing that at the first drop of her blood, I'd tell him everything.

Without another word, Tucker stood. He raised his knee and with one fast stomp, brought his boot heel to my phone, shattering the glass. It was garbage now. Then he walked to the man who'd taken me, and without breaking his stride, Tucker plowed a fist into the man's face before leaving the room.

Blood dripped from the man's nose, but he didn't make a sound. He didn't protest. He simply followed Tucker and the others out of the room, closing the door behind him as blood streamed from his face.

The lock from outside the door clicked. The light disappeared.

Cassandra and I were alone. Trapped.

She shuddered, bringing her knees to her chest. Her shoulders trembled but she didn't cry.

Tears wouldn't save our lives.

And as I succumbed to the black, I knew nothing would.

CHAPTER TWENTY

LUKE

"Scarlett," I called, bursting through the door.

No answer.

"Scarlett!"

Silence.

I sprinted through the kitchen and living room, taking the stairs two at a time. "Scarlett!"

She wasn't in the bedroom or bathroom. She wasn't in the office.

I ran downstairs as Dash, Emmett and Leo jogged through the door, but I didn't stop as I rounded the banister and ran to her room. "Scarlett!"

There was an edge to my voice. A crack.

Panic.

The world was spinning too fast and every step felt unsteady. Nothing in her room was out of place. Her bed was made. That citrus scent of hers laced the air even though she'd been sleeping in my room. Nothing was wrong, so where the fuck was she?

My heart raced as I scrambled for the dresser and ripped open the top drawer. It was full. So was the middle.

Where the fuck is she? I dragged my hands through my hair and ran for the living room, unsure where else to check —maybe the yard. But one look at Emmett holding a piece of paper and my worst nightmare came crashing down.

She was gone.

She'd left me.

I crossed the room and snatched the note from his hand. My pulse raced and my vision doubled so I closed my eyes and dragged in a breath. When I focused on the page again, the neat and tidy script was as clear as Scarlett's dazzling eyes.

She'd left me.

Fuck, I was going to pass out. This wasn't happening. This couldn't be happening. How? *Why?*

The adrenaline that had been coursing through my veins for the past hour was making it nearly impossible to focus and make sense of this. After Tucker Talbot had left us at the bar, I'd calmly walked to my truck and pulled out of the parking lot like I was headed for a lazy weekend drive.

But the minute the bar had been out of sight from my rearview mirror I'd turned on my lights and made the trip to Clifton Forge at 110 miles per hour. The guys had been behind me the entire way.

I'd known something was wrong. Tucker Talbot, that smug fucking bastard. I'd imagined the worst, coming home to find the house trashed or Scarlett dead. But this . . . this hadn't crossed my mind.

She'd left me?

In a note?

. . .

LUKE,

I can't let you do this. Not for me. It's asking too much.

*You're a good man. I didn't believe in good men until you.
I didn't know what love felt like until you.*

I'm sorry. I'm so sorry.

Forgive me.

I love you.

Scarlett

I READ it three times before my hand dropped to my side
and the paper floated from my grip.

"I don't . . ." My knees were shaking and I was seconds
from joining Scarlett's letter on the floor. Before I collapsed,
I shuffled to the living room and sank onto the edge of the
couch, letting my head fall into my hands.

"Where would she go?" Emmett asked, coming to sit
beside me. Dash and Leo followed.

"The FBI," I choked out. "Next door."

"Any chance that note is forged?" Dash asked.

"No, that's her handwriting." I had a dozen sticky notes
in the jockey box of my truck with grocery lists to prove it.

Dash paced in front of the fireplace. "It doesn't make
sense. Tucker, that son of a bitch, issued a challenge. He's
not letting this go."

"Then maybe it's a good thing she left," Leo said.

I lurched to my feet and cocked my fist back but Emmett
clapped me on the shoulder, shoving me back down. "Fuck
you."

"Sorry." Leo held up his hands. "Just saying, if the
Warriors knew she was here, maybe she's safer with the
feds."

I shook my head, dragging in a deep breath. Leo wasn't wrong. An asshole, but not wrong. There was only so much I could do to protect Scarlett, but I would have laid down my life to keep her safe.

And she'd left me without a goodbye.

That goddamn note didn't count.

What did she mean she couldn't let me do this? I'd agreed. Me. I'd made the decision to overlook the Warriors' crimes. Yeah, it wouldn't have been easy. But I could have lived with it.

I would have traded anything—my career and my badge —for a life with Scarlett.

"Fuck it." I shook Emmett's hand off my shoulder and stood, striding for the front door. The alarm panel had been disarmed, something I hadn't noticed when I'd come inside. Scarlett must have guessed the code.

"Where are you going?" Dash asked, following me outside.

I didn't respond. I just marched across my lawn to the house adjacent mine and pounded on the front door.

No answer.

"She's not here, man," Emmett said. "They would have gotten her out of here."

Well, I was going to track her down. I pounded once more and when there wasn't an answer, I turned the knob. The door opened and I shoved my way inside, braced for a fight.

Instead, I met a body in the barren living room.

"Shit." I flew across the room and knelt beside Birdy. Pressing my fingers hard into her throat, I held my breath, hoping to feel a pulse. It was there. Barely. "Call an ambulance!"

"On it," Leo said at my back.

There was a bullet wound in Birdy's chest. Blood pooled around her body, the edges of the black puddle on the carpet already beginning to dry. *Goddamn it.* This was bad. This would take a miracle.

"Find me a towel or something," I ordered and seconds later, Dash was holding one out for me to press against Birdy's wound. I did my best to staunch the trickling blood flow, but there was a lot of blood. Too much blood.

"Ambulance is on the way," Leo said, coming back inside to stand beside Emmett.

Dash crouched beside me. "I'll take over."

I let him replace my hands over the towel and stood, scanning the room as a jolt of terror raced down my spine. Where was Scarlett? The living room was empty except for a recliner and end table. A metallic scent clung to the air.

One foot in front of the other, I let habit and training take over as I checked the house. I searched every room, clearing them one by one, and when I didn't find a hint of Scarlett, I returned to the living room just as Emmett and Leo jogged inside.

A backpack was in Emmett's hand.

"Found this outside."

My heart dropped. No. Oh, fuck no. "That's hers."

She'd probably come over here to meet with the FBI but the Warriors had been waiting.

"There's a car across the street parked in the driveway. Engine's cold. The driver's side door is open and there's a phone on the ground."

"Which neighbor?" I pushed past them both and strode outside, not waiting for an answer.

The car with the open door was at the Clines' house.

They were a nice couple in their late fifties who loved camping in the summer. They'd borrowed my Yeti cooler once when they'd needed an extra for a two-week trip to Yosemite. And they bragged constantly about their daughter and her academic achievements.

That was Cassie's car.

She must have come here to study. I often saw her car in the driveway when they were gone and once, Dale had asked if I'd keep an eye out on the weekends she was here alone. Dale had asked all the neighbors to watch out for his daughter.

Damn it, this kept getting worse. Cassie wouldn't leave her door open or her phone on the concrete.

Had Cassie seen the Warriors? Had they taken her with Scarlett? Or would I find another body in a house?

The wail of sirens filled the air and I walked toward the curb. Down the street, the ambulance took the sharp corner and raced our way. A cruiser was close behind.

"What do you want us to do?" Emmett asked, appearing at my side.

"We have to get to Ashton," I told him. "They took her."

"Yeah."

"We need to check the house." I pointed across the street. "They might have nabbed Cassie too."

"I'll go," Emmett said and jogged away.

The ambulance parked in the driveway with a cruiser at its side. The EMTs poured out and Nathan shoved out of his cruiser, all eyes looking to me for direction.

"Inside." I jerked my chin for the EMTs to get moving. Then I turned my attention to my deputy. "This whole area is a crime scene. Call Chuck. Get him here to run lead. Breaking and entering. Attempted murder. Abduction." I pointed to Cassie's car. "Sweep the street. Go door to door and ask if anyone saw anything. Then call me with what you find."

"Where are you going?" Nathan asked as I turned and strode toward my own house.

"To get my girl." And I walked away—from the scene, from my job.

I marched through the front door and went to the sink to wash the blood from my hands. I dried them on my jeans just as Dash and Leo came inside.

Dash gave me a single nod and came to the sink to clean his hands too. Leo watched from the living room as I disappeared upstairs.

In my closet, I opened up my gun safe, taking out my spare pistol and tucking it into the hollow of my back.

When I came downstairs, Emmett had joined Leo. "Was Cassie there?"

He shook his head. "Place is empty."

"Fuck. Then they took her too."

Dash strode to the living room to stand beside his brothers, all three with legs planted wide and arms crossed.

A blockade to the door.

Were they going to stop me? I'd like to see them try. Because I'd take them all down if they got in my way.

I opened my mouth to order them to move.

Dash spoke first. "What's the plan?"

They were coming with me. A surge of relief rolled down my shoulders. "Do you think they knew Scarlett was here?"

"Probably," Emmett said. "That or they were here to take out the FBI agent, though they could have done that at any time. Scarlett might have interrupted them, but it's more likely they planned to kill the agent first, then go next door and grab her."

There was no guarantee Birdy would survive. I wasn't sure how long she'd been bleeding out but it had been a while.

"Why would Tucker risk this?" I asked. "With the video."

"Might have thought we were bluffing," Dash said. "Might have thought his guys already had Scarlett by the time we left the bar. Or he could have called his guys here in Clifton Forge before the meeting started, before he knew about the video."

The bastard had just been waiting. Our meeting had been the perfect opportunity to ensure I was out of the house and Scarlett was alone.

I swallowed hard, then voiced the question I feared the most. "Is she alive?"

Emmett and Dash shared a look. Leo's gaze landed on his boots.

Tell me she's alive. "Tell me."

"I don't know." Dash shook his head. "But I'll be real with you. He'll kill her before he spends his life in prison."

An icy cool seeped through my skin. A cold that tasted like revenge.

Tucker Talbot was dead.

I'd kill the man myself.

"I don't like that look," Emmett said.

I reached for my badge, unclipping it from my belt. The metal was heavy. The lights I'd left on this morning glinted off the silver and gold. I dragged my thumb across the smooth surface, then tossed it onto a couch.

That badge wasn't going to help me today.

I'd worried this morning that I was like Marcus Wagner. A good cop turned bad. No. That wasn't it at all. I just had something better to fight for. Love.

He'd lied and killed for his own selfish reasons. But it sure as hell hadn't been for love.

"We're getting her back," I declared.

"Can't just storm the Warrior clubhouse," Dash said. "We're outmanned and outgunned."

Yes, we were. Didn't change the fact that I was getting her back.

Scarlett had told me she loved me in a note. Nope. Not good enough. I was going to find her and hear those words myself.

And say them back.

Fuck, but I loved her. And if we both survived this, I'd tell her every day for the rest of her life.

She'd asked me on the river about my dreams. Well, they all required her.

My father had always told me that the Rosen men fell hard and fell once. He'd been right.

Be alive. Just be alive. I willed her to survive this. I willed her all the strength I had in my body.

I'm coming, beautiful. I'm coming for you. Hang on.

"How?" I asked. "Tell me how we do this."

"Their compound will be reinforced." Emmett rubbed a hand over his beard. "They'll be expecting us."

"We don't have the element of surprise either, though given how fast we got back here, they can't have much of a head start. Maybe an hour or two."

We'd race to Ashton. It was a three-hour trip that we could make in two or less.

"What about another fire?" Leo asked Dash.

Another fire? "What fire?"

Dash sighed. "Years ago, when Dad was alive, we burned down the Warrior clubhouse. My brother, Nick, helped. But their clubhouse is different now. Newer and built mostly out of concrete and cinder blocks."

And if Scarlett was inside, there was no way I'd put her in the middle of a damn fire.

Her backpack rested against Emmett's calf. "Did you check it?"

He nodded.

"The phone?"

He shook his head.

"Fuck." She'd had it on her. At least we had the backup. That alone might keep Tucker from killing her. "What do we do? There has to be a way inside." Maybe if I pulled in every one of my officers. Maybe if I enlisted help from the Ashton police too.

"Chief Rosen, before you get yourself killed—"

My eyes whipped to the front door and the guys spun around just as Agent Maria Brown crossed the threshold.

"—maybe you'll stop trying to shut me out."

I blinked. How long had she been standing there?

Maria walked past Dash, arching her eyebrow. "Mr. Slater."

"Should I know you?"

"No." She went to the couch, bending to pick up my badge. She inspected it, her eyes narrowing. Then she tossed it to me. "You're going to need this."

I caught it and arched an eyebrow.

"Luke, I'm on your side."

We'd see about that. "What do you want?"

"I'm your best shot at getting Scarlett back."

I crossed my arms over my chest. The guys all did the same, turning to face her.

Maria went to the couch, sitting ramrod straight. Those black slacks and suit jacket were as crisp as ever, but there was a frazzled edge to her today. The harsh knot that she normally wore in her hair was beginning to come undone.

"I don't want the Warriors to win," she said. "I've been working their case for the past three years. They're good. They know how to cover their tracks. There isn't a soul on earth I hate as much as Tucker Talbot."

Dash huffed a laugh. "Join the club."

"Scarlett Marks might be the only chance I have at putting him away for good," she said. "All I need is to get inside that clubhouse. I need a reason. And if the chief of police suspects that the Arrowhead Warriors have kidnapped an innocent woman from his community, then I have a reason. Give me five minutes to explain."

Easy choice. We were short on men and if the FBI wanted to bust into that clubhouse and rescue Scarlett, I sure as fuck wasn't going to stand in the way.

"Okay, Maria." I walked to the chair across from her. "I'm listening."

CHAPTER TWENTY-ONE

SCARLETT

I jolted awake, my head swimming as I looked around the dark room. It took me a moment to realize where I was, the dream I'd been having still fresh in my mind. *Luke. His bed. The scratch of his stubble against my shoulder. His arms banded around me.*

No matter how hard I squeezed my eyes shut, the dream faded, drifting away until I had no choice but to face reality.

I was stuck.

The Warriors would kill me in this cement room. Once the pounding music stopped. Once the people cleared out of the clubhouse. Once Tucker decided it was time.

The end was coming.

A lock of hair brushed the skin on my forearm and Cassandra shifted. Sometime after I'd passed out, she'd slid closer and fallen asleep herself. Her head rested on my shoulder and her coppery locks, something that even the darkness couldn't dull, brushed against my neck.

I'd deal with whatever the Warriors took from me, whatever punishment they delivered before ending my life.

But this girl . . . she was innocent.

So I rested my cheek on her head, hoping to give her the little bit of comfort I could. Before we both met our inevitable end.

My head throbbed but the ache was manageable now. My vision was clear and my mind alert.

The music from earlier boomed above and around us. If there'd been a party upstairs earlier, it had turned into a rave. Bodies were no doubt writhing against each other. Couples would be openly fucking in the party room. Men would be snorting lines of coke or smoking their drug of choice for tonight. Women—scantily dressed, drunk or high out of their minds—would be fawning over any male in a Warrior cut.

Why would Tucker wait? The perfect opportunity to murder two women was when everyone else was bombed.

Maybe he wouldn't kill us tonight. Maybe he was worried about the video backup I had saved. Or maybe he wasn't concerned about that video in the slightest and had a worse torture in mind than a quick bullet between the eyes.

Maybe Cassandra and I would end up in a trafficking ring. They'd get us addicted to drugs. They'd starve us to skin and bones. And someone would pay to own my body.

I chose death. If those were my options, I chose death.

Find me, Luke.

Save me.

Save her.

As if she'd known my thoughts were on her, Cassandra jerked and sat straight, blinking furiously. When she realized this wasn't a nightmare, her face paled. Her chin quivered. She'd been strong for me earlier, but now she was on the brink.

Now it was time for me to be strong for her.

"Hey," I said, my voice low and soothing.

"Hi." She scooted away and her gaze darted to my shoulder where she'd been sleeping. "Sorry."

"It's okay."

A loud cry permeated the music, making her flinch.

"They're having a party," I said. "I lived here for a while. With an ex-boyfriend. Saturdays are always crazy."

"Not mine," she whispered, drawing her knees to her chest. "I usually spend them working."

"What are you studying?"

"History."

History. That fit. Cassandra was young but there was wisdom in her eyes, and the subject suited her. She belonged in a library, surrounded by dusty books and tattered parchments.

"What do you want to do?"

"Earn my PhD. Write books. Teach. I like school."

"I always liked school too." I gave her a sad smile. "I only went to community college, but I would have kept going." If my father hadn't insisted I go to work for his company after earning my associate's.

"If we get out of here, I want to go to school," I said. We wouldn't get out of here, but the hope swelled regardless. "Maybe study interior design. I want to learn how to shoot a gun. I want to get pregnant on a rainy day. I want a nice home and to spend Sundays chasing my kids around the yard. I want to end each day with a smile."

Some of those had been Luke's dreams. Mine too. Because making his dreams come true *was* my dream.

"If we get out of here, I'm crawling under a rock and never getting out," Cassandra muttered.

I smiled and shifted so I could face her. "I'm sorry I got you into this, Cassandra."

"You didn't put me in that van."

"Yes, I did."

She shook her head. "My friends call me Cass."

"Cass." That was a pretty nickname. Simple but elegant. It fit her too. "Do you—"

The door burst open. Cassandra and I both gasped, our bodies lurching as we faced the couple stumbling inside.

Their mouths were fused and the man had his hands on her face as he shuffled them both into the room. He wore the Warrior vest over a stained white T-shirt. His hair was a bright blond, even whiter than Presley's. The strands curled around his ears and neck.

Ghost.

They called him Ghost because of that hair, though his skin had a natural tan. He'd played poker with Jeremiah on occasion and had come into our room upstairs two or three times. Ghost always had a cigarette dangling from his lower lip. He was the guy who loved fucking in public.

Had they come in here because we'd be a captive audience? Literally? Or had he, for once, decided to seek some privacy for his affairs?

The pair crossed the small room and collided with the cinderblock wall. The woman gasped as her back slammed into the hard surface. The door behind them was still open. Tucker and his men hadn't locked us in here. They hadn't needed to. With our arms bound and the party in full swing, we wouldn't have been able to make an escape.

The woman latched on to Ghost's mouth, moaned and slid her hand into his jeans. She was wearing a miniskirt that dangled an inch above the curve where her thighs met her ass. When she lifted a leg, there was nothing beneath that skirt.

Eww.

Ghost tugged at the strings holding a scrap of leather to her chest. The top fell loose and slapped heavy on the floor.

Cassandra squeaked.

The noise finally drew Ghost's attention. He blinked and squinted, trying to make sense of us against the wall. I guess he hadn't come in here for the audience after all.

"I know you," he slurred.

The woman only spared us a brief glance before curling her lip in our direction, then latching her mouth to Ghost's neck. Her hand in his jeans, stroking him, never slowed.

"Goldilocks." He snapped his fingers. "Right?"

I nodded.

"Heard you stole club money."

"No, I didn't. That was all Jeremiah." Why I felt the need to defend myself was a mystery. Maybe because I'd gone so long *not* defending myself. Now it seemed important. To end my days fighting.

"Ghost," the woman purred, dragging her bare thigh up and down his jeans. She wanted his full attention.

He grunted something, then gave her exactly what she wanted, sealing his lips over hers and thrusting his hips into her grip.

My stomach rolled. They were definitely going to have sex. It wouldn't be my first time as a witness, but judging by Cass's wide eyes and flapping jaw, she was about to get her first sour taste of live porn.

Ironically, not that long ago, I'd been innocent just like her. The first Warrior party had been an education. Except

I'd chosen to be there. This lesson was being forced on Cassandra, and I didn't want it to be her last memory.

"Hey." I shifted sideways, my movements stiff and slow, but when I was facing her, I nudged her foot with my own. "Don't look at them."

She blinked but didn't tear her eyes away.

"Cass."

Another blink, but this time she turned. "I don't want to die here."

"I know."

The woman Ghost had pinned to the wall unzipped her skirt, and the sound of the metal teeth unfastening filled the room. Minutes ago, it had been hard to hear anything over the noise of the music, but every gasp and moan and grunt from those two seemed to echo in this square space.

Cassandra's attention swung back to them just as Ghost unclasped his belt and sprang free. His jeans dropped to midthigh and the phone he'd had in his back pocket clattered to the cement floor.

I cringed as he drove into the woman, her fake scream an ice pick in my ears.

"Don't look at them," I whispered, nudging Cass's foot again.

Cassandra nodded and turned, mirroring my position.

The sounds of flesh smacking flesh, Ghost's grunts and the woman's cries were impossible to ignore. But Cass and I held each other's gaze and did our best to pretend it was just us in this room and the couple fucking in the corner weren't there.

"What's the feather for?" Cassandra asked, nodding to my hair.

"Oh." I'd forgotten it was in my hair. It hung tight to the

band that I'd used to secure it. "It's silly. But I thought it would help me be brave today."

"Brave for what?"

"To do the right thing."

It was long overdue.

Going to the police with that video was something I should have done months ago, but I wouldn't regret my time with Luke. Never. He'd turned the last days of my life into the happiest I'd ever known.

"What's your happiest memory?" I asked Cass. If in these last minutes or hours all we had were our memories, then we'd relive the best.

She leaned her head against the wall, a tear dripping down her cheek. "Traveling with my parents. We went on a trip to Redwood National Park. My mom had this idea to visit all of the national parks and that was the one she wanted to see first. We drove their station wagon and made a three-week trip out of it. That was before there was GPS, and my dad taught me how to use a compass and read a map. We walked beneath the trees and I have this picture of my mom hugging one of them. She looked like a toy compared to that tree, they are so big."

I envied the affection on her face. Cass had good parents, and they'd be devastated by this. I doubted my parents would ever learn how I'd died. "How old were you?"

"Ten. Every summer after that, we took another trip. They love to go camping and explore, but they always save the national park trips for me. I haven't been able to go lately with school." A shimmer of regret crossed her face. "Dad says I work too hard."

Movement at our sides caught our attention. Both of us looked over just in time to see Ghost pull out of the woman, take her by the hips and spin her around. Then he spit in his hand, rubbed it on his shaft and took the woman's ass cheeks in his hand, splitting them apart.

There was nothing fake or erotic about the scream that tore through the room as he penetrated her back entry. But she let him take her. She met my gaze as her fingernails dug into the cement wall.

Cass turned away, shaking her head as the tears fell in a steady stream down her smooth cheeks.

More questions. We needed more memories.

"What's your favorite part about school?" I asked.

"The true stories," she whispered, closing her eyes. "That's why I chose history. Because true stories are always the most powerful."

"Ghost, it's too much," the woman murmured.

He didn't stop.

If these walls could weep, we'd drown.

Had Tucker sent Ghost in here? Was this one of his tactics to terrify us? Because it was working.

I swallowed hard, scrambling for another question. Anything to keep the conversation going and block out what was happening in this room. "You said you wanted to write books. What kind of books?"

"Historical fiction. Or nonfiction. Maybe. I don't know." She shook her head violently. "I can't think."

"It's okay."

"No, it's not okay." Her chest shook as a sob broke free. "I don't want to die here."

But she would die here. We both would. "Me neither."

Cass's eyes lifted from her knees and she looked at me. Then a sad smile formed on her pretty face. "At least we won't be alone."

"We'll stay together."

More music. More grunts from Ghost. The pounding in my head was growing louder.

"It's your turn," she said. "What's your happiest memory?"

"Falling in love with Luke." I leaned my head against the wall again, picturing his handsome face in my mind.

"I've never been in love. What's it like?"

I opened my mouth to answer, to tell her about the gentle fall and the man who owned my heart, when the wall beside my cheek vibrated. A loud crack filled the room, replacing the noise from the music. On instinct, I tried to bring my hands to my ears to muffle the sound, but the tie at my wrists bit into my skin.

Then the entire room shook. The dim lightbulb swung on its cord, then *poof*, it went out.

Darkness.

"What the fuck?" Ghost muttered. His boots shuffled on the floor, then came the sound of something skidding our way. The phone. He'd kicked the phone.

The light was out. They'd left the door open.

I used every ounce of strength I had left to get to my knees. Then I leaned in, using my nose to feel for Cass's ear, bending in close.

There was no time to think or plan or contemplate. This was our only chance.

"Get up," I whispered. "Stay close. And run."

CHAPTER TWENTY-TWO

SCARLETT

I fumbled to my feet, unsteady. The floor swayed beneath me but I managed to find my balance as the heat from Cass's body pressed close. Stretching my arms as far as they would go behind my back, I felt through the air until my fingertips brushed against the hem of her shirt. I curled it into my fists, then tugged, walking us both toward the door.

My footsteps were slow but silent. Cass stayed with me, hovering close.

With the room cloaked in black, it was impossible to tell where we were headed. My shoulder brushed against a wall. Maybe it was the same wall where we'd been. Maybe we were moving closer to Ghost. But I kept going, my toes feeling ahead with each step before I planted the heel of my foot.

"Where's my fucking phone?" Ghost barked. The jingle of his belt buckle mixed with the commotion above us.

It was then that I felt it. I bent, dropping to my knees, and nearly collapsed onto my shoulder as I stretched. The muscles in my shoulders ached. The twist in my ribs pinched. But somehow, I managed to find Ghost's phone with my fingertips and draw it into my palms.

The music was gone but chaos had erupted above. Men were shouting. Women screamed. Then the first gunshot rang out. My entire body flinched as the sound of the blast lingered. But not for long. Soon it was replaced by another. And another.

It was war.

The noise covered everything, and I surged to my feet, moving forward, not trying to stay quiet. It probably wasn't safe outside this room, but it definitely wasn't safe inside.

Pop. Pop. Pop. The gunshots came in rapid succession until another deafening boom sounded, covering the shrill of my scream. The explosion was like the one that had shaken the walls and knocked out the power.

Cass and I both went down, crouching beside each other. I found her shirt again, gripping it tight.

"Go," I whispered, forcing myself to stand. "We have to go."

Whatever was happening upstairs sounded terrifying, but it would be better to die attempting an escape than waiting for our executioner to find us in that room.

A light flashed beside us, illuminating the room. We had Ghost's phone, but somewhere in her scrap of clothing, maybe a pocket in that miniskirt, the woman had stashed her own. She held it out, barely lighting the room. Ghost's eyes darted to the wall where we'd been huddled and when he found us missing, his eyes darted our way.

I was just one step away from the doorway. My heart leapt. We'd been going in the right direction. I bolted forward, taking Cass with me as I screamed, "Go!"

We lunged, making it out the door just as Ghost yelled,

"Fuck!"

I let go of Cass's shirt, bumping her in front of me with my shoulder as I dropped Ghost's phone to pull at the door's handle.

Hurry. My fingers slipped on the metal but I stretched, grabbing it again with all my might. Then I took a long step forward into the hallway, yanking the steel door with me and slamming it closed.

Ghost's fists beat on it from the inside. He went for the handle and I held it tight.

"Lock it." I pulled hard, holding the handle with the last shreds of my strength and leaning forward. I didn't weigh much but if I could just hold it for a minute. *Hold it. Hold tight.*

Ghost twisted at the knob, bellowing, "Let me the fuck out of here!"

The handle's square edges dug into my clammy palms but I didn't let go.

Cass shuffled in beside me, staring over her shoulder as her fingers fumbled with the sliding lock. She had to stand on her toes, but she found it and pushed. "Almost . . ."

The bolt slid into place.

I sagged. "Good job."

"Which way?" she whispered.

The hallway was as black as the room had been. I let go of the door's handle, holding my breath as Ghost continued to pound on the other side and rattle the lock. But it held. Hopefully it would keep holding for as long as it took us to get out of this basement.

One long breath was all I allowed myself before I dropped to the floor, again patting around in the darkness for the phone. I found it quickly, right beside my foot, and stood.

"Here. Can you take this?" I turned and stretched for her fingers, the two of us fumbling to make the handoff.

"Got it." She kept the phone tight and pushed the side button, turning on the lock screen.

The faint glow was just enough to get my bearings. We were in the basement, no surprise, but we hadn't been kept in the same room where Ken Raymond had been killed. That was two down from the stairs. Our room was three.

"Come on." I walked past her, hugging the wall as I moved. The phone's light went out and Cass continued to wake it up as we slowly crept toward the staircase.

While we'd been wrestling with the door, the gunfire had stopped. Dull footsteps and muted voices drifted over our heads but I couldn't make out any of the words. Ghost continued to pound and rage behind the door.

Who had fired those gunshots? What would we find upstairs? I gulped. I guess we'd find out. Because this basement was not an option.

The stairs drew closer. The door at the top opened to a hallway. We'd have to pass the individual rooms on our way out. Not all of the members lived here. Most of the senior members had their own homes. The brothers like Jeremiah, too cheap to get an apartment or those who wanted to be close for the parties, stayed here.

The rooms had windows. Small ones, but we could probably shimmy out. There'd be a drop to the ground, maybe eight feet, but I couldn't think of another option.

Beyond the rooms was the clubhouse common area. Whatever fight had broken out had to have taken place there and it would be crawling with people. Maybe littered with dead bodies too.

I gritted my teeth, taking the final few steps to the stairs.

"When we get up there, follow me," I whispered.

"Okay."

My legs trembled as I took the first step. I swayed, sucking in a deep breath. They were concrete steps, much like the rest of the clubhouse. Cold. Sterile. Harsh. A tumble from the top would mean another concussion or possibly a broken back.

"Be careful." I glanced over my shoulder. Cass's face was barely lit from the light of the phone.

She nodded.

I turned, ready to get the hell out of here, when the steel door above us flew open. My heart jumped into my throat and I backed up, pushing Cass backward with my bound hands.

She smothered the light of the phone, but not soon enough. The looming figure above us, dressed in black, raised an arm. Then the beam of a flashlight blinded me, forcing me to look away.

"Scarlett."

Scarlett. Even with the helmet covering his face, I knew that voice.

"Luke!" A sob broke free and the strength I'd had just a second ago vanished. My knees gave way, cracking against the floor as I fell.

He'd found me. He'd found us.

Luke's footsteps pounded down the stairs as he rushed for us. The flashlight clattered to the floor beside Cass just as the lights above us flipped on. The music that had been blaring before the power had been cut pounded as loud as ever.

Then it was gone.

And there he was, ripping the helmet off his face and the

gloves from his hands before taking my face in his palms, tipping my face to his.

"You came." I collapsed forward, my body shaking uncontrollably.

"Are you okay?" His hand went to the blood at my hair. "Where are you hurt?"

I choked down another sob and nodded, sucking in a deep breath. "I'm okay."

Beside me, Cass whimpered.

Luke dug in his pocket, searching. He came out with a pocketknife, flipping it open and severing our bonds.

I rolled my wrists, moving my arms as Cass did the same. "How?"

"Shh." He shook his head. "We'll talk later."

Luke reached for my legs to carry me, but I pushed on his shoulder and shook my head.

"Cass. Help Cass." My voice cracked. "Get her out of here."

Two more men came barreling down the stairs. They were dressed like Luke, covered head to toe in black. Cargo pants. A long-sleeved shirt. A thick vest. The same helmet he'd torn off.

It was tactical gear. One of the men's vests was emblazoned with three stark white letters.

FBI.

Luke had come here with the FBI.

A surge of relief raced through my body, the adrenaline boost giving me a second wind.

One of the men stood over Luke's shoulder.

"Help her," Luke ordered, jerking his chin at Cass.

The man took Cass's elbow, helping her to her feet. When she swayed, he picked her up in a cradle hold and carried her up the stairs. She looked at me over his shoulder, her eyes wide, her face pale.

I mustered a small smile before the agent whisked her out the door.

Luke swung me up and into his arms. "Is anyone else down here?"

Ghost's pounding answered that question.

The other agent brought a hand to the little black radio on his shoulder. "Johnson, come to the basement."

A voice, Johnson presumably, answered back instantly. "On my way, sir."

Luke gave the man a nod, then took the stairs without delay. The stench of stale alcohol and cigarettes and sweat filled my nose when we reached the hallway. Luke took a step to the right, toward the rooms and front entrance.

And there it was. Jeremiah's door. It was just a place behind a closed door but as we neared the room—third on the left from the mouth of the hallway—I knew I couldn't do this.

"Stop." I tapped on Luke's shoulder.

"What?" He slowed but didn't stop.

"Stop. Can you put me down? Please?" I met his eyes, so full of worry and fear it broke my heart. "I need to walk out of here on my own two feet."

I needed to walk past that door.

I needed to be the one to put this behind me, one step at a time.

Luke blew out a sigh. Then he pressed a kiss to my forehead, his eyes drifting closed. "Fuck, but you scared me."

I leaned into his touch. "I'm sorry."

"This is on Tucker. Not you."

"I'm still sorry," I whispered.

"Do what you need to do." He set me on my feet, then took my hand. "I'm here."

I leaned into his side, taking a moment to gather myself. Then I walked, not sparing a glance at the room that had once been Jeremiah's. I marched past two federal agents, both escorting men wearing Warrior vests and handcuffs toward the exit.

And I had my chin held high when I reached the massive open area where the Warriors held their parties. Beer and liquor spills puddled around the room. Plumes of smoke clouded the room, swirling around the too-bright florescent lights.

Spots of blood darkened the floor.

There were people everywhere. Federal agents in the same attire as Luke moved in and out of the double front doors. One agent had a Warrior pushed face-first onto the green felt of the pool table, working to get the cuffs around his wrists as the Warrior spewed a string of insults and threats.

For the number of people, it was surprisingly quiet in the room. Besides the one Warrior on the pool table, the others were silent, their jaws locked and mouths shut.

The flash of red and white and blue lights from beyond the door flickered into the room. Two EMTs rushed inside with a stretcher, hurrying to a man on the floor in the corner of the room. It was a Warrior, lying face down. His eyes were open, staring blankly at the boots of the agent crouched beside him.

Was he dead? I searched the walls, spotting a bullet hole to my left. Beyond that, the Arrowhead Warrior patch had been stitched onto a black flag and another bullet had ripped through its *A*.

The entire clubhouse had been raided. For every Warrior or party member there seemed to be two agents. More were probably outside with the men and women they'd already hauled out.

"Excuse me."

I jumped at the voice behind me and huddled into Luke's side as an agent skirted past. Behind him, two female agents escorted two drunk women, both in slinky dresses and teetering on their stiletto heels, out of a room.

Once they passed, Luke tugged on my hand. "Come on."

I nodded, taking a step, but froze when I met a dark gaze before me.

Tucker Talbot stood next to a female agent by the bar. His hands were secured behind his back. Over his shoulder, some of the liquor bottles had shattered, dripping amber and marigold onto the shelves.

Unlike the others, the agent at his side wasn't in tactical gear. She was wearing a black suit jacket cinched to her fit frame by a bullet-proof vest. Her pressed slacks draped to sensible heels. She was speaking to Tucker, reading him his rights, but his eyes were locked on me.

My heart thudded too hard, but I kept my chin high. I held his gaze and didn't falter.

Tucker Talbot would never make me cower again.

I'd testify against him. I'd give the FBI the video of him committing murder.

I'd live to see him go to prison.

"He crushed my phone," I whispered to Luke.

"We've got the backup," he said, then tugged on my hand again. Luke was done with this place.

So was I.

I held Tucker's gaze until he was in my periphery, then I

put him behind me, a problem for another day, and gripped Luke's hand tighter.

The minute we stepped outside, the cool evening air surrounded me, filling my lungs and chasing away the smell.

I breathed. For the first time in what felt like years, I breathed.

This wasn't over. There would be repercussions from this night, but for now, I was safe.

The parking lot was even more chaotic than I'd expected. The noise I'd missed in the main room seemed to have been waiting outdoors. Women cried. Men cursed. A couple were fighting a futile battle against being shoved into the back of a police car.

"Where's Cassandra?" I asked Luke.

He lifted his free hand, pointing to his truck parked at the very edge of the lot. She stood, shivering, with Ghost's phone in her grip and a wool blanket draped over her shoulders. The agent who'd carried her from the basement stood stoically by her side.

"She's okay. Thank God." I aimed my feet in her direction. Every step felt lighter. Safer. I floated. Until I realized I wasn't floating. I was falling.

"Scarlett." Luke caught me before I hit the ground.

Above me, the stars sparkled, swirling in the midnight sky. "Pretty."

"Scarlett. Stay with me." Luke shook me, his voice laced with fear. "Stay with me, beautiful. I need to tell you that I love you."

He loves me. I only had energy for a faint smile.

Then for the second or third time in a day—I'd lost track —the world went black.

CHAPTER TWENTY-THREE

LUKE

"Coffee?" Maria asked, holding out a paper cup filled to the brim with black, steaming liquid.

"Thanks." The first sip scalded my tongue, but I took another anyway. Caffeine was about the only thing keeping me standing at the moment.

Now that my heartrate was back to normal and the fear that had driven me through the night nearly gone, I was close to crashing. I would later, when I was home. When Scarlett was home.

I glanced over my shoulder into the hospital room where she was sleeping. The faint rays of dawn crept through the window. The light cast dancing beams on the waxed floor.

Scarlett's hair was damp and twisted into a knot on the white pillow. I'd insisted they wash the blood out after stitching the cut at her crown. The feather she'd had tied behind her ear was on the bedside table, next to my keys and wallet.

"How is she?" Maria asked.

"She's got a concussion. She's exhausted. But she'll be

fine. The doctor wants to keep her here for a few more hours, just to be safe."

When she'd passed out in my arms outside the Warrior clubhouse, I'd panicked. There'd been five ambulances in the lot, all having arrived after the gunfire had ceased. But instead of calling for the EMTs, I'd hauled Scarlett into my arms and driven her to the emergency room in Ashton myself.

The doctors had checked her from head to toe, but other than the wound to her head, she was fine. The Warriors hadn't touched her from what I could tell. She was tired. She'd been terrorized. But she'd recover, which was more than I could say for others after the events of last night.

Five Warriors had been shot and killed in the clubhouse raid. Two agents had been shot, though neither had been fatally wounded. The Warriors not being treated for their wounds at this very hospital were all in custody.

Maria hadn't fucked around.

After she'd sat down in my living room yesterday, I'd listened to her plan. In truth, it was a lot like the one I'd had in my head. Except instead of Dash, Emmett, Leo and me forcing our way into the Warrior stronghold, probably dying along the way, she offered up the power of the federal government.

She already had a large team here. Maybe it was because Ken Raymond had been killed. Maybe they'd already been preparing for a move on the club. I didn't ask.

My only request was to come along.

Maria had agreed as long as Dash, Emmett and Leo stayed behind. They protested, of course. They threatened to ride to Ashton anyway. Then Maria hit them with the logic they couldn't refute.

This was a federal raid.

If the Tin Gypsies came to Ashton, they would paint targets on their backs. Better to let the FBI take the blame and save themselves any repercussions.

So the guys had stayed behind while I'd driven to Ashton.

Fifty FBI agents. Twenty from the DEA. And me.

"What's next?" I asked, stepping back and leaning against the wall.

Maria had shown up at the hospital ten minutes ago, but before we'd talked, she'd insisted on getting coffee first.

She took a similar stance to mine on the opposite wall. "Next, we put them away."

"How are you going to do that?"

"Hopefully with video evidence."

My stomach dropped. "Scarlett's?"

"Maybe. But if I can get enough without it, I'll move ahead. Keep her out of it as much as I can. No promises, but I'll try."

"Appreciated." The less Scarlett was involved, the better.

"The prosecutors might ask to depose her about her abduction, but kidnapping is the least offensive charge on the docket. We're going to focus on the video surveillance we found at Tucker Talbot's home." She raised her coffee cup. "Good tip."

In addition to raiding the clubhouse, the judge had granted Maria a warrant to search for Scarlett at five personal residences—Tucker's and his senior leaders'.

Maria had ridden with me to Ashton yesterday afternoon. We hadn't talked much. She'd been busy coordinating her team, already in Ashton, from the road. But when she'd told me about the warrant, I'd suggested she search for video evidence.

Emmett had been right after all. Tucker had been recording the activities in the clubhouse to use against his men should they get out of line.

The son of a bitch would sink himself. Good.

"How's Birdy?" I asked.

"Last I heard, she was still in surgery."

"Think she'll make it?"

A wave of sadness crossed Maria's face. "It doesn't sound good."

"Sorry."

She nodded. "Part of the job. Doesn't get easier."

"No, it doesn't." I shook my head. "Tell me this. Did they come to my neighborhood for Birdy? Or Scarlett?"

"We're not sure. Maybe they knew Scarlett was next door and they came to shut Birdy down before anyone could stop them. Maybe they'd just figured out where Birdy was. She'd been undercover with Ken from the beginning. As soon as Ken was killed, we got her out of Ashton. I wanted to send her back to our field office in LA, but she refused to be reassigned."

"Can you tell me about Ken? Was that even his name?"

Maria shook her head. "I can't tell you much. He worked for years to get in with the Warriors. Finally did about ten months ago. Ken was going to smuggle them guns and ammunition. Black market stuff. I don't know what went wrong. One day, he reported things were good. Tucker and a couple others had come into the range to do some shooting. The next day, he was gone."

"Did he have family?"

"Just Birdy," she said.

"The two of them were together?"

"Partners in work and partners in life for over twenty years."

"Damn." I could imagine how Birdy felt, losing the person who owned her heart. She'd wanted to keep fighting, to punish the ones who'd killed her partner. And now she was fighting for her life.

Birdy had disappeared to the safety of my neighborhood, much like Scarlett, but the Warriors had still found her.

"Keep me posted."

Maria nodded. "Will do."

Scarlett showing up at Birdy's door had probably been lucky timing. Or maybe she could have stayed locked in my house and I still would have come home to find her gone. Regardless, when the Warriors had shot Birdy, then taken Scarlett and Cass, they'd given the FBI enough to go to a judge and request those warrants.

"What's the danger here?" I asked. "To Scarlett. Will they come after her?"

"Honestly, I don't know," she said. "Not a single Warrior wasn't arrested. Even the ones not at the party were taken into custody. But they've got allies. Tucker's lawyer is already fighting to get the video evidence dismissed."

"Will he get out?"

"Doubtful. I've got a team poring over the video footage. There's a lot, so I don't know exactly what it shows, but fingers crossed, it's enough."

That relieved some of my fears. Some. "Should Scarlett be in witness protection?"

Because if Scarlett was headed in to witness protection, then I'd be going along with her.

"I don't know if Tucker Talbot has any plays left," Maria said. "But—"

"No." Scarlett's faint voice drifted from her room.

I shoved off the wall, spinning for the door to find her sitting up in the bed, her blue eyes clear and bright.

She had the feather in her hand and was slowly dragging the pad of her index finger along the vane.

"You're awake." I crossed the room and dropped a kiss to her forehead, then pulled up the chair I'd been sitting in all night to the bed, putting my coffee aside.

Scarlett took my hand in hers, holding it on her lap, then looked past me to where Maria stood in the center of the room. "I'm not giving up my life after I fought so hard to take it back. I'm not going into witness protection."

"You could be in danger," Maria warned.

"Tucker doesn't stand to gain anything but revenge by killing me. You have other evidence, right? I'm just a piece?"

Maria nodded. "That's right. And even if you testified, it would be one of many nails in his coffin. But I've been watching Tucker Talbot for years. He's a vengeful man."

"If I disappear, he wins." Scarlett looked to me. "I won't let him win. I'll take my chances."

"Scar—"

"No, Luke. No more hiding. If Tucker decides to come after me, I'll fight. I'll keep fighting." She let go of my hand and brought hers to my face. Her thumbs stroked across my cheeks. "This is worth fighting for. Us."

I closed my eyes, giving one of her palms the weight of my head. "If he does come after you, he'll have to get through me first."

"And me." A spirited voice preceded its owner. Presley

breezed into the room. "Get out of the way, Rosen, so I can hug my sister."

I chuckled and stood. "Yes, ma'am."

Presley flew into Scarlett's waiting arms, the sisters holding each other tight.

Shaw was close behind his wife, carrying a tote bag with what looked like fresh clothes and shoes. "Hey."

"Hi." I held out my hand to shake his.

When Shaw and I had first met, he'd had this movie-star shine, a natural charisma that drew people in. It was still there, but since he'd moved to Clifton Forge permanently, I didn't see the man on-screen when I saw his face. I just saw a friend.

We hadn't hung out since Scarlett had moved to my house. And as Presley and Scarlett continued their hug, I knew that was about to change. Those two would be inseparable.

Maybe Shaw and I would have a chance to go fishing again. He was a good guy to have on the river. Didn't hook me in the eye. Didn't talk much either.

Though given how unlikely I was to let Scarlett out of my sight, the ladies would be coming too. We wouldn't catch a damn thing. Those two would chat the entire time.

I couldn't wait.

Shaw set down the tote bag and stood at my side, crossing his arms over his chest as he leaned in and lowered his voice. "Later, not today because that would be cruel, I'm going to remind you of the night you refused to let me get Presley. And later, because again, it would be cruel to say today, I'm going to call you a hypocrite and laugh in your face."

"I appreciate you saving that for later."

Shaw chuckled.

The night Jeremiah had held Scarlett and Presley hostage, I hadn't understood why Shaw insisted on entering that house. I did now. When the love of your life and your future was in danger, you didn't stand on the sidelines and hope for the best.

You pulled out all the stops to save her life.

A stream of people came into the room. Dash and Bryce led the way with Emmett and Leo close behind.

Bryce had a smile on her pretty face as she let go of Dash's hand and went to the bed and sat beside Scarlett. "I'm Bryce, Dash's wife." She lifted a bouquet of sunflowers. "These are for you."

"Oh. Thanks." Scarlett took the bundle, then blinked at the tall figures all looming at the foot of her bed.

"I'll take those." Presley grabbed the flowers and set them on the end table, then took up the free space at Scarlett's side.

"Genevieve and Isaiah couldn't come. They're babysitting our boys," Bryce said. "But they're excited to meet you when we get home. Genevieve is already baking cookies."

"They're the ones who live down the street," I reminded her.

"Ah." She nodded, then a look of dread crossed her face. "Cass. Where is she?"

"Home," Maria answered, stepping in between Leo and Emmett. "We took her home."

Scarlett relaxed. "Good. Then we'll see her when we get there."

"Sorry, you misunderstand." Maria shook her head. "She wanted to go home to Missoula. Where she lives. One of our agents drove her there last night."

"Is she okay?"

"She's tough," Maria said. "Like someone else I know."

Tough as nails, my Scarlett. She was as tough as they came.

"I've got to get going." Maria nodded to Scarlett, then to me. "Take care, Luke."

"I'll miss your daily visits."

She winked. "Liar."

"Stay in touch."

With a wave, she walked out of the hospital room, her heels clicking down the hall as she disappeared.

"Who else has the feeling that we haven't seen the last of the FBI?" Dash asked under his breath.

"Me," Emmett and Leo muttered in unison.

Me.

"One would think that when a motorcycle club disbands, the trouble stops." Bryce shook her head.

"You guys weren't this much trouble when you were a club," Presley muttered.

"We're the gift that keeps on giving," Leo teased.

The entire room erupted in laughter.

None of us blamed Dash or Emmett or Leo. They were as sick of looking over their shoulders as the rest of us.

I only wished we could walk out of this room and never look back.

But until time passed, until we could guarantee everyone was safe from the Warriors, we'd be vigilant. The Warriors might be broken, but they weren't gone yet. Not all of them would face long-term prison sentences. And when they got out . . .

That worry was for another day.

"Knock, kno—oh." Scarlett's doctor's eyes widened as

she took in the crowd that had gathered in the room. "Visiting hours haven't started yet."

The doc was met with blank stares.

"I'd really like to go home," Scarlett said. "I promise to take them with me."

"Then let's get you checked out and discharged." The doctor pointed down the hallway. "The waiting room is that way."

The men grumbled but trudged into the hallway. The women lingered and when it was clear that Presley wasn't leaving Scarlett's side, Bryce decided to stay too. Both of them stood by the window while I hovered over the doctor's shoulder as she checked Scarlett out.

"All clear." She squeezed Scarlett's foot and looped her stethoscope around her neck. "I'll have the nurse come in with discharge papers. Then you're free to go."

Two hours later, Scarlett showered and dressed in the sweats that Presley had brought along, then we were in my truck.

I'd hoped to have the three-hour trip home alone but Presley wasn't having it. "I missed my sister," she declared, climbing into the sterile and stiff backseat of my rig.

She scrunched up her nose but otherwise didn't complain about the uncomfortable ride. She just leaned forward nearly the entire way and talked to Scarlett.

Presley described the house she and Shaw were building. She told stories about the garage and life in Clifton Forge. I'd thought she was just making idle chatter, but as I pulled off the highway, it dawned on me.

This was Presley's pitch.

She wanted Scarlett to stay in Montana.

The minute we turned down my street, Scarlett sat

straighter. She looked to me and smiled. There were circles under her eyes again and she'd yawned a dozen times on the drive here. What she needed was a long night's rest, something I'd ensure she got.

After we ironed a few things out.

"It feels nice not to hide," she said as I pulled into the driveway. Before I could help her out, she popped open her door, then opened Presley's.

Without waiting for her sister to climb out, Scarlett walked out of the garage and into the sunlight. She tipped her face to the sky, her hair now mostly dry and dangling down her back in waves.

I hurried to join her as Shaw's Escalade parked on the street. In Ashton, Dash and Bryce had been in their truck, Emmett and Leo on their bikes. Now that we were home, I looked down the street to see the Slaters parked at Genevieve and Isaiah's house to pick up their boys. There was no sign of Emmett and Leo. They'd probably gone to The Betsy for a much-needed beer, even if it was before noon.

"Do you think she's okay?" Scarlett asked as I put my arm around her shoulders, pulling me into her side. Her gaze was aimed across the street where Cassandra's car was still parked in the driveway.

"We'll find out from her parents as soon as they get home." I hoped they'd been camping in a place with cell service.

Two houses down, one of the neighbors was mowing the lawn. When he spotted me, he raised a hand to wave.

I waved back.

So did Scarlett.

"You can always stay at our place if you're sick of this guy," Presley said as she joined us in the driveway.

Scarlett lifted her chin to meet my gaze. "Maybe he's sick of me."

"Never." I dropped a kiss to her lips. It was short. Too short. But we had time.

Presley might be lobbying for Scarlett to stay in Clifton Forge. I was simply going to insist upon it.

I doubted I'd be met with much resistance.

"It looks like you're in good hands." Presley pulled Scarlett out of my arms for another hug.

"The best."

"I'll come by tomorrow."

"Okay." Scarlett and I stood outside until Presley and Shaw were out of sight. Then she turned to the house, studying the exterior.

She didn't seem to be in a rush to go inside, so I put my arm around her again and pulled her close.

"I want to go camping on the river again."

"We can leave tomorrow." Nothing would make me happier than escaping the world for a week. Or two. We'd go somewhere new and I'd introduce her to my favorite places around Montana. Maria might have some qualms about us ditching town, but she had enough work to do with paperwork and lawyers, any questions she had for us could wait. "Maybe we can pick a place close to Missoula. Stop by and see Cass. And I can introduce you to my dad."

"I'd like that." A smile tugged at her mouth. "But we have to do a few things first."

"Okay. Let's hear it."

"First, I want to open all the shades in the house, and

unless we're going at it on the living room couch, I don't want them closed ever again."

I chuckled and kissed the top of her hair. "Done deal."

"I want to turn the dining room into a library where I can read and drink my coffee every morning."

"Just show me where you want me to build the bookshelves."

"I want to take that bush out there and move it there." She pointed to the shrub closest to the front door, then to the corner of the house. "Maybe add a couple of flowerpots to frame the front stoop."

"Better flow, right?"

"Now you're catching on." She wound her arms around my waist, holding tight. "I love you."

"I love you too." It was a rush to hear those words. To say them aloud. I hoped in the next fifty years that thrill would never fade. "Any other demands?"

Scarlett smiled. "Just one more."

CHAPTER TWENTY-FOUR

SCARLETT

"Here you go, baby." I set the plate of raw burgers beside the grill and stood on my tiptoes to kiss Luke's cheek.

He bent, turning in time to get my lips instead. "Thanks, beautiful."

"What else do you need?"

"Nothing." He opened the barbecue's lid and began putting on the patties, the meat sizzling as it hit the hot grate. "We'll be ready soon."

"Cass isn't here yet." I frowned. "Maybe she changed her mind."

"She'll come."

"I hope so."

I hadn't seen Cassandra since that night at the Warrior clubhouse. She hadn't returned to Clifton Forge since the kidnapping. Her parents had gone to visit her and check in. They'd returned her car. And when Luke and I had spoken to them, they'd given me Cass's number. But besides a handful of text messages, she'd been avoiding me. Even when we'd gone to Missoula and tried to arrange a visit, she'd made excuses.

When I'd spotted her car in her parents' driveway this morning, I'd texted her an invite for dinner. To my surprise, she'd said yes.

"Maybe I shouldn't have asked her over with so many people here." Our new deck was filled with friends.

Since I had the interior of the house the way I wanted it —for now—my focus over the past three weeks had been on the yard. We'd hired a local construction crew to build a deck. The landscaping we'd tackled ourselves. Luke had come home every evening from work and whatever I hadn't been able to do during the day while he'd been at the station, he'd helped me with after dinner.

The yard had been transformed in less than a month, and now that the project was mostly finished, we'd invited everyone over for a Saturday barbecue.

The deck stretched nearly the entire width of the house and was filled with planters and chairs and couches. My buying spree had been expensive, fast and so much fun. He'd scoffed at the number of seats, but as I looked around at our friends lounging comfortably, I made a mental note to get a couple more chairs.

"You guys need another beer?" Dash shoved up from the chaise where he'd been sitting, walking to the coolers we'd set against the iron railing.

"I'll take one." Leo raised a hand from his seat on the curved sectional.

Emmett and Shaw, seated beside him, both simply nodded.

And Isaiah, cuddling his four-month-old daughter,

Amelia, adjusted her sunhat with his tattooed hand and met Dash by the cooler. "Any more of those root beers left?"

Dash dug through the ice, pulled out a handful of bottles and stood, delivering them to the guys. He'd twisted the top on his own beer just as his sons, who'd been playing in the yard, bounded up the deck and collided with his legs.

"Can I try a drink, Daddy?" Xander asked.

"No."

The four-year-old didn't listen. He walked to the cooler, his hands sifting through the ice.

"Me too." Zeke, a year younger than his brother, started digging too.

"What's this one?" Xander tugged Luke's favorite amber from the ice and Dash snatched it out of his hand.

"Not for kids."

The look the boy sent his father was full of dare and challenge.

Emmett laughed. "God, I can't wait to watch him push every one of your buttons."

There was no doubt that the Slater boys were going to be a riot. They were already giving their parents a run for their money, but Dash and Bryce seemed to love every minute.

"I've got something special for you, Xander." I walked over and opened the other cooler, the one we'd filled with waters and soda and juice boxes. I found one for each of them, pushed in the attached straws and sent them on their way to the yard.

All they had to play with was a soccer ball and frisbee, but soon, the space would be more suitable for kids. Maybe a swing set and a slide. A covered sandbox might look nice beside the flower bed I was going to put in along the fence.

"Uh-oh." Presley came out of the french doors, followed by Bryce and Genevieve. "I know that face."

"Me too," Luke muttered from the grill. "It means another project."

I shrugged. "This yard needed me."

He chuckled and tipped his own beer bottle to his lips.

Presley held out two glasses, both filled with ice but different colored drinks. "Margarita or sangria?"

"Oh, I've got a beer inside." A nonalcoholic beer. I had it stashed in the mini fridge in the garage. I'd snuck in there earlier and poured one into a pint glass, hoping no one would see me or the empty bottles in the trash.

Luke and I had just found out two days ago we were expecting, and though I was excited to tell my sister, I wasn't quite ready yet.

For now, it was our secret.

We hadn't gotten pregnant on a rainy day—maybe next time, if we were so blessed. This house needed babies.

From what we could guess, we'd conceived right before the drama with the Warriors. Luke and I hadn't used a condom when we'd come home from the Smith River trip. We'd forgotten a few times in the tent too.

I liked to think we'd made this baby on the river.

Whenever it had happened, he or she had been made with love and would soon be joining the fray.

"Should we talk about the Warriors and get it over with?" Dash asked as Bryce settled onto his knee.

"Yeah." Luke closed the lid on the grill. Then he took my hand, fingering the diamond on my ring finger along with the coordinating wedding band, and led me to an empty chair.

I perched on the armrest as he settled into the seat, leaning forward with his elbows on his knees.

"I talked to Maria yesterday. Three guys are out on bail."

"Who?" Emmett asked.

Luke listed off the names. "From what she told me, they're some of the newest prospects. Not full members."

"Could be a problem." Dash shook his head. "If they're trying to get in Tucker's good graces, they might be willing to act out his revenge."

"I'll dig into them some," Emmett said.

"And get us some pictures so we know who to watch for," Shaw added.

"I've already got them inside," Luke said. "And I've passed them around to my team at the station so the officers on patrol can keep an eye out."

"Any word on Tucker?" Leo asked.

Luke nodded. "The judge didn't grant him or any of his senior members bail. They'll be in custody until their trials."

"And when is that going to be?" Genevieve asked, settling beside Isaiah and their daughter. She worked as a lawyer in town and I had a feeling in the coming months, she'd answer a lot of my questions.

"Maria said the prosecution is hoping to start them within the next few months," Luke answered.

Few months? That seemed like a long time to wait. But since we were talking murder and drugs and whatever else the Warriors were involved in, the process would probably be slow. I'd make it a point one of these evenings to visit Genevieve and Isaiah's house and pull her aside for some questions.

I didn't know how the criminal justice system worked, and though Luke was here, whenever I brought up the Warriors, his shoulders bunched and his forehead furrowed. Much like they were now.

We were all looking over our shoulders and the stress was weighing him down most.

It would be that way for a while. That was unavoidable. But I could ease the burden just a little by saving questions for Genevieve or having a list of projects to keep Luke's mind on other things.

The group went silent, each of us absorbing. All of our lives had changed since the Warriors had been arrested.

Everyone was on full-scale alert.

Shaw drove Presley to work at the garage each morning. Dash rarely let Bryce and their kids out of his sight. Genevieve and Isaiah were much the same.

And Luke . . .

Luke was terrified for his wife.

When he wasn't home, I had a protection detail. The Clifton Forge Police Department had few resources to spare, but one of his officers was stationed at the house during the day until Luke returned home each night.

I didn't go anywhere—to the grocery store or to lunch with Presley or to the backyard—alone.

He wouldn't hear me complain. I had no desire to cause him trouble.

Luke lifted a hand to cover mine and I met his worried gaze. "It'll be okay," I promised.

I had to believe that. We'd come too far to let the Warriors ruin our lives. We'd be cautious, but I wasn't giving up the future and hiding.

No more hiding.

"Anything else?" Emmett asked.

Luke shook his head. "That's it."

"Let's just stay vigilant," Dash said. "Tucker might be behind bars, but he's always going to be a threat."

"Until he's dead," Presley mumbled. "Maybe we should order a hit? Like that *Tiger King* guy."

"You do remember that I'm a cop, right?" Luke asked.

She laughed. "Pretend you didn't hear that."

Luke chuckled and ran a hand down my back before standing and going back to his station at the grill.

For today, the Warriors were not a problem. Tomorrow, that might be different, but all I wanted was to enjoy an evening with new friends and my husband.

The *one more thing* I'd asked of Luke before we'd gone on our camping and floating trip had been to swing by the courthouse so we could get married.

It had been a no-fuss affair. Presley and Shaw had come to stand as our witnesses. And when Luke had slid his mother's diamond ring on my finger, a ring she'd given him before she'd died, the two of us had exchanged vows.

I hadn't needed a fancy affair. I'd just wanted Luke.

My dress had been a simple white, strapless dress Presley and I had found at the one and only women's clothing store in town. After the judge had pronounced us husband and wife, we'd celebrated with dinner at Stockyard's.

Then we'd come home as Mr. and Mrs. Rosen.

The doorbell rang.

Cass.

"I'll get it." I jumped from my chair to race inside.

"Will one of you go with her?" Luke asked Dash.

Dash was already standing to escort me to the door since Luke was busy cooking.

"It's probably Cassandra," I told him as he turned the deadbolt. His tall body blocked the view, then he stepped out of the way so I could peer past his shoulder.

I smiled, my heart racing as she appeared. Then it twisted because she looked . . . awful.

For weeks, I'd hoped to see Cass's face. To somehow connect with her. She was part of the reason I'd gotten out of that room. Fighting for Cass had given me the strength to fight for myself. In the weeks that had passed, I'd worried for her, but I'd assumed that she'd be like me, moving on with her life.

Except standing before me was not a woman moving on. She looked tired. Hopeless. Lost.

Once, not that long ago, I'd been the same.

Her caramel eyes seemed hollow, her cheekbones too prominent. Her features were ghostly pale. The only thing bright about Cassandra was her auburn hair glowing copper in the sunlight.

"Hey." I forced a smile. "Come on in."

"I'll leave you two alone." Dash made room for Cassandra to enter, then he closed the door and flipped the lock again. With a small nod, he strode through the house, disappearing outside.

"Thanks for coming," I said, taking one of her hands. Her palm was clammy and her skin cold.

"I wasn't going to come," she confessed. "I saw all the cars outside and wasn't going to. But I wanted to see you. Are you, um . . . okay?"

"I'm okay."

A wash of relief crossed her gaze. "Good."

"Are you okay?"

She gave me a sad smile and tears flooded her pretty eyes. "No."

Then she was in my arms, holding on to my shoulders like she might fall if not for my bones keeping her upright.

Cassandra didn't cry out. She didn't make a noise. But she clutched me so fiercely it was difficult to breathe.

"I'm sorry." She let me go as quickly as she'd grabbed me, stepping away to wipe away the unshed tears. "I'm a mess."

"No, I'm sorry. Because of me—"

"It's not your fault." She shook her head. "I'm just . . . emotional. Things are changing so fast and I can't keep up."

"Changes?" I cocked my head. "What changes?"

"Well, I had to quit school. I'm moving back here. I need a job and an apartment because I love my parents but I can't live with them. Oh, and I'm pregnant."

My jaw dropped. "Pregnant."

She nodded. "I don't know if you remember or not. The story I told you in that, um . . . you know."

The basement. "Parts are fuzzy."

"I brought a friend home with me a while back. We went out, the one time in a year I went out, and had some drinks. There were these guys. She went home with one. I went home with the other."

"I remember now." That's what she'd told me when we'd been huddled together. When she'd been trying to keep me awake. "What guys?"

"Ugh," she groaned. "The wrong guys. I don't know how long you've lived here, but there used to be a motorcycle club in town."

Oh.

Shiiiiiiit.

"Cass—"

"I was the good girl. Always. In high school. In college. I've had two boyfriends, both in undergrad. I dated them each for months before sleeping with them. And I just . . . he was fun. He didn't look at me like a geek. I knew who he was. Every available woman in this town knows Leo Winter. He's the bad boy. I'm the good girl. And I thought for once it might be fun not doing everything that everyone expected me to do."

"Cass, I—"

"What was I thinking?" She raised her hands, her fingers splayed wide before they dove into her hair. "What the hell was I thinking? I knew he was trouble, but I let him screw me anyway."

This was a disaster. She was going to take one step onto my beautiful new deck and see Leo. I needed to disinvite her to this function. Fast.

"Maybe this dinner isn't a good idea. You're tired. There are other people here. How about we meet up for lunch this week?" *Please say yes.*

I moved closer, taking her arm, ready to steer her across the street.

Boots thudded on the deck beyond the french doors before I could shove Cass outside.

Damn it. Hadn't she seen Emmett's and Leo's motorcycles in the driveway? They'd been parked on the far side, beyond the other vehicles, but she should be paying more attention. Those bikes should have scared her away.

The french doors opened and I turned, praying it was anyone at all but . . .

Leo.

"Sorry." His voice carried through the living room. "Just gonna use your bathroom."

If Cassandra's face had been pale before, it went snow white. Her eyes darted between me and Leo.

An expression crossed his face as he took her in. He tilted his head to the side, his eyes narrowing on her. If he didn't remember her, I would castrate him on Cass's behalf.

"Hey," he drawled, still trying to place her. But he recognized her, that was for sure. "You're . . ."

"Cassandra," I gritted out. "The woman who was kidnapped by the Warriors."

Leo blinked, shaking out of his stupor. "What? That was you?"

We'd spoken Cass's name a dozen times in his presence. Clearly, he'd forgotten it from their hookup.

If my teeth were gritting together, Cass's molars were grinding diamonds to dust. "Would you give us a minute?"

"Um . . ."

Her nostrils flared. "Please."

"Sure."

She seethed as I backed away.

When I crossed paths with Leo, I gave him my best glare.

"What did I do?" he mumbled.

"I'm on her side," I declared and marched to the deck, opening the doors with too much force and slamming them closed behind me.

"What's wrong?" Luke asked, a spatula in his hand.

"You are never going to believe what just happened."

"WELL, THAT WAS A DISASTER." I heaved the throw pillows from the bed, whipping them toward the corner chair. Both the pillows and chair were new additions. I'd told Luke they were the last changes I was making to the bedroom, but this morning I'd woken up and decided it needed a new paint color.

I'd tackle this room first as practice before painting the nursery.

As hobbies went, interior design was going to have to be my specialty because clearly, hosting afternoon barbecues was not.

"Not a disaster." Luke gripped the collar of his T-shirt, yanking it over his head. Then he unbuttoned his jeans, kicking them off to reveal his strong legs and snug boxer briefs.

If I weren't so upset about the afternoon and evening, I would have spent more time enjoying the view. That taut skin. The strong, sinewy muscle.

Instead, I ripped the comforter off my side of the bed and plopped down with a huff. "Total disaster."

Cass and Leo hadn't returned to the deck, but their raised voices had been heard by all.

I hadn't had to tell anyone Cass's secret. We'd all heard her screaming, loud and clear.

Our group had given them privacy to talk, but they'd argued for so long that the burgers had grown cold. The rest of the food had been inside, waiting on the kitchen island.

Finally, the slam of the front door had echoed to the backyard. It had been followed by the rumble of a motorcycle as Leo raced away.

When I'd snuck a peek inside, it had been empty. Cassandra had retreated to the safety of her parents' house.

The evening might have been salvageable. We'd reheated the food and returned to the deck. But the mood had soured. Emmett had wolfed down a cheeseburger and made his excuses. We all knew he'd hunt down Leo.

I doubted it was to congratulate him on his upcoming fatherhood.

Genevieve and Isaiah had left next after Amelia had grown fussy. Dash and Bryce had taken their boys home before we'd had a chance to test out the new firepit and roast marshmallows.

The only two who'd stayed past dark were Presley and Shaw. Normally, I would have enjoyed an evening with my sister and brother-in-law, but somehow our conversation had drifted to Mom.

And Presley and I had gotten into a huge fight.

"Can you believe her?" I crossed my arms over my chest.

I'd told Presley that I was going to try and keep in touch with Mom. Maybe write her letters or something. Call the house when I suspected Dad was at work.

My sister had gone ballistic. She'd told me to give up on Mom because helping her was a lost cause.

"How could she say that? How could Presley just write Mom off? She's our *mother*." The surge of anger in my veins became a wash of tears. Freaking hormones.

Besides the one phone call, I hadn't reached out to Mom since I'd come to Montana. Maybe it was the pregnancy and the fact that soon I'd be someone's mother myself. But over the past three weeks, I'd put a lot of thought into my youth.

Mom wasn't a strong woman. She wasn't a warrior like Presley.

But she wasn't hopeless. She'd done what she could for her daughters. Presley didn't think it was enough. Maybe she was right. But that didn't change the fact that I loved Mom.

Luke slid into bed beside me, reaching for the nightstand to shut off the light. Then he pulled me into his arms, burying his nose in my hair. "Give it a day or two. Then you guys can work it out."

"She doesn't get it, Luke. She doesn't understand how

things were after she left. I had ten years with Mom. Ten. We only had each other. And she . . ."

The tears became a lump in the back of my throat.

Maybe it was foolish. Maybe it was a waste of time. But I wasn't giving up on Mom.

"She what?" Luke whispered.

"She got me out." I looked up at his handsome face. At the man of my dreams. "She got me out. Without her, I wouldn't be here. I wouldn't have you. I wouldn't have this life. I owe her everything."

Understanding crossed his gaze and he dropped his forehead to mine, holding me closer.

"I know Presley is worried. She doesn't want me to get my hopes up. And honestly, I don't think Mom will ever leave Dad. But Luke, what if?"

What if Mom had one fight in her? What if she came to Montana and found just a slice of the peace her daughters had found? *What if?*

"Then you call her. You write to her. You do what you need to do." Simple as that.

Luke always made the hard things seem easy.

He gave me courage to take on the world.

Whether the fight was against the Warriors. Or for our children. Or for my mother. With him here beside me, I'd fight to make our dreams come true.

An unexpected smile tugged at my lips. "I love you."

"I love you, beautiful."

"I didn't know it was supposed to be like this until you."

"Like what?"

"Like even when the days are shaky, as long as we're together, every day ends with a smile."

EPILOGUE
LUKE

Eight months later ...

"Chief Rosen," I answered my office phone.

"Three consecutive life sentences."

I always liked how Maria cut to the chase on our infrequent calls. "Any news on the others?"

"We're getting there. One by one. But we've got a long way to go."

The federal prosecutor assigned to the Warriors' case had pushed for Tucker's trial first. Most others were ongoing, but so far, the shortest sentence rendered was five years.

Fifty-seven Warriors were being sent through the criminal justice system to pay for their crimes. Murder. Drug trafficking. Kidnapping. Assault. The list went on. Some of them were already in prison, mostly those with shorter sentences and those who'd copped a plea for a reduced sentence. Others were awaiting trial. But at this moment in time, not a single member of the Arrowhead Warrior Motorcycle Club was walking free.

And if Tucker Talbot was spending his next three lives in a federal penitentiary, I would sleep better at night.

For a little while, at least.

I wasn't fool enough to believe it would last. He had connections to other clubs who might try to enact his revenge.

"If we're lucky, the judge's sentence for Tucker will set a precedent for the others coming," Maria said.

The other men being those who'd killed Ken Raymond and Birdy Hames.

Birdy had lost her life to the Warriors. She'd died on the operating table about the same time Scarlett had walked out of the hospital in Ashton all those months ago.

The one and only time I'd heard Maria's stoic and solid voice crack was when she'd called to tell me that Birdy hadn't survived. She'd taken the loss of two team members personally.

I would have too.

But death was the risk we'd agreed to when choosing a career in law enforcement. That didn't make it easier, especially when you were the one telling people to walk into dangerous situations and defuse them.

Sometimes the bomb just . . . detonated.

"Keep me posted," I said.

Maria didn't bother with parting small talk. There was just the simple click of the call ending.

I replaced the phone in its cradle and went back to my computer. The glare from the window behind me caught the screen so I stood and went to the glass. But before pulling the blinds, I took a long look at the river flowing behind the station.

It was the beginning of March and the snow had already

melted. Maybe we'd get another storm or two before we officially descended into spring, but the grass was already turning green. Montana springs were about as easy to predict as a March Madness bracket. Every year was different and each had a way of surprising you.

This time last year, we'd had snow everywhere. This time last year, I'd found Scarlett in the cookie aisle at the grocery store.

There'd been stress—a lot of stress—but without a doubt, this past year had been the best of my life.

The Arrowhead Warriors would try to fuck it up. But even if they got out of prison, even if Tucker orchestrated a retaliation effort from his prison cell, I'd fight.

No matter what that meant. No matter which side of the law that put me on. I was choosing the right side. I chose my wife, and my baby girl who would be here any day.

The robins chirped beyond the windows. The tree leaves rustled in the breeze. The last place I wanted to be was stuck at my desk doing paperwork. If I had time later, I'd cruise around town. I loathed traffic stops but in the past month, I'd written more speeding tickets than I had in the past five years combined.

The busy tasks helped me hide my fears so they wouldn't show when I got home. But no matter how many tickets I wrote, Scarlett's due date was rapidly approaching, and I couldn't seem to calm my nerves.

Could I keep them safe? Should we just disappear? Scarlett had suggested it once. Now that our daughter was almost here, I contemplated it more than ever.

How was I going to keep them safe?

If Scarlett was scared, she didn't let it show. Not about the Warriors or about becoming a mother. I'd expected some anxiety on her part, a hint of her uncertainty and fear, but she'd found this Zen during pregnancy. She was as steady as ever. And she was putting on a fearless face.

We both were.

She was determined not to let Tucker Talbot steal her future, and as much as I wanted to feel the same, the knot of dread never seemed to loosen.

Though hearing about Tucker's sentence had helped. I hoped she'd be relieved too when I reported home tonight.

Scarlett had thrown herself into our life. She'd settled into our home and neighborhood. She'd made friends. She was working toward her bachelor's degree in interior design online. She'd just finished her classes last week and was preparing to take the next semester off to be at home with the baby.

Whatever she wanted to do was fine by me. She'd tossed around the idea of opening her own business after graduating, possibly staging homes for realtors in town or offering freelance design services. She'd even mentioned event planning.

My wife had a talent for seeing a space and making it shine.

I was so damn proud of her. For school. For the way she wouldn't let her past define her future. For the way she'd handled her mother. We hadn't heard from Amanda Marks since Scarlett had started sending her letters. But every Friday on my way to work, I took Scarlett's latest to the mailbox.

I doubted we'd get a response. Scarlett had confessed she didn't either. Hell, maybe Scarlett's father was intercepting the letters. But she was sending them regardless.

There was no woman more quietly determined than my wife.

The unread emails in my inbox were calling so I turned away from the window and returned to my chair. I'd only made it through three when my phone rang again.

Scarlett's name flashed on the screen.

"Hey, beautiful."

"I'm at the hospital."

I was out of my chair so fast, I tripped on the wheelbase and crashed into my desk, barely catching myself by the elbows before hitting the floor.

The glass of water I'd refilled not long before Maria had called sloshed onto a shift report.

"Luke?"

"I'm coming." I brushed the water off the paper and kicked the chair away before it killed me. Then I spun around, searching for my keys. "I'm coming."

Where were my keys? I spun again. "Where are my keys?"

Scarlett laughed. "You have time."

"You don't know that." My voice rose, edged with panic.

"Don't drive crazy," she ordered, then ended the call.

Where the fuck were my keys? My head spun as I searched everywhere. I patted my jeans pockets. Empty. My desk. Nothing but papers, my sunglasses and a wallet.

I shoved the papers aside, some falling to the floor. Still, no keys.

"Fuck it."

I'd take one of the cruisers. Snatching up my wallet, I bolted from the office, whipping the door open with too much force. It bounced against the stop and clipped me in the shoulder as I nearly collided with Nathan.

He had his hand raised, ready to knock on my now-open door.

"Give me your keys." I held out my free hand.

My free hand, with my keys in them.

What the hell? I must have grabbed them, not even realizing I'd picked them up, when Scarlett had called.

"Uh . . . okay." He dug into his pocket.

"Never mind." I plowed past him, nearly knocking him down as I jogged through the bullpen.

Chuck was at his desk and when he saw me running, he shot out of his chair. "Is it time?"

"Yeah."

"Let's go!" he shouted, and the other officers sprinted into action. The room erupted.

I was the first out the door, but they were hot on my heels, dashing for their cruisers.

Two of them beat me out of the parking lot, lights and sirens flashing as they led the caravan to the hospital. Three more were behind me.

My heart raced so fast, the streets became a blur.

Thankfully, I didn't have to think, just follow the guys into the parking lot. My tires screeched as I took a corner too fast. The truck lurched as I slammed on the brakes beside the entrance.

Scarlett was standing on the sidewalk with Presley at her side, both shaking their heads. What the fuck was she doing outside?

Presley leaned in to whisper something in her sister's ear as she rubbed her own pregnant belly. She was due in a couple of weeks. Apparently, there'd been something in the water at our inaugural barbecue because not only was Scarlett pregnant, so was Presley. So was Genevieve. And so was Cass.

There were going to be a lot of babies soon.

I shoved the truck in park, not bothering to shut it off. One of the guys would park it and bring me the keys.

"Isn't this a little overkill?" Scarlett asked, waving a hand to the police cars lined up in succession.

"Kind of a waste of taxpayer dollars, Luke." Presley pulled her lips in to fight a laugh.

"Who drove you here?" I asked them both.

The sisters exchanged guilty looks. Both were so big that it was a struggle to fit behind the wheel.

"We'll talk about that later," I grumbled, taking Scarlett's elbow. Then I marched her toward the hospital's double doors, Presley waddling not far behind.

A chorus of claps rang out as my team whistled and cheered.

Scarlett cast them a beaming smile over her shoulder but I didn't slow. I raised a hand and disappeared inside to get checked in. It wasn't until Scarlett was in a bed, wearing a faded blue gown, that I finally breathed.

"You're freaking out," Scarlett said.

"Yup."

"Women have babies every day."

"Not my wife."

She patted the bed beside her hip. "Sit down."

"I can't." I paced between the monitor and the guest chair in the corner of the room.

"I'm going to leave you guys alone." Presley walked to Scarlett's side and took her hand. "Good luck."

"Thanks."

"If you decide to kick him out and want me to coach you instead, I'll be in the waiting room."

Scarlett rolled her eyes. "He'll be fine."

Presley shot me a doubtful look, then left us alone.

"What's wrong?" she asked. "Talk to me."

I didn't answer.

"Luke." Her voice was so gentle, so concerned, I wouldn't deny her the truth.

"I—" Before I could confess that I was nervous, Scarlett sucked in a sharp breath and gritted her teeth.

Her face twisted and she squeezed her eyes shut. "Ooof. That hurts."

I rushed to her side, taking her hand so she could squeeze my fingers. "Breathe."

She nodded, sucking in a breath through her nose. The green line spiked on the monitor as her contraction peaked. She'd had others since we'd been here, but this was the worst so far.

"Sorry," I said as the pain eased.

"For knocking me up?"

"No." I chuckled. "I promise to get my shit together."

"That would be good." She cracked her eyes open and brought a hand to my cheek. "We'll be okay. You'll keep her safe."

My jaw dropped. "How did you know?"

"Because I know you. That brave face doesn't hide anything from me."

"You're wearing one too."

"Yeah, I am. But just because I've got fears, doesn't mean I don't believe in my heart of hearts that we will be okay. You. Me. The baby. This is where our life is. I'm not giving it up. I'm not letting *you* give it up. So we'll fight for it, and you'll keep us safe."

Scarlett's faith in me was humbling.

She'd put me on a pedestal. Not that I minded, because I'd put her on one too. My parents had been that way, seeing the best in one another. Maybe that was the foundation of a solid marriage. Standing on your pedestals, eye to eye, together.

I took her hand from my face and brought it to my lips. "I love you."

"I love you too."

We sat like that, together, for the next twelve hours. She clutched my hand through the pain. I held a leg as she pushed. And we both wept over the miracle of our daughter's birth.

It was long after the sun had set and our baby girl had fallen asleep in Scarlett's arms that I finally wandered into the waiting room. It was crowded with familiar faces.

Presley was asleep against Shaw's shoulder. He spotted me first, raising his eyebrows in a silent question.

I nodded, unable to fight the smile that stretched across my face.

Two chairs down from him, Dash had fallen asleep too, his legs crossed at the ankle. On the small couch, my dad was lying with a hat tipped over his eyes. I'd texted them all hours ago that we were here and would send an update with news.

I should have expected the crowd. Our friends weren't the kind to wait at home for a text.

Dad would want to know, but soft snores were coming from beneath the ball cap's brim. I let him sleep.

Emmett, sitting across from Dad, turned when he heard

my footsteps and stood from his chair. "Congratulations, man."

I shook his outstretched hand. "Thanks."

"You owe me twenty," Shaw said. "We took bets on whether you or Leo would be out first."

"Leo's here?"

Emmett nodded. "Cass went into labor about eight hours ago."

If the timing worked out, our children would share a birthday. Scarlett would like that. She'd grown rather fond of Cassandra in the past eight months, treating her more like a younger sister than a friend.

Footsteps echoed down the hallway. Emmett and I turned to see Leo stride our way, his hands jammed in his pockets and his face pale.

"Everything okay?" I asked.

"I have a daughter." Leo blinked and raked a hand through his hair. "Holy fuck, I have a daughter."

I clapped him on the shoulder, laughing as I left him with our friends. I hadn't been the only expectant father freaking out, though compared to Leo, I'd handled it like a champ.

He'd make sense of it eventually. And maybe he'd finally open his eyes to Cassandra.

When I returned to our room, I tiptoed inside, not wanting to wake Scarlett. She'd wanted a natural delivery and by the time the baby had arrived with a wail, Scarlett had been exhausted. But as I pushed through the door, I found her awake, staring at our daughter swaddled against her chest.

"Isn't she perfect?"

I sat on the bed, leaning down to kiss Scarlett's forehead. "Like her mother."

"What if we named her Mary after your mom?"

My heart swelled so full it hurt. We'd found out the sex but had decided not to pick names until she was born.

Mary.

Mary Rosen.

If Mom was watching, she'd have one hell of a smile on her face.

"I'd like that," I choked out.

"Good." Carefully, Scarlett slid over in the bed, making room for me.

I kicked off my boots, then stretched out beside her, tucking her into my side. When I brushed Mary's hand, it opened just enough to circle my index finger and hold on tight.

Then Scarlett and I ended the day—the best day—with a smile.

BONUS EPILOGUE
SCARLETT

"Why do you have to be so short?" Mary muttered as she trudged into the kitchen, her pink basketball tucked under an arm.

"Sorry, baby." I fought a smile. "I tried. I mean, your dad was the tallest guy I could find."

She pouted as she pulled open the fridge for a sports drink. "Not tall enough."

My beautiful eleven-year-old daughter had inherited nearly all of my features. Blue eyes. Blond hair. Petite frame. Her brothers, on the other hand, were miniature versions of Luke. Dark hair. A dimpled cheek. Tall. Simon was nine and already stood an inch above his sister. Parker at six would surpass Mary before long too.

Maybe if her favorite sport was swimming or tennis, her height wouldn't bother her so much. But ever since Luke had given her a foam basketball when she was two, she'd fallen in love with the game.

He played with her constantly. The first thing she'd do when he got home from work was ask if they could shoot around before dinner. Simon and Parker would go out with them and I'd hover by the front door, watching with my camera ready.

When it was the five of us, her short stature didn't bother her so much. What she lacked in height, she made up for in energy and sheer determination to win, so she normally schooled her brothers. My girl was one hell of a shot and ball handler. Luke hadn't admitted it to her yet, but he'd told me on more than one occasion that soon, she'd outplay him.

Mary worked so hard, but on days like today, when the court in the driveway was crowded with not only her brothers, but cousins too, her height—and lack thereof—was hard to overcome.

Presley, Shaw and their kids were here for the day. Nico and Noah were outside playing ball. Their daughter, Natasha, was only four and too young, though she adored Mary and would follow her anywhere, including the basketball court, if we let her.

Natasha raced through the french doors and her face lit up when she spotted my daughter. "Mary!"

"Hey, Nat." Mary smiled and some of the frustration eased from her sweet face.

Presley came inside behind her daughter, our golden retriever Charlie trotting at her side. Since the other kids were all playing out front, she'd taken Nat to the yard to play with Charlie.

"How was the game?" Presley asked.

Mary shot me an agonized look. Not only did she love basketball, but she loved to win. She was exactly like Luke in that regard.

"Here." I walked around the island and opened the

freezer, pulling out two popsicles. "Why don't you girls go outside and have these. We won't tell the boys."

"Yeah!" Natasha beamed and nodded wildly.

Mary's scowl disappeared. "Where's Grandpa?"

"On the deck," I answered. He'd gone out to lay claim to his favorite chair.

After Josh had retired from the police department in Missoula, he'd moved to Clifton Forge. Luke and I had just finished the slowest remodel in history on the rental house. It hadn't been easy, but now it looked nothing like the dull safe house I'd crashed in once. Not a daisy in sight. And rather than rent it out, we'd sold it for bottom dollar to Josh.

That house had been my project after Simon was born, something besides chasing both kids around to keep me occupied.

My education hadn't been hurried, but I'd earned my degree online and now did the occasional design project around town. There were a handful of realtors who used me to stage houses when a new construction project was finished. My reputation was strong enough I could make a decent business out of it, but I didn't want work to consume my life.

I preferred the majority of my time to be spent here, at home being a wife and a mother. Besides, now that the kids were older, it was a full-time job rushing them to club meetings and sports practices every evening.

Mary took Natasha's hand and walked her outside, Charlie going with them, leaving me and Presley in the kitchen. Cheers and the echo of a dribbling basketball drifted in from the garage.

"Red or white?" I asked my sister, going to the fridge.

Call us uncultured, but both of us loved our wine cold, no matter the color.

"White." She went to the cupboard and took out glasses as I opened the bottle.

The two of us had built our own lives here. Presley had her work at the garage. I had my hobbies. Whenever Shaw's production company had a movie premiere or they wanted to spend time with his family, they'd take the kids and jet to California. Luke and I took our own crew on the river four or five times every summer.

But this was where Presley and I found ourselves most Saturday afternoons. Together. We'd be at one of our homes with the kids playing, our husbands talking or, like today, in the game. And the two of us would catch up over a bottle of wine before we made dinner.

"Guess what I heard?" Presley asked. "I stopped by the salon for a quick trim yesterday and all the girls were talking about that empty building at the end of Central. The rumor is we're getting a new Mexican restaurant."

"Oh, I hope it's true." We'd had one for years and it had been our favorite spot to meet and have tacos over lunch. But then the owners had retired and the restaurant had closed, leaving Presley and me craving homemade chips and guacamole ever since.

The thunder of feet warned us before the door to the garage flew open. A stream of boys burst inside, all racing for the fridge.

"Mom, we're hungry," Simon said, hauling out bottle after bottle of Gatorade for his brother and cousins.

Luke and Shaw trailed in behind the boys, each with a beer in their hand.

"Hi, beautiful." Luke kissed my temple as he pulled me into his side.

"Hi." I set my wine aside and wrapped my arms around his waist. There were a few flecks of gray in his hair these days. The crinkles near his eyes had deepened from years of laughter.

Years of falling asleep with a smile.

"How was the game?" I asked.

"The dads won." Shaw and Luke clinked bottles together.

The boys chattered around the kitchen as they collected snacks, then Presley shooed them outside with the girls. They disappeared just as the doorbell rang.

"Who could that be?" I asked Luke.

He shrugged, pinched my ass, then went to answer. Luke still didn't like me to answer the door, even though it had been over a decade since the Warriors had been arrested.

The voice he greeted was muffled, their words indistinct. Must be a neighbor. Except when he came into the house with an older woman trailing behind, it took me by surprise.

So did the cast on her left hand.

So did her face.

My mother's face.

Presley gasped.

My jaw dropped. "Mom?"

She nodded but didn't speak, blinking rapidly as her eyes flooded with tears.

I glanced past Luke, searching for another person, but there was no way Luke would have let my father into this house. Which meant Mom had come here alone.

For over eleven years I'd been writing to my mother. One letter, every week. I had no way of knowing if she'd received them. If she'd gotten my rambling updates on life in Clifton Forge. If she'd liked the pictures I'd sent her of the kids as they'd grown.

But I'd kept sending them all the same.

One letter, every week, sent with hope.

She'd aged over the years, but besides the cast, she looked good. Her once long, blond hair was now white and gray with sideswept bangs. But her blue eyes were the same color I remembered, the same color I saw in the mirror every morning.

The same color I saw in my daughter.

"Amanda, this is Shaw." Luke held out a hand to my brother-in-law. "Presley's husband."

"It's nice to meet you," Mom said softly, then looked up at Luke. "And you too."

"What are you doing here?" I asked, moving to my sister and taking her hand. She gripped it so tight, my fingers ached. But otherwise, she was too stunned to move or speak.

"I got your letters," Mom said.

My heart raced. "Good."

"Where's . . ." Presley couldn't finish her sentence. Not that she needed to.

"I left him." Mom fidgeted with the cast. "It was time."

"Are you . . . okay?" I asked.

She gave me a small smile. "I didn't think I'd see you girls again. And I was wondering"—Mom swallowed hard—"if I could meet my grandchildren."

I looked to Luke, who nodded, then I turned to Presley.

Her gaze was waiting. "I never thought . . ."

She never thought Mom would leave Dad. Neither had I. Not really. But I'd sent the letters anyway.

"They're outside." Presley let me go and rushed to

Mom's side. She didn't hug her but she took Mom's unin-jured arm and led her to the backyard.

My hand flew to my mouth and the tears I'd been too stunned to form a moment ago fell free.

Shaw put his hand on my shoulder, giving it a squeeze, then he followed behind his wife.

Then I was in Luke's arms.

"Oh my God," I whispered, burrowing into his strength. "I didn't think I'd see her again."

"I know." He pulled me close. "I can't believe it."

A giggle bubbled free. "She left him."

"Yeah."

"She left him, Luke." I hugged my husband so tight my arms strained. "She's here."

"We've got her now."

Yes, we had her now. Mom wouldn't fear for anything again. Whatever it took, we'd keep my father away. And I knew a police chief who'd be more than happy to throw that bastard in jail if he so much as set foot in Clifton Forge.

"Come on." Luke let me go and led me through the house, where we introduced our children to their grandmother.

When Parker looked her up and down, he turned to Mary. "She's short like you and Mom."

The entire deck burst out in laughter, much to my daughter's chagrin. But Luke wrapped her in a hug, some-thing that always put a smile on Mary's face. She was exactly like me, after all.

The evening passed with easy conversation. Mom sat and listened, asking a few questions, but mostly enjoying the kids' chatter and hearing firsthand about the lives her daugh-ters were living.

Shaw and Presley offered her a place to stay, and since their house was five times the size of ours, it made sense. So as darkness settled late on a Montana summer night, we said our farewells.

"We'll come over tomorrow and visit," I promised Mom, giving her a hug.

It was strange to have her in my arms, but after years apart, her hug was the same.

"Thank you, Scarlett," she whispered.

"For what?"

"Your letters saved my life. They gave me courage."

I held her closer. "I'm glad you're here, Mom."

"Me too. I'm so proud of my daughters. And grateful they married good men."

I smiled up at my husband over her shoulder. "The very best."

ACKNOWLEDGMENTS

Thank you for reading *Noble Prince*! When I originally planned the series, there were only going to be five books. But then I met Luke in *Riven Knight* and just knew he needed a story. When Scarlett came along in *Stone Princess*, there was no question that she was his.

Thank you to the amazing ladies who helped make this book shine: Elizabeth, Julie and Karen. Thank you Sarah for another gorgeous cover.

Thank you to each and every blogger who's helped me get the word out about this book and this series. Thank you to the members of Perry Street and all of my incredible readers. And lastly, thanks to my family and friends. You know who you are, and I hope you know how much I love you.

ABOUT THE AUTHOR

Devney is a *USA Today* bestselling author who lives in Washington with her husband and two sons. Born and raised in Montana, she loves writing books set in her treasured home state. After working in the technology industry for nearly a decade, she abandoned conference calls and project schedules to enjoy a slower pace at home with her family. Writing one book, let alone many, was not something she ever expected to do. But now that she's discovered her true passion for writing romance, she has no plans to ever stop.

Don't miss out on Devney's latest book news.
Subscribe to her newsletter!
www.devneyperry.com

Made in the USA
Middletown, DE
17 February 2023

25061792R00220